Vancouver at the Dawn

Vancouver
at the
Dawn

A TURN-OF-THE-CENTURY PORTRAIT

John A. Cherrington

HARBOUR PUBLISHING

Harbour Publishing
P.O. Box 219
Madeira Park, BC Canada V0N 2H0

Published with the assistance of the Canada Council and the Government of British Columbia, Tourism and Ministry Responsible for Culture, Cultural Services Branch.
Cover design by Roger Handling, Terra Firma Design.
Author photograph by Andrew W.R. Simpson II and Associates.
Printed and bound in Canada.

Photograph credits: CVA—City of Vancouver Archives; VPL—Vancouver Public Library. All other photographs are from the McLagan family collection.

Canadian Cataloguing in Publication Data

Cherrington, John, 1950–
        Vancouver at the dawn

        ISBN 1-55017-157-7

        1. McLagan, Sara—Fiction.   I. Title.
PS8555.H4482V35 1997   C813'.54   C97-910122-0
PR9199.3.C482V35 1997

THE CANADA COUNCIL | LE CONSEIL DES ARTS
FOR THE ARTS | DU CANADA
SINCE 1957 | DEPUIS 1957

To my father and mother,
Frank and Mary Ann Cherrington

"'Tis infamy to die and not be missed,"
(I thank thee, unknown poet, for that line.)
Let me imagine lips that I have kissed,
Will still, in memory, press these lips of mine.

When I shall journey to the Unknown Land,
Shall I some memories leave Death cannot kill?
Will men, with manly grip, still take my hand?
Will children listen for the voice that's still?

Death hath no sting for me, if when I sleep,
Children—and dogs—remember where I lie;
If, missing me, some gentle women weep,
And men, recalling me, shall heave a sigh.

If word I speak, or write, helps fellow man
To nobler, braver life; to aspirations high;
I shall not cease when I have filled life's span.
To be remembered thus is not to die.

> —from "I Shall Not Cease," by Francis Bursill,
> early Vancouver poet and journalist

❦

Preface

Sometimes history overwhelms us with its swirl of facts and events apparently unconnected to our own late twentieth-century world. At other times, the connections are so vivid that we feel déjà vu—when we look at a 1901 photograph of a cyclist tooling around Stanley Park, or when one's teenaged son exclaims with shock that his great-grandfather in the daguerrotype is wearing trendy wire-rimmed spectacles just like his own.

It so happens that the birth of the twentieth century coincided with a time of great change and upheaval in the western world. Vancouver was no exception, having recently become the western terminus of the national railway. I wanted to capture the sense of time and place in Vancouver, city of my birth, by way of a snapshot view of the era, hoping as well to discover some trends, habits and events which give Vancouver a distinctive character with which we identify today.

During the course of my research I met Lynda Orr, who is an interpreter at the Burnaby Village Museum and a passionate devotee of history. She urged me to consider writing a book on the life of Sara McLagan (nee Maclure), who in 1901 became owner and editor of the *Vancouver Daily World*. Sara was the first woman publisher of a Canadian daily newspaper, respecting which Lynda had produced a well-written paper. I had become aware of Sara and her intriguing life and career in the course of writing *The Fraser Valley: A History*, but there was insufficient material for a full biography. Why not then combine the two ideas, and capture Vancouver at century's turn through Sara's eyes?

I was and remain wary of writing history as an imagined memoir. The approach necessarily involves much speculation and educated guess. We know, for instance, that Sara had strong opinions on social issues and wrote many editorials for her newspaper, and that her hands-on approach to management left little room for editorializing that ran contrary to her own beliefs. Yet this memoir must be viewed as a work of historical fiction. As much as Sara's personal diaries and *Daily World* files have revealed her life and times for me, I take sole responsibility for errors of fact and interpretation.

Pioneers die; memories fade. The Vancouver scene at the dawn of our century was a very special time and place, and interpretations of that scene will differ. But perhaps, as Ralph Waldo Emerson put it, "there is no history, only biography."

Introduction

Vancouver rose from the ashes of the Great Fire of 1886 to become, by 1910, a prominent continental seaport. It was by no means a smooth passage. Born in the rowdy, bawdy Gassy Jack days of the Granville waterfront, the town which grew up around Hastings Mill was fuelled by a crude capitalism geared to exploitation of natural resources. Huge monopolies like the Canadian Pacific Railway dominated all development. Life was characterized by political turbulence, roller coaster cycles of boom and bust, and a shocking social underside. Squalor, violent crime, racism, prostitution, child neglect and drug and alcohol addiction were all virulent features of the cityscape. Prisons were filthy; ten-year-old boys were thrown into jail with murderers; men, women and children often worked seventy-hour weeks; hospitals were primitive; and deserted mothers and children frequently died of malnutrition.

The city's tawdry underside was balanced by its scenic setting of beaches, parks and West End mansions which boasted stone walls, manicured lawns and hedges, Chinese servants and monkey trees. From early times, Vancouverites exhibited a hankering for leisure. Stanley Park was a mecca; English Bay served as the Riviera. Tree-huggers first went on record in the 1890s when City Council sent out its policemen and mayor to halt tree-cutting on Deadman's Island off Stanley Park. Poor Theodore Ludgate, a Yankee sawmill owner, was utterly bewildered by the tenacity with which Vancouverites defended a few trees. The incident became known as the Ludgate Affair and gave birth to a conservation battle which still rages one hundred years later.

Certainly the Vancouver of 1901 was an exciting place to be. New inventions and technology promised an easier life. Ocean steamers disgorged China silk at dockside, along with hordes of Klondike miners who tramped and debauched their way about town. Down on Cordova Street, well-stocked polished bars slaked the thirst of workingman and visitor alike. Vaudeville farce flourished. At the Granville Opera House, international stars like Paderewski entertained the West End set. Incense lamps, fan tan and red lights beckoned one to a world of exotic delights in Chinatown and its environs. Streetcars jangled and fought their way along the streets, against horse-drawn livery wagons. And everywhere, cyclists flew about on cinder paths in spats and other outrageous attire.

Unlike genteel Victoria, raw dusky Vancouver experienced a prolonged paucity of women residents. Rough and ready young miners, labourers, fishermen and tradesmen poured west on the CPR trains to seek their fortunes. Few brought along wives or girlfriends. Vancouver society remained bereft of female participation until well into the 1890s, when a stirring of cultural nostalgia led to the birth of the Arts & Historical Society, drama, reading clubs and the opera. Women were defined by where they lived. East of Westminster Avenue (later Main Street) lived prostitutes, single working women and wives of workingmen. West of the line lived "good" society women who spent their time hosting at-homes and tea parties, supervising Chinese servants, attending church and appearing at costume balls.

The 1890s saw new worldwide trends in industrial relations. Throughout British Columbia, fishermen and industrial workers organized into unions. Even the city's bandsmen were union, as were journalists and press operators. Radical social reformers like Helena Gutteridge followed in the tradition of British socialism in lobbying for change. The suffragettes became a major force, and the Pankhurst radicals from England toured the province's cities thundering their message. The most powerful voice for the enfranchisement of women was the Women's Christian Temperance Union under the leadership of Maria Grant of Victoria. She and other reformers combined a plea for suffrage with a call to arms against alcohol.

Sailboats and other pleasure boats were a popular weekend sight at English Bay, seen here in 1900. Vancouverites often referred to the Bay as their "Riviera." (VPL 8217)

But for most women social reformers of the day, the right to vote was just one of many pressing issues. Gillian Marie notes in her article, "Writing Women Into British Columbia's History": "Historians have written about the suffrage movement, but in isolation, and not within the context of a wider social reform movement. This narrow focus gives the reader the false impression that suffrage is the story of women in the late 19th and early 20th centuries, that their only goal was the franchise, and that feminism died with the granting of suffrage. This interpretation ignores women's struggles for control of their own persons, their property, and their children. It also minimizes the impact of their demands for changes to the legal and educational systems..."

One of the most profound influences on Canadian women reformers was Lady Aberdeen, wife of the governor general and founder of the National Council of Women in 1893. Lady Aberdeen was an iron-willed, no-nonsense person who mingled equally well with prince and pauper. Her passion for reform was wide-ranging: working women and children, the aged and infirm, domestic servants, society girls, prison conditions, health facilities and education all received her energetic attentions. She was like a battlefield general the way she marshalled her troops throughout the land, establishing local Council cells in every city and major town and egging on her followers to investigate every social problem, organize shelters for the homeless, raise funds for hospitals and assorted charities, and lobby for legislative reform.

The National Council believed in a strong union of women everywhere to promote social goals and to invigorate the state by strengthening the family. Although supported by most members, suffragetism was not officially endorsed by the National Council until well after 1900. Lady Aberdeen in fact played a cunning game. By purposefully shunning the radical suffragettes, she set her sights squarely upon the male mainstream and their apprehension of the Pankhurst and radical Carrie Nation saloon bashers. The mission of her Council, she purred, was to simply strengthen Victorian social ideals. But her battle plans for Council troops were clear: "In all the reforms we devise, our first care should be to work for the quickening of the public and individual conscience, to make that conscience fulfil all of the obligations imposed; to take advantage of all the privileges granted by the present law; and when the law is found lacking, be sure that you will speedily obtain the legislation desired."

The exclusively male legislatures initially ignored the National Council. But as the power and strident pitch of the WCTU and other suffragette and labour groups intensified, fear set in amongst the politicians. Perhaps, they reasoned, the progressive women of National Council ilk represented a moderate path toward social change, since change now appeared inevitable. British Columbia in the late 1890s was the most backward province in Canada in social justice policy. And indeed the legislature continued to be obsessed with the old issues of trade, subsidies, railways, roads and Oriental immigration. Certainly Premier Semlin was no Lord Peel of Corn Law fame. But in 1897, activists succeeded in piloting a bill through the legislature which finally bestowed property rights upon women, known as the Married Women's Property Act. Close on the heels of this event was the granting of limited suffrage on a local level, as women were granted the right to run for school boards and to hold office on many municipal councils. In Victoria, the vocal Agnes Dean Cameron became the first woman school principal in the province's history.

Women social reformers were so successful that by the year 1925 many observers described British Columbia as the most progressive province in Canada. In the field of legislative reform, Helen MacGill, British Columbia's first female judge, and Mary Ellen Smith, first provincial woman cabinet minister in the British Empire, played prominent roles. The manifold efforts of the radicals, the WCTU and, above all, the National Council of Women, not only influenced the course of legal reform, but resulted in the organizing of charities, community support groups, and school and hospital construction projects.

An important facet of reform was the Canadian newspaper, which was until 1900 an almost exclusively male preserve. The only prominent early Canadian women journalists were Kit Coleman, a colourful and talented reporter for the *Toronto Globe*, and the novelist Sara Jeanette Duncan, who once wrote that she "doubted if women had a good nose for news." Both women trod softly in a male world; both would play key roles in the founding of the Canadian Women's Press Club in 1904.

Early women journalists in fact were mostly confined to writing about fashion, balls and theatre events. Their wages were low. Clare Battle recalls finding a job at the *Vancouver Daily World* after ownership had passed from Sara McLagan to Louis Taylor: "I was eighteen. I had always wanted to write, and now I had been given the chance. I was so happy that as I walked down Hastings Street it was as though I walked on air. And when I tell that I started newspaper work at four dollars a week, you may wonder if I lived on air as well. Did it matter? Not a bit. In those halcyon days, food was only of secondary importance. I remember I consumed masses of oatmeal, fish paste and bread..."

In 1900, Vancouver boasted two daily evening papers, the *World* and the *Daily Province*, and a morning paper, the *News-Advertiser*. These newspapers served a population of less than 28,000 people. At the *News-Advertiser*, popular novelist Julia Henshaw wrote social columns under the pen name of Julian Durham, it being the decided wisdom of the day that a woman columnist would not lend the same credibility to critiques of the Vancouver music, drama and cocktail scene as would a sophisticated Englishman, even a fictitious one.

Corner of Granville and Hastings, c. 1900. A newsboy leans on his bicycle at centre. (VPL 6677)

Over at the *World* offices at Homer and Pender, Sara McLagan and her husband jointly managed the paper they had founded in 1887. Sara's own social columns were written under the pen name of Lady Cook. But in the late nineties, Sara tired of all the tea party and fancy ball pap. Her liners concerning social evils became more strident in tone. By 1901, she had assumed sole control over publishing and editing the newspaper, while rigorously pursuing social and political objectives.

Sara possessed a deep social conscience. She was for many years regarded as the western lieutenant of Lady Aberdeen, and during the years 1898 through 1900, she served as president of the Vancouver Council of Women. As the proprietor of a major Canadian newspaper, Sara exercised enormous influence in an age when the print media were the chief source of news and opinion. In fact, her entire life from childhood onwards was devoted to spreading news of the world and pursuing her ideals of a better society. Her life and times were tumultuous, colourful, often traumatic.

This woman's accumulation of firsts is impressive: youngest female telegraphist in Canada; first woman publisher of a Canadian daily newspaper; first woman president of the Vancouver Arts & Historical Society. Perhaps more important than the statistics, however, is the subtle but definitive impact which Sara made upon her world. She commanded respect in a male-dominated power structure at a time when women were only just emerging from the closeted cocoon of Victorian society. Her life at the century's turn is a harbinger of the self-assured, pragmatic feminist of the late 1990s.

Like most pioneer women reformers, Sara McLagan neither sought nor received fame, fortune, or even recognition. By contrast, her brother Sam Maclure achieved lasting renown as one of the most eminent architects of British Columbia. Upon her retirement as publisher of the *World* in 1905, Sara passed quietly from the stage of history—her life and times to be remembered fondly, like the fading ambience of pre-motor-car Vancouver.

To understand Sara and her *World*, we must harken back to that pivotal year 1858, when thousands of shabbily clad American gold miners invaded the Hudson's Bay precinct now known as British Columbia in a mad scramble for gold on the Fraser River. Governor James Douglas of Vancouver Island immediately dispatched a plea to the British Foreign Office to proclaim the mainland a colony. Otherwise, he wrote, the entire region known as New Caledonia would soon become an American state.

Lord Lytton obliged, and on November 19, 1858, Douglas was sworn in as Governor of the new colony of British Columbia. The ceremony occurred on a soggy, drizzly day at Fort Langley, on the Fraser River, which Douglas had selected as his first capital. Douglas even began construction of government buildings at Derby, site of the first Hudson's Bay fort. But when Colonel James Moody and his Royal Engineers arrived a few months later, he demanded that Douglas reconsider his choice, because he believed that the low bank situation of Derby was indefensible against American naval attack. Douglas, proud but pragmatic, relented. The capital would be located at the ancient Kwantlen village of Skaiametl, which was renamed New Westminster.

The Royal Engineers of 1859 had included a genial Irishman named John Maclure who, with his mates, began clearing, blasting stumps and erecting buildings on the steep hillside. The engineers themselves lived in a camp called Sapperton. It was here that John's wife Martha and three-year-old daughter Sara disembarked from the brig *Thames City* in April of 1859, after a harrowing voyage around Cape Horn; the sturdy little vessel carried about one hundred more sappers, together with thirty-one women and thirty-four children—the first true European settlers of the new colony. Martha's initial impression of her new homeland was that she was "very far from civilization as I had known it."

The Maclures lived at Sapperton for some six years. During that time, Sara obtained elementary schooling, supplemented by home learning. Maclure and his fellow sappers meanwhile worked with Colonial Judge Matthew Baillie Begbie in maintaining law and order. They built roads, cleared land, erected buildings and bridges, surveyed the international border and performed other sundry tasks.

In 1863, the Royal Engineers disbanded. Most men and their families, including the Maclures, elected to stay on in the new colony. John Maclure was hired to help survey a portion of the Collins Overland Telegraph route through the Fraser Valley. The route had originally been designed to connect the United States with Europe via Alaska, but was abandoned with the successful laying of the underground cable beneath the Atlantic in 1866. British Columbia, however, was left with a working telegraph system connected with the outside world.

Upon being appointed Fraser Valley superintendent of the telegraph line, Maclure took up his military land grant of 150 acres on Matsqui Prairie, upriver of New Westminster near today's City of Abbotsford. The Maclure homestead, known as Hazelbrae, was situated at the crossroads of the historic Nooksack Trail and the Western Union Telegraph Line. Here the Maclures lived in virtual isolation, dependent upon local Natives for trade and steamboats for transport down the Fraser River. Sara's brothers and sisters were schooled at home. The family's land was subject to annual flooding. Land clearing was back-breaking, with roots and stumps having to be blasted with dynamite every few feet in order to create tillable soil.

Sara was the eldest of six children, and always the leader. She loved

the frontier life—the forays with her father and brothers; her canoe trips with Indian Jack; the hunting, fishing and riding bareback on her father's horses. Judge Begbie was a frequent guest at Hazelbrae. After a weary ride about the colony on jury circuit, he loved to let his hair down and go hunt and fish in woods and slough. Sara learned to converse with the great judge about both law and deer stalking.

Sara's special passion, however, was reserved for a magical black device with shiny keys which sat on the family's living room table. Although her father was the official operator, Sara quickly learned Morse Code and began taking over the operation of the telegraph machine, tapping out messages of world news to New Westminster whenever her father asked her to cover for him.

In 1868, Sara experienced a veritable ordeal by fire. That summer, the most devastating conflagration in the recorded history of the Fraser Valley struck hard, burning vast tracts of forest. When the approaching blaze threatened the Maclure home, where Sara was alone with her mother, John Maclure happened to be away at Fort Langley, repairing a section of telegraph line. Sara and her mother relayed buckets of water from the slough to douse flying cinders and dug a fire break around the house. Suddenly from indoors Sara heard the telegraph box ticking; she ran inside and tapped out a message to her father, warning him of the imminent danger. "Coming at once," he acknowledged; "well done, Sara." Sara and her mother took to a canoe when the forest flames threatened to engulf them. Then, when all hope for the house seemed lost, Maclure appeared with a number of Sto:lo friends and the bucket brigade managed to stave off the flames.

John Maclure was so impressed with Sara's coolness under fire that he completed her training to qualify as a full-time telegraphist when Hazelbrae was upgraded from a repair office to a full repeater station. The Hazelbrae station was a critical point in the North American service, for at this juncture the main line extending from New Westminster to Barkerville connected with the Western Union line to the United States. The Western Union superintendent touring the province in 1869 was startled to find that his key southern British Columbia station was being run by a thirteen-year-old girl. The company quickly confirmed Sara's appointment as full-time operator at a staggering monthly salary of $65. In this capacity, she

relayed to southwestern British Columbia the first news of the outbreak of the Franco-Prussian War and her own province's official entry into Canadian federation.

Sara's day began at 8:00 a.m., when she commenced the receiving and relaying of telegraph messages. She even hired and fired personnel, including repairmen and an office assistant. Sara gave her employees instructions each morning, dispatching the men to trouble spots along the line where ice or windstorms had struck the wires. She also handled all public requests for news and did her own bookkeeping. In March of 1872, for instance, she recorded paying 50 cents each to Indian Peter and Indian Jim for repairs to the line.

Sara was aware of her job's importance. In August of 1872 she sent her accounts to her supervisor, Robert McMicking, with a note requesting a salary increase. (At age fifteen, Sara was already making a wage greater than any other woman in the province.) McMicking agreed to increase Sara's salary to $100 per month, stating in a report to his employer, "Sara Maclure is an efficient employee and most zealous in her exertions to further the interest of the Company. This position has hitherto exacted a salary of $75 a month at another station, when the operator there was less efficient." McMicking also increased Sara's responsibilities and ordered all employees in the Fraser Valley to "obey her commands promptly and be zealous in carrying them out."

John Maclure was amused to learn of the regard in which his daughter was held. Her efficient management of the telegraph office allowed him to trundle about the province doing survey work, his real passion. Moreover, Sara's high salary, in keeping with Victorian tradition, was put to the use of the family—in this case, for the purchase and repair of farm equipment. Sara was secretly saving a special purse for the purchase of a piano, but when the family developed a dire need for an oxen team, she readily produced her hidden cash. The oxen became known as "Sara's Piano."

By age eighteen, Sara was a tall, handsome woman with long black hair which she wore pinned up in a bun. Her life, while never languid, had settled into a pleasant routine of congenial rural flavour, spiced with the daily excitement of spreading the world's news. But in 1875, this quiet existence came to an abrupt end. Technology had caught up with Hazelbrae.

Interior of a typical West End living room on Georgia Street, c. 1901. (VPL 4152)

That year, in order to save costs, Western Union ordered the closure of dozens of telegraph stations, made redundant by new, higher speed equipment. The Hazelbrae Station was no more.

However, in recognition of Sara's outstanding communication abilities, Western Union offered her the position of assistant manager of its prestigious Victoria central office. Sara accepted without hesitation. She loved Hazelbrae, but yearned to pursue her career.

Prior to and after arriving in Victoria, Sara trained and helped locate employment for her sister Susan and brothers Sam and Charles as telegraphists in different areas of British Columbia. But she had no sooner settled into Victoria than she was called upon to troubleshoot about the province, wherever telegraph offices were poorly run. For a time she was interim manager at the Yale office, where she completely reorganized procedures and dismissed troublesome, drunken employees. She even struck up a relationship with a local American hotel bartender who wrote her love poems and proposed marriage. She politely declined the offer.

Sara became well known in Victoria as an efficient and accommodating manager of news. She often forwarded items of special interest "hot off the wire" to politicians and newspaper editors. In 1881, when she was twenty-five, Western Union promoted her to the position of Victoria manager, thereby flouting the conventional bias in North America against women executives. In fact, American telegraph superintendents in the 1890s reported that they did not "call upon women to perform at the rate of 1500 words per hour and they do not expect such a service of them." Sara demonstrated a complete self-confidence and independence of spirit that impressed not only her employer, but also the likes of James Dunsmuir and other leading politicians and industrialists of Victoria.

Most impressed of all was John McLagan, co-founder of the *Victoria Times*. McLagan was a widower, recently arrived from Winnipeg. Slim, nimble, possessed of a ready wit and an engaging smile, McLagan was a human dynamo of energy, driven by an unlimited faith in technology, urban growth and the liberal ideals of Western civilization: the ultimate business booster with a social conscience. He had successfully established the Guelph Sewing Machine Company in Ontario, where he grew up. But his first and lasting love was newspaper publishing.

As a young boy, McLagan had read George Brown's *Globe* with awe. Brown had founded the first truly modern Canadian newspaper with his consistent coverage of political events and colourful leaders, and serialization of popular fiction. McLagan worked for a time at the *Globe* as a travelling correspondent. Later he became a printer, and in 1862 he published the *Guelph Mercury*. Then tragedy struck: his wife and four of his five children died in a diphtheria epidemic.

McLagan was devastated. For a period, he could only mope about, an emotional wreck. Then, endeavouring to blot out the memories, he did what thousands of other Canadians had done before him: he headed west, taking in tow his surviving son Jack. Upon establishing the *Victoria Times*, McLagan acted as managing editor and was joined in partnership by the Hon. William Templeton.

John McLagan courted Sara for only a few months before they were married in December of 1884. Sara immediately resigned her post as telegraph manager in order to assist McLagan with his burgeoning newspaper. To both her employer and her city friends, Sara appeared to succumb to Victorian mores of the day which dictated that a wife establish a home for her husband and provide a "stable refuge from the impersonal public sphere that men were now entering in increasing numbers." The truth of the matter was that Sara had mastered the telegraph management position and looked forward to the exciting challenge of running a newspaper.

The Government Telegraph Service, successor to Western Union, wrote to Sara that her resignation was a matter of "deep regret...and a loss to the public of a courteous and obliging servant." The political and business community, represented by MPP Robert Dunsmuir and David Higgins, staged a ceremony by way of public address to Sara for her special service to the fledgling province. She was heralded as "a most womanly woman and yet one of the very few who can talk politics with men without making them wish for an excuse to change the subject."

Sara worked with her husband on all aspects of *Times* management for four years. In 1888, McLagan was approached by senior officials of the Liberal Party of Canada, of which he was a member, who asked him to consider founding a newspaper in Vancouver. The politicians reasoned that after the CPR extended its terminus to the old Granville townsite, Vancouver would grow to rival Victoria as the province's major city. The only daily newspaper in Vancouver at the time was the staid Tory press, the *News-Advertiser*, run by Conservative MPP Francis Carter-Cotton.

McLagan eagerly grabbed at the opportunity to bring a *Globe* of the West to the mainland. It was an age when, as Susannah Moodie put it, "the Canadian cannot get by without his newspaper any more than an American could do without his tobacco." Moreover, an eastern Grit senator promised to loan $23,000 to cover startup costs; the remaining expense would be covered by Sara and John jointly.

The excited couple packed their bags and crossed the strait immediately, McLagan having arranged for his partner to take over sole ownership of the *Times*. Young Jack grumbled about this latest disruption to his life, but his father assured him that Vancouver would be much more exciting than staid old Victoria. Within a few months, on September 29, 1888—

two days after Stanley Park was opened—the first issue of the *Vancouver Daily World* rolled off the presses. McLagan's opening editorial began: "The *World* proposes first to conserve the very best interests of Vancouver, the Terminal City. It will cater more especially to the citizens of Vancouver…" Sara's odyssey had begun.

CHAPTER ONE

Flotsam and Jetsam

In its earliest years, British Columbia was a raw, uncouth, uproarious colony born in the haste and tumult of the Gold Rush. And I was there, from the time of the first shipload of colonists on the *Thames City*, right through the Great War. Many memories dance before my eyes—the huge trees, fires and floods, sternwheelers on the Fraser, colourful men like Judge Begbie and Governor Douglas, and most of all, toil and hardship. But the crisis point of my life and times, the time of trauma and excitement, was those dying years of the nineteenth century and the birth of the new. To those who came later, the early years of the twentieth century were a mere Edwardian hiatus presaging Armageddon. But to us alive in that dawn, life coursed swift and strong and vital through our veins.

It is not always easy for a person raised in the country to adapt to the life of the city. But to me there was something alluring about Vancouver from its humble beginnings. I reached port just after the Great Fire and cannot attest to its seedy Gassy Jack prelude. But as Wordsworth wrote, "Bliss was it in that dawn to be alive," and to a woman over thirty, it was even "very heaven." I suppose that there is some vanity here, for women were somewhat lacking in the town, which gave those of us in higher society much attention, some authority, and certainly countless charitable chores.

When I think back, it is as if my entire life was but a preparation for the challenges of 1901, when my own world fell apart. The whole of North

Newsboys pose in front of the Daily Province *offices, wearing many different kinds of hats. (VPL 16830)*

America was caught in a web of excitement over new inventions. Daily life was changing rapidly. Yet we all clung to the unchangeable icons and mores of the Victorian age. Even in Vancouver—still juvenile and strapping—we worshipped the Union Jack. Britannia ruled the waves and much of the world, and it was surely only a matter of time before Britain and her brash, upstart child to the south of us would dominate the entire globe with superior Anglo-Saxon values.

Turn-of-the-century Vancouver was indeed a fun place. I think of bicycle jaunts to English Bay, Sunday picnics at Stanley Park, and three-masted ships of the line in the Inlet. Of singing "The Last Rose of Summer" and reciting poetic favourites like "When all the world was young lad, and all the trees were green." Yet it was an age too of excess—in decor, dress and spending habits. Some of us emulated the theatre stars in our fashion, and we all followed the doings of the Astors, Vanderbilts and our very own Edward, Prince of Wales.

One could sit in the parlour's curtained bay window with the ladies and discuss bloomers and George Eliot and homeless mothers, and agree that the radical suffragettes were on the right track but a little too crude, while all the while the Victrola squeaked away in the background. Oh yes, and some women got into painting their faces with eye shadow, paste rouge, mascara and dabs of Velva Cream. Many wore spats—even men—and when we cycled to the beach the men took care never to mount their cycles until every lady was seated and ready to pedal.

The bicycle was the liberator of the nineties, especially for women. Not only were women more mobile, but fashion had to adapt. Some of us wore riding skirts with long gaiters. The more daring—and in Vancouver there were many—wore bloomers, causing even the normally liberal *Saturday Night* to complain, "The female who wears them is a fright… bloomers reveal the most shapeless lot of legs ever seen outside a butcher shop."

Most of my circle of women bore a strong social conscience. And while we may not have been blazing radicals like Sylvia Pankhurst or Helena Gutteridge, we thought of ourselves as "new women" in the tradition of Sara Duncan, Kit Coleman and, above all, Lady Aberdeen. "Pluck and plod" was our ethic. We thought we had good reason to believe that, as Laurier put it, the next century would be Canada's, and we had no doubt that Vancouver was destined to become a great city of the world. And until the late nineties, most of us had never even heard of the Boers of South Africa or a psychiatrist in Vienna named Freud…

From the time those Liberal Party hacks approached John in 1888, I was his partner in launching and running the *World*. Oh, I remember their promises. John was deeply absorbed in Liberal politics and would believe most anything that the eastern brass told him. Well, this Ontario senator did send out $23,000 all right as a loan to start up the paper, but the local party hacks raked $5,000 off the top and we were left with the full $23,000 debt to repay. My own personal savings which I brought to our marriage were significant, and were invested heavily in the purchase of presses and other equipment.

What kind of a town did we find on Burrard Inlet? By the time we arrived, about 10,000 people had dug themselves out of the ashes of the Great Fire and rebuilt most of the city. West End lots cost about $800; a choice commercial lot at Cordova and Water streets went for $1,500. One could buy a pack of twenty-one meal tickets at the Pacific Hotel for $5. Residents glowed with pride at the new Stanley Park, and a park tour was not complete without a viewing of the old wreck of the SS *Beaver* off Siwash Rock. A new waterworks system from the Capilano River gave us the purest water in the world. Victoria was envied, but we at least were assured that our lacrosse team could whip the capital boys; New Westminster was mocked as a has-been stump town possessed of surplus churches and a lacrosse team which we derisively labelled "salmonbellies."

Indians were still a common sight in the city, and from my Georgia Street window I would often watch paddlers from the Seymour and Capilano reserves cross the Inlet and beach their canoes near the *Empress* dock. Indians also still gathered together at low tide to harvest clams along the shore of Stanley Park, and once or twice a year there was an exceptionally low tide that brought out hundreds of Salish to partake in an ancient harvesting tradition of working the extensive clam beds through the night. This was a spectacle which I shall never forget—hundreds of figures working silently in the dusk with little spades, a sea of steady, glowing lights as the night came on. The Indians had made torches from fir gum and branches called "pitch sticks," which they slung across their canoes, the craft being covered with mud to prevent a fire. This allowed the harvesters to illuminate the exposed diggings. The dots of light lining the shore presented an eerie spectacle.

We started the dear old *World* as an evening paper, and quickly gathered a dominant market share over Carter-Cotton's morning *News-Advertiser*. John was versatile in all aspects of the printing trade and wrote decent editorials. Our offices were located at the corner of Homer and Pender streets. We contracted the construction of the building through my brother Sam Maclure, who was becoming prominent in the architecture field in Victoria. We proudly accepted accolades for the building on its completion as "possibly the best lighted and best arranged newspaper office in the Dominion."

John O'Brien was our first editor-in-chief, though no editor ever had a free hand; my husband and I frequently wrote the lead editorials and reshaped our editor's handiwork. Sam Robb was our top reporter; David Higgins, author and for several years Legislative Speaker, contributed articles. They were all characters. Higgins had come out to the region for the Fraser Gold Rush in 1858, and over sherry and rubber bridge, he regaled us often with tales of the West.

Cycling in Stanley Park was tremendously popular at century's turn. Note the formal dress. (VPL 5448)

Sam Robb was absolutely the most intrepid, indomitable character I have ever met. He once crossed Burrard Inlet in a canoe, after the ferries had all put into port to await the abatement of a major storm. Just as he approached the North Vancouver shore, he was swamped by a big wave and rescued by an Indian from the nearby Capilano reserve. He didn't get the story he was pursuing, but the tale of his ordeal on the inlet made excellent copy.

Sam's ragged moustache and unkempt hair were well-known features of the Vancouver street scene for many years. His appearance, however, made him persona non grata at certain uptown salons. For years, his abode was the old Clarendon Hotel. Here he used to place his dripping umbrella in the lobby rack to dry after coming inside from a typical Vancouver shower. It was always being stolen, so Sam painted the words "stolen from Sam Robb" on the inside of the bumbershoot. One day an unsuspecting guest picked up Sam's umbrella from the rack; he was accosted shortly after on the sidewalk by a policeman, who pointed out to the gentleman the white lettering inside the umbrella. "I guess I must have made a mistake," the man stammered. Sam was robbed no more.

For us, the enfant terrible of the nineties was Francis Carter-Cotton. This strident Tory publisher and longtime Vancouver MPP was scholarly, frugal and a good businessman. I can see in my mind's eye even now his wide white whiskers and broad forehead. He took himself very seriously, but could also be sporting in his editorials. Dry, though. He loved reporting proceedings of meetings, and his paper became known as the Hansard of BC. Such a stickler for procedure—he used to berate his reporters for failing to write "The meeting was then adjourned" at the end of every story about a public gathering.

But Carter-Cotton was very shrewd and innovative. He had obtained a monopoly on the morning Canadian Pacific telegraph reports, thus ensuring that no morning newspaper would ever compete with the *News-Advertiser*. In 1895, after we installed our own linotypes at the *World*, Cotton purchased the first lithograph machines and electrified his presses.

At first John and I were envious of Cotton's electric presses. But then it turned funny, for the story soon spread that every time a tram car passed by the *News-Advertiser* office at Cambie and Pender, the presses would slow down to a groan, due to loss of power. So Cotton installed a waterwheel, backed up by a steam engine for extra power. But something was always breaking down with his electrical operations until the city's power grid system finally emerged on the scene with good capacity.

Cotton was not only stubborn in his ways, but fearless. In 1894 he went to prison for a few days for libel, refusing to apologize for slights to the premier and other government members. His friend William Van Horne of the CPR wrote to cheer him in jail: "I think it was old James Bennett who once said that a newspaper man who had defended a dozen libel suits and served a term in jail was on the high road to success." Cotton blamed Premier Davie and my husband John for his incarceration, thundering a headliner with: "Mr. Cotton is still in jail; Messrs. Davie and McLagan are still running at large."

Cotton's acerbic attacks and John's equally vitriolic responses were all good sport. But the man who really got under John's skin was Walter Nichol, owner of the *Province*. This paper was a transplant from Victoria, said to have been removed to Vancouver at the behest of CPR interests who wanted a Vancouver press more sympathetic to their concerns. When it began publication in 1898, John dismissed the *Province* as "an obscure and very puerile publication from Victoria."

Nichol responded to the *World's* jab with a cut to the quick: "When Senator McLagan of the esteeemed *Vancouver World* smites the *Province*, hip and thigh, with his editorial jawbone, it is distressing indeed... Does he suppose for one moment that the Liberals of this province are prepared to bow down to the *World*, its man-servants, its maid-servants, its ox and its Senator McLagan?"

I suppose John deserved to be upbraided, but the "senator" razzing really hurt. After all of John's work for Laurier and his organization of the federal Liberal party in Vancouver, we had counted upon a senatorship—indeed, Laurier himself had hinted at it. Instead, John's ex-partner from Victoria, William Templeton, was appointed. John had no sooner recovered from his disappointment than illness struck in the form of the initial stages of tuberculosis, or consumption as everyone called it. Some days he was too weak to work.

Vancouverites were excited in 1898, what with the Klondike Rush on and ships sailing into and out of port every hour. We had experienced business recession in the nineties, but never looked back after '98. Tougher times loomed for us in the newspaper business, however, what with Nichol's new *Province* giving us stiff competition. My land, there were now three dailies serving fewer than 25,000 people, employing collectively over one hundred men and women.

Today, with our refined metropolis, it is impossible to imagine the incredible masses of men who washed through the city in 1898, bound for the Klondike. My friend Julia Henshaw described it well: "Down along the waterfront, all was life and bustle. Prospectors off to Atlin swaggered along in brand new corduroys, each man's heart aglow with hope, and his mouth full of prophecies concerning the placer claims he was going to locate in the new Eldorado. At the street corner, some returned Klondikers were pulling gold nuggets as large as marbles out of their pockets by way of illustrating northern yarns, and the crowded thoroughfares echoed with the hum of business... There a curbstone broker had pounced upon a citizen and was

View of West Georgia Street and Stanley Park, taken from the Hotel Vancouver at Granville and Georgia. Christ Church Cathedral is at middle left. Note the mowed boulevards and wood plank sidewalks. (CVA Van Sc P89 N88)

trying to sell him something that he didn't want, and on every side were heard quotations in stocks and the latest news from Dawson City, coupled with a hint at some rich strike just telegraphed from Kootenay."

The hope of becoming an instant millionaire was infectious, causing many steadily employed husbands and fathers to drop everything and set sail for the north. The lure of the gold fields was fuelled in part by the regular arrival into port of steamers such as the *Hating*. This ship was invariably loaded with gold that was ceremoniously transported in heavily guarded wagons to the city Assay Office.

Even Vancouver children got into the Klondike spirit. Noting the proclivity of prospectors for dogs, youngsters quickly learned to train stray mutts which they hitched up to little wagons. Then they sold the dogs to happy miners who were convinced of the dogs' ability to pull sleds over Yukon snow. Boats left the Burrard docks laden with hundreds of barking mongrels tied to the deck amidst the debris of multitudinous sacks and luggage. One evening, City Council considered whether sending these dogs off

Robertson & Hackett Sawmill, foot of Granville Street at False Creek, c. 1902. There were two other sawmills here at this time. At right are some small salmon fishing boats, tied bow to stern. They were manufactured by Alfred Wallace, a boatbuilder who in 1900 won a federal contract to build the government steamer Kestrel, shown partially constructed at left. (CVA Mi P68 N54)

to their harsh fate was cruelty, but when one alderman pointed out the volume of complaints against the poundkeeper over stray dogs in the West End, the matter was quietly dropped.

We tolerated the bedlam of miners in the city because of the prosperity it brought us. Overnight, whole new blocks of stores sprang up. There were Help Wanted signs everywhere. Recession had turned to boom. Retailer Charlie Woodward epitomized the surge, with his prosperous new dry goods store on Westminster Avenue (later Main Street). Woodward, like his competitors David Spencer and Timothy Eaton, did not believe in credit. "We keep no books," boasted Woodward, "and have no accountants, thereby saving thousands of dollars to those who patronize our store."

But in the wake of the boom, we forever lost False Creek for recreation, what with the emergent boatbuilding industry there and all the planing mills. Skid Row also flourished, and culture, education and living conditions there all lagged far behind the sudden prosperity experienced by the middle and upper classes.

As President of the Vancouver Council of Women, I worked with Lady Aberdeen to establish a training home for the Victorian Order of Nurses in Vancouver. This project was the result of a scheme devised after the Council had sent four nurses to the Yukon to help poor miners and their wives who fell ill or needed sustenance. Lady Aberdeen entrusted me to raise funds, and sent me a list of "what is suggested for each nurse for a year, over and above the rations provided by government."

The nurses were a great hit with the miners, trudging along to the goldfields with groups of men and doling out bannock, dried apples and coffee. The publicity which I gave the whole scheme in the *World* prompted city businesses to donate the requested funds, and in April of 1898 I introduced the four nurses at a Vancouver reception. In July, I brought Lady Aberdeen herself to town to announce the establishment of our training school. Skilled medical personnel in Vancouver were sadly lacking, and we stirred up so much enthusiasm that some eighty businessmen pledged financial support for a new nurses' training facility. (I later used that support to cajole City Council into building a new hospital.)

There was so little help for the downtrodden in those days—least of all for women, great numbers of whom were pouring into town in the wake of worldwide publicity about the Klondike Rush and Vancouver's leading role as supplier to the prospectors. To accommodate many homeless girls—and keep them off Skid Row—my church auxiliary established the first YWCA hostel in 1898 at 502 Pender Street. But many of these girls landed up in trouble. Those who did find work away from the Dupont Street brothels were paid pathetic wages for the most part. As I wrote in the *World*: "It is the disgrace of our civilization that no class in our large cities works so hard for so little money… as the working women and girls who are compelled to support themselves by the labour of their hands."

The city jailor would frequently call my home and ask that I come down to the lockup and console women or girls who had been brought in for sundry offences, there being no matron. I spent an entire night in the lockup comforting one young woman who had been brought in for debt— much like a Dickens tale. It transpired that the woman's husband had embezzled funds in New York, used his wife to sign assorted legal docu-

Dry goods stores flourished in 1898, when thousands of Klondike miners swept through town on their way north. This building at 326 Cordova Street was formerly the publishing office of the World *newspaper before the presses moved to Homer and Pender streets. (CVA Bu P311 N699)*

ments assuming responsibility, and then deserted her for parts unknown. In the morning I had Bowser, my own attorney, free her from jail.

As Vancouver had been razed in 1886, so old New Westminster perished in 1898. Fire broke out on the Columbia Street waterfront and spread rapidly. Residents ran terrified up the steep streets to escape the flames, grabbing a few meagre possessions. Flaming shingles sailed in the night wind, and canneries near the Fraser wharves blew up, causing cans of salmon to explode and hurtle shredded fish and shards of tin in every direction. By nightfall it was all over, and as the *Columbian* reported, "in the sickly sight of Sunday's dawn, thousands looked down on the smoking remains of what had been as beautiful, well built and well kept a city as there was on the coast."

That afternoon John and I raced by tram and then buggy to the smoking ruins and helped organize a relief committee. The helpless and the homeless were a pitiful sight. Ahead of the mainstream community in recovery were the city's Chinese, who, with aid from the Chinese Benevolent Society of Victoria, began on Monday to rebuild their Chinatown buildings brick by brick. John travelled back to Vancouver, but I stayed on that week, wired Lady Aberdeen in Ottawa for immediate assistance, and established the first Council of Women chapter in New Westminster.

The fire had made a deep impression on me. The acrid stench of smoke and fumes seemed to linger in my nostrils for days. It brought back painful memories of the great Fraser Valley fire of 1868 which nearly destroyed our Hazelbrae farm and in which my mother sustained severe smoke inhalation damage to her lungs. The key to every emergency was organization. I addressed my Vancouver Council thus: "I think that the New Westminster fire demonstrated to everyone the need of an organized body of women in every community ready to be called together for any emergency; for without such an organization we would have been powerless to act as promptly or as effectually in alleviating the suffering of the distressed families."

Yes, 1898 was a tumultuous year; but progress was made, to be sure. As co-owner of a leading daily newspaper I was able to move along my causes here and there, although it was only the year before that married women had been given the right to own their own property. Suffragettes were on the march, led by the intrepid Maria Grant of Victoria, who was elected the province's first female school trustee. Petition after petition was piled at the feet of the legislative members, seeking the provincial franchise for women. I certainly gave the cause editorial support, but at the same time took care to extol the virtues of good Queen Victoria so as to demonstrate that we weren't so radical as to want to destroy the social fabric or to use the franchise to vote against men as a bloc.

The *World's* sometime editor David Higgins, Speaker of the House, was certainly discomfited when the Bill of Enfranchisement was introduced in the Legislature by Dr. J. S. Helmcken in May of 1897. It happened, you see, that Mrs. Higgins' name was at the very top of the petition attached to the bill. Dr. Helmcken spoke jocularly to House members: "One of the great objections of some members is that they are afraid that the ladies will usurp the seats in the House, and that Mrs. D. W. Higgins, whose name appears first on the petition, might some day occupy the Speaker's chair." Higgins grimaced, covered his face, and never did reveal where he really stood on suffrage.

However, the Enfranchisement Bill of '97 was defeated, as it was again in 1898 when one Member, a Major Mutter, told the legislature that "it is a scientific fact that the brain of a woman weighed precisely two ounces less than a man."

In my Lady Cook column of the *World*, I wrote: "The tyranny of taxation without representation against which every Englishman feels justified in taking up arms the world over, is laid upon women still. How long is this grave injustice to continue? The extension of the franchise to women would do for them as a body what has already been done for the labouring classes; would remove a host of abuses; would give women a practical interest in the growth and prosperity of their country; and would sweep away those conditions which impede the increase of their self-respect and independence."

So the fight for political equality continued unabated. My Vancouver Women's Council supported Maria Grant and the WCTU on most of their social reform policies. I couldn't help but view their linkage of suffrage with liquor prohibition as counterproductive with male voters, but Maria was zealously committed to both causes, and completely fearless. Her 1898 call to arms helped to spur on each of our local women's councils to establish a committee to investigate laws affecting women and children generally.

Our committees studied four areas of reform: the legal status of women, care and custody of children, women in the workplace, and the treatment of women and juvenile criminal offenders. Our reports and lobbying of government bore immediate fruit. In 1898, the Legislature passed the Children's Protection Act, which allowed the Women's Council provincially to establish the Children's Aid Society. Volunteer funding would be supplemented by a grant from Victoria on a per child basis. In addition, abused and abandoned children were to be helped in an organized fashion.

We were still a long way from solving the problems of children and women, both within and outside of the family. It was not until 1917 and the granting of full women's suffrage that a mother gained equal rights to guardianship of her own children. A husband could, up until then, desert his family and still dictate the terms of his children's education—or the rotter could simply grab the children from the mother at any time. Equally obnoxious was a father's complete lack of legal responsibility for his illegitimate children.

The Klondike Gold Rush had deposited much flotsam and jetsam on Vancouver shores, some of which stuck around. Louis Taylor, for example, was an unemployed Michigan bank teller who had searched for gold near Telegraph Creek. He found nothing, became destitute and washed ashore in Vancouver in 1898 without having eaten a meal in thirty-six hours. He hired on checking freight for the CPR at $45 a month. A few months later he responded to a humorous editorial printed by Walter Nichol in the *Province*, in which Nichol bemoaned his paper route delivery problems.

Taylor was a resourceful young man with a gift of the gab. He presented Nichol with a plan to increase *Province* circulation and offered his services on a commission contract basis. Well, it worked out grand: *Province* circulation shot up, due to Taylor's reliable grid route delivery system. Soon L.D., as he was known to friends, was seen about town, swaggering about wearing his trademark red bow tie, an irrepressible smile on his face. This penniless ex-bank clerk was destined to hold office as Vancouver's mayor for much of his later life.

No less irrepressible on the Vancouver scene was Julia Henshaw, with whom I began cultivating a turbulent but lifelong friendship. Julia was a society hostess, novelist, journalist and botanist. In 1896 she hiked to the source of the Columbia and Kootenay rivers. In 1898 she achieved continent-wide fame with the publication of her novel *Hypnotized*. She was a frequent contributor to the *Province* and the *News-Advertiser*, writing mostly about the Vancouver society scene.

But Julia could also be very political, and I often clashed with her on her ultra-conservative views. In her books, anyone unemployed was just lazy. "There is bread and butter for all on the Pacific Coast," she wrote, "but it is not to be had for picking up—it must be earned by honest work.

Deadman's Island, photographed from Stanley Park, 1898. For centuries this piece of land was used as a burial ground by local Natives, and later it became a cemetery for indigent people of all races. But the island was most famous for the Ludgate affair. Ludgate, a Chicago entrepreneur, got a permit from the federal government to build a sawmill and log Deadman's, in spite of strong objections from aboriginal people and many other Vancouver residents. When Ludgate's crew showed up to cut the first trees, they were met by Mayor Garden and several police constables, who arrested them. The controversy raged for ten years. (CVA StPk P125 N138)

Employment can always be had by every able-bodied man and in Vancouver, abject poverty is scarcely ever heard of, and starvation unknown." I took her to task for those last lines, and invited her to visit the slums of Skid Row and the deserted mothers and children living in squalor around False Creek and other areas east of Carrall Street.

Julia's husband was a gadfly who loved entertaining so much that Vancouverites dubbed him "Afternoon Tea Charlie." He became most unpopular one night, however, after clothing his dinner guests in imported Parisian bathing costumes for an impromptu swimming party in his magnificent pool. The guests frolicked about for a time in the water, only to find that the swim suits dissolved completely after ten minutes. Julia was not amused.

The man whom Vancouverites tried to run out of town in 1898 was Theodore Ludgate. This ex-banker from Chicago arrived in Vancouver with the single-minded purpose of building a sawmill and logging off Deadman's Island, a piece of land regarded by the locals as part of Stanley Park. Despite protests from just about everyone, the federal government, as owner of the island, granted Ludgate a twenty-five-year lease to log timber there at a rental of $500 per year.

When Ludgate and his logging crew arrived to commence cutting trees, they were met by Mayor Garden and several policemen chosen specially for their conservationist sensibilities. The mayor read the Riot Act—though he was completely out of order—and then ordered Ludgate to withdraw. Ludgate ignored the mayor and had his workers begin axing the nearest big cedars and firs. At this point, the men in blue moved in and arrested Ludgate and his crew.

The Ludgate affair put Vancouver on the map as some ambivalent city on the West Coast whose inhabitants loved industrial growth, sawmill fumes, squalor and wealth side by side—but would rise in wrath to protect a single tree that formed part of the cityscape held sacred by all residents. Well, not quite all. Down at the old Savoy Hotel, workingmen at the bar sang: "Those West End mugs you would think they own the town. They would like to get that isle for a lawn tennis ground."

The Deadman's Island controversy simmered on. Rather than give up his rights, Ludgate sued in the courts. When John visited Laurier on Liberal Party business in Ottawa in 1899, he tried to get the Ludgate lease revoked, but the prime minister said that would not be possible. It was not until ten years later that the federal cabinet passed an order-in-council transferring the islet to the city, and by that time all of the big trees had been logged off.

Meanwhile, everyone ignored the protestations of the local Indians, who deplored the desecration of traditional burial grounds on the islet. For centuries, Indians had buried their dead at False Creek, Prospect Point and Deadman's Island. In the 1870s Chief Joe Capilano had thwarted an attempt by one John Morton, an early pioneer, to settle on Deadman's,

The News-Advertiser *composing room, 1895. The owners of the* News-Advertiser, *the* World's *major competitor for some years, prided themselves on leading the way in newspaper technology. They bought the first linotype machines to be used in British Columbia. (VPL)*

explaining that Morton would be uncomfortable living with the spirits of the dead. (Morton paddled over to the islet anyway, to take a better look; a quick tour revealed hundreds of cedar coffins perched in the trees and convinced him of the wisdom of Chief Joe's advice.)

In more recent years, Deadman's had served as a burial ground for indigent people of all races. Police Chief Stewart, who had supervised these burials, claimed in fact to have named the islet: "In 1885, when the present site of Vancouver was almost a wilderness, we had quite a large floating population of tramps, siwashes, Mexicans, and poor whites. We had then no burying ground, and our dead were taken over to New Westminster for interment. A number of deaths of people who had been in poor circumstances occurred… and I had the remains interred on what is known now as Deadman's Island. The name was used, I believe, for the first time by me."

There was no question that the city's scenic setting would continue to draw tourists, despite logging and sawmill activity. Some of the sights we

Many Native British Columbians lived off the reserves in shanties and shacks on the Vancouver waterfront. This family was photographed c. 1900. (VPL 13013)

tried to hide from visitors, such as the gambling dens of Chinatown. Oh, and just about anywhere in town you might run into a chain gang or two. While walking to the new Crofton private school one morning, student Ethel Wilson told her parents of passing the chain gang clearing building lots at Davie and Jervis streets. "The men of the chain gang," Wilson stated, "were all shackled. They were driven to work in a wagon with a team of horses and were guarded by keepers who cradled guns in their arms in traditional style. I was always a little afraid and did not turn to look at the chain gang, although I wanted to explore their faces, and understand why this had come about."

Cordova Street at night was also definitely off limits to respectable folk, since many pairs of gaudily rouged ladies in black roamed about there looking for business. A kinder portrait of the Cordova scene was painted by city poet John Elliott:

If ever I dream of the streets of heaven
I see but Cordova Street in Ninety Seven;
What if no Woolworths Five and Ten,
We had Russell and Macdonald's then;
And listen you Festival folk and know
We had a genuine burlesque show;
Ye old Savoy
You could enter and enjoy;
The show, some said it was not nice;
But at least it cost but a very small price...

Then across the street we march
And gaze at Andy Tyson's whale bone arch;
Then past Trorey's with the clock
You could see the time for half a block...
Then perhaps before we wander on
Go over and have a beer, have a big one,
With August Sehwan
Then across again to stand agog
At Mr. Musket's Tiny Dog.

But now we must hasten on
To try our luck with the Brothers Quann;
There was always a game in their old Balmoral,
Then turn the corner into Carrall;
And as our Omega
See Joe Fortes in the Bodega.

CHAPTER TWO

Fighting Joe Martin

From the moment John and I landed in Vancouver, the *World* consumed our lives. John was a tall, lean man, and his mind was ever quick. He loved a good argument, and he usually gave as good as he got. He was a trifle sensitive on the subject of Vancouver's stature and future prospects, refusing to tolerate criticism of his adopted city. In politics, he continued to be the leading federal Liberal organizer in the lower mainland, and despite his disappointment over the senatorship, he never swerved in his loyalty to Laurier.

John and I both had wanted children. Having lost all of the children but Jack from his prior marriage, John longed to rebuild his family. Well, Geraldine was born in 1886, followed by Hazel in 1887, Douglas in 1890, Doris in 1893 and then Margitte in 1894.

Tragically, Geraldine passed away in 1891 of scarlet fever. We buried her at Fairview Cemetery. John took it terribly hard; he had recurring nightmares of illness stealing away his loved ones all over again. He remained morose and withdrawn for many months after her death. I gradually coaxed him out of depression, but afterwards he drove himself harder and harder at the office, completely unmindful of his tuberculosis symptoms.

John wanted his son Jack to get along with our children, but Jack remained sullen and withdrawn. I tried hard to befriend him, but he bitterly resented me and his half-siblings. John found him a job at the paper, but after a while Jack quit and went to work on the Burrard docks as a stevedore. This pained John, for he loved the boy, but it was clear that Jack would not be living with us for long. John was often stern and sharp with Douglas during this period. He told me that if Jack was a failure, then it was his fault as a father and he had best keep Douglas on a short leash.

We lived in a two-and-a-half-storey frame house on Georgia Street which overlooked Burrard Inlet. It was a typical West End upper middle class home of the times, with a covered porch, gabled end facing the street, and several bay windows. Visitors to the city commented that such homes were a blend of San Francisco modern and southern Ontario city house.

Not all of the homes on our street were so conventional. A potpourri of sizes, shapes and designs dotted Georgia in the 1890s—very individual and not always tasteful. One *Province* correspondent in fact labelled my neighbours' homes "outré," describing them as "miserable little houses, architectural monstrosities, the row of mustard pots on Georgia Hill—at the bottom of which is a pepper-box (of dirty white shade), then come the mustard pots, of colour violent enough to knock you down, save at the top of the row—where the condiment has evidently become a trifle dry and consequently of a duller hue; truly every prospect pleases and only this cruet-stand and such like enormities are vile."

Although the venerable Anglican Christ Church Cathedral stood only two blocks away, we attended St. Andrew's Presbyterian, which was five blocks east on Georgia and Richards. The church was a focal point for not only religious but considerable civic social activity. The annual St. Andrew's Ball was for many years one of Vancouver's gala events, attracting all of the city tycoons, naval officers in full dress uniform, and the cream of West End fashionable women in their handsome gowns. My favourite dress for these occasions was made of green velvet and silk with violets. Taxing affairs, mind you. John was president of the church society and invariably we were the last to leave for home in the pre-dawn hours.

I did not have any strong theological views; but I regarded the church as an important element in maintaining stability and public morality—even if I didn't always share the preacher's dogma. Our church acted as the Liberal counterbalance to the Tories' Christ Church, where Sir Charles Hibbert and Lady Tupper reigned (not necessarily in that order). Our

The Honourable Joseph Martin, a quixotic and charismatic man, served as Premier for a few months in 1900. Prime Minister Laurier refused to endorse this Liberal firebrand, who drew so little support from legislative members that he had to appoint nonelected Cabinet members—including a grocery clerk named Ryder, whom Martin met as a stranger on a train. Ryder alighted from the train as Minister of Finance. (CVA Port P1756 N1074)

church building was of a striking appearance inside. The high ceiling was nicely frescoed, while the seats were arranged in tiers like an amphitheatre, sloping toward the pulpit. A huge gallery extended all around the rear and sides of the auditorium.

The minister who presided over St. Andrew's from its inception was the fiery Ontario born Rev. E. D. McLaren, enemy of sloth, drink, gambling and debauchery. McLaren provided good theatre every Sunday. Gentle Mayor Garden lived in terror of McLaren's regular admonitions to City Council about the slack enforcement of gambling and prostitution laws down on Dupont Street. But McLaren was also a compassionate man behind the rhetoric, and he worked hard with my Council of Women for many worthy causes, including the founding of the Children's Aid Society.

Middle and upper class society yearned for culture in the hitherto bawdy port on the inlet. And, like the economic boom which came with the '98 gold rush, culture arrived on the tide as well. The CPR-owned Opera House stood just behind the old Vancouver Hotel at Georgia and Granville. This magnificent building seated some 2,000 persons and boasted a stage measuring fifty by seventy-five feet, set against a magnificent oil-painted backdrop of the Rockies. The sign at the entrance doors read: "We do not require ladies to remove their hats in the theatre as is the custom in the United States. Ladies in British Columbia know that gentlemen cannot see through felt and feathers."

Star after star from the New York and London stages performed at the Opera House, and we began to take for granted the likes of Melba, Paderewski and Sarah Bernhardt. One local favourite was Pauline Johnson, the most famous Indian poet in Canada, whom Vancouver adopted as its very own. Pauline belonged to my Council of Women and she also served as a National Council executive member on behalf of Indian women of Canada.

I can vividly recall Pauline Johnson reading her inspiring poems to a packed house one evening before the century's turn—why, even staid old Sir Charles Tupper stood up in his box and applauded wildly. On another occasion Pauline appeared and forcefully delivered two new poems, "Canadian Born" and "Riders of the Plains." The audience remained hushed for quite a time during this rendition, completely nonplussed at her subtle parody of Ottawa high society. Then the house broke up in laughter when Pauline mimicked a pompous railway director who praised the loyalty of Vancouver to the CPR.

Mark Twain toured the city a few times—a lovable, companionable man with bushy moustache and blue eyes. He always reminded me of Bill Miner, the twinkle-eyed American train robber who staged Canada's first train holdup in 1904 at Mission. Twain was completely uninhibited, though he spoke with a slight nasal twang. I recall one night at the Opera House when he had a bad cold. Everyone laughed so at his pronunciation that he had to keep pausing to be heard in his recital of *The Tragedy of Pudd'nhead Wilson*.

I admired and pitied Twain. The grand old man of American humour had lost his fortune many years before in a business venture. In order to repay his debts, he had embarked on a nine-year world lecture tour. Sam Robb interviewed Twain in his hotel room prior to his last appearance in Vancouver. "Are you preparing for your lecture tonight, Mr. Clemens?" he asked. Twain looked thoughtfully at the candle burning on a table by the edge of his bed. Then he replied, "I am preparing my entertainment by the light of other days." Twain returned home from his ramblings later that year, his lecture tours forever behind him. We enjoyed and laughed at his book of experiences entitled *A Tramp Abroad*.

Occasionally we would attend the Savoy Music Hall, built in 1898 on Cordova Street. Young Al Jolson played there, and in March of 1899, the infamous "Klondike Nugget," Gussie Lamore, appeared. (Respectable folk stayed away.) Then there was the Alhambra, opened in 1899 at the corner of Pender and Howe.

The Alhambra catered to vaudeville. It seated eight hundred people—in plebeian chairs, mind you, not at all like the cushy velvet seats of the Opera House. Theatre patrons there would often yell insulting remarks when the act deteriorated—which was often—like "Supe, Supe" and "23 Skidoo," all the while throwing crackers, peanuts and orange peels onto the raised stage. Although the Alhambra was not generally suitable for family folk, we did go once to watch Charlie Chaplin and another time to celebrate Queen Victoria's birthday.

Competing with the Alhambra for working class patronage was the

Grand Theatre on Cordova, which was also built in the wake of the
Klondike Rush. Here the vaudeville acts emphasized Elizabethan humour.
Seats cost only 25 cents, and it was common for miners, loggers and mill-
workers to congregate there—after fortifying themselves with spirits from
the numerous bars nearby—to lustily sing "On the Banks of the Wabash"
and "Oh, Susannah." The local favourite was "City of Sighs and Tears,"
which struck a chord with lonely men seeking the comforts of the Dupont
brothels:

> Down In the city of sighs and tears
> Under the gaslights' glare,
> Down in the city of aching hee-arts
> You'll find your momma there,
> Walking along where each painted face
> Tells its story of wasted yee-ars.

To counterbalance the cruder aspects of leisure in the city, women
banded together in 1894 to form the Arts & Historical Association. My
friend Gertrude Mellon was the initiator of the Association (though not
the first president—only a few men attended the meetings, yet all of the
presidents were male until I was elected in 1901). Gertrude wrote of the
civilizing mission of her culture enthusiasts: "This Association had its
inception when Vancouver was in a state of transition from the primeval
forest; when the frogs in the marshes kept their nightly vigil, relieved by the
buzzing of the nighthawk and the noiseless passage of the bat; while the
denizens of the forest were slowly but surely yielding the rights they had
maintained for centuries past, until the day arrived when the forerunner of
civilization, the iron horse, came screeching into the city, sweeping away tra-
ditions of 'Gastown,' 'Happy Jack,' and the last relic, the Princess Louise
Tree—and with it the usual concomitants of all the usual nationalities, all
bent towards one goal—the participation in the wealth of a glorious heritage not yet encroached upon by the hand of Man. It was because certain
people in that early community believed that, if no restraining hand was
put forth, eventually a harvest of corruption and unhealthy surroundings
would result, that this Association was formed."

Fine homes of the West End, early 1900s. Well-groomed terraces and stonework were de rigueur. *(VPL 7141)*

What with my duties at the *World* and a heavy burden of club work, our household would have collapsed without the cool, efficient Chinese servants who acted as complete domestic managers. Chief of these for many years was Louie, a short, thin man who never stopped smiling—and could do anything. He cooked, cleaned house, gardened, and took the children everywhere. Like many West End families, we took him very much for granted. At the end of a long, exhausting day, Louie would just disappear into the night, returning to some hovel in Chinatown on Pender or Cordova, where some three thousand Orientals lived.

All better-off households boasted at least one Chinese "domestic." In this we were hypocritical, I suppose. We enjoyed our servants as part of the family; we shopped frequently in Chinatown for fresh poultry and vegetables, and even mingled socially with the better educated Chinese. Their clog shoes, tight alpaca pants, pigtails and shaved heads added colour to our streets that was much appreciated by tourists. Yet we said and published

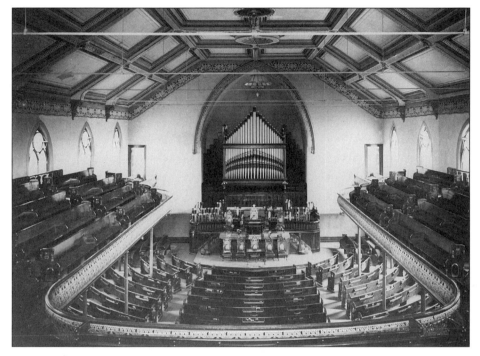

Interior of St. Andrew's Presbyterian Church, where Rev. McLaren thundered forth many a sermon against vice and the "pink cocktail" gin parties which some West End hostesses held instead of Sunday afternoon tea. Although catering to the well-heeled, St. Andrew's was considered second in social standing to the Anglicans' Christ Church, where Tory bluebloods like Sir Charles and Lady Tupper worshipped. (VPL 7518)

hateful things about the Chinese as a group, wanting them permanently disenfranchised and kept out of mainstream business.

On city streets, young men were known to taunt Chinese men and pull their pigtails, or "queues." Some queues were plaited, others braided; and a dressier man draped his queue over his arm, under the armpit, and then over the forearm. Back in 1886, when a white gang rioted over Chinese workers clearing the forest west of Burrard, many Chinese men had been cruelly tied together by their queues. Dozens of these poor men were then herded like cattle into wagons and shipped from Chinatown next day to New Westminster—standing up all the way.

Our family cycled or walked to Stanley Park on Sundays, or we lounged at English Bay, careful not to expose too much skin in summer. (Of course, only workingmen sported tans.) Sometimes we rowed across to

Kitsilano Beach for a picnic. Then there were the Sunday evening band concerts at Alexandra Park.

As much as I still loved my childhood home at Hazelbrae, I was intoxicated with the salt breezes and mosquito-free environment so different from the heavy verdancy of the Fraser Valley. "Stanley Park," I editorialized, "is heaven on a bright sunny afternoon, when the birds are singing and all nature is rejoicing, and the green swards are peopled with laughing, romping children, while their elders sit in pleasant shade spots and listen to sweet music. At such a time Atheist and Deist meet on common ground and say, 'It is good to be here.'"

At English Bay, the wonderful beach was complemented by fine recreation facilities catering to the city's "respectable" class. The English Bay Club featured an upgraded beach house and pavilion. Two long verandahs joined to make the finest dance floor in Vancouver, where the "ozone laden breezes will ever provide freshness and comfort." Card rooms, a restaurant and a cozy smoking and reading room for gentlemen offered club members pleasure, while some twenty bedrooms upstairs accommodated overnight guests. The mayor and his aldermen haunted the place so much that we joked about the real business of the city being carried on at beachside.

All too often, though, nature was slotted only for Sundays, the rest of the week being a mad blur of hustle and bustle. Of course, I was a chief offender, but liked to editorialize with Wordsworth's lines:

> The world is too much with us; late and soon,
> Getting and spending, we lay waste our power:
> Little we see in nature that is ours:
> We have given our hearts away, a sordid boon.

Leisure activities near the close of the old century came to be increasingly dominated by the culture of the bicycle. At city hall, the CPR depot and numerous hotels, long bicycle racks were installed. At Granville and Pender there was even a riding school, surrounded by a high wooden fence that screened nervous novices from gawkers. Bicycle meets were held at Brockton Point regularly. Dotting the city were numerous cycling paths on

Joe Fortes, seen at English Bay teaching children to swim. The popular Trinidadian was employed by City Council as official swimming instructor and lifeguard until he died in 1922. All Vancouver mourned. (CVA Be P115 N68)

all the main streets, surfaced with cinders and running between gutter and wooden sidewalks, about six feet wide.

Cyclists and pedestrians frequently quarrelled. Part of the problem was that until streets were paved, the macadam or plank surface loosened as the bicycle rolled over it and water spurted upward, dirtying the rider's clothing. So cyclists took to riding the sidewalks, especially in the evening hours. Well, this was illegal, as was riding without a light at night. Police Court was kept busy hearing numerous charges against cyclists, not to mention personal injury lawsuits in the higher courts.

Rough bush predominated in the area west of Burrard, an area we still regarded as wilderness. We picked blackberries on Bute Street. A muddy wagon track ran past St. Paul's Hospital; Beach Avenue was a mere ten-foot-wide trail and huge stumps stood everywhere. Of course children loved it, and West End mothers lived in fear of their children being hit by stray bullets of hunters. Douglas and his friends ignored the city by-laws prohibiting hunting and prowled about with their .22s in search of squirrels, ducks, and grouse.

City Council hired the beach guard, Joe Fortes, as special constable to patrol the English Bay area and stop the shooting, but Douglas and other hunters usually evaded Joe. When they shot ducks from a rowboat—a favourite pastime—Joe would come running out of his cottage yelling "Youse 'rrested!", whereupon the boys would just duck down in the boat and let the tide drift them away out of Joe's reach.

Joe Fortes was one of the most colourful characters of early Vancouver. English Bay Joe always wore a broad smile, and he loved children. At age seventeen he had landed in England from his native Trinidad, and there he became an expert swimming instructor. His career was enhanced when he won the gold medal awarded by the City of Liverpool for the fastest time running a three-mile course along the Mersey River. He took ship to Vancouver, where he soon became a bartender at the old Bodega Hotel at Carrall and Cordova—though he himself was a teetotaller. In the Great Fire of 1886, Joe played a leading role in aiding and comforting the homeless and injured.

Year after year, Joe gave his free time to teaching Vancouver children how to swim. It was a common sight for bathers to see Joe leading a long line of youngsters through the West End bush to English Bay. He believed in the adage "sink or swim." Timid youngsters would stand on the raft moored in the water, egged on by Joe bellowing, "Jump! I tell you jump! If you don't jump off that raft, I'll throw you in!" They usually jumped.

After many years of Joe donating his services for free, City Council decided to hire Joe as Vancouver's permanent lifeguard and swimming instructor. He lived for some time in a cottage above the beach, from which he would often emerge to run down the beach, his voice booming a warning to a child who was swimming too deep. Joe died at a young age in 1922, and the funeral was one of the largest in the city's history. Not a dry eye was seen in the church when the organ spewed forth "Old Black Joe." Ironically, next to the beach which Joe patrolled for much of his life, people of colour were banned from the public pool.

Aside from the odd holiday trip to Hazelbrae to visit my parents, or to Victoria on business, our family seldom travelled. We did enjoy the annual railway excursion to the Fraser Valley, sponsored by the *World* for Vancouver businessmen and their families. In September of 1898, we loaded some 1,100 people onto nineteen rail cars at the CPR station and set out for Agassiz. Despite showers, the group enjoyed the lavish food spread we provided and a tour of the Agassiz Experimental Farm. I hosted

Looking west on Georgia Street at Thurlow. Note the arc streetlight. Residents complained of their insufficient numbers, dimness, and propensity to die in strong winds. (VPL 33)

thirty friends and prominent city celebrities for lunch off the train at a friend's farm. On the return trip, liquor flowed freely, and I had to move my children to another compartment to avoid the awful cigar smoke.

As much as I enjoyed my work as President of the Council of Women, there was just too much to do and so few of us who were socially active. The same female faces kept popping up for different causes. I had my hands full at the office, and would have cracked had it not been for Louie managing the household and the support of Marie McNaughton and Madame Martin. Marie and I enjoyed each other's company for reading and philosophy sessions once a month. She was later elected as a School Board member and singlehandedly succeeded in obtaining for Vancouver its first policewoman in 1912.

The dying years of the century were frantic and chaotic, the air full of excitement and uncertainty. Despite editorials to the contrary, Vancouverites celebrated New Year's Eve in 1899 as if 1900 were the first year of the new century, rather than 1901. Kaiser Wilhelm in fact main-

Genteel living on West Georgia Street, c. 1900. Then as now, Vancouverites loved their plants and gardens. (VPL 4153)

tained that 1900 was the twentieth century, and had all his cannons fired to usher in the new age.

Well, it certainly did feel different to write "1900" on stationery. And superficially at least, the city and our own *World* were booming. The very first shipments of prairie grain left Vancouver, promising a great future for our status as a port. Reader circulation was up, a modest profit being made. But I saw trouble brewing in the newspaper business. We always seemed to be undercapitalized. Our archaic linotype machines were equipped with only one mold of single-column measure, which was most inadequate for effective advertisements. The *Province* and *News-Advertiser* were innovating faster than us.

Then there was John's illness, hanging ominously over us. None of Vancouver's doctors could prescribe anything other than palliative pills and rest at Harrison Hot Springs, lounging about in the sulphur pools. John would have none of that. He coughed and staggered about, never letting up. He was becoming very testy with the *World* staff, and I often had to intervene to smooth things over with employees.

Amongst the wealth and excess around us, I saw too the increased poverty on the east side—above all, the abused children, some of whom were worked to the bone in False Creek mills. Noticeable too was the rising tide of anti-Oriental hysteria, which hysteria the *World* helped fuel. Political debate on these issues was shrill, the quality of our legislators mediocre. Dominating the political landscape of the province were various bickering factions which could be described as neither Tory nor Grit. Into this vortex stepped the most enigmatic politician of the day, Joe Martin.

I first heard of Joe Martin when John mentioned that one of Laurier's top Liberals in Manitoba was moving to Vancouver in order to establish a law practice. Shortly after the 1896 federal election, John invited Martin over to dinner. Louie prepared a wonderful West Coast salmon, Joe having let it be known that he enjoyed fish. Well, we talked late into the night, Martin all afire with ideas—he hated the CPR, and would lobby for a new competitor railroad, preferably run by his good friend, Joe Hill. He stabbed the air often with his trademark cigar. He was a bearded man, with hawklike nose and piercing eyes. Charming, mind you. You never knew whether a scowl or a smile would etch his wolflike countenance, but you soon learned that it would be one or the other!

When we first met him, Martin was still gloating over his recent victory over the Benchers of the Law Society, who, he said, had opposed his admittance to the BC Bar because of his Liberal affiliations. Their opposition had actually been based more on his troublemaking antics while politicking in Manitoba. It seemed that Joe had been elected as MPP in that province and then proceeded to ignore parliamentary decorum by accusing the Speaker of the House of bias. But he later became attorney general, fought the CPR's rail monopoly, resigned and was then elected federally as Winnipeg's first Liberal MP in 1891. A forceful rhetorician, he made his mark in the Commons. He gained notoriety as a "Red" Liberal, and grudging respect as a champion of western Canadian rights.

The turbulent politics of British Columbia in the 1890s were a perfect milieu for Martin. Over after-dinner brandy, he spoke to John and me of fighting the vested interests. (Ironically, he acted as counsel for the CPR in Vancouver, his client foolishly thinking that this would neutralize him in the political arena. The retainer would not last long.) His first goal was to organize party lines for provincial elections. Following the founding convention of the BC Liberal Party, Joe was elected as MPP from Vancouver, along with Tory Carter-Cotton, as "Oppositionists." In Joe's mind this meant opposing both the existing opposition leader and the premier.

The 1898 general election ended in chaotic hysteria, with cries of gross election day irregularities. The lieutenant governor of the day was one Charles McInnes, a dour doctor from Nova Scotia who had paid his political dues; McInnes now called upon Charles Semlin, a Cariboo rancher, to form a government. To do so, Semlin needed support from both Martin and Carter-Cotton, and both of them accepted Cabinet positions in the new administration, Martin serving as attorney general. Thence began a roller coaster ride of theatrical disasters for the government. Martin heated up matters from the start with his bombastic baiting of Carter-Cotton at every turn. Then he took to holding court in his office with cronies each week, boasting through a haze of cigar smoke that he would be the next premier.

Some of Joe's political initiatives were far-sighted. He introduced legislation which established a form of Torrens land registration system for the province, and he increased the efficiency of the courts. But Martinesque fiascoes also occurred. He drew up and passed through the Legislature an anti-Oriental immigration bill which excluded Americans as well as Orientals! Washington formally protested, and the federal Cabinet, embarrassed beyond measure, disallowed the legislation. Another time Joe travelled to Rossland in an attempt to mollify mining operators who were smarting from his government's new mining regulations. During the course of his speech, Martin was heckled repeatedly. Enraged, he stepped forward on the stage, raised his fists and shouted that he "would not be silenced by hoboes in evening dress." Someone in the audience shouted back, "You are the hobo!"

Chinese vendors on Pender Street, early 1900s. Chinese residents were prominent in the grocery trade, in the laundry business and in domestic service. To most white Vancouverites, Chinatown remained an exotic, mysterious world apart. (VPL 6729)

Martin had even antagonized my husband, trying to exclude John as President of the Vancouver Liberals. Despite John's many kindnesses and loyalty to Martin, Joe paranoiacally saw him as being Laurier's federal agent working against him. In November of 1898, Joe tried to pass a resolution at a Vancouver gathering that would have prohibited the "packing" of meetings. John easily rallied his troops against the motion and Joe was sent packing from the meeting. Joe's career seemed to turn to ashes when Premier Semlin, tired of his antics, expelled Joe first from the Cabinet and then from the caucus.

Martin bided his time on the opposition bench, needling Semlin and making friends with a new man in the House, coal tycoon James Dunsmuir. He accused the new Finance Minister, Carter-Cotton, of fraudulently altering government documents relating to the Deadman's Island controversy. Then, by one vote, Martin rallied the opposition forces and combined with my old friend David Higgins to bring down the government on a comparatively minor redistribution bill. To everyone's shock but Martin's, Lieutenant Governor McInnes dismissed Premier Semlin and his government. Our Victoria correspondent reported that Martin sat there beaming like the Cheshire cat.

The Legislature immediately passed a motion condemning McInnes's actions in dismissing Semlin, and then assembled next day to hear the lieutenant governor's response. To the collective horror of members, Joe Martin rose from his seat and announced that McInnes had asked him to form a government! Whereupon the Assembly passed a motion of no confidence in Martin by a vote of 28 to 1. When McInnes tried to speak, Dunsmuir led all of the members but Martin out of the chamber in protest—leaving Joe hunched over in his seat, alone with McInnes. Above them in the gallery, a crowd jeered.

McInnes stumbled through the motions of prorogation, while Martin sat nervously biting his lip. Then McInnes literally ran out of the Chamber. Immediately, all of the members marched back in and took their seats. Dunsmuir and others shouted their disgust at McInnes's attempt to help his old friend Martin, who was referred to by one member as "that buffoon." In the midst of this chaos, a page boy suddenly rushed into the chamber and announced that South Africa's Ladysmith had just been relieved by the British Army, and the Assembly exploded with cheers. The events of this day in the Legislature had no parallel in the history of Canada.

In need of a Cabinet, Premier Martin anxiously flailed about for supporters who would serve under him. He visited John one afternoon at the *World* office and, desperate to mend fences now, offered him a high post. John declined, but he yielded to Joe's beseeching eyes and promised to support him in the pending provincial election. Lacking credibility within the Legislature itself, Martin wanted John to bring the federal Liberal Party over to his side so as to fight the election along party lines and win endorsement from Prime Minister Laurier.

John wrote to Laurier for his blessing to Joe's proposal. In response, the prime minister replied that he was reviewing McInnes's unseemly actions in the House and that it would be improper for him to interfere with provincial election matters. Further, wrote Laurier, Martin had "placed himself in collision with our policy at Ottawa" by pledging to exclude Japanese in addition to Chinese immigration, when the Laurier government had expressly approved of Japanese immigrants. However, Laurier added: "While unable to support Martin, I will take no part against him."

John crumpled Laurier's letter in disgust. Tempers flared everywhere over Martin's clandestine ascension to power. Our own *World* editor, J. M. O'Brien, resigned in a flap, distressed at John's and my support for the quixotic premier. Martin himself was unperturbed by Laurier's rebuff and all the controversy. "I well enjoy a David versus Goliath role," he told me one evening, "and I'll trust in the people."

What a strange, lonely man! Of Joe's cabinet of six men, only one fellow was an elected MPP, and his minister of finance was one Cory Ryder, a grocery clerk whom Martin had appointed extemporaneously on a train ride, after Ryder—a total stranger—complimented him on his tenacity. For three months prior to the general election, this Cabinet of Curios bumbled along.

I will give old Joe Martin this much: he put on an incredible show. Despite Laurier's position on party lines, Joe called a meeting of the federal Liberals in Vancouver to override the prime minister and invoke the party name for his election bid. What a fiasco! A fight broke out and the police were called to restore order on the floor.

The ensuing election campaign was dirty, to say the least. The *Province* claimed that Martin had accepted $100,000 from Joe Hill in return for Martin's alleged promise to give the Great Northern Railway a Coast to Kootenay route. Martin ignored such attacks and managed to assemble twenty-seven men to stand for election on his ticket. He "gave them hell" at stormy meetings around the province, and in the words of Judge Howay, celebrated historian of the day, Joe's effort was "comprehensive, his campaign strong, vigorous, brilliant." Martin declared himself a radical, but in 1900 that word connoted the unwanted baggage of anarchists, atheists, vegetarians and nudists, and so we at the *World* described his philosophy as simply "Martinism."

CHAPTER THREE
1900: Toward the Vortex

Martin almost made it. As the returns rolled in on election night, June 9, 1900, the *World* sent bulletins around the province. Well, most of our staff was out at the polling booths, so from six o'clock I worked alone at the office telegraph set for five solid hours without a break. It looked like Joe had been re-elected in Vancouver, but that his candidates were having mixed success elsewhere. At least Carter-Cotton was going down to defeat.

At about eleven o'clock while working the telegraph, I heard a stir in the corridor. Then in strode Joe Martin himself. He was haggard, his shirt crumpled, but his eyes defiant. "Sara," he said calmly, "go get some dinner for yourself; I'll handle those keys for a time." I protested, "But Joe—" "But nothing," he said. "Go on, you're worn out; besides, you know that I'm an old brass-pounder."

So British Columbia's premier sat down at my desk and worked the telegraph keys for the next hour, noting up the returns. The tide was now clearly flowing against his forming a majority or any government, though no particular faction had more seats than the Martinites. When I returned around midnight, he was guffawing loudly. He wordlessly showed me his transcription of a private message sent from one of his closest campaign workers to a friend, which message gleefully heralded the "elimination of that arch traitor Martin." Joe sighed and stood up. "That's all right, Sara," he said, "such is life." With that, he strode out, cigar planted firmly between his teeth.

The election aftermath saw Martin toppled, McInnes fired by Laurier, and James Dunsmuir appointed premier. I personally got on well with the premier and his mother Joan, who took a real interest in our Council of Women work. I was grateful too for my brother Sam getting a key commission when Dunsmuir hired him to design and supervise construction of his Hatley Park mansion. Up until then, Francis Rattenbury had got all the press, though in my view Sam showed a much better eye for detail. Sam had been commissioned to work with Rattenbury as co-designer of Cary Castle, the new Government House, but he fell ill in the early stages of draftmanship. Rattenbury carried on with the project. (A fire had destroyed the earlier structure in May of 1899; the ludicrous McInnes had escaped with just the clothes on his back.) The opportunity was not without its cost: Sam suffered a nervous breakdown over the project.

The cool, businesslike hand of Premier Dunsmuir did little to obviate the effects of that year's unsettling events. We were all in a fog, confounded by the social and international conflicts that pressed about us. Most unsettling and news dominant was the Boer War, which had broken out in 1898. At first we thought this was just some series of bush skirmishes, but after a time it became apparent that these Dutch farmers were ripping up General Gordon's boys pretty badly. Mind you, the war did help the newspaper industry. The *World's* circulation shot up to 10,000 copies and we rode high for a time with the greatest circulation of any western Canadian daily.

Canadian participation in the Boer War was, I am sad to say, largely precipitated by the enormously potent news coverage given by the big Canadian dailies. The *Montreal Daily Star* was particularly effective in using shrill, Empire-rallying invective and jingoism to promote the conflict as a glorious cause, and the paper urged all Canadians of age to enlist. The *Star* even went so far as to "personally insure" the lives of Canadian soldiers.

On October 24, 1899, our city ceremoniously saw off seventeen young male volunteers at the CPR station—the first Vancouverites ever to go to war. J. L. Luscombe, city butcher, arrived at the station with his cart, attached to which was a long flagpole flying the Union Jack. Tied to the

Sara McLagan, woman of the World.

head of the pole was a large bunch of maple leaves, while at the foot was a real boar's head, through which was rammed a menacing butcher knife. The crowd laughed it up at the sight. The mayor even presented to each soldier $25 on behalf of a "grateful Vancouver." One of the young soldiers was Victor Odlum, son of world-famous inventor and scholar Professor Odlum, who built an estate in the backwoods of Grandview. Victor became one of Canada's most celebrated war heroes as a general in World War One.

In late February of 1900, the *World* received news that two of these Vancouver volunteers had been killed at the Battle of Paardeberg, together with several comrades from the British Columbia contingent. Flags in the city flew at half-mast, and the sock troopers of women redoubled their knitting efforts for the lads overseas. (Whenever disaster occurs in wars, it seems that women are relegated to knitting more socks and canning more jam.) A short time later, word flashed that Empire troops had been relieved from siege at Mafeking, and citizens built a bonfire at the corner of Cambie and Hastings, the blaze from which burnt a huge hole in the wooden pavement.

We still held so much faith in the Empire and its civilizing mission that we never thought to question the morality of any conflict involving Britain. The popular ditty around town was "At Britain's side whate'er betide." *Harper's Weekly* even urged Americans to mourn the increasing pile of British defeats in South Africa "if we have a proper pride of race." It was inconceivable that the upward tide of progress begun in the mid-nineteenth century could be tempered or halted—railways, steamships, the telegraph, electric lights, steam engines, knitting machines, telephones, and now even x-rays for surgery all promised a new life of efficiency and comfort. The *World* joined with the *New York Times* in anticipating a still brighter dawn of civilization, nurtured by Anglo-Saxon nations taking up Kipling's "white man's burden."

The United States adopted the gold standard in March of 1900. Huge money deals became regular fare this year. J. Pierpont Morgan formed the giant US Steel, buying out Carnegie to form the world's first billion-dollar corporation. Henry Adams pronounced his Law of Acceleration, stating that he feared that any official who stood near him might hold a bomb, such was the force of increased technology: "So long as the rate of progress held good, these bombs would double in force and number every ten years... Power leaped from every atom... Men could no longer hold it off." Even in detached Vancouver we felt a sense of awe and anxiety at the material and technological forces being unleashed about us.

Oscar Wilde died that year in Paris, an emaciated wreck. Nietzsche died mad in Germany. The International Exposition in Paris turned into a gaudy display of technology that included coloured fountains, steel towers, moving sidewalks and rapid-fire machine guns. Max Planck propounded the quantum theory of energy, destroying Newtonian thought. Freud wrote *The Interpretation of Dreams*, which helped destroy Victorianism. In China, the Boxer Rebellion led to the massacre of 1,500 foreigners and threatened the trade of the Great Powers. King Humbert of Italy was shot to death by an anarchist. In our own country, there existed massive political and labour unrest, and the worst fire in Canadian history left 15,000 people homeless in Ottawa and Hull.

Such was the state of the world's mad tea party. There certainly were enough Tweedledees and Tweedledums strutting about town—all those dandies in their Homburg hats, Prince Albert coats and gold chains. The sole object it seemed was to make money, the more of it the better. But the peaceful accumulation of wealth proved far from inexorable in that summer of 1900. For the racial and industrial strife which erupted were to send shock waves through genteel society.

In July, thousands of Fraser River fishermen staged a strike against the canners' association. The canneries had tried to control salmon prices and the number of fish boats on the water, whereas fishermen sought better prices and open access by independent fishermen to canneries of their choice. Caught in the middle of this dispute were 1,700 Japanese fishermen, who comprised some one-third of the industry. These men spoke little or no English and resided chiefly in Steveston. In order to survive, and threatened by cannery owners urging them to defy the strikers, many Japanese continued to fish. Raging white strikers responded by slashing nets and threatening physical violence. The militia was hastily called in from Vancouver. The strike was finally settled, but a new era of industrial relations had dawned. Competition among the various racial groups actually provided the impetus to union organization, and not just in the fishing

The first Vancouver residents to serve in battle overseas. These seventeen soldiers are seen posing in front of the drill shed at the foot of Beatty Street on October 29, 1899. The next day they left for South Africa and the Boer War. (CVA Mil P7 N48)

industry. Japanese were excluded from white unions; the Asiatic Exclusion League flourished; Victoria childishly flouted federal immigration authority by illegally imposing a head tax of $500 upon each Japanese entering the province.

John and I disagreed somewhat on the race question. Neither of us thought twice about the low wages we paid Louie and our other houseboys; but John and other white businessmen and union types became paranoid, fearing the competition of Orientals in the work force because they accepted lower wages. In fact, John got so carried away that he had to settle a libel suit brought against the *World* by the *Province*, after John alleged that the rival paper had fired many of its white employees and was replacing them with cheap Japanese workmen. It was the first and last time anyone at the *World* ever apologized to Nichol's rag.

But paranoia over Oriental competition wasn't just a male response.

I well remember two women walking out of the BC Cannery plant on Homer Street in 1900 when the manager hired on four Japanese to wash and scrape a large rush shipment of carrots. In a *World* interview, the manager apologized to Sam Robb, and assured Sam that the Japanese were hired temporarily for just this one job. The women employees were welcome to return and their wages would be secure.

The hysteria of Vancouverites over Chinese opium dens reached a peak in 1900, fuelling racism even more. The Chinese actually handled their own opium smoking in moderation, but it seems that young white males began visiting the Chinatown dens en masse and many became addicted to the drug. Raids became commonplace. Public cries for stiff penalties against the Chinese operators spurred City Council to direct the Chief of Police to exercise a heavy hand.

We were all fascinated by the mystery and exoticism of eastern depravity. John sent a reporter down to glimpse firsthand the actual process of opium smoking: "The smoking paraphernalia is usually arranged more or less tastily on a large tray. The smoker rolls a little ball of the dark brown, sticky substance on the sharp end of a long needle, and twirls it rapidly as he makes the symmetrical band. Then over the lamp flame it is cooked, the ball being twirled and turned, to keep it in perfect shape… Then the dope pill, about the size of a pea, is placed in the big hollow pipe. And if you are not too frequent a user of opium, you will soon fall asleep."

White Canadians' fear of Orientals increased even more with the bizarre murder of Steveston Police Chief Alex Main. The chief had been hunting for stolen goods in an area of Chinese cannery workers' shacks. His mutilated body was found in the neighbourhood—legs almost severed at the knees, neck brutally slashed. Yip Chuck and Chanyu Chung were arrested for the murder. Chung quickly confessed to his part in the affair, but nailed Yip as the real culprit. Yip, he said, had cracked open Main's head with an axe, cut his throat and then slashed him with a bush hook.

The rage of the local white community was not ameliorated by the fact that fifty Japanese residents of Steveston asked the police if they could take the Chinese defendants out and kill them, nor by Chinese residents' offer of a $200 reward for the arrest of a third defendant wanted in the murder. Nichol's *Province* created the stereotypical Chinese bogeyman: "Yip

Chuck is one of the ugliest looking specimens of a bad Chinaman ever landed in British Columbia. His face is of the blackest of his race, his upper teeth protrude, his eyes are fierce, and his hair is like that of a barbarian." (Now readers really could relate to that popular Victorian caution to children, "The Chinaman'll get you if you don't watch out!")

Yip Chuck was hanged after a speedy trial. The hangman bungled the trap door; he later admitted he was suffering from a severe hangover after a night of boozing around New Westminster bars. Chuck was kept in terrifying suspense for some eleven seconds before plunging to his death. The thick manila rope broke his neck instantly.

The Oriental issue that year tore at the heart and soul of our society. Tommy Homma, a Japanese hotel proprietor, applied for placement on the provincial voters' list and was refused. Afraid of federal repercussions— Ottawa being partial to cultivating Japan's friendship—Dunsmuir and his Cabinet thrashed about desperately for a means to deny Japanese residents the vote. His government passed another Immigration Act, this time requiring any immigrant to be able to write a European language in order to vote. Since few Oriental immigrants could read or write English, they were virtually excluded.

In the 1900 federal election, Liberal George Maxwell won his Vancouver seat with the help of Japanese electors (male only, of course). Carter-Cotton winced in horror: "The blow has fallen; the majority cast their vote for Mongolian naturalization and Maxwell." Crusty Carter-Cotton had an even greater horror of women's suffrage.

The women's suffrage movement in BC was in fact bogging down. And no wonder. Leading suffragettes like Maria Grant and Cecilia Spofford insisted on tying temperance to the vote. WCTU floats appeared in every parade, with a huge temperance banner flying next to the Union Jack; perched on the float were fair young maidens in white, garlanded with flowers, and young children singing hymns. And as if that weren't enough, we had preachers in every church telling women about their duties to the home—why, I just about walked out of a Sunday service at St. Andrew's one time when Reverend McLaren sermonized on "The Ideal Woman." Ugh!

The firebrand Agnes Cameron, BC's first school principal, spoke in

A working mother makes dinner in the kitchen of her modest Fairview home, c. 1900. (VPL 13015)

disquieting terms to my July National Women's Council convention: "You can't open your school room door for a breath of fresh air without someone with a mission falling in... The WCTU has succeeded in introducing into the schools the formal teaching of the effects of alcohol. A child now is to be kept in the narrow way of self-restraint by dangling before him a hobnailed liver and by intimidating him with visions of the tobacco heart. He trembles and joins the Band of Hope."

A New Brunswick delegate to my convention, Winnifred Johnston, wrote an interesting monologue for us on her impressions of Vancouver, part of which I printed: "After the fire of 12 years ago, the city was built far more substantially, and now its business blocks and streets are far finer than Victoria, which is fat, fair and forty... In the West End there was nothing but stumps two years ago, and now you find block after block of fine residences. In fact, the town has come out as far as it can in this direction, to

Stanley Park, and must move eastward to spread further. They build the houses first and put the streets up afterwards, and it looks very odd to see a beautiful house surrounded by stumps and thick underbrush. There is a lane built through the middle of each residential block, so that delivery wagons need not stop at the front door or the maids do their spooning over the front gates. The houses are not as uniformly ugly as those adorning the back streets of Fredericton…"

In fact, as Mrs. Johnston noted, Vancouver builders were imaginative, and most houses being constructed now were graced with broad verandahs, bay windows, Japanese gables, lower storeys of stone and upper of fancy shingles. Terraced lawns and flower beds flourished around most West End homes. In spring, as one rode along on a bicycle, the scent of honeysuckle was almost overpowering.

Like most visitors to town, Mrs. Johnston was fascinated by Vancouver's diverse population: "Vancouver is a fine place for girls, but a new young man here isn't as important as at home. The woods are full of them! You go down streets Saturday night and pass group after group of young men and very few girls. Young men coming West to seek positions not only have to compete with women in clerical work, school teaching, etc., but with Chinese and Japanese cheap labour. The Chinese fill most of the kitchens of Vancouver, and also keep a number of shops, and do dress-making and tailoring… The country is not wholly given over to Orientals; there are a lot of real old Scots here, as you would have seen if you had attended the Scottish games last Saturday at Brockton Point."

The effects of uncontrolled growth in our fair port were beginning to tell. Vancouver City Council took some feeble steps in 1900 to control development by passing the very first building by-law. But the big debate at the council table revolved around the sewer on Broughton Street which emptied into English Bay: should a huge septic tank be placed on the beach? Dr. Hoops argued vehemently that bathing would be ruined at First and Second beaches, while Sir Charles Tupper and supporters presented a petition against the septic tank. This stalled the tank for a time.

Julia Henshaw called me a troublemaker for stirring up social issues all the time, and I guess I did blow my top one day when I told her that she would do well to develop a social conscience. I was not a little peeved that

Carter-Cotton gave Julia an entire page each week in his *News-Advertiser* to talk about the high society news of the city. She certainly scooped the *World* in this department. Well, I thought, let her gloat and glorify the upper crust elite of Vancouver—even if it means that she publicly berates me (as Lady Cook) in her paper for misdescribing some evening gown worn at one of Lady Tupper's fashionable parties. I responded tartly to her criticism: "This paper endeavours to give a complete list of persons at every function of note, and one is happy to say that the *World's* list of dresses worn is not confined to a small elite."

We printed good hard stories about the underside of the city that I stand by today, which meant less time spent covering ladies' receiving parties. Take, for instance, the city jail. I have recounted the fact that there was no matron for girl or woman prisoners. And male inmates—why, they were treated like animals throughout their entire incarceration, most of them shackled continuously in irons. The condition of teenage boys in jail was particularly pitiful. Sam Robb visited the city cells one day to find two small boys serving time for petty theft—both of them thoroughly emaciated. They were not allowed to exercise; only a tiny bit of light filtered into their cold cell: "The atmosphere is always damp and chilly, for the rays of the sun descend no further than the top of the twelve foot fence which surrounds the enclosure... To keep their bodies warm, the frail young boys huddle around the stove in the passage. In the darkened corridor, the spirit of life is dwarfed. Only two months of their sentence have been served, and if now they are only ghosts of their former selves, in six months they will be— what? A little daylight and exercise is all that is needed to bring back the health that has fled and check the disease that is fast creeping upon them..."

I myself had no doubt that either tuberculosis or pneumonia would attack these young boys' bodies if conditions were not improved. Not a day passed when I failed to caution John as to his failing health, and while some days he sparkled like his old self, I could see him slipping. Fearing the worst, we both pragmatically prepared for his demise. To avoid estate complications, John had his solicitor transfer all of the shares of the World Publishing Co. Ltd. to me.

After a bad bout in April, John's consumption seemed to go into remission for a time, but it flared up again in the summer. Doctors came and went at our Georgia Street home, applying ice-cold poultices to his head one day and steaming hot cloths the next. But nothing seemed to relieve him of his head pain and general inflammation. His pulse was often rapid and his temperature high.

John had became increasingly irritable during Martin's election campaign, and he had collapsed into an exhausted, depressed state after Joe lost. He had staked his reputation on Martin, and now people treated the ex-premier as a bumbling accident of history. John shouted at *World* employees. He cried at night. Our new editor, Mr. Donald, rebelled against this abuse and resigned. I intervened and called a meeting at Mr. Bowser's law office; there I requested that I take over as president of the newspaper, and that John stay away from active management—in particular, the editorial desk. John agreed to this, as well as to the installation of my brother Fred as treasurer and comptroller.

The changes in management paid off. I quickly lured Donald back to the editor's job. Fred proved a tremendous help, managing the paper's finances with a stern hand, eliminating the chaos of hand-to-mouth living and uncertainty as to our true revenues and expenses. Still, the financial picture was far from rosy. Profits were shrinking, for John's strident Martinist editorials had alienated some of our readership, and I discovered too a number of *World* debts that just couldn't be paid off in the short term, despite better management.

The financial picture of the *World* in fact was suddenly so bleak that I wrote in desperation to a newspaperman in Toronto—one E. L. Pattison—about selling an option to purchase the *World* to Pattison's principal, a Mr. Keenleyside. Pattison responded: "I was glad to learn that everything is now running smoothly and that you have succeeded in persuading Mr. McLagan to act in accordance with your wishes. I notified Mr. Keenleyside that for the present neither the whole nor any portion of the *World* stock could be purchased. He asked that you give him the management of the business, and let him pay a few thousand dollars into the paper with the right to buy control of the stock, say within five years… I think this would also meet with Mr. McLagan's views, as well as enable you to raise a few thousand dollars that might come very useful at the present time. Mr. Keenleyside is a reliable and thoroughly experienced newspaperman…"

I stared at Pattison's letter. John thought it best that we bring in fresh blood and wind things down, in view of his precarious health and our urgent financial needs. I should have been relieved at Pattison's offer. Instead, I just sat thinking about all the toil and tears we had shed for the *World*, of John's dream of creating a western *Globe*. Then I hid the letter away. I climbed the long stairs to the big bedroom where John lay reading and approached his bed. "John," I said, "we have quarrelled a little lately; but come what may, I have decided that we must hang on to the *World*."

John threw aside his newspaper and looked up at me, astonished. "But the debts?" he stammered. "Don't you worry," I said, "I am taking the morning ferry to Victoria, and I expect to come back with a commitment for funds to see us through. I know that the banks will refuse me, but we are not without our friends. Now just get some rest." John lay back, wheezing, a thin smile on his tortured face. "My Sara," he whispered.

The next day I travelled to Government House in Victoria, where I met with Joan Dunsmuir. I explained my predicament, and she committed immediately to a generous loan. I told her that the loan must not compromise the *World*'s editorial policies, but that she could rest assured that I would lead no crusade to reinstate Martin in her son's legislative chair. It was only while riding back to the mainland on the ferry that evening that I realized something had changed: I enjoyed running things and I knew that I could run the *World* on my own, with Fred's help.

We kept my presidency of the *World* secret because it wasn't considered dignified in those days for a woman to usurp even an ailing husband in running anything. Well, that was just fine; I could chuckle behind the scenes. Not that some of the staff didn't suspect, of course. Sam Robb winked at me and called me "Chief" when I came down to the office. But I felt so energetic about it all that shortly after I returned from my meeting with Joan Dunsmuir, we hosted a big dinner for key *World* staff. I helped Louie cook up a feast of oysters, tomato soup, broiled salmon with parsley sauce, roast chicken, peas, salad and a strawberry almond dessert. Over claret and smokes, Sam Robb regaled the boys in our parlour with story after story. Everyone laughed loudest when Sam told how he had bribed a porter to sneak an interview with Rudyard Kipling down at the CPR station.

The CPR Depot, always a busy scene. Here drivers with horses and buggies wait to pick up passengers disembarking from a steamship. (VPL 2981)

John also eased our family situation at this time by finding his son Jack a job in Dawson City. The position was guaranteed for two years. I wished Jack all the best, secretly hoping that he would return to Vancouver with greater maturity and a friendlier disposition toward his extended family. Alas, this was not to be.

Meanwhile, even with Jack settled, our money and health problems were putting pressure on us. I told no one of my neuralgia attacks. John's gloom and pain led me to send all of the children out to Hazelbrae with Louie for most of the summer. Children and grandparents loved it all. They romped about farm, slough and forest. I kept in touch by sending each day by train a package containing a newspaper, clothes and sweets, plus my traditional note to Mother about the previous day's events. The loyal CPR engineer, Mr. Mowat, obligingly dropped off my package at the front gate of Hazelbrae (about ten feet from the track), slowing down the train just enough for the package to be thrown accurately without mishap.

The freedom of life in the country fired Douglas with a burning passion to escape city life and go into farming. One late afternoon that fall, Douglas's principal called at our home to tell us that Douglas was often truant from school. We had it out with the boy and John became very cross, warning Douglas of dire punishments should his truancy and poor marks continue.

Then, on one snowy December afternoon, Douglas failed to come home from school. Frantic, I notified the city police and we went down to scour all of the boy's favourite haunts around English Bay. Darkness fell. The family glumly huddled in despair over a late dinner, as Douglas was nowhere to be found. Then late in the evening, a telegram from Mother arrived at the door advising that Douglas was at Hazelbrae—cold and wet, but otherwise intact.

It turned out that while Douglas had been enjoying himself sleighing up and down a West End hill, he decided to abandon the city school life for the country. So he boarded a tram for New Westminster, took the steamboat from there to Mission City, and then walked across the rickety, slippery Mission rail bridge. The train came along as he was walking across, so Douglas had to hang from a girder high above the dark, churning waters of the Fraser River, an experience which I recounted for *World* readers a few days later: "The iron structure sent out a warning clang as the monster leaped the first span... Paralyzed, the little lad stood for one moment; the next he vaulted over the slight railing. He grasped the iron girder and closed his eyes. There was a mighty blast of wind and smoke and the red glare of fire flashed. Then a great silence seemed to cover all, and a sobbing but thankful boy kneeled and wept aloud his misery. When Douglas reached Hazelbrae, nine miles away, Grandfather Maclure slapped his thigh and chuckled, 'Aha! He's game—he's a true son of the heather!'"

My parents dispatched Douglas back to Vancouver the next day by train from Mission. Down at the CPR station, John embraced the boy warmly as he stepped off last—and there were many tears of joy. There was no retribution and Douglas went back to school without further misadventure. But the boy had served notice: he wanted to become a farmer.

In keeping with my new duties, I personally penned the Christmas editorial of the *World* that year: "The last Christmas season of the 19th century has come around. The signs point to storms ahead but fortunately people are so constituted that they can forget for a time the stress of life in these fin de siècle days. It is good for us to be able for a few days to cast dull care aside and be happy at the feast of Christmas. This is a time for particular rejoicing that the future is hidden, that the past is beyond the power of change, that the present is ours to enjoy... Millions of people today call themselves Christians, but how many in Vancouver who have two coats impart to him that hath none?

"We in Vancouver pride ourselves on the fact that gaunt want does not stalk our streets at night, that none is compelled to find a bed on a door-step or refuge from the rain in a hay-loft. Do we enquire very closely to see whether our pride is justified? It is a fact that shipwrecked sailors tonight are waiting for some purse-strings to be untied, that hungry men are dependent upon the Christian for a Christmas dinner. Ask Mrs. Machin at the Free Library if this is not the case. She has a sheet of paper at the library on which the charitable are asked to help to give deserving people a square meal. This morning there was a wealth of whiteness on that sheet; by Christmas night, we hope, there will be a wealth of dollars. If each citizen who has been blessed with fair fortune will give a little, then Christmas will be gladdened for many in this city."

As we drifted toward midnight of the dying century, the portents of trouble were many. On December 31st, however, Vancouverites celebrated the return of the first set of Boer War volunteers, home from bloody battles that had not shaken the Empire's resolve to emerge triumphant in its first real test since the Crimean affair. And what a magnificent New Year's Eve celebration this wrought around town!

> Home again, for the war is done,
> They have come from the South afar,
> Browned and bronzed in the tropic sun
> And scarred with the shafts of war.
> They have knit the Empire: firm and fast,
> By the deeds which their hands have wrought;
> Yes, a bond which shall forever last,
> The blood of our sons has bought.

The returning troops were mobbed at the train station, where Lieutenant Lafferty and his men alighted from a locomotive bedecked with

A snowy day on Hastings Street, c. 1900. (VPL 2452)

Union Jacks. Schoolchildren, civic officials and the local militia then marched the veterans to the tune of "The Maple Leaf Forever" up Cordova Street to Cambie, then on to Hastings, and up Granville to the Theatre Royal. The city shops closed. Thousands lined the route or manned windows overhead. At the theatre, the stage was immersed in flags, bunting and flowers, and waitresses attired in Red Cross uniforms served the hungry throngs at long trestle tables.

That New Year's evening, John and I attended the Opera House with Madame Martin and watched the mayor present gold watches to each of the Boer veterans. Private Bonner opined, "I am not sorry that I went, but I am honestly glad to be back home again... but as far as the acquiring of territory is concerned, I would not give Vancouver for the whole of South Africa."

Our family stayed up to see in the new century. The Chinese put on a fabulous fireworks display, only slightly dampened by the onset of a heavy snowfall around eight o'clock. At midnight, freighters in the Inlet blew their whistles and horns. Revellers tramped about the city streets, shouting and laughing.

I lay awake long after John's rasping wheeze signalled a deep sleep. Tomorrow, our first 1901 edition of the *World* would proclaim the new century as upon us. I thought of the khaki-clad lads who had left town not a year before, and their mates who had not returned. I thought of the war that was still raging, the burnt-out towns and homeless villagers of the veldt. But most of all, I thought of the hardened, battle-worn look in the eyes of the young heroes on the Opera House stage—of cynicism, perhaps; of innocence robbed. What exactly was our legacy to Canadians of the new century?

CHAPTER FOUR

1901: Winter Sorrow

Vancouver greeted the dawn of the new century with a glistening white devil-may-care air. A foot of snow bathed city streets, which were deserted in the morning; even the streetcars were idle. By afternoon, though, the pleasant tinkling of sleigh bells was heard, and a motley collection of sleighs of all sizes and shapes appeared downtown, contraptions which would have horrified proper Torontonians. Douglas and not a few of his friends, I am sad to say, hurled their fair share of snowballs at the passersby on Georgia Street.

John was well enough to sit downstairs and receive a dozen or so guests for our New Year's Day at-home, but he remained very pale, withdrawn and weak. I busied myself with *World* affairs, meeting with staff and assuring them that all would be well; we would press on in spite of their old chief's illness. I appointed Sam Robb as city editor at this time, laid additional duties upon Fred, and shared chief editorship duties with the recently hired Harold Sands. (Donald had finally left, claiming too much interference with his editorial positions.) There was now no question in my mind of John ever returning to manage the business—either he let me have a completely free hand or we would sell the *World*.

Perhaps it was John's illness or maybe I still smarted over her caustic criticism of the *World's* costume ball piece, but Julia Henshaw and her cliquish snobbery began to irritate me beyond measure. So, as a spoof in response to all her banal plaudits of high society hostesses and their receiving lines, I published a social register listing some 218 Vancouver hostesses and their weekly receiving days and hours—including my own. I meant it to be facetious, but Lady Tupper and others congratulated me on the *World's* new "social awareness."

In order to shock the city's smug snob set, I revelled in publishing stories about the underside of life in Vancouver. The Tuppers and Henshaws were aghast at my focus on the "low life": "The old man was sitting in a Granville street car the other evening, and anyone could see that his had been a hard day's work. The very fact that the poor old fellow seemed on the verge of prostration appealed to the pity of fellow passengers, and they made way for him so he could rest his worn-out limbs. As he sat down, his gnarled hands wandered nervously over his forehead, as if his 62 summers burdened his very soul down. At the post office, two ladies got on… They had fine clothes, and to judge from their talk, they lived in the West End. The only vacant seat was next to the old man, and as they gracefully deposited their luxurious persons, the one nearest the old laborer drew her dress in carefully in fear of contamination. One woman then audibly stated, 'Deah me, why don't they have special cahs for these working creatuahs? It is getting too horrible that a lady cawnt ride in a cah without getting a dress spoiled. They ought to have special cahs, with the place for these working people in the rear. It is simply disgusting.'"

Vancouver was still small enough that all of the social and personal items that one normally associates with rural weekly newspapers could be dished up to our readers. For years, we ran a "Daily City Gossip" column. Some samples:

> J. Anderson was yesterday fined $50 for smuggling and $10 for using abusive language to the landing waiter at the CPR wharf. Anderson was caught bringing a choice piece of silk, in the form of a lady's wrapper, off the *Empress*.
>
> It is said that there were two whales in the Inlet yesterday. They came in on Saturday and the monsters could not again find the narrows.
>
> Joe Fisher, well-known Calgary rancher, arrived in the city

Thursday with a shipment of horses. Half the carload were shipped today to Nanaimo to work in the mines. The others are now on sale at the stable in the rear of the Granville Hotel.

A man in the West End has his dog trained to steal the papers off his neighbour's porch.

Another round-the-world tramp struck the city yesterday. It is time these pestiferous nuisances were stopped.

Rev. R. G. MacBeth entertained an appreciative audience at Eburne last evening with his reminiscent talk on the Northwest Rebellion.

Thomas Shirley states he will hold the city liable for his typhoid fever illness, alleging that the officers of the health department were negligent…

My daily life began to follow a predictable pattern. After seeing the children off to school, checking on John in his bed and instructing Louie and Tring on the day's chores, I headed down to the *World* office on Homer, usually walking along Georgia to Granville, and then taking the tram along Hastings Street past the post office. As soon as I entered the office, I smelled the musty, inky scent of the presses, heard the click clacking of machinery and the familiar old tapping of the telegraph keys.

John's office was a trifle large for my needs, but I admit to a thrill at sitting down at the big mahogany desk and commencing the checklist of our daily stories. One of the reasons that we went through so many chief editors at the *World* was because John and I had always insisted on a proprietary approach to each editorial and story. I scanned everything for content, accuracy, grammar and spelling—in fact, my proofing of each edition later got me in trouble with the Proof-Reader's Union. My eyes and ears were Sam Robb; for the city editor is the field commander, running to and fro to meet and direct the reporters, demanding the story on a suicide on Carrall Street or a drowning in the harbour. Sam knew that I wanted human interest stories and he got them, regularly.

The staffers were always deferential toward me. My warm but businesslike relationship with them did not change after gaining the presidency and sole ownership later on. In any case, I never stood on formality: they

Squatters find shelter in tents at the foot of Columbia Street on the Vancouver waterfront. The people pictured here are likely transients. Resident squatters erected shacks and shanties. (VPL 9525)

all knew that I just wanted the job done well. We had some mighty good times down at the World, when I think of it. Sam kept us all in stitches with his humorous stories. Known for his ability to entertain and graced with tousled hair and ragged moustache, he was dubbed Vancouver's Mark Twain by World staff. Copy men and reporters alike often crowded into my office to hear Sam's latest scoop on the waterfront—for even after becoming city editor, Sam insisted upon rooting out many stories by himself.

The most unusual character associated with the *World* was Francis Bursill, whose pen name was Felix Penne. Bursill lived in a shack in the South Vancouver woods. But he spent his days downtown. Sporting a scraggly grey beard and carrying his customary bundle of newspapers under arm, he strutted about town and for a time kept a salon on Pender Street, near Cambie—a huge, barnlike room cluttered with furniture, books and pictures. Here he entertained friends over a glass of whiskey. I

Imposing and smartly dressed, two Vancouver policemen pose while on duty, c. 1900. Major Matthews, founder of the City of Vancouver Archives, identified the man on the right as Constable Malcolm McLennan. (CVA Pol P8 N5)

am told that it was a decidedly Bohemian atmosphere, though Bursill loved all art and literature. And he was a good writer. I persuaded him to contribute a regular column in the *World* on literary matters.

Bursill founded both the Vagabond's Club and the Shakespeare Society. The Vagabonds met monthly at his salon. God knows what they accomplished. But one night the organizing committee planned a gala evening of fun and sport involving a make-believe trial of Bursill on a charge of murdering some city resident. Bursill turned up as usual, wearing a special velvet coat he reserved for formal occasions and smoking a Havana cigar. Not being aware of the planned events, he became apoplectic when the frock-coated Vagabond clerk formally read the charges to him of having committed a gruesome axe murder. As poor Bursill rose trembling to protest his innocence, he unconsciously threw his burning cigar into his coat pocket. Smoke rose, then flame. The velvet coat was shed and soon lay ruined on the floor. Bursill angrily ejected everyone out of the salon; the Vagabond Club was no more.

When I had finished my daily office business, I usually made a sweep through the press room. I especially liked to check out the telegraph machine, and in a pinch willingly took up my old trade. The dynamics of the newspaper office were exciting: news coming in over the wire and by telephone; composers crying out for copy; the copy headed and sent to the rattling machines—or "up the spout," as we said. Men dressed in black vests and bow ties sat in a row at these machines and cut the copy into "takes," dropping it out in the little metal bars soon to become type. Then the heads were added, advertisements and stories finalized, and all was rushed to the make-up man, who turned the lot into forms—here the page was made up as a balanced product.

The stereotyper received the form from the make-up man and placed it under moistened matrix paper. The whole piece was then put under the heat and pressure of the steam table, and left to cook. The finished matrix emerged and was placed in a mould, and the molten metal was turned inward. The final step saw the plate being rushed to the press room and stuck to the press rollers. Thousands of copies were churned out each day, and dozens of paper boys came in to hurry the papers to city streets. The grind was constant, the work tedious. A newspaper office never sleeps, for the drive to scoop the competitor and sell more papers is relentless. As the Hearst people say, "Nothing succeeds like circulation."

My first project of the new century was to inaugurate a regular women's page in the *World*. My Lady Cook articles were not enough. I wanted to strike a balance between the bland social and fashion news of the day and the deeper issues affecting women in society—including social injustice. But I did not want to preach too radically at men as a group. I sympathized with the renowned female journalist from Toronto, Kit Coleman of the *Daily Mail*. While supportive of various women's social causes, she believed it would be counterproductive for women to "rush into print" everywhere, pouring invective on men, for men could quickly become "condescending, patronizing, or mercilessly sarcastic." Backlash against women's political activity was in full swing as a result of the fanatical actions of characters like Carrie Nation, who in 1901 was smashing saloons with her hatchet in Kansas.

The management demands of the *World* caused me to reduce my club commitments. My three-year term as President of the Council of Women was up and I was grateful for a respite—I was exhausted with meetings. But it was not all drudgery. Fred and I slipped off to the Opera House at least twice a week to see plays and opera—though I must say that the much-touted "Belle of New York" was disgusting vaudeville farce. "Tess" and the "Prisoner of Zenda" were much better. John lay most of the time languishing in his bed, his odd trip uptown leaving him exhausted and depressed. But I refused to be disconsolate; life is full of challenges and we just have to live it as best we can with the cards we are dealt.

Then, on January 19th, 1901, our whole world changed. Sam rang me up in the late afternoon to advise of a telegraph report stating that Queen Victoria was mortally ill. Well, we all prayed; we spoke in hushed tones. This went on for three days, the whole city immersed in a bleak fog of anxiety. At 10:15 a.m. on the 22nd, we received word over the wire of the Queen's death.

All businesses in the city immediately closed as word spread. One didn't need a proclamation for that, it was just something one did out of respect. Public and other buildings were draped in black crepe, and bells from all the city churches tolled ceaselessly. We all wore black armbands in

A lazy Saturday afternoon at Second Beach at the turn of the century. (VPL 5449)

public. Streets were deserted—except for the bars, which provoked out-raged mourners to question saloon owners' patriotism. Even the CPR trains were draped in black. Businesses competed with one another to pro-duce the most lavish, artistic mourning displays. It was generally agreed that the Hudson's Bay Company store on Granville Street won this contest.

There were few Canadians alive who had not grown to maturity with Victoria as their queen. She was outspoken on public issues, though in shunning the cause of suffragetism, she certainly did not typify the "new woman." But most people, including most suffragettes, viewed her as a dis-tant mother, a bulwark of ideals, strength, decency. Her death filled us all with deep sadness. Perhaps our grief and apprehension were also related to the perceived inadequacy of the Queen's successor, her profligate, philan-dering son, Edward the Seventh. I pondered all of this as I joined with my children and two thousand other Vancouverites in a memorial service at the Opera House.

The day after the Queen died was so cold that I told Louie to take the children skating on Trout Lake. When I reached the office that morning I

Chinese and Sikh immigrants are detained for questioning aboard ship at Vancouver Harbour, early 1900s. (VPL 3027)

decided to use the occasion of the Queen's passing as a catalyst for a project I had had in mind for many years—a new and proper city hospital. The existing decrepit structure did not even have a children's wing. So I composed a quick editorial directed at City Council. "What could be more appropriate as a memorial to the late Queen," I wrote, "than the erection of a modern hospital, with a special ward commemorative of the fallen heroes of the field of battle."

The city's medical doctors supported me unanimously, as did the Council of Women. I persuaded the Victorian Order of Nurses to agree to direct the $1100 we had collected for a nurses' training centre toward a brand new hospital instead. With this startup pledge in hand, I appeared one evening before City Council to argue my case. The reception was cordial. Clearly some councillors were annoyed at being cajoled by a woman, but they could not deny the need, and indeed the populace was pushing hard for Vancouver to join with the rest of the Empire in erecting some socially useful memorial for the late Queen. It took some time, but my efforts proved successful, resulting first in the incorporation of the Vancouver General Hospital Society, and second in a new hospital in Fairview.

The centre of Vancouver continued to move southwest from the old Granville site at Water and Carrall streets. Smart new buildings were erected up the hill toward Georgia Street, away from the grime, smoke and eyesore of Hastings Mill, where sailing ships still loaded their cargoes. The cream of the Vancouver elite at this time built their mansions at the foot of Howe Street, the short stretch of which was known as "Blueblood Alley." Here the harbour view could be enjoyed without even seeing the several Kanaka hovels still standing on the beach at Coal Harbour.

We all spoke derisively of the Kanaka shacks; they offended our notions of progress, contrasting sharply with the West End mansions springing up nearby. Indian and white families also squatted on shoreline lands—including the Cumming family, the oldest of the squatters. Jim Cumming was a Scot fisherman who married a Bella Coola Indian named Lucy in the early 1870s. They settled east of Brockton Point at a time when the Park was still a military reserve. Jim died in 1897, but Lucy and their children, Agnes and Timothy, continued to reside in the old cottage, which was regarded as an intriguing artifact by the thousands of tourists and locals who travelled the Park drive in their carriages.

At about the same time Jim Cumming first squatted, Mary Ehiu and her husband, both Kanakas, took up land on Coal Harbour that backed northward to Georgia Street. As much as I deplored the unsightliness of Mary's shack, I empathized with her ongoing fight to retain her land. After her husband died, Mary successfully resisted a real estate developer's lawsuit to dispossess her, when a Supreme Court judge upheld her squatter's rights in July of 1899. Despite the judgment, this nasty developer destroyed Mary's fences, ruined portions of her orchard, and burned at least two of three shacks that stood on her property. Mary implored City Council to protect her and her family from these antics, but she finally succumbed to the vicious persecution and left her land for only nominal compensation.

The Fairview and Mount Pleasant districts meanwhile expanded the city in other directions, and there was talk of even South Vancouver and

Looking north on Main Street from Broadway, c. 1901. (VPL 6718)

Point Grey becoming part of Vancouver proper. Outside the West End, one could always see horse-drawn drays on the streets coming and going, loaded with the household goods of families on the move. And everywhere in the downtown environs there were workmen digging ditches along the roads, building wooden sidewalks and burning stumps.

The slaughterhouses and mills lining False Creek were cesspools of disease and polluted water. Yet we turned a blind eye because industry was badly needed and, after all, we had Stanley Park. But one form of pollution that I could not tolerate was spitting. I ordered spittoons removed from *World* offices, banning the practice completely. I suspected, you see, that John's tuberculosis could well have been contracted as a result of this disgusting practice. Listen to my tirade in the *World*: "The anti-spitting notices with which the street cars are placarded have been instrumental in curtailing the filthy habit in the cars. Spitting in all public places is not only filthy, but dangerous to public health. It is recognized as one of the most prolific means of propagating disease in every community. An eminent authority has stated that consumption would soon be completely eradicated if the

The YWCA (Young Women's Christian Association) building, early 1900s. (VPL 7727)

human sputum could be intercepted and cared for just after it leaves the mouth… We must forbid expectoration on the sidewalk, in public halls, conveyances, on floors, carpets, and in dark corners of hotels and private houses. Ladies are advised to wear shorter skirts and people who must expectorate should use paper handkerchiefs which should be burned after using."

A few days after publication of my anti-spitting editorial, John took a turn for the worse. He could no longer retain his food and grew very weak. I did prop him up one afternoon to watch a great bicycle race progress down Georgia Street, but he was clearly failing fast. Easter Monday dawned gloriously warm and sunny. Mother sent lilies of the valley from Hazelbrae with a sealed trout box containing Father's fresh catches. But alas, John was unable to enjoy any of this. He babbled terribly about destroying his old will, though I assured him that it had been revoked automatically by his making a new one.

Doctors came and went, shaking their heads in dismay. Madame Martin stayed with us to provide comfort and extra help, and a constant

The front page of The Daily World *on April 11, 1901, announcing the death of John McLagan. The newspaperman and political power broker was lauded by friends and opponents alike as a man indefatigably committed to the future greatness of Vancouver.*

stream of callers stopped by to check on John's condition. Well, I stayed with him to the last, and the sound of his breathing was torture to the ears. When the doctors told me on April 10th that John was near the end, I rang up Reverend McLaren and asked him to come by. After the minister was finished, I shooed everyone downstairs, sitting next to the bed with John's hand in mine until it grew cold in death. His last words to me, spoken when he was virtually unconscious, were "Canada, Canada." I placed a lily on his chest and then plodded slowly down the stairs, the thick mahogany boards underfoot literally groaning and creaking in the chilly quiet of death's aftermath.

The following day, Mother and Father and my brother Charles arrived. Charles attended to the funeral arrangements. We laid John out in an open casket in the parlour and posted Louie and Fred at the door for the customary two days of viewing by friends and acquaintances. The children were devastated, confused. For my part, despite my grief, I was glad John was out of pain at last, noting in my diary, "The dear one looks so peaceful and happy, I dare not wish him back."

Reverend McLaren held the funeral service in our home. The house filled to overflowing, and I was comforted by not only good friends like Marie McNaughton and Madame Martin, but even Carter-Cotton, who stopped by to sympathize with my loss and called John "a very worthy opponent." Father, Charles and Douglas headed the funeral procession to St. Andrew's Church, where hundreds more attended a public memorial service, including the entire City Council and *World* staff. All of the flags on public buildings flew at half-mast as the black, horse-drawn hearse was escorted across the Westminster Bridge to Fairview Cemetery. There John was buried next to our beloved daughter Geraldine.

Mayor Townley sent condolences to me from City Council, writing: "We feel that no one man has done as much as Mr. McLagan to advance Vancouver's welfare." The press generally heralded John as a man of indomitable perseverance, restless energy and impetuous disposition, who spoke his mind fearlessly. Walter Nichol eulogized that "Canadian journalism loses one of its most venerable representatives… In the growth of Vancouver he exercised a personal influence which no one could gainsay."

The night of the funeral I slipped exhausted into a deep sleep at ten o'clock. I awoke early to a bright morning with fragrant flowers filling the house, while outside the cold, pale waters of Burrard Inlet glistened in the sun, beyond them the white mountain peaks tinged with the pink hues of dawn. But this dawn held no cheer, no solace. For the first time in my life, I felt truly alone. Within the first one hundred days of the new century, I had lost my queen and now my husband.

Later that day I stood with Fred at the edge of John's grave. The planing mills of False Creek whined in the distance and seagulls soared overhead in the stiff breeze. Suddenly I remembered the pledge I had made to myself. I would carry on; the *World* presses must continue to spin under the McLagan masthead.

After a long period of silence, Fred gently tugged at my arm and guided me to the waiting carriage. "Dear Fred," I smiled, "take me downtown." "Home?" he asked. "No, Fred, to the office, silly, I have work to do." "But Sara," Fred pleaded, "don't you think you should rest—""Just drive, Fred," I said.

The horses whipped us along. I could smell the tangy salt air, mingled with the acrid scent of the mills. Perhaps, after all, I thought, this was what the new century was all about. The old bulwarks were gone; life was changing. The nation, Vancouver, and Sara McLagan were all on their own now. And we had damn well better make a good show of it.

CHAPTER FIVE

Oriental Breezes

A few days after the funeral, Fred and I headed for the countryside for rest and reflection. At Hazelbrae, we walked the familiar country paths. The woods were full of trilliums and bleeding hearts. And there on a side table in the kitchen lay my old telegraph set, the keys worn but shiny. In the slough near the house, Father and I angled for cutthroat trout. When the train came by, a familiar package was thrown toward our gate, containing the *World's* latest sheet. After a few days, Fred and I travelled on to Harrison Hot Springs, where Fred lay for hours in the mineral baths to relieve his rheumatism.

When we returned to the city two weeks later, we were surprised to find that Madame Martin had completely re-wallpapered my home with cheerful bright floral patterns. The girls and Douglas threw themselves upon me in a tearful reunion, and though I could not hold back my tears that day, we all picnicked near John's grave, reflecting on the uncertainty of existence. Doris was a special joy that evening, filling the house with song from the old piano.

The will was read later that week at Bowser's law office, where it was confirmed that I was the sole heir of John's estate except for a $500 bequest to his son Jack. We had wired Jack in Dawson when John was slipping away, but he had not made it down for the funeral. Later we learned that Jack had married a Miss Frances Wood of Dawson. I wrote in my diary, "We conclude that he no longer considers that we are interested in his actions."

Police Chief J. Stewart. Stewart suspended one constable for being "overzealous" in carrying out unauthorized raids on Chinatown gambling dens. The Constable incurred the Chief's wrath by escorting reporter Sam Robb and Rev. McLaren through some thirty dens, resulting in a detailed World *article describing trap doors, fan tan games and opium smoking. (CVA Port P1787 N1200)*

My brother Sam was spending more time in Vancouver on business these days, so he came often to dinner. We laughed about how in 1889 I had engineered his and his fiancee's elopement to Vancouver from Victoria. I had arranged for Daisy to dress in black, disguised as a haggard old woman. As she boarded the boat for Vancouver, she barely eluded the frantic clutches of her brother, who was determined to return her home to Mother. Now Daisy was achieving some fame in her own right as a painter.

Sam's talents as an architect meanwhile were becoming known throughout the Pacific Northwest, and he was now being pressed on all sides by Vancouver businessmen for Maclure-designed homes. His first major contract was for the lumber broker H. G. Ross, who wanted a huge frame house built on Comox Street.

But the commission that established Sam's enduring reputation in Vancouver was his design of "Gabriola" for Ben Rogers, an industrialist who founded the BC Sugar Refinery and later owned the first motor car in the city. Rogers had talked City Council into giving him fifteen years of tax exemption and ten years of free water in exchange for building a refinery complex. He asked Sam to build a home for him on Davie Street, using mostly Gabriola Island quarried stone. This extravagant home became the model for other tycoons of the city—two and a half storeys, hip roof, a huge gazebo-like verandah and eighteen fireplaces. The house featured friezes of intricate carved stone picturing sea horses and Indian profiles, a unique terra-cotta overmantel for one of the gargantuan fireplaces, and stained glass window work unmatched in Vancouver. After Gabriola, Sam never looked back. He soon opened a full-time office in Vancouver and even after taking on partners, he experienced difficulty in keeping up with the clamour for designs from the bluebloods settling in the West End.

Joe Martin would still show up unannounced at my home or at the *World* office, ever a source of comic relief. Joe was still leader of the Liberal opposition against Premier Dunsmuir, but was engaged in a rather quixotic stratagem of supporting Dunsmuir against the large bloc of other opposition MPPs who distrusted Joe. In fact, Joe behaved as if he were still attorney general, introducing ten bills in the Legislature at one sitting and securing passage of seven of them. He became so influential with the inept Dunsmuir that he finally achieved his longtime objective of government endorsement of a coast-to-coast Kootenay railway for his friend Joe Hill, competition at last for the CPR.

Our *World* editorials in fact wailed constantly about the paternalistic monopoly of the CPR—personally I still boiled over Carter-Cotton's exclusive CPR telegraph contract—and many Canadians viewed Vancouver as nothing more than a CPR company town, filled with Chinese coolies left over from railway building. Lally Bernard of the *Toronto Globe* had this to say about the Vancouver of 1901: "The new residential part of Vancouver bears a strong resemblance to the least magnificent part of Newport, Rhode Island... Standing in front of picturesque residences I saw several of these little lads clad in loose, white garments which showed in strong relief their ivory-coloured faces and the inky black of the long pigtail which reached to their feet. These were the footmen of the richer inhabitants of Vancouver, and very charming page boys they were, as they slid noiselessly over the highly polished floors in their queer little paper-soled shoes. They were entirely in keeping with the general surroundings, although British Columbians will tell you that the atmosphere of the province is distinctly English. Vancouver presented to the traveller nothing in the least reminiscent of the Motherland, save one building, the Badminton. All else seemed so extraordinarily new and suggestive of the American town. It is impossible to think of Vancouver apart from the CPR, as the city seems in truth 'the power of the line.'"

Bernard's *Globe* article rankled. We were a CPR town, and bitterly resented it. And unlike genteel Victoria, with its rambling gardens, stately carriages and high teas, we were akin to San Francisco: a rough, strapping, uproarious port city flexing its youthful muscles—with horse dung littering our streets.

In fact, only the sea breeze kept the stench of dung from driving me mad. Drays, carriages and commercial teams clopped along side by side with streetcars. Hundreds of City workhorses were stabled at False Creek. Horses did the city work—there was even a large stable behind the Hotel Vancouver. Runaway teams of horses would often come charging up Granville Street from the CPR wharf, and cowboys would gallop down Georgia, scaring ladies in their carriages. I railed at City Council about its

Kitsilano Indian Reserve, c. 1907. The caption on the archival print of this photograph identifies the people as August Jack Haatsalano and his wife Swanamia and daughter. The view is toward the east, near the foot of today's Chestnut Street. (CVA In N17 P35)

lack of a sanitation policy for problems like horse manure and dead cats decomposing on downtown streets.

Sanitation aside, Vancouver aspired in 1901 to a triple crown objective: to become a leading world seaport, to rid itself of the CPR and to drive out the Chinese. Alas, our city became obsessed with the latter. Although comprising less than 10 percent of Vancouver's population, the Chinese remained the focus of appalling racism and hatred. In this, it was generally the lower classes who led the charge. Jobs were scarce. The Chinese shared their mean tenements on Pender, Powell and Cordova streets with one another, and many of them trudged each morning to West End homes like mine, where they worked for low wages. It was not just racism that fanned the flame of discontent, however, but also hostility to immigrants who temporarily took up residence solely for the purpose of earning sufficient money to return to their native country. Add to that their tremendous efficiency, diligence and poor remuneration, and you needed little but a small spark for the situation to explode.

I know my own position was hypocritical. I suggested in the *World* that we needed good English girls to serve in West End homes. Yet I made no effort to find any; in fact, I regarded Louie as part of the family and trusted him with my daughters' lives every day. He was the best nanny and

Chinese track gang working at the foot of Columbia Street, early 1900s. (VPL 7742

cook in the city. Yet we cruelly made fun of the Chinese as a group, never stopping to consider the effect of our ridicule upon the individual. In a typical item, I deadpanned in my social column: "A Chinaman who was a passenger on the *Empress* came into port in a wooden box filled with lime. He was dead."

The police regularly harassed the Chinese fan tan clubs and opium dens by means of elaborately contrived raids. But it was hard for Anglo-Saxons to disguise themselves with pigtails. They sometimes tried their hand at braiding the silk covers of umbrellas and tying these to their heads, but only succeeded in making themselves look ridiculous. More often than not, the men in blue would pretend to be Sikhs, and go about wearing high turbans, old clothes and fake beards. This generally got them past the Chinese guards posted at the houses of iniquity.

The entire issue of police raids on Chinese gambling blew up into scandal in 1901, when Police Chief Stewart suspended one Constable McAllister for carrying out raids without his permission. It seems that the good constable was overzealous in his war against gambling dens, and in his off-duty hours was prone to haunt the Chinatown area, even giving guided tours to anyone who wanted to view vice firsthand. Sam Robb and my good minister, Reverend McLaren, were escorted about the dens by McAllister

Chinese bandwagon, c. 1900. Major celebrations in Vancouver such as Royal Visits were considerably enhanced by the panoply of Oriental decorations and band music provided by the Chinese community. (VPL 6716)

just prior to his suspension. Some thirty houses were visited, centring upon Dupont Street.

Sam's report was intriguing: "At this place is the largest game in Chinatown. The interior equipment is arranged with a view to the minimum chance of arrest if an alarm is given. There are trap doors and stairs leading to different exits. The house is a veritable labyrinth... The next place visited was the row of gambling houses on the alley leading to the Chinese theatre, off Carrall Street. The ministerial party made a run on the first one, but the door closed... and by the time the end of the row was reached, every place was closed up tight. There was an excited jabbering among the Chinese whenever any force was used to enter. Around the corner, one of the houses was open and no game was in operation. Inside, half a dozen Chinese were lounging around smoking and enjoying an evening's comfort. One or two were laid out with the opium paraphernalia. There were a couple of tables used for Chinese games, one for fan tan and the other chuck-a-luck, while a third was based on the blackjack principle. The

"Gabriola," the mansion of sugar tycoon Ben Rogers, and a masterpiece of design by Sara McLagan's brother, Sam Maclure. The address is 1531 Davie Street. (VPL 7161)

minister made a detailed examination of the system by which the door-keeper controls the alarm and closes two or three sets of doors by one pull of the string. McAllister pulled the string and the minister gasped for breath as the doors swung forward. Then the reverend praised the fine mechanism and skill of the Chinese… Another house nearby was the subject of a raid some time ago, and all the Chinese jumped out of the rear windows, some falling ten feet to the ground below…"

Aside from zealots like Reverend McLaren and Constable McAllister, Vancouverites only condemned the gambling dens for corrupting young Anglo-Saxon men and they couldn't care less about what the Chinese did among themselves. After all, it was in the arena of the workplace that the Chinese were a threat; their culture and habits were exotic, colourful, even appealing to much of the community. Chief Stewart's own ambivalent view ultimately prevailed. The number of gambling raids declined. Besides, the police were hopelessly ill-equipped to even make a dent in the gaming trade. I recall one morning, after a big raid had netted four accused gamblers, Louie told me that the joke running in Chinatown was that just before the policemen arrived at the house, some forty gamblers escaped through a trap door in the floor. "Alle samee potatoes—poured down," smiled Louie. When the policemen left, these men climbed back up the ladder to resume their leisurely games.

The police were initially as ambivalent in their approach to the opium trade as they were toward gambling. But here there was a more determined public will. Reverend McLaren was joined by other ministers in the city in pursuing the war against drugs, but the real leader in this crusade was a young grocery clerk named Harry H. Stevens, who lay-preached at the Mount Pleasant Methodist Church. H.H., as he became known, had a gift of the gab. His efforts against raw opium—which, he said, was carried brazenly through Vancouver streets in open baskets—led to the formation of the city's first Narcotics Control Squad. Carter-Cotton took Stevens under his wing, gave him plenty of ink for his crusade, and helped him climb the hierarchical rungs of the Conservative Party. Stevens went on to a distinguished career in Canadian politics as one of the favourite sons of the West.

The furor of anti-Oriental feeling in British Columbia led Prime Minister Laurier to appoint a Royal Commission to investigate Chinese and Japanese affairs on the West Coast. The Commission began hearings in Vancouver in mid-March. Storekeepers, union men, policemen, canners, fishermen, industrialists and Indians all testified in one long emotional drama that involved only a few Orientals. Along with much racist rhetoric, the witnesses urged against any further immigration, chiefly on the grounds that the Oriental worker, who accepted low wages, deprived white workers of a livelihood. Cannery and mill owners argued that they could never compete with American operations without low-paid Oriental workers. White fishermen were even more bitter, complaining that Japanese fishermen held 1,759 fishing licences compared to 1,142 for whites. Indians agreed. Chief James Harry of the Squamish and Seymour Creek bands stated that the Japanese could live more cheaply than anyone else "on a spoonful of rice and a little perch."

The Commission was startled one morning to hear the eloquence of Won Cumyow, official translator for the Vancouver Chinese community. With quiet dignity, Cumyow systematically destroyed the arguments of the white witnesses: Orientals, he argued, fill a need in the marketplace and allow industry to compete internationally. "Many of the opponents of the Chinese," he said, "are new arrivals in the Province, who have very little idea of the facts. Some of these men are unwilling to work themselves and they misspend their earnings they do make, yet they are eager to run down the Chinese, who are willing to work hard and are very careful of their hard earned money. Chinese contractors are honest, drunkenness is rare; families stay together—and were it not for the unfriendly reception here, most Chinese would bring their wives and children over to stay… The Chinese are not a burden to the state, even operating their own city hospital for the indigent sick."

Despite Cumyow's logic and the pleas of industrial leaders, the Royal Commission recommended at the conclusion of its hearing that the head tax on Orientals be increased from $100 to $500. Laurier had already quashed similar provincial legislation, and refused this request as well. So the Chinese continued to arrive at dockside by the hundreds.

The Chinese Empire Reform Association appeared in Vancouver at this time and began to swing public opinion outside of labour circles toward a more tolerant viewpoint. Using Cumyow as interpreter, Anglo-Saxon leaders were invited regularly to address members of the Association at the Chinese Opera House, and later the ritzy Oriental Club at Hastings and Carrall. The Association also sponsored intellectual debate, plays and opera, and it favoured the modernization and westernization of China.

These developments coincided with a trend among Chinese immigrants to wear western style dress on Vancouver streets. Hair queues were becoming rarer. There was still a long way to go, and indeed flareups of violence instigated by the powerful Asiatic Exclusion League would blacken Vancouver's reputation for years. But the seeds of conciliation, of the acceptance of a diversity of cultures living in harmony, were planted in our port city by the quiet-spoken clerk, Won Cumyow.

Vancouverites had traditionally been more tolerant of the local Indians, indeed depended upon them when emergencies occurred on the water. How many times did some Sunday dandy dressed to the nines capsize his canoe off Stanley Park or English Bay and have to be rescued by an alert Indian? True, there was some resentment over the Indians squatting along Coal Harbour, but as Louis Taylor pointed out, these derelict shacks

Chief Joe Capilano and other Chiefs arrayed in traditional costume, on the North Vancouver ferry wharf, just before Chief Joe embarked for England in 1906. The Chief obtained an audience before King Edward VII, to whom he related Native land claim grievances. (CVA In P41 N23)

mainly housed Kanakas and "half-breeds," who were of course considered much inferior to our full-blooded Salish.

When some politicians and developers agitated for removal of Indians from their North Shore reserves, the popular Capilano Chief James Harry joined with Chief Joe Capilano in the fight for Indian rights. In an interview with the *World*, Chief Harry said: "It is hardly fair. For we have a right to the land, as we were the owners long before the white people had ever seen it. We are content with what has been devoted to our exclusive use, although it does not nearly approach the extent of land we are entitled to under the Act. At the Mission, we have 37 acres, which allows 20 feet to each family, whereas the Act calls for 160 acres. At Seymour Creek the allotment is about ten acres to each… This being the case, I do not think any agitation to have us deprived of the small heritage left us, should be continued…" I gave prominence to this declaration of Chief Harry with the headline: "Indians' Unanswerable Argument As To Right Of Possession." The Indians stayed.

Greater discord erupted over the Kitsilano Indian Reserve. City Council members wanted to rid the city of this reserve and thus take over the entire beachland area extending from False Creek to the tip of Point

Mary Capilano, wife of Chief Joe Capilano, was an imposing and forceful figure in her own right. She was often seen paddling her canoe across Burrard Inlet and skillfully traversed the dangerous First Narrows current. (VPL 2689)

Grey for bathing and picnic grounds suitable for the white mainstream. As well, white settlement could then proceed southward from the beaches.

Kitsilano Beach was named by Professor Charles Hill-Tout after one of the Squamish chiefs, Kateseelanogh. It had been known formerly as Greer's Beach, after the eccentric Sam Greer, who had occupied a large block adjacent to the reserve. The provincial government also supported City Council in desiring to force the Indians off of their land. The government agent stated that "my government is determined to get the Reserve, by fair means or foul." Thus, tribal leaders knew that they could but fight a delaying action, and so began moving band members to other reserves. The Indian dead were exhumed from their graves at the First Avenue and Fir Street cemetery and the bones moved to other reserve cemeteries.

Chief Joe Capilano was by far the most prominent Salish chief in the lower mainland of British Columbia in the early years of the new century. Joe had been asked by Father Durieu in the 1890s to leave his Seymour Creek Reserve home and establish a church on the Capilano Reserve to the west, where the Catholic religion had not yet taken hold. Joe agreed to tackle the task and assumed gradual leadership of the Capilano band, whose members did embrace the Catholic faith. What Durieu did not foresee was that in the process, Joe would become the leading Indian activist in the province. A man seldom overawed by technological advances, Joe had returned home from his first trip on a train—travelling as far as Port Moody with musket in hand—with the comment, "train not go so fast."

Capilano Joe was adept at mingling with white society without losing touch with his heritage. Toiling in shingle mills by day, he regaled visitors by night with tales of the past, reminding many of his white guests— including *World* reporters—that there had been some ten Indian villages on Burrard Inlet and Point Grey when whites first arrived, and that now there were only three miserable reserves. Many of his tales were compiled by Pauline Johnson and published in her *Legends of Vancouver*. (In 1906, Joe travelled to London and was received by King Edward VII, to whom he presented a petition regarding Indian land claims. He paraded about London streets with fellow chiefs, clad in full regalia, at one point creating a stir when he raised his arms in Hyde Park and declared, "This would be a great hunting ground." But he received only vague promises of redress from the King.)

Joe's wife, Mary Capilano (Layhulette) was granddaughter of a Yuculta princess. Mary was a handsome woman possessed of a hearty laugh, kindly disposition, and enormous vitality. As a child, she had travelled with her father by canoe to Fort Langley, where Indians traded otter pelts and salmon for Hudson's Bay blankets, utensils and tobacco. Her first impression of a European came when a burly, bearded trader picked her up, tumbled her in the air and then set her trembling form down in the canoe. Mary was loyal to Joe and his needs yet very independent. She was often seen paddling her dugout across the Inlet on her own, traversing the dangerous First Narrows current with alacrity. When a reporter interviewed her one day about how she reconciled traditional Indian religion with Catholicism, Mary simply pointed toward the sky and said, "Many churches—One Sagulee Tyee." (One God.)

The deportation of the Kitsilano Indians proceeded far more smoothly than had the eviction of Sam Greer. Greer's lands, which he had occupied for several years on the basis of a deed from some Indians, were claimed by the CPR as railway property. According to company lawyers, Victoria had settled certain differences with the railway in 1891 by granting the CPR some 6000 acres, among which was Greer's 160-acre spread, the English Bay shore of which was known as Greer's Beach.

Sam was barraged with demands from the CPR to vacate his house and land. He refused to move. When Sheriff Tom Armstrong finally arrived to physically remove him and his family, Sam raised his rifle and shot the sheriff in the arm. He was promptly arrested for assault, then tried and jailed. Most Vancouverites were indignant and supported Sam all the way in his subsequent legal battles with the huge railway. But he ultimately lost in the courts, and the CPR sold off the Greer acreage for residential lots once the Indians next door had been evicted.

As we have seen, paranoia over Oriental immigration was matched only by Vancouverites' obsession with the power of the CPR. Aside from the Kitsilano lands, the CPR held title to a vast number of city lots. When Council decided to purchase the Cambie Street site for our new hospital, Dr. Wilson asked why the CPR did not aid the City Hospital "as the CPR

Vancouver's first resident automobile. (VPL 4217)

magnates did in Montreal." The question proved purely rhetorical, there being no reply.

When Andrew Carnegie donated $50,000 for a public library in Vancouver in 1901, we fought tooth and nail with the CPR to persuade them to donate a mere 80- by 120-foot lot for the building. The CPR demurred, and eventually wiggled out of the situation as a result of City Council's division over the appropriate location. (We finally built the library at Main and Hastings Street, after East End councillors insisted that it be accessible to more than just the West End rich. As a result, the library came to be patronized largely by vagrants and drunks who often collapsed thankfully over the reading tables.)

Even on the water, Canadian Pacific reigned supreme. Three majestic *Empress* ships plied the waters between Vancouver and the Orient. And how the scents of tea and mahogany and the silk bales piled high on the Howe Street wharf excited us! Crowds always gathered to greet the arrival of an

Empress ship. Often the Hotel Vancouver burst at the seams when tram-loads of tourists arrived in town to await an *Empress* liner bound for Australia or China. The great hotel contained 205 rooms, 75 of which boasted baths attached. And the cultured gentleman and lady could slip next door to the Opera House at night to watch a play, assured that their iced champagne bucket would arrive at their box exactly midway through the performance.

Canadian Pacific vessels also dominated the runs between Vancouver and Victoria. Their elegant cuisine and wood-panelled dining rooms added to the charm of my occasional visits to the capital, where Sam and Daisy would meet me at the dock. It was all very genteel. Except of course when ugly incidents involving race or disease intervened.

Occasionally, boats loaded with Orientals—or, as later happened in 1914, Sikhs aboard the *Komagata Maru*—were greeted by hostile crowds seeking to stop passengers from landing because of their ethnic origin. Smallpox scares only heightened anti-immigration sentiments. One day the CP vessel *Premier* arrived from Victoria at the Howe Street dock, carrying some passengers believed to carry smallpox. Policemen stood on the dock and prevented passengers from disembarking. One determined soul was punched in the nose by a bobbie as he tried to wedge his way down the gangplank. A brawl ensued, and the Vancouver fire brigade charged down and trained a powerful spray of water on the Victoria passengers—who in turn activated the ship's hose and barraged the waterfront. Finally the vessel sailed away from the wharf—and tricked the local constabulary by making a beeline for Johnnie Baker's Clearing near Brockton Point, where passengers hurriedly disembarked and dispersed before the police arrived.

Not so elegant, but beloved by the working classes, were the garish black and orange funnelled Union Steamship boats. These vessels serviced trade up and down the BC coast. But on weekends, the *Comox, Capilano* and *Lady Rose* picked up eager families at the Main Street wharf and ferried them to favourite picnic grounds up Howe Sound or to summer cottages at Sechelt and Halfmoon Bay.

Saturday night brought the Union Steamship booze cruise for young unattached men and women. Bowen Island was never the same after these weekend sprees—and people today talk about the lascivious twenties! Such debauchery led me to run several editorials as to the need for club and recreational facilities for young people in Vancouver that would offer wholesome evening entertainment. And I didn't mean the Alhambra Hotel or the cat-houses of Dupont Street.

CHAPTER SIX

The Last Rose of Summer

Who has truly lived without tasting a Vancouver spring? May blossomed gorgeous in 1901. "Out here in the West," I wrote, "the trees are dreams of beauty as their tender green leaves open out to the warm sun that floods the world. The boulevards and lawns are golden with dandelions, and the flowering currant is all abloom. As one comes down the road in the soft gloom of night, its delicious fragrance greets one —there is nothing to be seen in the dark, neither leaf nor flower, but everywhere is the ravishing sweetness pouring out on the still night air. All day long the birds chirrup and sing—the robins whistle like mad things, and under the blue and gold sky the fruit trees in the orchards and gardens rise in radiant bloom like great bridal bouquets."

Provincial politics, alas, were not so prosaic, but rather continued on their chaotic course. Premier Dunsmuir vacillated on every issue, distracted by labour and safety problems in his coal mines. Joe Martin continued to play out his farcical role of opposition leader; while Tory gladhand Richard McBride emerged this year as the new leading light.

Dunsmuir viewed his role as premier much as the Duke of Wellington had viewed his—to maintain stability. He was utterly incapable of dealing with citizens, politicians or unions. He hated his job. He was a lame duck kept in office solely by MPPs of all political stripes who were terrified of Martin, much preferring a rich, impotent tycoon to a professional buffoon, even if the buffoon had savvy.

Martin's game of puppetry with Dunsmuir was wearing thin. Though he was but a caretaker, the premier no longer needed Joe's support on most bills. Martin was fast losing support from his own party as well. He was the Liberal Party leader in name, but he lost when he ran for the prestigious position of Honorary President of the Vancouver Liberals—vacant since my John had died. The tide was out for Fighting Joe, and he would soon lose his status as opposition leader to McBride. Even this provoked a spectacle: a game of musical chairs for the opposition leader's seat ensued when Martin refused to move to the backbenches.

So Joe began to devote more and more of his time to the practice of law in Vancouver. Once he left the political scene, it was never so colourful. An old friend, Donald Barr, wrote aptly of Joe: "Whenever his name was mentioned, such rancor was aroused that I usually got nothing but profanity. He is a man not to be ignored, and I can imagine his quiet, incisive voice from the body of a public meeting being the precursor of a riot. Something in him arouses all of the virulent antagonism of the human race."

Springtime also saw Carter-Cotton announce his retirement from provincial politics. Much as we had crossed swords over the years, I must say that I admired the bewhiskered old man, and even said so in an editorial. Not that Fred and I felt any less piqued when Carter-Cotton spoiled the *World's* promotional campaign involving the Buffalo Exposition trip. You see, we had thought to run a contest whereby a reader holding a subscription to the *World* would write in to us and give the name of his favourite Vancouver teacher—with readers' votes weighted according to the length of their paid subscription period. New subscribers were sought after to participate, of course, and the teacher receiving the most votes would receive an all-expense-paid trip to Buffalo, where the world exposition was making history.

Unfortunately, Carter-Cotton and Walter Nichol ganged up on us to spoil the party. They managed to convince all but six of Vancouver's seventy-six teachers that it would be unseemly and unethical to allow their names to stand. Cotton wrote: "As in any other line of commercial activity, a newspaper should seek and secure public support on its own merits as a purveyor of news and an exponent of public opinion. To be compelled to bid for advertising patronage, or for additions to the list of subscribers by all sorts of fakes and side-shows, is to show that its management lacks that ability, knowledge, and expertise which it should possess."

Well, I blew up in fury at this torpedoing of my scheme. We ended up sending Miss R. M. Macfarlane to Buffalo, and she sent back decently written accounts of her trip which we published. Unfortunately the subscription campaign fizzled: the expenses of the trip far outweighed revenue from new readers, and worst of all, everyone knew that Miss Macfarlane, while a good person, was not Vancouver's favourite teacher.

Even so, our readership remained well ahead of the *News-Advertiser*, which was fading fast. But Nichol's *Province* was pulling ahead of us—that upstart, tawdry journal, the CPR's toady—why, it would print most anything to sell copy. When the *Cobbledick*, a huge Fraser River gold dredging barge, had problems upriver of Lytton one day, the *Province* headlined with a wild tale of the vessel snapping its cable and careening down the Fraser Canyon with several men aboard. "The doomed men were hurled through boiling and seething whirlpools," screamed their liner. In fact, the barge's captain was snacking on beer and biscuits at the Lytton Hotel and the old scow was quickly brought to shore with no damage or injury to the crew.

Nichol's circus poster even had the audacity to label me a traitor for our plaudits recognizing the Boers as brave foes. "Those brave fellows," wrote my editor, "brigands though they are, compel the honest admiration of every man for their splendid courage…" Despite my outrage at Nichol, however, I could not deny that, yellow journalism aside, Louis Taylor was doing a marvellous job of improving the *Province's* subscription rolls.

By mid-year, I was comfortable in my role as the first female proprietor and editor-in-chief of a daily newspaper in Canada. Not that my senior editors lasted long. The latest recruit was Harold Sands, a quiet, decent man who liked to ply his sailboat up and down the coast.

In my fervour for proof-reading all *World* items, I began to run afoul of organized labour. One day I was informed by Proof-Reader's Union chairman W. H. Hunt that I was "scabbing" if I proof-read my own paper, as the union required its own people to perform this task. Now, all but my most senior employees were union and I proudly boasted the union label, but as I saw it, the *World* was mine to proof-read if I chose.

I wrote to Hunt: "I beg to request that the decision of the last meet-

The editorial staff of the Vancouver Daily World, *1901, with the newspaper office in the background. Harold Sands is at far left, next to reporter Sam Robb. The wood plank sidewalk of Homer Street, between Hastings and Pender, can be seen at left. (CVA Str P84 N81)*

ing be reconsidered in view of the fact that I am desirous of continuing to read the proofs myself, having found it more advantageous to the business for various reasons... Should however I find it advisable to discontinue at any time, I hereby agree to appoint someone satisfactory to the Union. I am most anxious to maintain friendly relations with the Union and hope that nothing will occur to disturb them." Well, the union did reconsider, and eventually agreed with the terms of my letter. (The dispute was not fully resolved until 1904.)

Other union matters were not so easily resolved in this tumultuous year. Over 74,000 steel strikers went out in the United States. The miners struck at Rossland; and in Spain, even the King's cooks took to the picket line! In June, some 5,000 CPR trackmen went on strike across Canada, 700 of whom worked the BC section. Although special police constables were sworn in to protect railway property and to guard track and tunnels, few people took the trains and there were several bitter incidents of violence. The dispute wore on for many months.

The summer heated up again in the fishing industry, with racially motivated violence being perpetrated by white strikers against Japanese fishermen. Indians joined with the white fishermen in harassing Japanese boats, with dozens of Salish war canoes circling in waters off the Terra Nova Cannery. Eleven Japanese boats were attacked by white fishermen, the vessels seized and the Japanese themselves dumped ashore on Bowen Island, stranded without food or shelter. Police ultimately made arrests, but the accused were acquitted of the charges by an all-white jury.

My sympathy lay with the unions, despite my condemning of all violence. Working conditions in this province were simply appalling. It is no wonder that everyone organized, right down to the Vancouver City Bandsmen.

Even the telephone operators went on strike, and not just for higher wages. Picture this: If an operator missed even half a day's work because of illness, she had to pay another woman to replace her—or she risked being fired, never mind paid sick leave. It riled me that we wallowed in this churning cauldron of social misery and industrial unrest, while the bluebloods of Vancouver just kept playing their games, having fun in the Vancouver sun, seemingly oblivious to the hardship and violence in our midst. Carter-Cotton even alleged that there was no hostility between the canners and the striking fishermen. I responded tartly: "Perhaps the *News-Advertiser* sees them sitting up at night making love to each other."

In Dickens' opening lines of *A Tale of Two Cities*, the writer speaks of "the best of times, the worst of times." Well, that sums up 1901. While Japanese were being attacked on boats around us and homeless orphans died of malnutrition, Vancouverites spent a bacchanalian week of celebration to honour the century's first Dominion Day. British warships came to harbour, colourful parades and sports events were held, and we experienced the most marvellous evening lighting all along the main streets of the city for the entire week, with incandescent electric arc lamps burning forth a canopy of bright light weird and wonderful. (City Council debated whether it should leave the Hotel Vancouver block in total darkness, since the penurious CPR refused to contribute a red cent to the lighting, but the aldermen relented for the sake of decorum and respect for hotel guests.)

The British Marines bought up all the tobacco in town; their colourful uniforms were seen everywhere swaggering and strutting about the streets on the prowl for local women. Sports events were highlighted by Angus McLeod, famous Scottish cyclist, who showed up the local boys as he flew around Stanley Park in his colourful red and white uniform, a small silk Union Jack tied about his waist. And at Hastings Driving Park, the horse races were most exciting, marred only by the fining and suspension of Tip O'Neill, a popular jockey, for deliberately throwing a race with his pony Bessie Trimble.

Amidst this revelry, I sought to bring Vancouver's social conditions into perspective. "In our social columns today," I wrote, "we give some idea of the joyousness of the week and we… pay a cordial tribute to the naval men who entered so heartily into the events. The warships left the harbour this morning and the Inlet seems to have grown larger, so conspicuous are the gaps the *Warspite* and its consorts left behind. But while the wives of our prominent men have been vying with each other in displaying new gowns, the CPR strikers are still fighting for a living wage and the fishermen have not come to terms with the canners…" Needless to say, I was fast becoming persona non grata at Lady Tupper's receptions!

I cannot blame Lady Tupper and her friends for trying to emphasize culture and to smooth the raw diamond which was Vancouver. How it rankled to hear eastern Canadians jest about our opium dens and bawdy houses. So the Opera House continued to shake with packed performances every night. Sir Henry Irving and Ellen Terry were now the latest rage. And higher society men and women gave game and champagne parties at the Dutch Grill, while others organized grand balls, receptions and endless at-homes. Fred and I even tried dancing the Kangaroo Droop and Alexandrian Limp. Reading clubs flourished—we read Dickens, Twain and Kipling. How we all loved Kipling—Tory and Grit alike; we were surely more patriotic about the Empire than the British themselves.

I was elected the first female President of the Arts and Historical Association, now the prime cultural body of the city. We all tried to appreciate the new art forms suddenly in vogue, but few of us succeeded. Tom

The view south on Granville from Hastings Street, c. 1908. (VPL)

Thomson and the later-to-be-famous Group of Seven painters were just not our club's cup of tea. Even Emily Carr was shunned—being, after all, a woman and from Victoria.

Vancouverites much preferred the bold strokes, dash and realism of John Innes and our very own John Radford. Radford had settled in the city during the nineties and was rapidly becoming an icon among art lovers. He was bearded, with blazing blue eyes that sparkled as he spoke of his life passion. All summer and fall, Radford trudged about the province painting landscapes, and each spring he held an exhibition of his works downtown. He detested modern art from eastern Canada, and he characterized Tom Thomson and his friends as men who painted "mountains that resembled ice-cream cones."

Radford's invective was matched in intensity by his great painter friend, John Innes—the most famous western Canadian artist of the early century. Tall, distinguished and handsome, Innes had a leonine head, a well-trimmed beard and a strong resemblance to Kaiser Wilhelm. He hailed from Ontario, but painted western scenes and drew illustrations which attracted international recognition. He had arrived in Vancouver by horse from Calgary in 1899, dismounting down on Hastings Street. What a stir he caused, with his saddlebags full of canvasses! He left town after a short stay to serve in that cursed Boer War, but returned eventually to make Vancouver his home. For many years, no West End home was without an Innes work proudly displayed.

My personal affairs were in such a bustle, what with the *World*, social events, charity drives and the like, that I simply had no time to feel lonely. I shudder to write this, for poor John's sake. But there simply wasn't time. Then there were the girls to fuss over, though I must confess Louie ran a tight ship at home and never let them mess the house or remain idle. What a nanny! I would never have traded Louie—but surely there weren't many like him. The time I did have at home was spent in leisure moments, playing duets on the piano with Hazel, singing "Pop Goes the Weasel" and "The Last Rose of Summer" with little Margitte; turning on the Victrola and lounging about on the antimacassar after a hard day at the office. And we still went as a family to hear Reverend McLaren give his thundering oration at St. Andrew's most Sunday mornings.

As for Douglas, he was now out on the farm at Hazelbrae, permanently. For some time I had struggled to keep the precocious boy in the city. But his restless nature told me enough. He still loved the farm. After John died, we had a little talk about his future, and it was decided that he would go to an agricultural college after high school. In the meantime, he could attend the Mission school and live with my parents at Hazelbrae. Oh, I dearly missed the boy, despite his stubborn ways. Julia Henshaw assured me that it was the right thing to do; he needed to spread his wings towards a future. Well, since starting school in Mission, his marks had improved— and what was more important, my father said with a twinkle in his eye, so had his marksmanship.

So caring for the children on my own, thanks to Louie and my parents, became rather easy. Nor did I lack friends. Aside from family, where men abounded, my women companions were all from the clubs—all, that is, except for Julia Henshaw. Julia was charming, egocentric, iconoclastic, intellectual, Tory; one of the few great women I have truly known. And as much as we still sparred over social issues—even in print—she began to nurture my respect and close friendship. Her range of interests was

John Radford, a Vancouver artist who in the 1900s became very popular for his natural BC land-scapes. He later ridiculed Tom Thomson and the Group of Seven artists as being men from the east who painted "mountains that resembled ice-cream cones." (VPL 21053)

Julia Henshaw. The fiercely independent Vancouver author traded barbs with Sara McLagan in newspaper wars, but eventually the two women became best friends. They served together in Red Cross relief work in war-ravaged France. (CVA Port P1073 N943)

Francis Carter-Cotton. The Tory MLA was publisher of the News-Advertiser, *chief rival of the* World *for many years. (CVA Port P1125 N548)*

Lady Charles H. Tupper, regarded by many as the First Lady of Vancouver at century's turn. Little of social importance in the city escaped Lady Tupper's hand. Invitees to her receptions knew that they had truly "arrived" on the social scene. (CVA Port P1080 N641)

astounding: botany, mountain climbing, novel writing—she did it all. I began attending her pinochle parties. Then we exchanged at-homes, laughing over our tea at how we had traded barbs over the years about fashion and snobbery.

Like Kit Coleman, Julia was very much for women's rights, but she well understood the limits of male sensitivity, beyond which women risked losing their hard-fought gains. Hence Julia frowned upon the Pankhurst and WCTU-style suffragettes. So I was startled when in midsummer Julia published her latest novel, a romantic piece entitled *Why Not, Sweetheart?* The plot was centred partly in Vancouver, and despite its bland title, the book caused quite a stir about town.

Julia's novel satirized the English snob who views all Canadians as mere colonials. But she went further and delved into the relationship between the sexes: "They were sitting at breakfast at the Hotel Vancouver and had more than once looked across at each other during the meal—he eyeing her with the semi-interested, but wholly critical glance so characteristic of the British tourist; she subjecting him to that shrewd scrutiny with which Western girls invariably 'size up' strangers."

The colonial lady in the novel whose fair hand is at stake is one Agnes Arbuckle, who surprises her English suitor with her "new woman" independence of thought. When an elderly English squire—with whom I had always associated Julia and her conservatism—questions whether Agnes is thinking too much about political matters, Agnes responds vehemently: "Indeed. There is a terrible lot of harm done in this world by people who do not think. A door is always open or shut. Either we bachelor girls must try to think and act understandingly and for ourselves, or else we must be content to settle down to a tabby-cat and weak-tea existence for the rest of our lives." The old squire jerks up in his chair at this retort and states: "But as long as your sex is beautiful, and men are men, love and devotion will always be a woman's heritage." Agnes responds: "That is one of your chivalrous speeches which remind me of lavender and knee-buckles. But alas, the end of the 19th century wears golf stockings, and the smell of sweet herbs is not upon it… In the old days, you were masters of the situation, but now the chestnut tree is waving over the grave of that very meek and impossible 'she.'"

"My God, Julia," I sputtered over tea one day. "Your novel is the talk of the town. Whatever happened to the Tory in you—next you'll be joining up with the Pankhurst crowd!" "Well I might, Sara," Julia laughed, her eyes twinkling, "well I might. But for now, I'll stick to confining my 'new woman' outbursts to my novels, much as you only turn vitriolic in your *World* editorials."

"Touché, Julia," I retorted. "But I am not at all sure that this inflammatory language about woman's independence promotes harmony between the sexes in the manner you have always sought. For instance, when your heroine is finally won over by her beau, Joseph Kingsearl, you make Agnes sound positively anarchistic—here, I'll read the passage: 'When Joseph… won her whole love, and because he could not bend her will, the girl, with all her sweet graciousness and belief in the graciousness of men, died; and in her place there arose a woman strong in the consciousness of her own powers, and constantly on the defensive to do battle for her own sex. Thus it came that she rode roughshod over anything masculine, and never wearied of trying to make other girls hold their heads up.'"

Julia would not confirm it, but I was certain that the Agnes Arbuckle of her novel had been inspired by the outspoken teacher-principal from Victoria, Agnes Deans Cameron. When Victoria school trustees proposed in the spring to raise the salaries of male teachers only, Agnes organized the women teachers and confronted the trustees, attacking the Board decision as retrogressive and demoralizing.

Agnes Cameron was a wonderful rhetorician. "Women teachers are of one mind," she thundered, "that it is a vicious principle to establish any such basis of payment or salary as that of sex." Then she turned her guns on a popular British education journal which discriminated on the basis of age, specifying in its job placement ads that "no one over forty need apply." "What do they do with their schoolmistresses," wrote the thirty-eight-year-old Cameron, "when that fatal milestone is passed? Kill them off? One wonders."

This was all too much for the Victoria school trustees. In June they suspended Agnes for allegedly disobeying a rule whereby written promotion examinations were to be replaced by oral tests. The motion of suspension was made by one Mr. Belyea, who was outspoken in his opposition to women principals. Public pressure helped reinstate Agnes this time, but shortly thereafter she was formally suspended again, for allowing students to use rulers in drawing class. The outcry against what became permanent dismissal was so great that a Royal Commission was struck, which held hearings and supported the dismissal after exhaustively examining students' drawing books. Agnes fought back by running for school trustee and topping the polls. Although her teaching career was over, she went on to become one of Canada's foremost journalists. Her grossly unfair treatment at the hands of a male-dominated educational structure inspired many moderate feminists to become more radical—certainly more active.

Agnes Cameron and I got to know one another better in later years, after the 1904 formation of the Canadian Women's Press Club, of which I was a founding member. Agnes was indomitable. She travelled everywhere, writing articles for many newspapers and journals, including the *London Daily Mail*, and she wrote a book of her harrowing adventures journeying to the Arctic Circle, entitled *The New North*. She shocked contemporary society with her approval of polygamy as practised by the Eskimoes—provided, she said, that it was based upon practical necessity. "There are," she wrote, "no seductive 'Want Columns' in the daily press of the Eskimo to offer a niche whereby unappropriated spinsters may become self-supporting wage-earners as chaste type-writers, school teachers, or manicurists." Indeed, without a male hunter for a husband, a single female Eskimo might well starve to death.

Prostitution, not polygamy, was a heady issue in turn-of-the-century Vancouver. Many citizens were not prepared to accept the unofficial tolerance of the Red Light District that flourished on Dupont Street, where hundreds of prostitutes plied their trade. A young woman who earned between $3 and $7 per week as a department store clerk could make $50 to $200 per week serving the needs of the many single men of the city, not to mention the hordes of itinerant miners passing through. Unattractive, less sought-after women often supplemented their nightly revenue by doing laundry work by day.

Parents whose children attended the Strathcona and Central schools were especially incensed that the police failed to shut down the brothels. But as long as the women confined their trade to Dupont Street and Chinatown, they were left largely undisturbed. Later, when several whores

Cyclists from the Terminal City Cycling Club take a rest south of Prospect Point, c. 1892. The Park Road in Stanley Park, paved with white shells from Indian middens, was ideal for riding. Other roads were rough, potholed and uneven except for the cinder bicycle paths installed along certain city streets. In group rides like this one, buglers maintained order. (CVA Sp P18 N33)

moved to Park Lane in the Mount Pleasant district, the East End Improvement & Protection Association warned, "The public nature of the area would make the existence of the restricted district therein intolerable." The police responded with a few notable arrests, which stemmed the outward tide.

On some weekend evenings, as many as fifty men might be seen congregating outside a large brothel, necessitating a call about town for more women to be fetched for duty. On a tour of Shanghai Alley one night, *World* reporters noted that there were so many patrons waiting for service that the women did the choosing as to which men should be allowed inside. Our correspondent reported: "As quickly as visitors to the place left, the occupants of the room attired in the briefest of skirts, with the decolleté apparel to the limit, took their choice from the waiting crowd milling about the door."

It was my strong view that we would only solve the rampant prostitution epidemic in our city if we improved opportunities for young women.

As for the men, the lower classes had nowhere to go but gambling dens, whorehouses and bars. Not that all the bars were seedy. It was natural for a young worker to frequent a bar where he could purchase a schooner or beer for 5 cents or two glasses of whiskey for a quarter. And many of our bartenders were conscientious professionals, dressed in vest and tie.

But there were plenty more mangy, poky bars about the city. It was alarming to see crowds of young men roaming aimlessly about the streets at night. I editorialized: "It was painfully evident that Vancouver has not risen to the opportunities for making glad the evening hours. On Dominion Day night, there was nothing for people to do save to listen to the plashing of the waves at the Bay or the sighing of trees in the Park, or the stamping of the foot on the sidewalks of Hastings and Cordova Streets. A little joviality before retirement conduces to good sleep, and if the municipality provided the amusement, it could be made clean, wholesome and yet delightful. And there might be money in it for the City."

Of even greater concern in my mind was the need to create better working opportunities for young women migrating to the city by providing a sheltered atmosphere of support. To this end, I organized a petition by the Council of Women asking the CPR to donate two city lots as a site for a home for women who arrive in town "seeking situations." Again the CPR declined, and the project languished. What doubly disturbed me was the lack of support from wealthy West Enders who deplored the brothels, but did not want to dirty their hands with a solution that involved any cost to them. Maria Grant and the WCTU supported me, but lacked funds and membership interest. Too many of their members were obsessed with issues like chocolate liqueur bars being sold at confectioneries. Moreover, most WCTU members went berserk every time a woman's flesh was even slightly bared in public. Take, for instance, the Great English Bay Scandal.

Originally, a big boulder resting at the foot of Denman Street marked the division between the men's and women's bathing areas on the Bay. Men bathed to the east, women to the west. Over time, women invaded the men's beach. That was fine for the prudes, so long as women wore those old-fashioned suits with flounces about the waist with stockings and sandals. But one day a daring hussy was caught actually bathing without her stockings—sheer naked from the knees down!

Well, the WCTU published the hussy's name and the woman successfully sued the WCTU for libel. Immediately afterwards, an Englishwoman was accused by police of using the men's bathing house at English Bay, and she responded: "Oh well, no harm done; and besides, they do those sorts of things out here in the West."

While such incidents set West End matrons abuzz, society people remained aloof from the goings-on east of Granville Street. Not that activities were always so chaste in our quarter. One Sunday morning, Reverend McLaren lashed out at the pink tea parties which, he stormed, were becoming all the rage with the wealthy. (It seems that gin cocktails had replaced high tea at some West End residences.) His sermon was a preface to the war he was about to wage against music halls coming to town.

City Council submitted the matter of licensing music halls—which were popular in the United States and catered to beer drinking and raunchy vaudeville stuff—to a general plebescite. Our fiery-eyed minister thundered rhetoric about moral depravity, arguing that miners and loggers didn't need such temptations. He noted that women would be banned from the establishments. "Let us have the same moral standards for young men as for young women," he boomed before Council. "What kind of a performance do you expect when there are no ladies in the audience to restrain by their native modesty the low actors upon the stage?" McLaren then cited the experience of Seattle, where music halls had turned into nothing more than booze palaces. The plebescite resulted in the defeat of the music hall bid by a wide margin.

At this time, Bernard McEvoy told Canadians in a letter to the *Mail and Empire* that British Columbians were unstable: "There has been a flock of the immoral people who want to be rich in ten minutes without working, and the sad infection of the epidemic that these people suffer from is visible everywhere. Many British Columbians appear to me to live too much on tiptoe. They are expecting to make a lucky strike somehow. They find it difficult to settle down into that calm industrial activity by which alone a great province can be built up."

McEvoy's missive enraged Vancouver society. We had turned down the music halls at least in part because we wanted to show easterners that we really were moral, cultured folk. But it appeared that there was nothing we could do that would convince Toronto of how sophisticated we had become. Well, we reasoned, Vancouverites may as well settle back and do what we do best—enjoy ourselves. So we planned for a gala Street Fair in August. Meanwhile, City Council authorized a monster Gun Club crow shoot in Stanley Park. The hunt was designed to help rid the city of those vile feathered predators that attack songbirds and recently had even killed some young black swans.

What annoyed everyone most of all, as the prime summer bathing season approached, was the hundreds of dead salmon washing ashore on city beaches. You see, there was a huge run of fish on the Fraser River that year and the canneries were handling all they could, so fishermen often just dumped their glut of fish overboard. For weeks, the stench at English Bay was intolerable for bathers. In fact, it was so bad that the notorious Peeping Tom of Stanley Park—noted for his daily spying on ladies bathing at Second Beach—simply folded up his tent and fled the city. And believe me, it wasn't often that perverts left Vancouver!

CHAPTER SEVEN

Royalty and Revelry

It was impossible to slake the thirst of Vancouverites for celebration and fun in 1901. Victoria Day, Dominion Day, the Street Fair in early August, royal visits—we could not be satiated. Although many of these celebrations were rooted in our sentimental attachment to Empire, we were also becoming entranced by the American fads and fashions sweeping the continent. Our socially conscious citizens believed that Vancouver should emulate the St. Louis Carnival or the Mardi Gras of New Orleans. As a Street Fair organizer explained in the *World*:"The typical county fair of the East is rapidly becoming obsolete and the street fair is supplanting it. The fair is always held upon some prominent thoroughfare near the heart of the city... It is the agricultural fair transported and brought to town. Each day should be a special day and every night should have its special feature. On the afternoon of the second day all school children are admitted free. On women's day the popular fancy suggests a floral parade and baby show. Then comes a day for fraternal societies, labor unions, etc..."

City Council roped off the entire area between Pender and Hastings Streets and between Howe and Burrard. Circus acts, European villages, and exotic Oriental dancing girls entertained visitors all week long. Several indignant church women marched angrily out of the German village tent when cries of"more beer, more beer!" rang out drunkenly. Jugglers, comedians and Scottish pipers performed to the delight of thousands. An Arab sheikh, Hadji Sharif, showed his world-renowned gun-spinning and shooting prowess. And for 60 cents you could watch the high dive by Professor Rose from a height of sixty-five feet into a five-foot-deep tank of water.

Close on the heels of the Street Fair came the biggest event of the year, the Royal Visit to Vancouver of the Duke and Duchess of York (and later King George V and Queen Mary). Louis Taylor chaired the citizens' committee; Mayor Townley and his council rushed about to raise funds for monster displays of affection for the future monarch, even ordering forty thousand Chinese lanterns from Hong Kong for harbour lighting. My Council of Women arranged to present the royal couple with a photographic history of the city. But bickering and wrangling soon broke out among everyone as to who would have access to the royal presence.

Mayor Townley in his wisdom had decided behind council's back that he alone would represent the City and, together with a select elite, would entertain the Duke and Duchess at the luncheon scheduled for the ceremonial opening of the new Drill Hall. The aldermen would be left to cool their heels with lesser members of the Royal Party. Well, the aldermen went berserk. "I am indignant beyond measure," cried Alderman Foreman, "and I characterize the action of the reception committee as arrogant, impertinent, and insulting."

Townley was a pompous Tory who, as a full British colonel, had established Vancouver's first official militia battalion. We ran the full story of Council's rage against him under the liner "Above The Salt." Feeling the heat, Townley finally relented and reluctantly agreed to permit the aldermen to dine with the royal visitors.

The royal party arrived at the CPR station on October 1st. Taylor had arranged for a huge Welcome arch, shaped like a turretted castle, to be erected over the platform. After alighting, the Duke and Duchess rode in their own carriage to the courthouse, cheered on by thousands of ecstatic Vancouverites lining the streets. The Chinese and Japanese communities built their own street arches which at night came to life as masses of green jade with diamonds, reminding one of tea gardens and graceful dances. Thousands of flags hung from shop windows, and bunting streamed from every telephone pole. All was splendour and gaiety as the Duke, in his dazzling blue naval uniform, stepped out of the coach escorting the Duchess. The Duke scored well with the throngs crowded about, frequently touching his hat and bowing to the men and boys, who doffed their caps, and to the women, who waved flags and handkerchiefs.

The royal couple toured the Hastings Mill, which was processing logs for shipment to the Orient. At the Drill Hall prior to the luncheon, Duchess Mary broke down and cried when she spotted pictures of her two sons on her dressing table, placed carefully in frames by Mrs. Dana of the Reception Committee. The Duchess sobbed to Mayor Townley, "Everywhere I have gone, I have been handed bouquets, and now I am here, and at home. Oh, how I do long to see my boys." At that moment the Duke entered the room and embraced her.

Later that afternoon, the royal couple travelled in their carriage around Stanley Park to view the big trees. Townley triumphed here: by persuading the Duke and Duchess that only a local dignitary would be able to enlighten them as to the botany and big cedars, he broke precedent and became the first commoner ever to ride in the royal carriage. (Louis Taylor learned from Townley's technique. A few years later, when Taylor was mayor, President Theodore Roosevelt and his wife arrived in town for a brief visit. Taylor "kidnapped" the Roosevelts from the CPR station, right under the noses of the civic reception committee, bundled the couple off the platform into a waiting limousine, and climbed into the back seat. Louis then ordered the driver to take the Stanley Park tour, where he picnicked quietly with the pair. A few hours later he returned to dockside, just in time to pack the Roosevelts off on the boat to Victoria. Meanwhile, bewildered Council members clad in their fancy striped pants and top hats morosely ate their official lunch at the Drill Hall and dispersed.)

Even the outwardly joyous signs of celebration could not hide the black clouds swirling about us in 1901. Just before departing for Victoria, the Duke and Duchess heard, with all of us, the terrible news of an explosion at Premier Dunsmuir's Nanaimo coal mine which had killed some seventeen men. During the entire provincial tour, violets were carefully placed on the tables at all royal functions in memory of Queen Victoria. Many citizens still sported black armbands. The Boer War dragged on and everyone whispered about the besmirching of Britain's honour, as horror stories of

Sara McLagan in a garden corner.

Louis Taylor. He purchased The Daily World *in 1905, and later served as Mayor of Vancouver for some eleven years. "L.D.," as he was known to friends, was fond of cigars and red ties. (CVA Port P149 N854)*

the concentration camps in South Africa were published. And the *Islander* disaster still lay heavy on the city.

On August 15th, the CP flagship *Islander* struck an iceberg just out of Skagway and sank, killing more than sixty-five passengers and crew. Many women and children drowned after stopping to dress. (The yellow rag *Province* sensationalized the incident by claiming that they had been pushed aside by men scrambling for the lifeboats.) Still, evacuation of the stricken vessel proceeded smoothly. Captain Foote dutifully went down with his ship, which was *de rigueur*, and one Vancouver survivor told of finding a baby next morning strapped in a blanket, floating in the water on a life preserver, alive and well. Yet Vancouverites were shocked that their well-known and beloved *Islander* could have sunk in fifteen minutes. She was supposed to be unsinkable. Ah, well; so life was indeed still hazardous, despite all the modern inventions. And imagine that saucy Professor Odlum predicting that we would one day see flying ships above English Bay!

The gloom deepened when, on September 13th, President McKinley died from an assassin's bullet, after lingering in pain. The memorial service held at the Vancouver Opera House on September 20th rivalled in size the memorial for our late queen. It seemed like my entire life this year was spent attending either funeral services or gaudy festivals and fêtes.

President McKinley's demise was made especially poignant by the fact of his progressiveness. If the late queen's passing signified the end of Victorian ideals, prudery and stability, McKinley's life had symbolized the brave new world of democracy, gadgetry and the hopes and dreams of the masses. And how atrocious that the vile act of murder was perpetrated at Buffalo—scene of the exposition that shone as a beacon toward the modern way, where Edison's new storage battery promised electricity for every house and every city street. Here, for the first time in history, electrical display lighting had been used, stunning visitors with the 405-foot Electric Tower that dazzled the night sky with 3,500 light bulbs. We stood agog at the Buffalo display of countless other inventions in medicine, engineering and transportation. Motor cars and aeroplanes were said to be on their way. Greater freedom was foretold by an exposition chariot which raced about the fair carrying several women dressed in garb which represented humanity's ideals.

As a raw port city inundated with riffraff, Vancouver continued to seethe with labour unrest, racial tension and class division. Yet an amazing civility prevailed as well. Violence was confined largely to the hardened criminal element and although no society lady from the West End would be caught walking east of Carrall Street, we began to pride ourselves as a city on our Chinatown and even the Japanese community, particularly after the incredible displays of loyalty demonstrated by the Orientals during the Royal Visit.

Tourists meanwhile were enjoying the city's exotic eastern ambience, while avoiding the Dupont Street sin houses at night. Carter-Cotton admired the patience, discipline and hospitality of the Chinese: "The Chinaman is an artist at enjoying himself. He does not plunge into orgies. His New Year's celebrations, like the Indian Passion Play staged at Chilliwack this year, attracted thousands of onlookers. The fireworks were splendid, even though European white sensibilities were a little jarred by the discordant tones of a tom-tom, gong, and cymbals resembling a pair of huge tin trays."

In September of 1901, Won Cumyow resumed his battle against prejudice by applying for his name to be placed on the provincial voters' list. The local bureaucrat in charge tersely rejected the application, whereupon Cumyow appealed to the Collector of Votes in Victoria: "In September I made application to you to have my name put on the List of Voters for the Vancouver Electoral District. Since that date I have repeatedly looked over the list, but my name does not appear. Kindly let me know at your earliest convenience why my name has not been placed on the list and oblige." Cumyow lost his appeal, but continued to lobby for political equality.

The Chinese in fact were becoming more self-confident in their struggle to attain respectability amidst white society. White residents were surprised at how the Chinese fought back against racism. In August, Wing Thong and Jim Crosby drove up with their horses and rigs to the public drinking fountain on Westminster Avenue at the same time. Thong's horse proceeded to bite one of Crosby's team, and in the ensuing fracas Thong and Crosby pelted each other with punches. Thong sustained a black eye and bloody nose, while Crosby suffered a badly chewed thumb and arm. Charges and countercharges were laid, but at Police Court both men appeared, laughed, and told the judge that they had made up their differences. The charges were withdrawn.

Haughty West End bigots were also finding that the Chinese could use the courts to defend their rights as readily as Europeans. One Mrs. Keefer hastily accused San Sue and San Chat of stealing her purse: the bag had gone missing after the two Chinese men had called on the home to pick up laundry. They were immediately arrested, only to be released a few hours later when Mrs. Keefer found her purse in the same room in which the theft was alleged to have occurred. The Chinese men sued for $10,000 in damages for false imprisonment, and although the suit was not successful, this and the Thong/Crosby affair suitably impressed Vancouverites that Orientals would stand up for their rights at every turn.

As if our bobbies didn't have enough to do with breaking up drunken brawls, chasing thieves and fighting the opium trade, the police, aided by the city health inspector and by-law enforcement officer, found crime in every city street. Health Inspector Joseph Huntly religiously persecuted homeowners for keeping trash in their yards, failing to hook up to the sewers, and keeping more than one cow in their backyards. He even charged a young woman for trying to sell him a Bible without a licence. The woman had to post $100 bail to get out of jail and only got free of Huntly's clutches after obtaining a letter from her Ontario employer confirming her sales position. (Huntly later decamped from the city in the night, and it turned out that the Skagit County sheriff had been chasing him for some time for fraud and failure to pay wife support in Washington.)

Not a week passed without a man being charged with using insulting language to a lady. Many parents were charged and convicted under a new law that required them to send their children to school. Cyclists too were prosecuted if they dared to deviate from the myriad riding rules: "In Police Court yesterday, a young man was fined $5 for coasting with his feet on the pedals. He advanced the plea that he was going but very slowly, but the magistrate decided that this was a case in which speed did not cut any figure." And God help you if you were caught riding a bicycle on the sidewalk. One must stick to the roads or designated cycle paths, though boorish teamster drivers frequently drove their rigs onto the cinder tracks with malice in their hearts.

Arrival of the Duke and Duchess of York at the CPR Depot, September 30, 1901. The Royal Visit of the future King George V and Queen Mary sent Vancouverites into ecstatic convulsions. Some 40,000 Chinese lanterns were purchased from Hong Kong to light the harbour for the royal couple, and the city was draped in bunting. (CVA Port P17 N212)

The servant girl problem in the West End often led to the courts as well. One society lady went through thirty-five girls in one month, deeming them all to be either incompetent or thieves; she pursued various charges of theft unsuccessfully. In Police Court, one Miss Agar pursued a charge of insulting language against an elderly man named Carson. It seems that Carson had brought the young woman from England with his son and used her for purposes other than domestic work. When his son won the lady's affections and Carson was no longer welcome in her bedroom, the father grew violent with jealousy. Magistrate Russell admonished the elderly man for parading this dirty laundry in public and said that he doubted that Miss Agar had "debauched his son" as alleged—since, said the magistrate, any debauchery had already been accomplished by Carson himself.

These morality cases were all very amusing, though I am sure that Reverend McLaren and his brothers in the ministry fretted about it. Most residents were more concerned by the robberies, murders and purse-

Shooting gallery on Cordova Street. (CVA SP P74 N78)

snatchings that were becoming daily events in our town. Now, I know that every generation thinks that crime is always on the rise, but the Vancouver of 1901 saw the most incredible outbreak of burglaries and purse-snatchings. No one was safe. People in the West End closed tight their windows at night to stop cat burglaries. Many of the criminals were transients passing through from 'Frisco or the Klondike, like the infamous Stella Nelson, known along the Pacific Coast as Queen of the Pickpockets. When she stopped in town in October, Stella was "clothed in sealskins and silk and adorned with numerous nuggets." She was interviewed by the *World*, and she stated, "I've had a lovely time—four months in Nome, Alaska—arrested four times a week, but they couldn't prove a thing." Stella passed on to Seattle, but not before she had thoroughly charmed our own Chief of Police.

We were in fact a highly litigious province. The Vancouver courthouse was built in 1890 on the Pender Street side of what is now called Victory Square. An addition fronting on Hastings Street came into use in

1894, much more elaborate with classic columns and domed by a statue of the Greek goddess of justice. But the two courtrooms were simply inadequate for the torrent of litigation. I suppose it was better than the American West, where disputes tended to be settled in the streets with six-guns; but my God we were quick to drop writs on someone for any affront.

Lawyers abounded in the city. The two best-known barristers were Sir Charles H. Tupper and Joe Martin, who regularly staged slugfests before Judge Bole, the police magistrate. Tupper was arrogant, brilliant, eloquent beyond measure; whereas Martin was, well, Martinesque—bombastic, accusatory, fiery, always capable of infuriating the judge. One day, Martin appeared for several defendants charged with theft. In arguing that the summonses to the accused were improperly completed, he stated that his clients in the dock should be forthwith released from custody. Judge Bole curtly denied Martin's plea. Without hesitation, Martin packed up his briefcase, advised the judge he was wrong, and escorted his astonished clients out of the courtroom. Tupper, who was waiting for his own case to be called, stood agape while the judge turned beet red with fury. Then the judge summoned the sheriffs to pursue and re-arrest the prisoners, who were found skipping along Hastings Steet. Judge Bole growled to Tupper, "I ought to arrest Martin too."

On another occasion, Martin was accused of removing evidence from the courtroom—a little black account book belonging to his client, Desiré Brothier, a brothel madam. When the prosecutor angrily confronted Martin with an allegation that he had tampered with evidence, Joe quietly suggested that the lawyers all retire to the judge's private chambers, where it took under two minutes to convince the judge that the missing book's contents were best kept secret. The brothel madam went free.

In these days just prior to the motor car's debut, transport fascinated everyone—the new CPR engines drew crowds daily and the smart new Park & English Bay tram cars carried up to 4,000 people on Sundays. Even the chain gang rode in class now, with the appearance of John Grady's Blue Bird coach. Every day Officer Grady transported twenty prisoners to their place of work in a long wagon decoratively painted an imperial blue with shafts and gear a glowing carmine colour. The coach was drawn by Pete, a veteran fire engine horse, dressed in a new leather harness.

Mayor Thomas Townley. After trying to exclude other City Council members from dining with the Duke and Duchess of York during the 1901 Royal Tour, Townley managed to break protocol and ride with the couple in the royal carriage around Stanley Park. He may have been the first commoner ever to have done so—on the pretext that only he could enlighten the royal guests as to the botany and big trees of Stanley Park. (VPL 3482)

Downtown eastside streets were always full of activity. The dust often swept in clouds up Cordova, and windows there frequently had to be closed all day. When some merchants sprayed water in front of their shops to counter the dust, pools would form, causing pedestrians to complain. Walkers would encounter a merchant extolling the latest shaving soap, and a variety of street vendors. On every corner, someone tried to sell you something; books were especially popular in the new age. And everywhere, political radicals and evangelists stood on their soapbox.

I recall one Sunday anarchist orator at Carrall and Hastings who attacked the *World* for confusing anarchists with socialists—a charge I viewed as unfair, since we had taken pains to point out that socialists held themselves aloof from violence and based their tactics on moral suasion. Well, this was shortly after McKinley's assassination, and when this orator began shouting that the late president was no martyr, it proved too much for two Americans standing in the crowd. The Yankees marched forth and physically removed the spouter from his box, then gave speeches themselves against anarchism, to the cheers of the throngs who prevented the anarchist from responding.

One of the keys to becoming more civilized in the modern age, we believed, was paying more attention to cleanliness. Dirt and filth led directly to disease, and so when it was rumoured that some Chinese laundrymen spit upon their customers' clothes to dampen them when ironing, we had a collective fit. The health inspector served thirty summonses one month upon Chinese launderers for violating the spitting by-law. The whole issue became so inflamed that the Toronto writer and inventor Bernard McEvoy was summoned by our Health Board to introduce his new patented apparatus for disinfecting clothing and bedding.

The Health Board was also overwhelmed by the sufferings of destitute families, many of which sustained serious illness. Numerous penniless people lived on False Creek, including one Mrs. Ray and her eight children. Mrs. Ray was found ill in bed, her children largely unclothed, in conditions of absolute squalor, and only a few turnips in the house for food. The health officers passed such cases on to organizations such as my Women's Council, the Victorian Order of Nurses, the YWCA, and the Salvation Army. We did what we could to feed and clothe these people, and several of us also organized a city branch of the Red Cross. But as I editorialized at Thanksgiving, "This city is full of striking examples of the fact that charity may begin at home, but that reform is generally practised on someone else."

The new women's writer for the *Province*, Mollie Glenn, became so disgusted with a prominent Vancouver businessman who deserted his wife and children that she publicly scolded the wretch: "A rumour is afloat that the family of a well-known man in town has been sadly neglected, in fact are in destitute circumstances, while the man in question has been entertaining at dinner and acting the part of genial host to all but his worthy family." We took up a collection for the family concerned.

It broke my heart to see the number of tramps who not only lived homeless in filth, but died without notice. I had my reporters hunt down these stories, like old George the hobo: "George Richardson, the one-legged tramp, was buried yesterday afternoon. There were no friends to follow his mortal remains to their last resting place, neither was there a minister to read a service. Truly George Richardson was a wanderer on the face of the earth." Then there was Richard Burke, the street corner evangelist who regaled passersby with pamphlets and cries of "Repent!" Burke now lay dying of stomach cancer in hospital, his family destitute.

Our institutional care for those in need remained pathetic. Deserted wives often resorted to prostitution to feed their children. Judges threw up their hands in dismay with young offenders, saying in open court: "What am I to do—I have no place to send them other than jail!" The government held to a policy of delay, linger and obfuscate regarding the building of a juvenile reformatory.

The Salvation Army meanwhile did its best to shelter people, but had a most unlucky autumn. First the wind blew down the brick chimney at the Stanley Park shelter, causing much damage. Then a black stallion in the shelter's stable chewed through its halter and attacked all the other horses. In the ensuing melee, several horses were injured and the stable was knocked apart. The Sally Ann Band paraded through downtown streets regularly, particularly in the Chinatown district, where it succeeded in waking up loggers, miners and other patrons of the brothels at an early hour. The popular Sally Ann picnics were held at Hallelujah Point, site of the nine o'clock gun, which has fired daily at nine p.m. since its arrival from

England in 1894. The gun was originally installed in order to flash signals to sailing vessels that allowed the captain to take a tide reading.

The Alexandra Orphanage in Fairview housed some fifty-four children. For Thanksgiving 1901, Mayor Townley and the sugar baron Rogers sent large turkeys and barrels of sugar and syrup. This orphanage was forever associated with my friend Sarah Bowes, its matron for many years. She also published a monthly pamphlet for the downtrodden called "Home Cheer." Although she was a Methodist and a fierce WCTU fighter, I admired her pluck and would sometimes visit her home on Hastings Street for tea. She worked hard for my Council in its successful lobbying for the Children's Aid legislation. Ever sporting a radiant smile, Sarah conducted many of the services at the old Homer Methodist Church, all without any male objections, and she regularly visited the Dupont (later Pender Street) red light district to counsel and console working girls there. She was, in my view, Vancouver's first and foremost social worker.

Our current city hospital was so overcrowded that patients were sometimes turned away. The owner of the Metropole Hotel complained to City Council that a seventeen-year-old boy had been confined to his establishment for appendicitis because there were no beds at the hospital. Council partially reimbursed him.

I met regularly with Lady Tupper and others to discuss fundraising ideas for the planned Fairview hospital. As the premier hostess of the city, Lady Tupper was very helpful—in fact, she was indispensable for the success of various social causes. (Though I daresay that in 1901 she was just as excited about the mansion known as Parkside that my brother Sam was designing for her on Barclay Street.) But much of the startup funding was raised by my Women's Auxiliary. I wrote in the *World*: "They stood resolutely on street corners, and even invaded Chinatown, where the response was generous. Greatly daring, the women gathered their sweeping skirts about them and stepped into the saloons, risking ribald remarks of drunken sailors. Their bravery was rewarded with quantities of dirty crumpled bills. The treasurer washed and ironed this precious currency and then hid it under the stair carpet of her home until it could be banked the following Monday."

The ambulance service was about as slow and inefficient as a donkey express, and for a time in 1901 the drivers wouldn't even take the rig out from the livery stable unless payment was assured in advance. Often the narrow wheels of the ambulance became mired in mud on side streets, and patients were known to have jumped down and helped the driver push the carriage out. But what a fancy carriage it was! Thanks to the efforts of Mrs. W. Griffin, the city acquired a glass-windowed coach painted green with gold stripes, equipped with a rubber mattress, three silver lanterns, a zinc-lined water tank and two prancing steeds. (Alas, ambulances got off to a bad start in Vancouver. A couple of years later, when the new motorized ambulance went for its trial run, it knocked down a pedestrian—an American visitor—in front of Fader's Grocery on Granville and killed him instantly. So the very first passenger to ride in the new ambulance was transported to the morgue.)

As for a sanitarium, the New Westminster Asylum took care of all of our mentally ill patients. Those cases not warranting confinement were treated by Vancouver doctors, who believed that rest in the country offered the best tonic. One day I published a note from the owner of the St. Alice Hotel in Harrison Hot Springs, who wrote that the hotel doctor was "willing to treat almost any form of disease, yet insanity is barred," and he would be pleased if "no more patients were sent by Vancouver doctors, principally for the benefit of guests who wish to sleep."

Most well-to-do families of our day owned their own domestic medicine chests, the contents of which were usually a potpourri of both good and dubious folk medicines, supplemented by a few reliable pharmaceutical drugs. (Don't forget that every newspaper ran ads claiming that Carter's Little Liver Pills cured all ailments.) These chests were usually made of cedar or mahogany; some held glass and scales, a small glass mortar and pestle. Common to every chest was opium or some derivative. My chest contained such potions as cascara, laudanum, quinine for fever, rhubarb (a purgative), aspirin for lumbago, neuralgia and rheumatism, and huge bottles of castor oil for use as a laxative. Having grown up on a farm, I had acquired much knowledge of pharmacology over the years, but remained wary of many quack remedies.

For children and babies, we kept a separate medicine cupboard. Here is my published advice to mothers of the day: "Keep witch hazel for lumps

Children's Aid Society foster home, early 1900s. Sara McLagan was one of many Vancouver residents who worked unceasingly for better facilities for orphans, the homeless, the ill and the aged. (CVA Bu P383 N330)

and bruises, wine of ipecac for croupy nights, and a bottle of lime water and oil for burns or scalds. For colds and hoarseness prepare a half-pound jar of lard and turpentine. Mix these in equal quantities and melt over hot water… a tablespoonful can be heated and rubbed on a child's back, chest, neck and soles of his feet. A box of mustard is useful for hurried plasters; a bottle of vinegar for bruises; a package of absorbent cotton, a roll of bandages; tincture of iodine for chilblains, ginger or peppermint water for colic; chlorate of potash for sore throats, oil of cloves for toothache… It is a good plan for a mother to ask the advice of her doctor for simple home remedies."

What with Kipling's *Jungle Book*, P. T. Barnum's circus, and Teddy Roosevelt's big game hunting, society this year became entranced by beasts and exotic pets. Joe Martin acquired a delightful grizzly bear cub in Barkerville and donated it to the city zoo, where the animal became a favourite. While performing a live act at the Savoy Theatre in November, one Madame Schell was mauled by a huge lion, to everyone's horror but obvious fascination. She survived. Then there were the cobras and rattlesnakes on display at the McDowell shop at Cambie and Cordova, writhing around in the store window and egged on inside by a stick wielded by Professor Eaton, who entertained a large crowd of people peering in from the street.

Less exotic, but important enough to merit *World* liners, were pet birds and mice, the birds alas too often escaping their owners:

> Art Saniger, the pigeon fancier, recently let loose two homing pigeons from Port Haney. They were too far away from home and got lost. Mr. Saniger would be glad to have them returned if found...
>
> Anyone who chances to find a gray parrot will be rewarded by returning the bird to 217 Howe Street...
>
> George Trorey, the jeweller, has recently imported a choice consignment of real German mice. It must not be inferred that the rodents from the Fatherland have been deliberately imported to enter into competition with native-born and truly British mice—on the contrary, they came by accident, as stowaways in a shipment of fancy shades which they depended upon for papery sustenance during their long voyage. The shades are evidence in that connection...

The rivalry among Victoria, New Westminster and Vancouver has always been keen. New Westminster resents having lost its status as capital to Victoria and its commercial hegemony to Vancouver; Victoria smugly ho-hums its genteel superiority to both mainland cities; Vancouverites believe that their city is far swankier than the stump city to the east and sleepy Tory Empress-ville to the southwest. Sports have brought out both the best and the worst in this rivalry, and the contests among city squads in 1901 were as supercharged as the politics. Vancouver's baseball grounds were officially opened in May on Powell Street, where the first season of the BC Amateur Ball League commenced. Thousands of fans attended the inaugural game with Victoria, and R. G. Macpherson, a Cordova druggist, presented a 5-dollar pair of military hairbrushes to batters hitting home runs.

But the real game of the day was lacrosse. From 1896 to 1904, the New Westminster Salmonbellies reigned as provincial champions. Vancouver's YMCA team frequently defeated the Victoria squad at the Brockton Point field, but usually fell to the Salmonbellies. On October 1st, the bloodiest, most disgraceful sports match in BC's history was played between the two teams at Queen's Park in New Westminster. Vancouver lost 7–1, but not before police were called to break up vicious fights on the field. W. Gifford smashed Archie MacNaughton over the head with his stick, perrmanently disfiguring him. Gifford himself suffered internal injuries from a stick, while numerous other players sustained broken ribs and cuts and had to be carried off the field to waiting ambulances. Hundreds of spectators left the grandstand, shaken by the blood and gore on the field. Eastern Canadian newspapers had a field day satirizing the "barbarous" Canadian West.

Aside from baseball and lacrosse, Vancouverites loved horse racing, boxing, cycling and boat races. To the horror of church ladies, wrestlers would climb into the ring now at the Opera House for Saturday bouts; and to their equal disgust, men and boys played billiards on Sundays at east side parlours. Seattle promoters even brought cockfights to town. When one incensed alderman discovered that cockfighting was taking place just two blocks from the police station, the police chief smiled at him reassuringly and advised, "We fined the owner of the cockfight premises $25." Such slaps on the wrist failed to halt the fights.

One didn't have to visit the Dupont Street gambling joints to take in other traditional games of chance. Slot machines abounded in the city's saloons and hotels from the early nineties, at first taking the form of mere vending machines where the odd extra cigar plopped down for a nickel. Then musical slot machines arrived, and over lunch many clerks, tradesmen and shop owners began visiting bars to have a beer and sandwich and drop a few nickels into the machines in the hope of reaping a dollar in coin. Even policemen got into the act, which ultimately helped justify City Council's decision to fire Chief Stewart, whose softness toward east-side gambling

Native war canoe and harbour ships preparing for the 1901 Royal Visit. (VPL 1853)

houses was well known. By the fall of 1901, every slot machine in the city had been ripped out by Council's order. (Ironically, Council remained tolerant only of Chinatown gambling.)

Respectable women of course never frequented the bars which housed the slot machines or the billiard parlours. We did try out the new game of ping-pong, which was all the rage. Then there appeared in town the progressive luncheons, where each lady rotated courses among, say, five hostesses and homes. But as the new century unfolded, the proper perameters of a "real lady's" actions were becoming somewhat blurred, what with our greater participation in social causes and politics, and the freedom of movement occasioned by the bicycle. I believed then and still believe that it was the woman's character beneath the veneer of social niceties and fashion that made a woman a lady—and I said so in my *World*: "The real lady settles her debts, does not forget her liabilities, would as soon commit murder as cheat, and actually considers an engagement a binding duty. She has a soft voice, pleasant manner, and confesses to being older than her children. She is the daughter of evolution, and the survival of the fittest. If she has nerves, she does not show them. She has the courage of her opinions and the moral courage to deny herself. In short, she possesses all the qualities that make a gentleman."

Julia Henshaw and I argued about the latest fashions and the tendency of many "modern" women to wear boisterous hats and outrageously decolleté dresses, and their proclivity for chain smoking in restaurants. Smoking was made fashionable by the example of Alice Roosevelt, the president's daughter, who epitomized the Gibson Girl image of chic self-confidence and beauty. Alice would party until dawn, was utterly unabashed, and was known to push senators into swimming pools for a laugh. America and the world loved her. Her father proclaimed, "I can do one of two things. I can be President of the United States, or I can control Alice. I cannot possibly do both."

I didn't mind a certain amount of spunk, but many women and men exhibited just plain bad taste. I lectured to Vancouver women in the *World* on what not to wear: cheap jewellery any time, white petticoats on muddy days, bright red with a florid complexion, a broad belt on a stout figure, conspicuous bicycle costumes, cheap trimmings on a good dress, cheap lace on anything, diamonds in daytime, theatre bonnets with street suits, dotted veils with weak eyes, pointed shoes when cycling, the new tight sleeve on a long thin arm, tan shoes in mid-winter, boots with buttons missing, soiled white gloves on shopping trips, gaudy colours in cheap materials, horizontal stripes on a stout figure and untidy frocks for breakfast. Finally, I counselled, stay away from the nest of bird feathers in your hats—it's gauche, and I agreed with the Audubon Society that fashion should not dictate the needless slaughter of egrets and other poor birds.

As with cycling, the activity of hiking brought new fashion injunctions to women. The Vancouver Mountaineering Club—which included Julia Henshaw and other women who insisted they could go wherever men went—organized numerous hikes up local mountains, including an annual scaling of the Lions. The men dressed in worn clothes, hob-nailed boots and puttees. Women had it rough: "The appearance of the lady climbers was even more hideous than most of the men. Forced by the laws of polite society to wear a skirt reaching to their heels and clothed above in some form of blouse with long sleeves and high neck, the picture was completed by a pair of heavy nailed boots peeping from below the skirt. Some form of hat was also necessary to cover the long hair. Of course, the skirts had to be discarded at the first opportunity, bringing into view a pair of bloomers which ballooned out at the waist and draped over the knees. A more unsuitable garment for brush could hardly be conceived. It simply invited every snag to grab it, with some disastrous results. On the return trip, the cached skirt was resumed for crossing the ferry… Woe betide the young lady who, through accident or failure to locate the cache, found herself skirtless. A rule of the ferry company forbade any lady to board the boat in bloomers and on one occasion an unfortunate bloomer girl had to send word across and have a relative come over with a skirt to enable her to get home."

My own coiffure suffered much in 1901, as I buried myself in the business and editorial affairs of the *World*. I was too exhausted to attend the theatre most nights and couldn't have cared less about what was fashionably in or out—the latest trend calling for a soft puff round the face, broken by a few little curls at one side and loose knots arranged to wind about the nape of the neck, one large rose to be worn to one side—pshaw! As if fresh roses are available year round in Vancouver!

My days were so frantic that I raced home from the office at noon on my receiving days—my official at-homes on Georgia Street were the first and third Wednesdays of the month—without time to even change my clothes. Thank God for perfume! And then I had to put up with the inane conversation of West End ladies of leisure who couldn't comprehend the complexities of running a newspaper business.

The current debate among the high tea set touched upon a few raw nerves of mine. What was acceptable for women in the workplace? Was daring Alice Roosevelt to be emulated? In April, the journal *Independent* posed the argument that "men wanted a girl who has not rubbed off the peach blossom of innocence by exposure to a rough world." Rubbish, I argued; women can hold their own and still be feminine working in that rough world. That doesn't mean that men will accept Carrie Nation smashing saloons, or the 160-pound schoolmarm Anna Taylor shooting Niagara Falls in a barrel.

The *World* was taking much heat lately over our reluctance to disclose the names of certain young criminal offenders and victims. You see, the press and publicity given in a 28,000-strong town could ruin a young adult's career and harm the family. Nichol's yellow rag certainly was not holding back—unless it happened to be politically astute for the owner. Hardly a day passed without family members approaching me or my editor to plead that their dear one's name not be published.

Take the young man who is caught stealing from his employer's till (this actually happened at the *World*). He is the son of a widow; his mother's happiness and his own future depend upon the editor, who must choose between protecting the errant boy and scoring a juicy news liner. Take also the woman caught shoplifting. She has heretofore been respectable. She has a family of grown children and a steady, hardworking husband. Besides, she took only a pound of tea or a stove lifter. A gambling house is raided and a number of fine young men are lined up next day at Police Court. They stand to lose their jobs if an employer reads of their escapades. A silly girl elopes with a married minister; the minister is hauled back by an angry father, chastised, and sent packing from the province. Why publish these youthful indiscretions and shame those who deserve a second chance? No, I thought, I will continue to shield those miserable social predators and demons for the sake of those young souls and their families who do not deserve to suffer more—even if that means the loss of subscriptions. If the public wants rank sensationalism, there are other papers in town.

CHAPTER EIGHT

A Brighter Dawn

Perhaps I should have stooped to rag journalism. The *Province* was pulling out in front of the *World* by an ever-increasing margin. Our circulation held steady, but Nichol's readership grew with the population. I huddled with Fred and took measure of our operations, even consulting with Professor Odlum for advice. I was not happy with my editorial chief, and Odlum suggested that his son Victor, recently returned from South Africa, might do the job. So I chatted heart to heart with Harold Sands and we agreed that Victor Odlum would take over his spot as chief editor in early 1902.

I had one other serious staffing problem at the *World*: Sam Robb. Yes, dear old Sam. He just couldn't stay sober these days. Time and again I had to send him home in a hansom when he showed up drunk at the office. I had heard stories of how he would go every evening to the Badminton Hotel with Dr. McGuigan for four or five nightcaps of whiskey. Finally I called him into the office and told him he was fired—but that he could come back to the paper once he proved that he could stay sober. Well, God knows he tried. But that rascal Dr. McGuigan knocked him back off the wagon.

One day after I fired Sam I learned that McGuigan had met him on the street and offered to buy him a drink. Sam replied, "No, sworn off; no more." "Well, then," smiled McGuigan, "at least have a drink of milk with me." Sam agreed, and the doctor escorted him into the nearest saloon and asked the bartender to pour Sam a glass of milk. McGuigan grasped the glass, sniffed it and said, "Sam, this stuff has got millions of microbes in it; you've got to kill the microbes before you drink it." Sam queried, "How?" McGuigan then motioned the bartender to pass a bottle of brandy, and he poured the liquor into the milk, stirred it well to kill the microbes, and handed it to Sam. Sam downed the glass in one long gulp. "How is it?" asked the doctor. "Good," grunted Sam. "Then," said McGuigan, "it must have killed those microbes all right."

At about this time, I tried to bolster readership by introducing new columns and formats, including "The Very Latest," flashes and tidbits of world news which ranged from the sublime to the ridiculous. Some samples:

It is officially denied that there is a case of plague at the West London Hospital...

Miss Vanderbilt-Wackerman has been arrested as a wandering lunatic in London; it is believed that with good care she may recover her reason...

Negotiations are in progress between Great Britain and Nicaragua, looking to the recognition of the sovereignty of Nicaragua over the Mosquito Coast...

Dr. James Braithwaite in the *Lancet* suggests that excessive use of salt in one's diet is a chief cause of cancer...

Nine street car conductors of Montreal have been arrested for playing a game of stud poker...

Danish chocolate exporters are seeking a weapon wherewith to retaliate against the USA for import tariffs...

The *London Times* denies that the Trans-Siberian Railway is anything like completed...

Another Chinese has been murdered as a result of the Wong Chin feud in San Francisco...

As autumn leaves fell about the city, residents retreated from their verandahs indoors for their evening parties and Sunday teas. Little did we know that the advent of the motor car on Vancouver streets was just

Sara McLagan and her daughters, c. 1901.

around the corner and would forever destroy the tranquil gentility of verandah parties. But would real streetlights ever illuminate all the roads? We
had a few arc lights here and there, but electric posts didn't arrive until
1906, and the arc lights kept dying in the wind. (These lights were only
slightly improved over the first bulbs erected on Hastings, Cordova and
Carrall streets—carbon lights of 16 candle power; the joke was that one
needed a candle to find the electric light, which light was a mere "red worm
in a glass bulb.") City Council in fact ordered the police to report any streetlights which blew out during the night so as to force the Electric Light
Company to rebate to the City 22 cents for every light down.

Between the unreliable streetlights and the hordes of dogs running
wild in the West End, my neighbours had plenty to complain about without even touching on the sensitive topic of whether the city should allow
Sunday band concerts at Stanley Park and English Bay. My own pet peeve
was people who failed to arrive at the Opera House on time—why, the first
number of Monsieur Nachez at the Albani Concert was simply ruined for
those of us in the orchestra stalls by the tardy arrival of several preening
bluebloods who obviously attend theatre chiefly to be seen and heard!

Trends in West Coast cuisine impressed me about as much as bird's
nests in ladies' hats. French cooking was all the rage, as was imported lamb
from Australia. But I couldn't convince the locals that visitors loved our BC
salmon—as did I. Salmon in fact were so plentiful in 1901 that a 5-
pounder sold for 5 cents. Giving a salmon to someone marked the recipient
as indigent. It was considered *déclassé* for a West End hostess to serve
salmon to guests, the fish being considered as mere subsistence fare "fit only
for siwashes."

Fishing regulations in fact were nonexistent—except for the law prohibiting Indians from selling fish commercially other than under contract
to canneries. Loggers and others regularly dynamited Capilano River pools
to secure salmon or steelhead for dinner, often killing dozens of surplus fish
which were left to rot. Thousands of salmon still swam up Brewery Creek
from False Creek, past Westminster Avenue as far as the Tea Swamp in
South Vancouver. When big runs came up the Brewery, fishermen used
scoop nets, pitchforks and gaff hooks to catch as many as a dozen salmon
in half an hour.

Yet our little city was certain of its destiny. The new Carnegie Library plans were finalized in September, and excavation began at the corner of Hastings and Westminster Avenue. Mayor Townley succeeded in persuading the provincial government to relinquish ownership to the city of the flats at both False Creek and Coal Harbour. (Whether this would help the mayor win next January's civic election against retailer Charles Woodward was hotly debated, since Townley was alleged to be in a conflict of interest as a result of holding the additional office of Registrar of Land Titles.) So the expansion of False Creek sawmills was assured, as was the inflation of lot prices. Even out in Fairview, building lots were going for $500.

Vancouver had become a speculator's haven. The city was so famous for its "potential" that even Rudyard Kipling purchased several city lots on spec. Writing of Vancouver in his book *From Sea To Sea*, Kipling says: "A great sleepiness lies over Vancouver as compared with an American town. Men do not fly up and down stairs telling lies, and the spittoons in the delightful hotels are unused; the baths are free and the doors are unlocked. You do not have to pick up a hotel clerk when you want a bath, which shows the inferiority of Vancouver... Moreover, the old flag waves over some of the buildings and this is cheering to the soul. The place is full of Englishmen who speak the English tongue correctly and with clearness, avoiding more blasphemy than is necessary, and taking a reasonable length of time to down their drinks."

The shadows lengthened. Hallowe'en came and went, with rowdyism kept to a minimum. (In past years, a favourite prank of youths was to exchange flags on all the consulate poles, with the stars and stripes flying at the Japanese residence and vice versa.) One resident did send this missive to the *World*: "If the boys who carried off the gates at the corner of Bute and Barclay Streets will be good enough to return them this evening, they will receive a reward."

Snow fell early in December. Children sledded and tobogganned down Burrard Street from the Christ Church Cathedral corner, and down Granville from Georgia. Those without sleds slid on makeshift pieces of tin, washboards or their backsides. Dogs travelled too. Ed Eggleton of my staff tramped with a friend along snow-covered sidewalk boards in front of the United States Consulate one morning on a stroll. Eggleton observed a

Interior of the old Vancouver Opera House on Granville Street. The stage featured a drop screen and an enormous background oil painting of Banff's Three Sisters. Numerous world celebrities performed here, and even Mark Twain appeared for a reading of his works. (CVA BU P7 N132)

huge dog rolling about in the snow. "That's a St. Bernard dog," he said to his companion. "Never heard of it," replied the friend. Eggleton turned to his companion agape. "Why, Charlie, don't you know that St. Bernard dogs rescue travellers in danger of perishing in the snow?" His friend paused; then, carefully eyeing the big dog—which by now had shaken off some snow and headed up the hill—he asked, "what do they do when they find the travellers?" "Well, in the Alps," said Eggleton, "the dogs have little silver tankards of brandy hanging on their necks and these spirits revive the traveller from the cold." Eggleton's friend, a country iconoclast, shook his head dubiously. "They do, they do," insisted Eggleton. "Why, if that's true, then," said his friend, a gleam in his eye, "do you suppose, Eggleton, that if you and I were to lie down here in the snow by the sidewalk, do you think that dog up there would have sense enough to bring us a drink?"

The snow was followed by a period of cold, clear weather, rendering Trout Lake frozen for skating and even the salt water down by the Inlet wharves caked up. One frosty morning I paused on Cordova Street to watch an *Empress* ship arrive at the dock: "Just inside the CPR wharf, a solitary gull was perched on the ice, one foot cuddled among its feathers... It drew the attention of the passengers of the ship to the fact that the ice was hard enough to form a covering on salt water. (Actually, the numerous sewer drains emptied here in such abundance that, while the water was far from fresh, the brine content was somewhat emasculated.) Fresh from the enervating heat of China and the tropics, the passengers found the exhilarating air of early morning Vancouver extremely invigorating, and they came down the gangplank with colour in their faces and a ring in their voices."

That same afternoon, one thousand Vancouverites clustered at the CPR station to bid adieu to twenty more local lads bound for the South African war front. The war puzzled all of us. How could these Boer farmers, even with their great bravery, hold out for so long against the might of the British Empire? When Mayor Townley received a private letter from city native Major Bennett, an earlier volunteer, he delivered it to me privately with a request to publish selective portions. I greatly offended Colonel Worsnop and the local militia by publishing even part of the letter, since the major implied shortcomings in the British Army: "Things are so unsettled in South Africa, and the constabulary in a bad mess. Instead of doing police duties, we have been bundled right out into the field with no equipment except what we left Canada with, about one-third the horses—very poor green horses—and most of the men as green as the horses... We are told by General Baden-Powell that everything will be lovely bye and bye, but in the meantime brother Boer is as active as a flea. We had several scraps, and on the 11th had rather hard luck in running up against Dewet, who had 500 men, with only 65 men from the two troops on this post against it. My troop of 24 men lost heavily. I had 4 killed, 4 wounded, and 11 men captured, but we knocked out 25 Boers. My men fought like devils... but those of us not killed or wounded had to give up against great odds. I was captured by General Dewet himself... I like it however and am in fine health... but give me Vancouver."

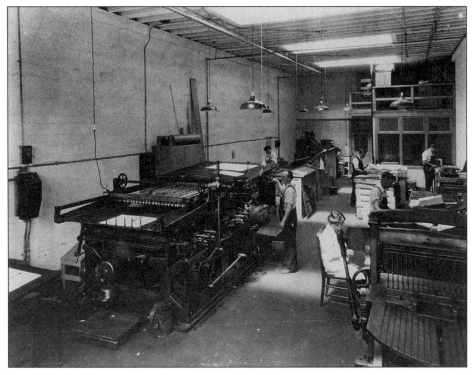

Typical news press, Homer Street, c. 1903. At right front is a cutter. (VPL 10697)

Christmas approached. The rain melted the snow quickly and caused flooding. (Death, taxes and rain are the only constants in this town.) The year and the new century had brought us death, disaster, war and world unrest, not to mention burglars on bicycles. But it had also brought low prices, Children's Aid reforms, a new library, hospital approval, great engineering advances, improved lighting, and material prosperity for many.

On December 16th we received word from St. John's, Newfoundland that Marconi had succeeded in transmitting wireless signals across the Atlantic from England—some 1,700 miles away. The world press wrote in awe of this achievement as the most wonderful scientific "discovery" of modern times, heralding a new age of communications.

Now, progress is only relative. Many of my fellow Vancouverites believed that despite all these doings, the most significant event of the year was the capture of the largest Capilano River trout in BC history—an 11-pound rainbow, reeled in above the dam by old Madison the fisherman.

Streetcar in snow, Granville and Pender streets. Skating on Trout Lake was a popular pastime in cold weather. (VPL 7136)

Hundreds of Izaak Walton fishing fans paraded down to the Avenue Hotel, where the monster trout remained on display in the window for weeks. Trust Vancouverites to measure world events in leisure terms.

The city was a sea of dazzling lights, as Christmas shoppers patronized shops ablaze with store lighting for the first time in history. Electricity was indeed the new-found tool of the decorator, and shoppers went wild, comparing the city to exotic San Francisco. The *World* reported: "The Terminal City Club was ablaze of electricity last night and the radiancy was brilliant last evening between 5:00 p.m. until midnight in the shops, when the last tired store clerk was able to put on his rubbers and go home."

The store lighting displays were used "in all sorts of devices, from the arc of wood to the revolving ball. It shone from the model of the free library, from the snow-covered sides of the toboggan slide in the big drygoods window... And the lights were multi-coloured. The many unique novelties are fitting reminders that this is the twentieth century, and even good old conservative Santa Claus must substitute the automobile soon for the reindeer sled if he hopes to keep up with the times."

The new lighting helped Vancouver merchants do a record business that Christmas. The most popular children's gift was model Boer fighters and red and khaki British soldiers. Of course, not all children would be so fortunate as to receive store presents. In this regard, I bustled about helping various charities in their labours to bring good cheer to the indigent and the homeless. On Christmas Eve, I ran my traditional editorial: "Vancouver is growing to such an extent that it now has its very poor, for whom provision has to be made. For those who are in straightened circumstances, or in jail, or in hospital in this city, there will be aid tomorrow to let them pass at least one day of pleasure."

The Salvation Army and Friendly Aid Society ensured that jail inmates, Alexandra House orphans, Rescue Home girls and widowed families received food, gifts and cheer. At the free library, Mrs. Machin devoted herself to the many men she saw every day coming in from the cold—out of work and down on their luck, for whom she arranged Christmas dinner and evening musical entertainment.

Mind you, our city jail only contained sixteen men on Christmas—a record low—of whom only nine were regulars. These men included the old souse Ginger Granville, who knew the cells very well. As the *World* reported, "Ginger has complimented Chief Jail Cook Grady in days gone by on the excellence of the plum pudding. Frederick, a man of colour, who is doing a few months for supplying liquor to Indians, has also been in jail before. (He is welcome, says Grady, because he is a good helper cook.) Lawrence Smith is glad to be in Grady Castle. He thanked the magistrate a few days ago for sending him there over Christmas."

These prisoners were overheard by our *World* reporter singing their own special Christmas ditty: "We're all froze out poor labouring men; we've got no work to do-oo." The ditty originated as a result of the tradition begun by the late Mayor Oppenheimer of giving prisoners Christmas Day off from their forced labour.

Fred, the girls and I took the Christmas Eve train to Hazelbrae. My God, it was wonderful to see Douglas again and my parents looking so well. And to breathe the deep, clear country air. There were ducks and geese everywhere on the Matsqui marshes, local birds who refused to fly south in the winter. I walked about in the afternoon to the old blind where I used to watch Judge Begbie shoot his prey. There too were the old burn marks on the huge cedar stumps by the barn, where the devastating fire of '68 had been contained. And the old house, still standing, with the big spruce tree all decorated and shimmering in the parlour; the kitchen with the wood stove burning—and yes, the very same table where I had sat as a young girl working the keys of the telegraph machine.

My brother Sam was held up in Victoria, but we were joined at Hazelbrae by Charles and his family, who arrived with bundles of gifts, the wind tousling their hair as they hurried in from the train stop. Christmas Day itself brought a terrific storm. The wind howled and rain pelted against the window panes. Turkey dinner was cooked over the stove in the old manner and served by candlelight at noon, the day being so dark. The gloom of the storm simply heightened our spirits, and Papa let the brandy flow in good measure afterward, as we all gathered in the parlour to discuss politics and Sam's latest mansion designs.

Telegraph and telephone lines remained out for days; the storm had even cut off rail service. When I was finally able to return to Vancouver three days later, I was greeted by devastation. The storm experienced in the Valley had been of hurricane force in the city—the worst in recorded history. Broken salmon cases and other debris, thought to be the remains of wrecked ships, floated along the shoreline at English Bay. Shop windows were blown in; fallen trees lay sprawled on every street. Roofs were torn off; chimneys toppled. Every telephone post and flagpole in the city was down.

CPR steamers had been badly damaged and the city wharf at the foot of Burrard Street had broken in two. The electric lights which had so recently presented a fantasy wonderland to shoppers were all out, globes were smashed and wires snapped in every quarter. At English Bay, most boats were destroyed or damaged, and the bathing pavilion had been rendered a wreck of splinters. The English Bay Cannery had completely collapsed.

As Vancouverites reeled from the hurricane's blow and began cleanup, perhaps the strangest sight was the hundreds of residents who beachcombed for salmon cases still washing ashore at English Bay. The *World* reported: "A large proportion of the Fairview population turned out in working clothes and in many a household last evening canned salmon was served at tea time, on which neither freight duty nor storekeeper was paid... Not content with carrying away a few odd cans as souvenirs of a mysterious wreck, the residents came down with wheelbarrows, baby carriages, go-carts, sacks and baskets, and gathered the harvest. One enterprising citizen had, when evening came, a pile of twenty unbroken cases filling his sacks, and he returned with a wagon in the darkness of night to take home his treasure trove." One case of salmon had been storm-blown by the waves some thirty feet into the air, and lodged in a tree.

On New Year's Eve, I watched the cleanup of the city wharves from my bay window, as the militia men and labourers hauled in boats and wreckage. The dykes of Sea Island had just burst, causing incredible devastation of farmland—the entire island had become a huge lake; all Delta towns were under water, the canneries at Steveston and elsewhere destroyed. Well, at least no one lost their life, I mused. I told the children not to worry, we would recover. Time to wind up the old Victrola and contemplate both the past year and the future.

Margitte jumped up on my knee as the stirring lines of "Auld Lang Syne" died away on the Victrola. "We've come through the first year of the new century, child," I smiled. "Now repeat after me: "Bliss was it in that dawn to be alive; but to be young was very heaven.'" Margitte stammered, laughed, and finally got it right.

Alas, I had forgotten most of Wordsworth's poems. Well, in this century's dawn I had experienced much pain and sorrow with the loss of my husband. Canadians had lost a queen, soldiers at war—perhaps, like the returning Boer veterans, even their innocence. Yet I, a matronly widow, still lived and breathed and yes, loved in this dawn. And while it was not quite "very heaven," it was enough. My heaven remained locked in the soul of my childhood years at Hazelbrae, fingering the mysterious telegraph keys of the little black box on the table, spreading news to the world. Wasn't it I who first flashed word to New Westminster that British Columbia had just joined Confederation—when there was no Vancouver?

The Victrola was quiet. Twilight engulfed the Inlet. The workers on the dock had all tramped away home. Bare hulls, smashed and battered

John McLagan's photograph, as it appeared in the World *in 1903, with other flagship photos.*

from the storm, lay silhouetted on the shore like beached whales. I thought of the Homer Street presses, sitting quietly now as Fred left the office, the night reporters scurrying in. In the morning, I would give orders to change the masthead of the *World*. Since John's death, the name of the proprietor had been omitted on the editorial page, contrary to custom. Male business friends had cautioned me that a woman's name had never appeared as the "chief" in a major Canadian paper, and that readers might lose confidence in a paper they knew to be run by a woman.

Well, it was time for all of that to change. Sara McLagan was here; she was a woman; and she damn well intended to keep publishing the best newspaper west of Ontario—spreading the news, her way.

Epilogue

The years rolled by. The *World*, though outpaced by the *Province*, maintained a strong readership base, thanks to Sara's hands-on management and Fred's fiscal expertise. Sara found the demands of the job to be physically draining, in part because she insisted on taking a lead role in writing editorials and shaping storylines. She reaped some reward in 1904, when she was invited to become an inaugural member of the Canadian Women's Press Club. The journalists present at the founding meeting described Sara as the most powerful woman "press lord" in Canada.

Sara was approached in 1905 by Louis Taylor, who offered to purchase the *World*. Fred's health had seriously deteriorated; her own health was unstable. She quickly accepted Taylor's offer of $65,000. Her stepson Jack surfaced inconveniently at this time and, hearing of the impending sale, brought court action against Sara, demanding a portion of the sale proceeds on the basis of a claim against his late father's estate. On the eve of the court's judgment, Sara wrote to her mother of her apprehensions: "This has been a trying day for many reasons, full of doubts and fears as to what the future may hold, but I am going to try to throw care to the winds now and look on the bright side... I believe everything is arranged to pay the sale amount to me tomorrow, so that this is practically my last day with the dear old *World* after many years of joys and sorrows."

The judge dismissed Jack McLagan's action as frivolous, noting that

Sara had put much of her own money into the launching of the newspaper, and he lambasted Jack for wasting the court's time. The sale was allowed to proceed. *World* employees sent a gift to Sara with both a birthday greeting and a parting message: "It is the hearty wish of the employees of the *World* that you have many happy returns of this your birthday. The members have one and all had the most pleasant experience of your constant sympathy with them in their work and cordial and unsparing acknowledgments of their efforts to maintain the high standards of journalistic achievement which you have set in Vancouver…"

Immediately upon completion of the sale, the new proprietor, Louis Taylor, opined in the *World*: "Mrs. McLagan, as every staff member knows, was a womanly woman. She sympathized with those who were in trouble and was ever willing to expend both time and money in lending a helping hand to the suffering and the needy… Time and time again she threw her columns open to aid a worthy cause. By the kindly course she pursued, she won many friends, some of the warmest of whom were in her own office. But Mrs. McLagan's life had another side—she was a prominent figure in the public eye. As a leading member and ex-president of the Arts & Historical Association, and as a very active worker in several women's organizations, she was frequently in direct contact with all types of people, and on every occasion bore herself with credit… Day after day she has attended the office from early morning 'til late in the evening, striving in every way possible to produce a paper which would reflect in some measure the high journalistic ideals she ever held before her."

Sara returned to Hazelbrae to unwind. Near the family farm, at the foot of Sumas Mountain, she and brother Charles discovered whitish lumps of fire-clay which were assayed as being of extremely high quality. Sara quickly arranged to purchase 640 acres of surrounding land from the federal government at $1 per acre.

Sara and her brothers then formed the Clayburn Brick Company. A narrow-gauge steam railway ran the clay down the mountain to a large plant which the siblings built at its base, across from which an entire company town grew up—a store and neat little brick bungalows surrounded by rambling English gardens and white picket fences. Within a few years, Clayburn bricks achieved national renown. The new Hotel Vancouver and other landmark buildings were constructed of the buff-coloured, high-quality brick.

Following John Maclure's death in 1907, Sara returned to live part-time in Vancouver, where she continued to participate in Council of Women activities, the Press Club and numerous other charitable organizations. But the onset of world war in 1914 brought new challenges and pain. In 1916, she travelled to California to live for a time with her youngest daughter Margitte and her husband. When the United States entered the war, Sara took a job as a telegraphist for a shipbuilding company. After only a few months on the job, she learned that her beloved son Douglas had been killed in action in France.

Devastated, Sara returned home to Vancouver. By this time, her best friend was Julia Henshaw, and the latter was herself in France running a Red Cross civilian relief unit. Julia invited Sara to help her there—and to search for Douglas's grave. This was just the tonic that Sara needed, and she set forth at once for Europe.

Julia had personally organized a Canadian sector in the most devastated areas of France, comprising the Vimy, Arras and Cambrai regions. The Red Cross unit established advance food depots, distributed medical supplies and clothing, and provided transport to desperate civilians fleeing to other parts of the country. Julia's unit was battle-hardened from serving during the last big German offensive of 1918.

At age sixty-three, Sara found herself helping to evacuate villages lying in the path of war—bundling the aged and wounded off to Paris, giving first aid, and caring for homeless children. After the Armistice was declared in November of 1918, Sara assisted in postwar reconstruction and relief.

At Christmas 1919, Sara wrote of the yuletide cheer her unit sought to bring to a charred and ravaged countryside: "In addition to the usual bundles of supplies, 550 families were given a gallon tin of Canadian peaches, six tins of port and beans, six cocoa and coffee tins, chocolate bars, and tobacco… The Christmas tree was truly unique, it having been impossible to find a green one in the devastated region. Some bare branches were nailed to a pedestal and trimmed with a few sprays of ivy and holly. It was pathetic to see the joy of the poor children over the trifles which had been gathered from wrecked homes, including small vases and wooden shells… Each child was given a bundle of clothes and a package of candy from our doctor."

Sara also lauded the stout-hearted people of Arras who "by the last harvest, transformed the battlefields to acres of waving grain and flourishing market gardens, and in between grew the poppies immortalized by John McCrae." But she never found Douglas's grave. Her solace was her volunteer work and selection as one of only six Canadians representing Canada in London at the unveiling of both the Cenotaph and the Tomb of the Unknown Soldier. Over the stones of that tomb, she noted, every future British monarch must tread in order to be crowned.

Sara returned home in 1919 to become Superintendent of the Vancouver Old People's Home, a post she served at tirelessly for many years. When cancer attacked her body, she ignored it, blithely spreading good cheer to the lonely and infirm in her charge.

We catch up with Sara in 1923, at her Vancouver home…A tall, regal figure in a burgundy silk dress fusses with her teapot. To the east, down Georgia Street, Sara peers out at the stately spire of Christ Church Cathedral. To the south, black smoke spews upward from False Creek as it always has, and Sara thinks of the gases filling men's lungs at the great mills there…

Ah, but the old town is progressing. Trade, trade and more trade, she laughs to herself; never-ending progress. She stirs her tea and glances out the big bay window toward Burrard Inlet, watching an outward-bound freighter laden with wheat. Originally dubbed Stevens Folly after the grocer clerk turned MP who sponsored its construction, the big new grain terminal is now being applauded as indicative of Vancouver's proud status as the major port of west coast North America. Less praiseworthy, Sara muses, is the crass claptrap boosterism of that cursed gadfly Louis Taylor, Vancouver's oft-time mayor—still wearing his gauche scarlet ties and smoking dirty cigars. And to think that he sits in my chair at the *World*, she sighs.

Sara picks up a newly published book that Fred has given her, *The Black Candle*, which exposes the gruesome drug trade, prostitution and seediness in Vancouver's streets. And who is listening, she thinks. Why,

Sara McLagan's immediate and extended family, 1904. Sara stands with her daughter Hazel and (left to right) brothers Fred, Charles and Sam. Her father and mother, John and Martha Maclure, are seated just in front of her in the second row. At far left and right of the second row are Sara's daughters Margitte and Doris, and her son Douglas is sitting on the floor, front row right, beside the dog. (CVA Port P984 N449)

until 1921, Taylor and his civic cronies didn't even recognize a need for women's public toilet facilities, much less worry about teenage whores!

Ah well, she smiles to herself, the world is one big treadmill. You work, do your bit, pay your social dues, and then get off. But she has had, she muses, one jolly good run. She opens her copy of the day's *World* and laughs aloud at the clean-shaven men photographed on the front page in their bell bottoms, dancing the Charleston with women smeared with lipstick and rouge. They are all escaping, she smiles, trying to flee the wreckage of the war to end all wars. And imagine us all believing that the little Boer scuffle would be the last bloody conflict of western civilization, presaging a twentieth century of refinement and enlightenment!

And why shouldn't the young and not so young try to blot out the carnage with wild abandon? We haven't tried the Bohemian way yet. Maybe prudery and sobriety simply hide the warts and acne of a violent, vainglorious, chauvinistic society. Could Kipling possibly have foreseen the disaster to his beloved Empire?

Sara McLagan on duty with the Red Cross in France, 1917.

The sky turns crimson and gold over Stanley Park as dusk approaches. Sara stares out the window, enthralled. A seagull lands on the ledge. You can see the end of the old era coming, she ponders. We all thought that science and technology—supported by Victorian values—would build Utopia. Motor cars, aeroplanes, new drugs and countless gadgets represented a leap in Mankind's fortunes. Or so we thought.

Sara opens the window to throw a few bread crumbs to the waiting gull, then draws back and winced in pain from the cancer which wracks her body. Well, she has braved the storm, fought her battles—even old Carter-Cotton has given her that, bless his Tory soul. And she has watched a colony become a province, a smouldering ruin become a city; she has witnessed world war and the fall of the old order.

Sara dozes in her chair, her tea growing cold beside her. Outside, a stiff breeze ripples the heavy canvasses of the luxury yachts moored at dockside. Across the Inlet, a lone paddler in a dugout canoe sets forth upon frothing waves toward the city. A noisy motor car sputters along Georgia Street below. Overhead, the seagulls squawk and soar in the gathering dusk.

Sara McLagan died on March 20, 1924. Just a few weeks after her death, the *World* ceased to publish: it was absorbed by the well-financed *Vancouver Sun*. Both woman and newspaper had laid firm roots of service and journalistic excellence for future generations.

Acknowledgements

This book would not have been possible without the encouragement and research assistance of my collaborator, Lynda Orr, who persisted in convincing me that Sara's story deserved to be told.

The City of Vancouver Archives staff was particularly helpful and professional in facilitating this project; they administer a wonderful facility which would have made founding archivist Major Matthews proud of his city.

Thanks to the Vancouver Public Library Special Collections staff for expediting photographs.

Special thanks go to Gerry Leiper for his generous assistance in collating research materials.

To Doria Moodie, great-granddaughter of Sara McLagan, my thanks for giving me generous access to Sara's diaries and the family records.

I acknowledge my usual debt to the staff of the Public Archives of British Columbia.

Finally, many thanks to my Harbour editor, Mary Schendlinger, for her thorough and objective comments on the manuscript.

Chapter Notes

Epigraph

"I Shall Not Cease," from "The Gold Stripe," Vol. I, Amputations Club of BC, p. 160.

Introduction

"Historians have written about the suffrage movement": Gillian Marie, "Writing Women Into British Columbia's History," in *In Her Own Right: Selected Essays on Women's History in British Columbia*, ed. B. Latham, p. 2.

"In all the reforms we devise": Lady Aberdeen, National Council of Women, *Women Workers of Canada: Report of the Fifth Annual Conference*, p. 366.

"I was eighteen. I had always wanted to write": Clare Battle, Letter to the Editor, *The Vancouver Sun*, Sept. 29, 1959.

"They did not 'call upon women to perform'": S. Tillotson, *Canadian Telegraphers 1900–1930: A Case Study in Gender and Skill Hierarchies*, p. 144.

"A most womanly woman": B. Latham, *In Her Own Right*, p. 5.

"The Canadian cannot get by": "Mrs. Moody's First Impressions of British Columbia," in *BC Historical News*, ed. J. Greschko, Vol. 11, pp. 3–4.

Chapter One

"The female who wears them.": J. Callwood, *The Naughty Nineties, 1890–1900*, p. 76.

"I think it was old James Bennett": Unpublished letter, Sept. 12, 1894, City of Vancouver Archives.

"Down along the waterfront": J. Henshaw, *What Now, Sweetheart?*, p. 45.

"It is the disgrace of our civilization": "Working Women and Girls," in *Vancouver Weekly World*, Dec. 6, 1888, p. 4.

"The tyranny of taxation": *Vancouver Daily World*, Jan. 9, 1897, p. 7.

"Those West End mugs": J. Elliott, City of Vancouver Archives, July 19, 1963.

"In 1885, when the present site": J. Stewart, City of Vancouver Archives, AM0054.

"The men of the chain gang": E. Nicol, *Vancouver*, pp. 110–11.

"If ever I dream of the streets of heaven": J. Elliott, unpublished poem, City of Vancouver Archives 1364.

Chapter Two

"Miserable little houses": *Vancouver Province*, March 14, 1896.

"Are you preparing for your lecture tonight": Unpublished paper, "Goodman—A Family History," City of Vancouver Archives, p. 49.

"City of Sighs and Tears": J.S. Matthews, *Early Vancouver*, Vol. 3, p. 258.

"The Association had its inception when Vancouver": N. Robinson, "History of the Arts, Historical, and Scientific Association," City of Vancouver Archives, PAM 1944.9, p. 12.

"Stanley Park is heaven": *Vancouver Daily World*, May 20, 1901.

"The world is too much with us": W. Wordsworth, *Miscellaneous Sonnets*.

"People of colour were banned": The Crystal Pool colour bar remained in force until 1946.

Laurier letter: Unpublished letter, April 4, 1900, original in private Moodie family files.

Chapter Three

"personally insure": D. Fetherling, *The Rise of the Canadian Newspaper*, p. 68.

"If we have a proper pride of race": W. Lord, *The Good Years*, pp. 3, 7.

"So long as the rate of progress": H. Adams, *The Education of Henry Adams*, Boston: Houghton & Mifflin, 1918, pp. 494–95.

"The smoking paraphernalia": *Vancouver Daily World*, Oct. 13, 1900.

"You can't open your school room door": *Victoria Colonist*, July 27, 1900.

"After the fire of 12 years ago": *Vancouver Daily World*, Sept. 19, 1900.

"This paper endeavours to give a complete list": *Vancouver Daily World*, April 12, 1902.

"The atmosphere is always damp and chilly": *Vancouver Daily World*, Dec. 11, 1900.

"The last Christmas season of the 19th century": *Vancouver Daily World*, Dec. 22, 1900.

"I am not sorry that I went": *Vancouver Daily World*, Dec. 31, 1900.

Chapter Four

"Condescending, patronizing, or mercilessly sarcastic": B. Freeman, "'Every Stroke Upward,' Women Journalists in Canada, 1880–1906," *Canadian Women's Studies*, p. 55.

"What could be more appropriate": *Vancouver Daily World*, Feb. 5, 1901.

"The anti-spitting notices with which the street": *Vancouver Daily World*, April 4, 1901.

"Canadian journalism loses one of its most valuable representatives": *Vancouver Daily World*, April 11, 1901.

"We feel that no one man has done as much": *Vancouver Daily World*, April 12, 1901.

Chapter Five

"A Chinaman who was a passenger on the *Empress*": *Vancouver Daily World*, April 18, 1901.

"Many of the opponents of the Chinese": *Vancouver Daily World*, May 11, 1901.

"It is hardly fair": *Vancouver Daily World*, Oct. 12, 1901.

"Train not go so fast": *Vancouver Province*, March 26, 1910.

"Many churches—One Sagulee Tyee": N. Robinson, unpublished paper, City of Vancouver Archives, AM 0054, 013.007111.

Chapter Six

"Out here in the West": *Vancouver Daily World*, May 26, 1901.

"Whenever his name was mentioned": S. Jackman, *Portraits of the Premiers*, Sidney, BC: Gray's Publishing Co., 1969, p. 132.

"As in any other line of commercial activity": *Vancouver Daily World*, June 13, 1901.

"Perhaps the *News-Advertiser* sees them sitting up at night": *Vancouver Daily World*, July 15, 1901.

"They were sitting at breakfast": J. Henshaw, *What Now, Sweetheart?*, pp. 25, 28, 33.

"There are no seductive Want Columns": A. Cameron, *The New North: Being Some Account of a Woman's Journey Through Canada to the Arctic*, New York: D. Appleton & Co., 1910, p. 219.

"The public nature of the area": Correspondence of an Association, June 15, 1906.

"As quickly as visitors to the place": *Vancouver Daily World*, 1906.

"There has been a flock of the immoral people": *Vancouver Daily World*, Aug. 30, 1901.

Chapter Seven

"The typical county fair of the East": *Vancouver Daily World*, July 5, 1901.

"In September I made application to you": Cumyow to Cunningham, unpublished letter, May 15, 1902, City of Vancouver Archives.

"debauched his son": *Vancouver Daily World*, Sept. 6, 1901.

"A rumour is afloat that the family": *Vancouver Province*, March 17, 1900.

"willing to treat almost any form of disease": *Vancouver Daily World*, June 19, 1901.

"Keep witch hazel for lumps": *Vancouver Daily World*, June 22, 1901.

"Art Saniger, the pigeon fancier": *Vancouver Daily World*, Oct. 28, 1901.

"The real lady settles her debts": *Vancouver Daily World*, Aug. 31, 1901.

"The appearance of the lady climbers": F. H. Smith, "Cabins, Camps, and Climbs," *The Mountaineer*, 50th Anniversary, 1907–57, Vancouver: Chapman & Warwick Ltd., 1958, p. 3.

Chapter Eight

"No, sworn off; no more": Unpublished paper, "Sam Robb," City of Vancouver Archives, 3915, fiche.

"A great sleepiness lies over Vancouver": Reprinted from *From Sea to Sea*, in *Vancouver Daily World*, Sept. 19, 1901.

"That's a St. Bernard dog": *Vancouver Daily World*, Dec. 11, 1901.

"Just inside the CPR wharf": *Vancouver Daily World*, Dec. 11, 1901.

"Things are so unsettled in South Africa": *Vancouver Daily World*, Aug. 30, 1901.

"The Terminal City Club was ablaze": *Vancouver Daily World*, Dec. 24, 1901.

"Ginger has complimented": *Vancouver Daily World*, Dec. 24, 1901.

Epilogue

"This has been a trying day": Unpublished letter, private Moodie family papers, May 31, 1905.

"It is the hearty wish of the employees": Unpublished letter, private Moodie family papers, April 1, 1905.

"Mrs. McLagan, as every staff member knows": *Vancouver Daily World*, June 1, 1905.

Selected Bibliography

Baker, Edna. "Pages From The History of the Vancouver Branch, Canadian Women's Press Club," unpublished manuscript. Vancouver BC: 1957.

Bingham, Janet. *Samuel Maclure, Architect*. Ganges BC: Horsdal & Schubart, 1985.

Brock, Peter J. "Fighting Joe Martin In British Columbia," M.A. Thesis, Simon Fraser University, 1976.

Callwood, June. *The Naughty Nineties, 1890–1900*. Toronto: Natural Science of Canada Ltd., 1977.

Cruikshank, Connie. "The Maclure Story," unpublished paper, n.d.

Davis, Chuck and Shirley Mooney. *Vancouver: An Illustrated Chronology*. Windsor ON: Windsor Publications Ltd., 1986.

Fetherling, Douglas. *The Rise of the Canadian Newspaper*. Toronto: Oxford University Press, 1990.

Freeman, Barbara. "'Every Stroke Upward,' Women Journalists In Canada, 1880–1906," *Canadian Women's Studies*, Vol. 7, No. 3 (Fall 1986).

Gough, Lyn. *As Wise As Serpents*. Victoria: Swan Lake Publishing, 1988.

Hale, Linda. "The British Columbia Women's Suffrage Movement, 1890–1917," M.A. Thesis, University of British Columbia, 1977.

Harris, Christie. "Sara Maclure, Telegraphist," unpublished transcript of CBC play broadcast October, 1942.

Hastings, Margaret. *Blue Bow and the Golden Rule: Provincial Council of Women of BC*. Burnaby BC: Provincial Council, 1984.

Henshaw, Julia. *Why Not, Sweetheart?* Toronto: Geo. Morang & Co. Ltd., 1901.

Howard, Irene. "The Mothers' Council of Vancouver: Holding the Fort for the Unemployed," in "Vancouver Past: Essays In Social History," ed. R. A. McDonald and Jean Barman. *BC Studies* (Spring 1986).

Howay, F. W. and E. O. S. Scholefield. *British Columbia From Earliest Times to the Present*. Vancouver: Clark Publishing, 1914.

Johnson, Pauline. *Legends of Vancouver*. Toronto: McClelland & Stewart, 1961.

Keller, Betty. *On the Shady Side: Vancouver, 1886–1914*. Ganges BC: Horsdal & Schubart, 1986.

Kerr, J. B. "Journalism in Vancouver," *British Columbia Magazine* (1911).

Kluckner, Michael. *Vancouver: The Way It Was*. North Vancouver: Whitecap Books Ltd., 1984.

Lamb, Bessie. "From Tickler To Telegram: Notes on Early Vancouver Newspapers," *BC Historical Quarterly*, Vol. ix, No. 3 (1945).

Lamb, Bessie. "The Origin and Development of Newspapers in Vancouver," M.A. Thesis, University of British Columbia, 1942.

Lang, Marjory and Linda Hale. "Women of *The World* and Other Dailies: The Lives and Times of Vancouver Newspaperwomen in the First Quarter of the Twentieth Century," *BC Studies*, No. 85 (Spring 1990).

Latham, Barbara, ed. *In Her Own Right: Selected Essays on Women's History in British Columbia*. Victoria: Camosun College, 1980.

Local Councils of Women of BC. "Woman's Life and Work in the Province of British Columbia," Government of BC, 1909, City of Vancouver Archives.

Lord, Walter. *The Good Years: From 1900 to the First World War*. New York: Harper & Brothers, 1960.

McLagan, Sara. Unpublished diaries and personal papers. (Dorit Moodie Family Collection.)

MacGill, Elsie G. *My Mother the Judge*. Toronto: The Ryerson Press, 1955.

MacGill, Helen G. *Laws for Women and Children in British Columbia*. Vancouver, 1939.

_____ *The Story of Vancouver Social Service*. City of Vancouver Archives, 1943.

MacGregor, D. A. "Adventures of Vancouver Newspapers 1892–1926," *British Columbia Historical Quarterly* 10:2 (1946).

Morley, Alan. *Vancouver: From Milltown to Metropolis*. Vancouver: Mitchell Press, 1969.

Matthews, James S. *Early Vancouver*. Vols. 1–7, CVA.

Nicol, Eric. *Vancouver*. Toronto: Doubleday, 1978.

Ormsby, Margaret. *British Columbia: A History*. Vancouver: Evergreen Press, 1958.

Orr, Lynda M. "Sara Ann McLagan, 'A Woman of the World,'" unpublished paper, October 1993.

Saywell, John T. *The Canadian Journal of Lady Aberdeen, 1893–1898.* Toronto: The Champlain Society, 1960.

Schwesinger, Gladys. *Recollections of Early Vancouver in My Childhood, 1893–1912.* Vancouver: Brock Webber, 1965.

Smith, Dorothy B. "Early Memories of Vancouver," *BC Historical News* 17:3 (1984).

Strong-Boag, Veronica. *The Parliament of Women: The National Council of Women of Canada, 1893–1929.* Ottawa: National Museums of Canada, 1976.

Tillotson, Shirley. "Canadian Telegraphers 1900–1930: A Case Study In Gender and Skill Hierarchies," Ph.D. Thesis, Queen's University, 1989.

Vipond, Mary. *The Mass Media in Canada.* Toronto: Lorimer, 1989.

Woodcock, George. *British Columbia: A History of the Province.* Vancouver: Douglas & McIntyre, 1990.

The Province (Vancouver), various dates.

The Vancouver Daily World, various dates.

His Majesty's Fourth

Moe Quinn

PublishAmerica
Baltimore

ISBN: 1-4137-9464-5
PUBLISHED BY PUBLISHAMERICA, LLLP
www.publishamerica.com
Baltimore

Printed in the United States of America

Prologue

In the seventeen hundreds, France and England fought three wars. The last war, during the reign of King George of England, was known in Europe as the Seven Years War. In North America it was called the French and Indian War. It lasted from seventeen fifty-six to seventeen sixty-three. Both the English and French had Indian allies who raided French and English settlements. Rape, murder and burning were common practices on both sides. To protect the lives of the settlers, forts were built. Fort number four was the northernmost fort in the Connecticut River Valley. The fort at Charlestown, New Hampshire, was not a large military fort. It was known as a fortified settlement. A group of houses forming a rectangle with a stockade fence ten to twelve feet high surrounded the buildings. When an alarm was sounded, the settlers would gather up livestock and families and run to the safety of the fort. Through the fort passed many soldiers using the Crown Point Road, which ran through what is now the state of Vermont, but was known then as the New Hampshire Grants, or the Wilderness, for there was nothing but wilderness from the fort to Montreal, Canada.

Chapter One

The heavily loaded birch bark canoe rode low in the water. The paddle dipped into the water, pushing the canoe effortlessly through the light mist-covered water of the Connecticut River. A smile spread across Mannasas Buck's handsome face as he watched a large salmon rise from the water and snatch a low-flying butterfly in its mouth. The fish splashed back into the river and left a ripple that was steadily advancing toward the canoe, while overhead a large hawk circled around on the air currents, his keen eyes looking for breakfast. A blue heron, half hidden in the cattails, was ready to spear an unsuspecting bullfrog with its sharp beak. The crows heralded the presence of the canoe on the river as he passed by with a rustle of wings, circling overhead and landing in the pine trees on the other side of the river.

Mannasas Buck, known as Bucky to friends and foe alike, was a handsome, blond-haired twenty-five-year-old man. He was five feet ten inches tall and one hundred and eighty-five pounds of solid muscle, with wide shoulders and a narrow waist. He had a short stubble of a beard and shoulder-length hair. Bucky wore a deerskin shirt and trousers, with deerskin moccasins that came up to his knees. Bucky was at peace with the world that beautiful June morning. His canoe was loaded to the gunwales with prime furs from his fall, winter and spring trappings, taken from the northernmost part of the New Hampshire Grants. Rounding a bend in the river, Bucky could see the tower and roofs of fort number four. Digging the paddle into the water with force, sending the canoe surging ahead, Bucky guided the canoe toward the boat landing. It had been a long, lonely winter, and he was anxious to get home and swap stories with his friends.

Johnny Scott was a large boy for his fourteen years. Johnny was five feet seven inches tall, and weighed one hundred and forty pounds and growing. For the last few days Johnny had spent all of his free time up in the fort's tower, looking up the river and hoping for Bucky's return. Having spent all of his fourteen years on the frontier, Johnny knew all to well the dangers that could befall anyone who got careless. Johnny brushed his black hair from his eyes as the canoe rounded the bend in the river. Recognizing Bucky, Johnny let out a yell, ran down the stairs of the tower and was standing by the river boat landing with a big smile on his face as Bucky's canoe beached itself on the shore.

"Hi, Johnny," Bucky said as he stepped from the canoe and tossed the paddle to Johnny.

"Hi! Gosh, it's good to see you, Bucky," Johnny replied.

"Looks like you grew up some during the winter," Bucky said as he put his arm around Johnny's shoulder.

"I guess so; at least that's what Ma says. She tells everyone that I really shot up the last couple of months.

"How's your ma and pa? I'll bet your pa wintered just fine, sitting beside his cider barrel with your ma stocking up the fire. My mouth's been watering for a glass of his good cider all winter long," Bucky said, pretending to wipe his lips.

"Bucky, Pa is dead."

"What! Dead? How? When?" Bucky asked, a look of shock in his eyes. "My God, Johnny, he was the best friend I ever had."

"I know. He died about three weeks after you left. It was about the last of September when he came down with the fever. Ma and Doctor

Hastings did everything they could. He just got weaker and weaker. Then one night he died."

Bucky stood by the river, looking across the tree stump-studded field surrounding the fort. Those trees he and Charlie Scott help to cut down made the fort more secure from attack by the French and Indians. A mental picture of Charlie formed in Bucky's mind. He was a large man at six feet two and at least two hundred and twenty-five pounds. When he laughed, his voice could be heard a half-mile away. How could something you couldn't even see put a man like that into the ground? Charlie's wife, Marie, was a dark-haired woman of thirty hard winters. She was five years older than Bucky and five years younger than Charlie, with large black eyes that shone when she smiled. She was as pretty to look at as any wildflower in God's garden, even though she faced the hard life on the frontier during those harsh and dangerous times.

"Want some help with your furs?" Johnny asked, breaking into Bucky's thoughts.

"Huh? Oh, yeah, I sure could use some. What's your ma going to do? I'll bet she has all kinds of fellows calling to court her."

"She did for a little while, but she chased them all away. Ma is trying to sell the cabin and land, but no one wants to give her anything for it. My aunt in Boston wrote and told Ma that she could get her a job in an inn where she works as a cleaning lady, and me a job cleaning stables. Bucky, I don't want to spend the rest of my life shoveling horse shit! I want to see the St. Lawrence River and those large lakes that you and Pa always talked about."

"You don't think you would like to shovel shit?" Bucky asked with a grin.

"No, I don't, and I remember Pa telling Ma that Auntie was nothing but a cheap whore. I don't want Ma doing anything like that."

"No, Johnny, I don't want that either. How did my cabin winter? Did you take good care of it?"

"Sure did, Bucky. I kept the roof shoveled off and a small fire going all winter."

It took Bucky and Johnny three trips to carry the furs to Clem and Sue's trading post. The trading post was a two-room lean-to. One room was for the store and one for Sue's dining room. The dining room was also a place for the locals to drink hard cider or rum and tell each other lies. In the back of the store was a storage space and Clem and Sue's meager living quarters. There were two doors to get into the trading post, one into the dining room and one into the store, with large double doors connecting the two rooms. The trading post was about one half-mile from the river and one hundred yards east of the main gate of the fort. It was a popular place for food, drink and conversation.

"That's the last of them, Clem," Bucky said as he threw the last bundle of furs on his pile of furs in the corner of the storage room.

I won't be able to look them over and give you a price for a couple of days, Bucky."

"That's all right, I'll be here all summer."

"If you need anything you can put it on the books."

"Thanks, Clem, but I think I'm all set for a while."

"Hey, Bucky, how would you like to trap that?" Clem asked as he looked over Bucky's shoulder.

Bucky turned and watched Mary Stearns walk up to the counter with long, easy strides and a pleasant smile on her lips.

"Morning, Clem. Hi, Bucky. When did you get back?'

"Today, about three hours ago," Bucky replied as he looked Mary over from head to toe. His look brought a light flush to her cheeks. It was a look that she enjoyed.

Bucky had admired Mary from afar for a long time. Mary was as tall as Bucky, with blue eyes that looked straight into yours when she talked to you. It made some men uneasy, but it always sent Bucky's blood rushing through his body. He liked it. Bucky had never seen her legs, but he just knew they were long, and were being hidden by the long homespun dress that also hid her small waist and firm breasts that moved every time she took a breath. Everything just seemed to go perfectly with her waist-length red hair. Bucky thought Mary was the prettiest woman he had ever seen. The Indians that traded at the fort called her "woman who has hair like flaming maple in the fall."

Bucky glance away as Ben Stearns walked into the store and up to the counter. Ben Stearns was a man who looked like he was born sucking on a sour pickle, and had a personality to match. Bucky didn't like him, and neither did anyone else in the settlement.

Glancing around the room, Ben said, "Give me a pound of shot and powder, and put it on my bill."

Snatching the powder and shot from Clem, Ben put them in a sack and grabbed Mary roughly by the arm.

"Come on, woman. We can't stand around here and talk all day. We have work to do."

"That son of a bitch. If it wasn't for Mary I would stop his credit," said Clem. "Too bad you didn't meet Mary before he did. You would make a nice-looking couple."

"Forget it, Clem. I'm not the marrying kind."

"Someday you will, Bucky. Someday you will get tired of sleeping all alone out there in the woods."

"Who says I am sleeping alone? Haven't you ever heard of woods pussy?" Bucky asked as he steered Johnny toward the dining room.

Looking around the dining room, Bucky saw Sue, all five feet two inches of her, and just as big around, working in the kitchen. The way flour was flying around, Bucky suspected that Sue was making bread. Creeping up behind her, trying to be as quiet as a fart in church, Bucky poked her in the ribs. She let out a scream you could hear halfway to Boston. Spinning around, Sue let out a squeal of joy and hugged Bucky in a fond embrace.

Johnny laughed when he saw the floured hand prints on Bucky's back, and the front of him all covered with flour.

"How have you been, Mama Sue? It looks like you lost weight," Bucky said as he poked her in the side with his finger.

"The more for Clem to love," Sue replied.

"Ha," Clem said and walked back into the store.

"What have you got today?" Bucky asked, lifting the top from the big iron kettle sitting on the stove.

11

"Venison stew," Sue replied.

"Do you think you could spare a couple of bowls?"

"And bread too?" Sue asked.

"Yes, and bread too," Bucky replied.

"Go sit down and I will fix you right up," Sue said, reaching for two bowls and filling them to the top with steaming venison stew. Sue set the table and placed the stew and bread, along with a tin of fresh churned butter, on the table. Then she sat down beside Bucky and Johnny.

"I worry about you, Bucky, out there in those woods all by yourself with this crazy war going on. Those damn Indians are running wild all over the place. Nobody's safe anymore. We even had some folks burned out and murdered not more than five miles from here."

"I know, Sue. I have seen their signs all over the place. Don't worry, I plan on keeping my hair," Bucky said as he put his arm around Sue's shoulder and gave her a big squeeze.

Later, after stepping out of the dining room and into the June midday sun, Bucky looked around.

"Johnny, I'm going over to the fort and have a few words with Captain Burroughs. Tell your ma that I will be over later this afternoon."

"Come for supper. I know Ma will want you to."

"All right, I'll be there."

"Come early, Bucky," Johnny pleaded.

"Sure, Johnny, I'll be there early."

Chapter Two

After wiping a piece of bread around the plate and popping it into his mouth, Bucky got up from the table.

"Marie, you are the best cook in the world. Leave the dishes, we will pick them up later. Let's take a walk down to the river."

Marie, Bucky and Johnny walked down the path through the woods that led to the Connecticut River, where Charlie and Bucky had spent many a summer day, especially when the salmon were running.

All the settlers along the river caught them by the sackful. They would eat their fill until they were sick of them. Then they would smoke and salt them away for winter eating. For some, in the dead of winter when game was scarce, that was all they had to eat. The Connecticut salmon were so plentiful that the settlers used them as fertilizer in their vegetable gardens.

Bucky took out line from his pocket and, after cutting three poles, he tied the line to the poles while Johnny turned over rocks and picked up fish worms. They sat on the riverbank and talked about happier times with Charlie. With the approaching darkness almost upon them, Bucky gutted and cleaned the mess of perch they had caught in the cool, clean, clear waters of the Connecticut River.

Darkness had settled in when they had reached Marie's cabin. They could hear the faint sounds of a fiddle playing, floating on the air currents of the peaceful June evening.

"Ma, they are having a dance at the fort tonight. Do you care if I go?" Johnny asked.

"No, have a good time."

"See you tomorrow, Bucky?"

"Sure will."

As Johnny disappeared into the darkness, Bucky turned toward Marie.

"He's a good boy, Marie."

"He's not a boy anymore. He has grown up fast since Charlie died."

"How have you been doing?"

"I haven't had a man since Charlie died. Sometimes I go to bed and cry myself to sleep. I'm a young woman. I loved Charlie, but I need someone."

"There must have been some coming around."

"Yes, a few, but all they wanted was someone to cook for them and take care of their kids. I don't want a husband, I want you. I want you, Bucky. I need to feel you inside me for one night."

Grabbing Bucky by the hips, Marie pulled him down on top of her.

Bucky reached down and pulled Marie's dress up to her hips and moved his hand up to her thigh, then stopped as Marie moaned in anticipation.

"I'm sorry. I'm sorry, Marie. I just can't do it."

"Why? Is it because I am not an Indian? You think I won't be as good as your woods pussy?" Marie asked sarcastically.

"No, I'm sure it would be great, and I wish I could. I'm sorry, but I can't. I feel like Charlie's watching us." Bucky stood up, reached down and picked Marie up and set her on her feet. He held her for a few seconds, then turned and walked away into the night.

Marie walked into the cabin and sat down. Putting her face into hands, she cried from shame and frustration.

***

Bucky was on his bed, fully clothed and unable to sleep, which gave him plenty of time to think. He was up before first light and walked to Marie's cabin. Waiting outside, Bucky watched the sun come up. Hearing someone moving around inside the cabin, Bucky finally knocked on the door. The door swung open, and Marie stood facing Bucky with a musket in her hands.

Throwing up his hands, Bucky said jokingly, "Don't shoot, me white man."

Marie stepped outside, closed the door and propped the musket against the outside wall.

"Oh, Bucky, I am so ashamed," Marie said with downcast eyes.

"Don't be, let's forget last night."

Marie shook her head in agreement.

"Marie, I have a proposition to make to you and Johnny. I don't know how much Charlie told you about me. Knowing Charlie, as closed mouth as he was, I don't imagine he told you much. Let me tell you the story of my life. My ma died when I was born. We lived in London, England. I wouldn't say that we lived; survived like pigs was more like it. I can remember being cold and hungry most of the time. My pa, older brother and sister worked in a small shop, making shoes. The owner cheated them out of most of their wages. He even charged them for the coal to heat the place. One day when I was ten, my pa gathered us all together and told us that we were all going to Boston, a city in the colonies. He had indentured all of us to a man named Ely for seven years."

"I have heard of him," said Marie. "His name is Sam Ely. Everyone around Boston knows him. He owns a large farm, an inn, a shoe factory and other businesses in Boston. He is a very rich man. I always heard that he was fair to the people who worked for him."

"Well, I don't know about that, Marie, because about one day out from Boston we got caught in a bad storm. It blew our sails to shreds, and we lost our rudder. The storm blew us onto the rocks off of the coast of New Hampshire. Just as the ship started to break up, Pa threw me overboard and told me to swim as hard as I could. I can't remember anything. I came-to the next day, bouncing around in the back of a wagon. Cyrus Buck found me on the beach more dead than alive. He pumped the water out of me and took me home with him. Old Cyrus lived about three miles from the ocean, right next to the Boston to Portsmouth Road. I told him how my pa had indentured us to a man named Ely. He told me to keep my mouth shut. That if anyone came around he would tell them I was his grandson, Mannasas Buck.

"Did anyone come looking for survivors?" Marie asked.

"Oh, I guess they did. For at least two weeks Ely and other groups of people searched up and down the shore. They didn't find anyone. I guess I was the only one to survive. It's too bad that Pa's dream of a better life ended the night we hit those rocks. I lived with Cyrus for four years, until I was fourteen years old. He was real good to me. Cyrus taught me to read and write. He taught me how to find my way by the stars and sun. He had spent most of his life on the sea. Cyrus would spend hours telling me stories about the sea and all the places he had sailed to. After every storm we would go to the seashore and collect whatever washed ashore from the ships that met their end on the rocks offshore. Any bodies that washed ashore, Cyrus would clean their pockets of money and anything else of value, then give them a decent burial. Our house had everything, the very best dishes, cups, pots and pans, the best furniture, the finest cloth and rugs in the world. We had them by the cases. Cyrus's house was large, more than twice the size of Clem's store. He had not one but two full stories. He had built it from the finest lumber that washed ashore. I would still be there if Cyrus hadn't up and died. We just finished making six bedrooms upstairs when Cyrus caught a cold. It turned into pneumonia, and he died. Before he died, he showed me a letter addressed to a John Pope, Esq. He made me promise that if anything should happen to him that I was to bury him overlooking the ocean, then bring the letter to John Pope in Portsmouth the same day. Cyrus had left everything to me. The house, one hundred acres of land, and quite a large sum of money in one of the money houses in Portsmouth was all mine. I didn't want to stay there alone without Cyrus, and at fourteen I didn't want to be an inn keeper. I could see those mountains off in the distance, and I wanted to see what was on the other side of them. So I made a contract with Peter Wells, my neighbor, that if he would take care of the house he could use the outbuildings and fields. Once a year I send him a small token of cash for his troubles."

"How did you meet Charlie?"

"By being stupid. Somewhere between here and Concord I stopped at a trading post like Clem's. I was hungry, so I went in to eat. Being young and foolish, I guess I wasn't too careful with the way I showed my money. When I left, two men followed me. When I got down the road a ways they jumped me. What they didn't know was that Charlie noticed them eyeing my bag of money. Charlie knew what they were after, so he followed them."

"That was just like Charlie, always helping someone."

"I can tell you, Marie, if it wasn't for Charlie I wouldn't be here today. He let out a yell, and they took one look at big Charlie running at them with a musket in his hands and took off faster than a rabbit with a fox on his tail. I didn't realize it then, but that day he took me under his wing. He listened to my plans. He didn't laugh at them but gently guided me in a different direction. The rest you know. He taught me everything I know about trapping. He talked me into buying the land next to yours and helped me to build a cabin, because he said everyone should have a place to come home to. Charlie showed me what was behind those mountains. He showed me those great lakes, the St. Lawrence River, and all the little rivers and swamps where beaver were like fleas on a dog. He taught me French, and we spent time in Montreal. We spent two years with the St Francis Indians, trapping and exploring the whole area until Black Hawk, that murdering, thieving savage, took a disliking to us and stole our traps to drive us out. I guess we were lucky to get out with our scalps. Now, Marie, I want to pay Charlie back by helping you and Johnny. Marie, your cooking is the best in the world. Nobody makes bread, pies and doughnuts like you do. I will trade Cyrus's house, land and everything in it for your land and cabin. Marie, I don't want you going to Boston and working in some whorehouse."

"You have been talking to Johnny, haven't you?"

"Yes, I have. Marie, you could have your own place like Clem's, only better. I don't want the place. I don't want to be an innkeeper, and I sure as hell don't want to taste or smell saltwater again. This is where I belong, and Johnny too. I will take Johnny as a partner and teach him everything Charlie taught me. I will make a mountain man out of him."

"Bucky, it sounds too good to be true, but I can't do it. I don't have the money to get started."

"I will get you started. We'll go into Portsmouth, where you can buy what you need. I will draw the money from the money house. You can pay me back with ten percent of your profits."

"I would never be able to do it alone, with Johnny staying with you."

"You won't have to. The person who is keeping an eye on the place, Peter Wells, will help you for a fee. I guess I have taken all of your excuses from you, Marie. Do you want to talk this over with Johnny?"

"We don't have to, Bucky," Johnny said from the loft window. "Ma, this is what I want. I want to stay with Bucky."

"You're just like your pa. I guess it wouldn't be right for me to try and change you."

"Bucky, you're the best friend anybody ever had. I will never be able to repay you," Marie said, with tears in her eyes.

"You don't have to, Marie. When do you want to leave?"

"When can we leave?"

"You gather up the things you want to take. I will be back in an hour with Clem's horse and wagon," Bucky replied.

As Bucky drove Clem's horse and wagon over to Marie's cabin, a big smile spread across his face. He just knew that once Marie and Peter Wells saw each other, that Marie's frustration would come to an end.

Chapter Three

"That was a nice thing you did for Marie," Clem said to Bucky, who was sitting in the store in a rocking chair, his feet upon a small barrel.

"It was nothing. I was glad to get rid of the place; it's a weight off of my shoulders."

"Ha, don't act hard to me! I know you too well. In some ways you're softer than fresh horse shit," Clem said, making Bucky laugh.

"I'll be glad to get back in the woods. Nobody knows all your business there."

"That reminds me, Bucky, I've got something to show you." Walking to the back of the store, Clem returned with a bundle of furs. Taking a fox fur from the top, Clem held it up for Bucky to see.

"Ever see a fox fur like this before?"

Bucky stood up and took the fur from Clem.

"Yes, I have seen this before. When did old Moe Hood come in?"

"Moe Hood? I haven't seen Old Moe since last summer!"

"Who brought these furs in?"

"The Morse brothers, Jim and Ike. Why do you ask?"

"Because those bastards stole them from old Moe."

"Are you sure?"

"You are damn right I'm sure. I stopped and saw Old Moe when I came back two weeks ago. We polished off a jug of cider. He showed me that pelt and told me how he had seen that fox running around. Moe told me he spent weeks trying to trap him. He said he was beginning to think that fox was smarter than him. He was real proud of that pelt. Neither of us had ever seen a fox like this, with those streaks running through his red fur from head to toe. Clem, Moe would never give up these furs without a fight. Besides, Moe always put his mark on his furs."

Turning the pelt inside-out, Bucky pointed to an "M. H."

"Clem, that is Moe's mark. I know, because Old Moe can't write. I showed him how to make those initials. If those bastards have hurt Old Moe, I'll kill them."

Looking into Bucky's eyes, Clem knew that it was not an idle threat.

"Those Morses are lazy, good-for-nothing bastards. A few years back Charlie and I took them on as partners, along with four Frenchie friends from Montreal. We went up the St. Lawrence River, through the Great Lakes, and then snuck into Hudson Bay country up near Thunder Bay. We planned on hunting and trapping for two years. Jim and Ike wouldn't do a lick of work around the camp or on the trap lines. So we kicked them out of camp. They cried and said that we would be sorry. We think they went to the nearest Hudson Bay Fortified Trading Post, because the next thing we knew the place was swarming with Frenchies and Indians. We gathered up what we could and got the hell out of there with them right on our ass. We beat them to the St. Lawrence. After about a half day on the river, Charlie came up with a plan to outsmart them. We pulled to shore, unloaded the furs and hid them in the bushes, turned canoes around and paddled back up the river. When we met them coming down the river, they stopped and asked us if we had met anyone going down the river with canoes loaded with furs. Charlie said, 'Yes, about a half hour ago.' They dug their paddles in and took off like a preacher after a sinner. When they got out of sight we turned around and went back to where we had stashed our furs. We knew that we couldn't go to

Montreal, for they would be looking for us, so we divided the furs. The Frenchies went their way, and Charlie and I cut cross-country, dodging Indians all the way, until we got to Crown Point. We sold our furs to some trader for real cheap. Charlie and I were just too damn tired to carry them any farther. That was the last time I saw Ike and Jim Morse."

"What are we going to do?" Clem asked.

"Have you paid them for the furs yet?"

"No," Clem replied.

"Can you hold off paying them for a couple of days? Johnny and I will go and check up on Old Moe, and I want them here when I get back. Will you tell Captain Burroughs what I suspect?"

"Don't you worry, Bucky, I will take care of everything back here."

Chapter Four

The canoe glided smoothly up the Connecticut River. Johnny and Bucky's paddles were moving in perfect time, raising, then dipping into the water with powerful strokes. *We are making good time,* Bucky thought to himself as he looked up at the noonday sun. *Charlie taught Johnny real well. Another year and I will be hard-pressed to keep up with him. He is pushing me almost to my limit,* Bucky thought with a grin on his face.

"Bucky, look over there. What do you make of that?" Johnny asked, pointing toward the New Hampshire side of the river.

Johnny's question interrupted Bucky's thought. Looking in the direction of Johnny's outstretched arm, Bucky said, "I don't know. It's a fire of some kind. It's too little smoke for someone burning brush, and too large for chimney smoke. I don't like the looks of it. I think we better check it out."

"Maybe it's that young couple that stopped at the fort last fall. I heard Clem tell Pa that they bought some land up this way. Pa said it was up near Old Moe."

Bucky and Johnny moved quietly through the woods until they could see a small clearing. Creeping up to the clearing, they could see a small log cabin, its door open and hanging by one hinge. The roof had burned, and its wall were smoldering, sending smoke spiraling lazily up into the sky. There was a body laying face down near the door. Bucky and Johnny advanced slowly toward the cabin, with every nerve taunt and eyes darting around the clearing. Bucky rolled the body over onto its back with his foot.

"Do you know him?" Bucky asked.

"Yes, that's him," Johnny replied, looking down at his face with his wide open eyes staring back at him.

"Damn Indians," he uttered, half to himself.

"Didn't you say there was a young girl with him?"

"Yes, but I don't see her."

"I don't think this is the work of Indians, but if it is, they may have taken her with them. I'll check inside the cabin. You look around out here."

Bucky had just stepped through the cabin door when he heard Johnny exclaim, "Oh my God! Bucky, come here."

Bucky walked around the side of the cabin wall and saw Johnny coughing, gagging and throwing up. Bucky stepped around Johnny and looked on the ground in back of the cabin. Bucky looked down at the body of a young girl who might have been pretty at one time but was beyond telling now. She was completely naked, her clothes ripped from her body and thrown every which way. She had been raped, Bucky guessed, probably many times. When they had all they wanted from her, they hacked her to pieces with an ax. Bucky saw blood spatters on the ground nearby. One arm was completely cut off. What was left of her head was almost cut off, just hanging by a small piece of skin. Her whole body was covered with cuts from the ax that someone had kept swinging until their arms were too tired to lift the ax again. Bucky walked over to where Johnny was sitting on a stump, his face as white as a sheet.

Bucky put his hand on Johnny's shoulder and said, "Johnny, this is something you will never get used to. Your stomach will get hardened to it, but if you are human, you never will. If you feel up to it, see if you can find a shovel and dig them a grave. I'll take care of the bodies so we can give them a decent burial."

Looking around the burned cabin, Bucky found a piece of white cotton canvas folded in the corner of the room. Bucky wrapped the young girl in the canvas and carried her to the shallow grave that Johnny had dug. Bucky looked but couldn't find anything to wrap the young man's body in, so Bucky took hold of the young man's feet and started to drag him toward the open grave. Bucky, looking down at the heels of the young man's boots, suddenly stopped.

"Damn!" Bucky exclaimed. "I should have noticed that before. Johnny, I am sure this was not done by Indians."

"How can you be so sure?"

"Because there are no signs here that say Indians. Look around, what do you see?"

Looking around Johnny said, "Nothing."

"That's right. If the house wasn't burned down you would think they went for a walk in the woods. I know Indians, and Indians don't do this. Look at those chickens running around loose. They would have killed them and roasted them over the cabin fire. Also, do you notice any arrows sticking into anything?"

"No, not a one," Johnny replied.

"Right. Very few Indians own muskets, but they are experts with a bow and arrow, tomahawk and knife. Seeing as how there was only a man and a woman here, they would have crept up on them and bashed their heads in with a tomahawk. They would lift their scalps to bring back to their village and hang them from their lodge poles. To an Indian that is a sign of bravery, and also for every English scalp they bring back, the French fatten their purse. Knowing Indians like I do, I suspect that a few French scalps have graced the lodge poles of quite a few Indian villages that the French have paid for. The one thing I overlooked was staring us right in the face. The only moccasin prints around here are mine. Now look at those boot prints right there," Bucky said, pointing at the boot prints in the soft soil around the cabin.

"It left a print like a 'V' in the dirt. Do you see any marks on these?" Bucky asked, holding the dead man's boots up for Johnny to look at.

"No," Johnny replied.

"I know who killed these folks, and I am going to see them hang. It was the Morse brothers. I have watched Ike Morse sit around all day cutting notches in a stick. I have also seen the stupid bastard cut notches in the heel of his boots. His hobby is going to get him hung this time."

Bucky and Johnny buried the young couple side by side and covered the gravesite with stones to keep the animals from digging the bodies up. Johnny said a short prayer that Marie had taught him, while Bucky scooped up a perfect boot print, put it in a pan and covered it with grass. Bucky didn't join in the prayer. It wasn't that Bucky didn't believe in God, because he did in his own way. It was because he was in a hurry to get to Old Moe's. He was afraid of what they would find. Bucky and Johnny hurried to the river. Bucky sprinkled water on the grass that covered the boot print and put the pan in the front of the canoe. When they reached the bottom of Ottouquechee Falls they beached the canoe on the Grants side of the river. They carried the canoe inland a short ways and covered it with brush.

"You're wondering why we didn't carry the canoe around the falls?" Bucky asked with a grin, seeing the look on Johnny's face.

"I am wondering."

"Charlie and I figured this out years ago. We stashed a canoe above Ottouquechee Falls and one above White River Falls, so whichever way we were going we would always have a canoe waiting so we wouldn't have to carry a canoe around the falls. It saves a lot of time coming and going. Pretty smart of your pa and I, wouldn't you say?' Bucky asked with a laugh.

The late afternoon sun was just starting to go down in the west as Bucky and Johnny paddled up the White River.

"Bucky, how much farther?" Johnny asked.

"Not much. We are almost there, about a mile I'd say."

"Don't you think we should head for shore and scout the rest of the way by foot?"

"I don't think we are in any danger, Johnny. I think it is safe to go right in. I believe the danger is back at Clem's trading post, swilling down rum with stolen money."

They paddled in silence for a while as their eyes scanned both sides of the river. Bucky broke the silence.

"Over there, Johnny, see the opening on the left side of the river? That's where Moe's cabin is. Keep your eyes open," Bucky added as an afterthought.

Bucky was out of the canoe before it hit the shore. Johnny was beside him in a split second with his musket held tightly in his hands and his mouth as dry as a maple leaf in October. They stood there looking at Moe's cabin and the open clearing in front of it. Bucky knew the layout of Moe's place very well. He and Charlie had spent many a day with Moe, drinking rum and cider until they were so bleary eyed they couldn't have seen an Indian if one stood in front of them. Moe's cabin was built into a dirt bank. The three walls showing were built of stone, with a heavy log roof covered with sod. Moe always said that he felt as safe here as in his mother's arms. The door was wide open, with no sign of life showing.

Bucky whispered to Johnny, "You take the left side of the clearing and I will take the other. We will meet at the cabin."

Johnny started to move through the clearing. He had taken about a dozen steps when he came across a pool of blood. Looking to his left, Johnny saw a body laying in the underbrush.

"Bucky, over here!" Johnny called. Bending down, he put his hand on Moe's neck. "I think he's alive, he's still warm!" Johnny exclaimed excitedly. Johnny was dragging Moe into the clearing when Bucky came running over.

Ripping open Moe's shirt, Bucky exclaimed, "They shot him! The bastards shot him in the back! He's lost a lot of blood. We have got to stop the bleeding or he's a goner. Doctor Hastings back at the fort is his only chance. I hope we aren't too late."

Bucky ran to the cabin and came back with a blanket. He cut the blanket into strips.

"Johnny, hold him up in a sitting position while I try to stop the bleeding."

Bucky made two thick pads, one for the wound in Moe's back and also for the one in front. Taking another strip of the blanket, he wrapped it tightly around the two pads and secured it with a piece of rawhide.

"God, Bucky, look at his head!" Johnny exclaimed.

"That's what a musket butt will do to you, Johnny. They clubbed him after they shot him just to be safe."

Bucky carried Moe to the canoe and placed him down in the middle. Running back to the cabin, Bucky returned with a blanket and a metal dish. He put the blanket over Moe, then took the dish and scooped up a boot print with a 'V' in its heel, covered it with damp grass and put it in the canoe. Bucky and Johnny pushed the canoe away from shore and started back down the White River. When they reached the White River Falls, darkness had set in. The sky was clear and the moon shone bright. Bucky and Johnny, working as a team, had no trouble getting around the two falls, each taking turns carrying Moe. They didn't talk much to each other, for they knew they were in a race against time. They made good time coming down the Connecticut River after they got past Ottauguechee Falls, but even then it was past midnight when they sighted the outline of Fort Number Four. Reaching shore, Bucky picked up Moe and put him over his shoulder.

Turning to Johnny, he said, "I am going to bring Moe to my cabin. You go get Doctor Hastings and bring him there. Don't say a word to anyone."

Bucky laid Moe on the bed and covered him with a blanket. Moe's head was sticking out from under the blanket, and to Bucky it looked like death had already set in. Bucky busied himself by building a fire to get the dampness from the cabin.

"Where the hell are they? What's taking them so long?" Bucky had just gotten the words out of his mouth when Johnny and Doctor Hastings walked in. Doctor Hastings walked over to the bed and pulled the blanket down.

"He hasn't moved or said anything since we found him, Doctor," Bucky said.

Doctor Hastings just nodded his head as he examined Moe.

"I need hot water. I have got to clean up these wounds," he said as he rolled up his sleeves.

To Bucky and Johnny, Moe looked better after Doctor Hastings had cleaned him up and changed his bandages.

"One thing in his favor, that musket ball went right straight through, so it's a clean wound. He has lost a lot of blood. You have got to keep him warm and hope he doesn't get pneumonia. If he does, he's gone. I don't know how long he'll be out from that whack on the head, but when he does wake up he is going to have one hell of a headache," Doctor Hastings said as he washed his hands.

Chapter Five

Bucky, Johnny and Clem sat in Captain Burrough's kitchen, sipping a cup of tea Mrs. Burroughs had brewed for them.

"You make a great cup of tea, Alice," Bucky said with a smile.

"It should be. That's some of my best Irish whiskey she put in it," Captain Burroughs said, giving Alice a loving look.

"I thought you needed something good after that rot gut whiskey Clem sells you," Alice replied.

The men had a good laugh at Clem's expense as Alice walked from the kitchen.

"Well, Captain, how do you want to handle it?" Bucky asked.

"I will officially arrest them and charge them with the murder of the young couple and the attempted murder and robbery of Moe. Where are they now?"

"They have been spending most of their time with the Indians down by the river, drinking rum and chasing after any of the young Indian girls that get close to them. Right now they are over at the store, waiting for Sue to make them breakfast. I told her to drag it out as long as she could," Clem replied.

"We might as well get it over with. If you boys are ready, let's get them before they get wind of what we know and hightail it into the hills."

As Captain Burroughs, Bucky, Johnny and Clem walked into the dining room from the store entryway, Bucky ordered Johnny to stand by the door and not let either of the Morse brothers out.

Captain Burroughs, Bucky and Clem advanced to the table, with muskets held ready. Ike and Jim Morse were sitting on opposite sides of a small table with their feet propped up on a chair. They smelled of stale rum and unwashed bodies. The last time their bodies felt water was when they got caught out in the rain. Ike and Jim looked at them with sulking eyes. Looking at the muskets pointed at them, Jim Morse was the first to speak.

"Clem, can't you get your old lady to move faster?"

"What's this all about?" Ike asked, pointing at the muskets leveled at him and Ike.

"Ike and Jim Morse, I am arresting you and holding you for trial for the murder of Carol and Pete Smith, and the attempted murder and robbery of Moe Hood. If Old Moe doesn't pull through, it will be three counts of murder."

Jim jumped for his musket that was leaning against the table. Bucky was faster. He stepped forward and swung his musket barrel across Jim's forehead. Jim fell to the floor, out cold, with blood running down his face. Bucky put the end of the musket barrel between Jim's eyes.

Captain Burroughs jumped forward and put his hand on Bucky's chest. "Don't do it. Don't do it, Bucky. Save him for the trial."

Bucky slowly moved the musket away. The knuckles on his hands holding the musket were as white as snow. He unclenched his teeth and slowly let his muscles relax.

Ike jumped up and started to run for the door. Johnny met him and swung the flat of his musket butt into Ike's stomach. You could hear the smack and whoosh of air from Ike's lungs throughout the room. Johnny followed through with his swing, sending Ike into a gasping heap beside Jim.

"Get them up. We will lock them up in the storeroom at the fort. Can we hold the trial here, Clem?" Captain Burroughs asked.

"Sure can," Clem replied with a smile, visualizing all the extra business he would do.

"Good, I will see if I can get Ensign Sartwell to defend them."

"Don't need anyone to defend us. We will defend ourselves," Ike gasped.

"Suit yourself. Trial begins Monday morning at ten. Now get them the hell out of here," Burroughs ordered.

Chapter Six

Bucky and Clem stood down front in the makeshift courtroom, watching the people file in. Bucky watched Mary and Ben Stearns walk into the room and take seats down near the front of the room. Mary's eyes wandered around until she spotted Bucky, then a large smile crept across her face. Bucky returned her smile and nodded his head in acknowledgment.

"I'll bet you would give all of next years furs for just one peek up her dress," Clem whispered, to Bucky.

"Why, you old bastard, aren't you getting too old to be thinking of that?"

"You are never to old for that," Clem replied with a laugh, giving Bucky a slap on the back.

The courtroom soon filled to its capacity with people standing three and four deep around the room, and people spilling outside were hoping to hear and maybe get a peek of the goings on inside.

"Where in hell did they all come from?" Bucky asked.

"They came from all over. News travels fast, and this is big news. This is something they will tell their children and grandchildren for years. I wouldn't want to miss it."

Clem was interrupted by the shouting from outside.

"Here they come! Give them to us, Captain, we'll take care of them for you. Let's hang the bastards now. Murderers! Scum!"

Captain Burroughs stepped into the courtroom with the Morses close behind, followed by Captain Spaffard, Lieutenant Parker, Lieutenant Willard and Ensign Sartwell. Captain Burroughs pointed to two vacant chairs in the front of the room. The guard detail pushed the Morses toward the chairs and roughly sat them down and untied their hands.

Ike and Jim looked around the courtroom nervously. Jim, with a bloody bandage around his head, and Ike, his eyes large as an owl, listened to the threats being shouted at them inside and outside the courtroom.

Captain Burroughs called Clem over. "For God's sake, Clem, can't you open the windows? This place stinks."

Clem walked over to the windows and opened them wide. The people outside immediately crowed around the windows, shutting off any air that might flow through.

"All right, everybody, settle down," Captain Burroughs ordered as he banged the table with the hammer that Clem had supplied him.

"This place smells like an outhouse. We are packed very close in here, so let's respect each other. If you have to expel gas, go outside."

"Better outside than inside,. Captain," shouted a young man standing in the back of the room who suddenly let out a loud fart.

"Get that son of a bitch and throw him out!" Captain Burroughs shouted to the people in the back of the room. The crowd roared with laughter as they pushed the young man out of the door.

"Goddamn it, if you don't have any respect for each other, at least have some for the king's court. Any more of this horse shit and I will clear you all out of this courtroom."

The room grew so quiet that you could hear the floor boards squeak as the spectators shifted their feet.

Captain Burroughs banged the hammer on the table, making everyone jump.

"This court is now in session. The court of King George versus Jim and Ike Morse. Captain Spaffard will handle the prosecution. The Morses are acting in their own defense."

The crowd, knowing that the Morses couldn't read and write, couldn't suppress their laughter. Captain Burroughs rapped for silence and continued. "We need a jury, and I will pick them. When you are picked, go sit in the chair on my left." Captain Burroughs randomly picked twelve men from the room.

"Are there any of you men who do not think you should be on this jury?"

The men responded by shaking their heads.

"Captain Spaffard?" Burroughs asked.

"They seem fine to me; I have no problem with them."

"Jim and Ike, do you disapprove of anyone on this jury?"

"What in hell difference does it make? We aren't going to get a fair trial anyway," Jim replied.

"You will get as fair a trial here as in any of the other colonies," Captain Burroughs said sternly.

"Captain Spaffard, if you are ready, bring your first witness forward."

"Thank you, Captain. I call Clem Ross as my first witness. Clem, did Jim and Ike Morse leave any furs with you?"

"Yes, they did. As you know, I buy and sell furs as well as food for the stomach, clothes to keep the body warm, ball and powder also."

"Just answer the question. You aren't here to sell your goods," Captain Burroughs said, interrupting Clem, which brought a snicker from the crowd.

"Yes, sir, that they did," Clem replied, with a wink at the people in the room.

"Do you remember seeing this pelt?" Captain Spaffard asked, holding up the fox pelt with the unusual design.

"Yes, it was on top of the pile of furs they brought in for me to look at. They were real proud of that one. Ike said they should get more money for that one."

"What happened next?"

"About four hours later Bucky came into the store, and I showed him the fox fur. I asked if he had ever seen a fox fur like that. Bucky said, 'Yes. Where is Old Moe? When did he come in?' I told Bucky that I hadn't seen Moe. Bucky said that the fur belonged to Old Moe, that Old Moe showed it to him two weeks before, when he stopped at his cabin on the way down the river. Then Bucky said he knew it was Old Moe's fur, because his mark was on the inside. He showed me a small 'M. H.' stamped in the pelt. I checked the rest of the furs, and they all had Moe's mark on them. Bucky said the bastards must have stolen them, since Old Moe would never let the furs go without a fight. That is what Bucky said when I told him who brought them in."

"That's a lie. We didn't steal them, we bought them from Moe Hood," Jim said, jumping to his feet.

"Sit down. You will get your chance to speak later," Captain Burroughs shouted so he could be heard above the crowd.

"What happened next?" Captain Spaffard asked.

"Well, Bucky asked me if I would not pay Jim and Ike for the furs for a couple of days. He wanted to keep them here while he and Johnny Scott went back up the river to Moe's cabin to check up on his well-being. He also asked me to tell Captain Burroughs that he feared those two bastards might have done Old Moe in," Clem said, pointing at Ike and Jim.

"Burroughs, he has no right to call us names. We have done nothing wrong!" Jim shouted.

"You're right. Captain Spaffard, instruct your witnesses to watch their mouths."

"Sorry, Your Honor, I was just repeating what Bucky said," Clem said, bowing to Captain Burroughs.

"Sit down or go sell some beans or something," Captain Burroughs said, then waited for the laughter to die down.

"Call your next witness, Captain Spaffard."

"Yes, sir, I would like to call Bucky as my next witness. Bucky, after your conversation with Clem, you and Johnny Scott started up the Connecticut. Tell us what happened that day."

Bucky leaned back in the chair and looked directly at Mary Stearns. The sun was shining through the open window. Its rays were landing on Mary's red hair, which seemed to light up the whole room. Mary returned his stare with a smile.

Captain Spaffard followed Bucky's eyes and spotted the sun shining on Mary's hair.

"Mary, will you put a hat on? You are blinding us over here," he said jokingly.

The crowd laughed. All but Ben Stearns, who sat there like a bump on a log.

Bucky shifted his eyes to the Morses and began.

"Johnny and I pushed real hard. We were making good time when Johnny noticed smoke on the Grants side of the river. It didn't look right. It seemed to be smoldering, not like brush burning. Johnny said there was a young couple homesteading up that way, and with all the Indian war parties roaming around, we decided to check it out. What we found wasn't pretty. There was a young man laying face down in front of the cabin. He had been shot in the back. There was a young girl laying in back of the cabin. She had been hacked to pieces with an ax that was nearby. I think she had been raped, but I couldn't tell, since there wasn't enough of her to tell. We buried them in their front yard right near a bed of wild flowers."

The crowd that was in a laughing mood a short time before was now in a somber mood. Some of them remembered the young couple who had stopped at the fort for a few days.

"Was it Indians, Bucky?"

"No, it was not Indians. They didn't even do a good job of making it look like Indians did it. They didn't even do a good job of burning the cabin down. It just smoldered away. They did not scalp either one of them. There were no arrows or moccasin tracks around. This was done by white men."

"You keep saying 'they.' Do you think there was more than one man?"

"I think there were two. We will prove it before this day is over," Bucky said, looking directly at the Morses.

Captain Spaffard walked over to a table and came back with a plate full of dirt. "Bucky, do you recognize this?"

"Looks like a plate full of dirt to me," someone wisecracked. No one in the crowd laughed; they were not in a laughing mood anymore.

"Yes, that is a boot print that I picked up near the young girl that was killed. If you look, there is a 'V' mark in the heel."

Captain Spaffard showed the heel print to the jury.

The people in the courtroom craned their necks to look. He placed it on the table.

The Morses started to squirm in their seats. Jim gave Ike a dirty look. Ike moved his feet around as if trying to hide them.

"Go on, Bucky, if you please."

"Johnny and I really put the paddles to the river and got to Moe's place late in the afternoon. The cabin door was open, and there was no sign of life. We started looking for what we thought would be Moe's body.

"Johnny found him laying near some brush. He was alive, but just barely. He had been shot in the back. The ball went straight through, and he had lost a lot of blood. Someone had whacked him on the head with a musket butt. I didn't know if he would be alive when we got to the fort, but we had to try. I bandaged his wounds the best I could, and we got back to the fort after midnight. I carried him to my cabin while Johnny went and got Doctor Hastings. He's still alive as of this morning. Doctor Hastings said that if he comes down with pneumonia he's gone. He hasn't come to yet. Doctor Hastings said he doesn't know if he ever will."

"Do you recognize this, Bucky?"

"Yes, it's a boot print that I took at Moe's place. It has the same mark as the other one, and if you take off Ike's left boot you'll find that 'V' matches the one in the left heel of his boot."

"Captain, could we see that left boot?"

"Ike, take your boots off," Burroughs ordered.

"I don't have to, Captain. I have rights too, don't I?"

"Take off those boots or we will take them off of your dead body," yelled a huge frontier farmer.

Ike took one look at the man and yanked off his boots.

"Suffering God! Don't you ever wash?" Captain Burroughs asked as the stench filled the room. "Hurry up and do what you have to do and give him back his boots."

37

Captain Spaffard took the left boot and put it up to the two dirt prints.

"They are a perfect match. These prints were made by this boot." He held them up so that everyone in the room could see. He tossed the boot to Ike. You could hear a murmur going through the crowd.

"Let's hang them now. We have heard enough, so let's get it over with. Let them dance on the end of a rope!" yelled members of the crowd in the makeshift courtroom.

"I will have none of that talk here or I will clear this courtroom. Anyone making a move toward the Morses will be shot," Burroughs said, and slammed a pistol on the table for effect.

"Bucky, Clem, come over here," Captain Burroughs ordered.

"This crowd is getting ugly, I may need your help to protect the Morses. Can I count on your help if I need it? If they hang, it is going to be done right."

"You can count on us," Bucky replied.

"Do you have anything else, Captain Spaffard?"

"No, I am done. You can give the Morses a chance to try and lie their way out of this one."

"Ike, Jim, are you ready to defend yourselves?" Captain Burroughs asked.

"Yes, Captain, we are," Jim replied.

"The floor's all yours," Burroughs said.

"Thanks, Captain," Jim said as he stood up and faced the crowd in the room.

"Folks, Bucky has painted an awfully dark picture of Ike and me, but it is not true. Now we are not saying that we were not at that young couple's place, or at Moe's either, because we were. That is why Ike's boot print was found in the ground by Bucky. You see, Ike and I had been trapping farther up north, and we had a good supply of furs when we were jumped by a small Indian war party. Barely got away with our scalps."

Ike sat in the chair and nodded his head in agreement to everything Jim said. He then stood up beside Jim and added, "Those howling savages stole everything from our camp and left us with only the clothes on our backs and our muskets."

"You never owned anything else anyways," Clem said.

"Clem, one more outburst like that and I will have you removed from this courtroom."

"You can't, Captain. I own the place."

"I can and I will," Burroughs said, glaring at Clem.

"As I was saying before I was interrupted by that fool—" Ike said, looking at Clem.

Clem's face turned white and he took a step toward Ike. Bucky put his arm out and held Clem back.

"As I was saying," Ike said, giving a sideways glance at Clem. "We outsmarted those howling savages and made for Moe's, where we knew we would be safe. We offered Moe a fair price for his furs, and he took us up on our offer. This is why Bucky found our boot prints around Moe's cabin, and also why we had Moe's furs to sell to Clem. When we left Moe he was alive and well. As for that young couple, we didn't know anybody was homesteading in the area. It has been some time since we have been down this way. We were following the river down when we heard someone chopping wood. We found a young couple working hard, clearing the land of brush and trees. We stopped and passed pleasantries with them and had a meal of fried salmon and fiddle heads, then continued on our way. They were alive and kicking when we left, and of course that is why our boot prints where there too."

Clem nudged Bucky with his elbow. "Johnny wants you."

Bucky looked up and saw Johnny standing by the door, motioning for him to come outside. Bucky expected the worst, for Johnny had stayed with Moe.

"What is it, Johnny?" Bucky asked.

"Old Moe just came to, and he is raising hell."

Bucky ran to the cabin and burst through the door. He was greeted by, "Jesus Christ, what are you trying to do, hatch chickens in this place? For God's sake, Bucky, open some windows."

"I guess you are going to live," Bucky said with a smile.

"Those Goddamn Morses aren't going to live when I catch up with them. How did I get here?"

"Ike and Jim tried to sell your furs to Clem. Johnny and I went to check up on you, found you more dead than alive, and brought you down here. We have Jim and Ike on trial right now over at Clem's store for the murder of the young couple that were homesteading near you, also for the attempted murder and robbery of you."

"Oh no! They didn't kill those nice kids, did they?"

"Yes, they did. I won't tell you how; you would not want to know."

"I helped them survive last winter. They were long on ambition and short on knowledge."

"Do you feel like facing the Morses?"

"I would like to, but every time I try to get up I get weak and dizzy."

"How do you feel now?" Bucky asked. He had rolled up a blanket and put it behind Moe, getting him into a half-sitting position.

"Not bad, just a little dizzy. It seems to be going away," Moe said, blinking his eyes.

"Good, I think I can get you to the trial."

Jim Morse was telling the people in the courtroom how he and Ike wished that Moe would regain consciousness, when he was interrupted by laughter outside the courtroom. A few seconds later Bucky entered, pushing a wheelbarrow with Moe inside it.

"Did I hear you say that you wished Moe was here? Well, you just got your wish," Clem said with a laugh.

"You bastards! You two rotten bastards! You tried to kill me, and from what I hear you robbed me of my furs and only God knows what else. Goddamn it, someone get me a musket and I will kill the cock suckers right now."

"Watch your talk, Moe. We have ladies present," Captain Burroughs said.

"To hell with the ladies, those bastards tried to kill me, Captain."

"You bastards, I mean Morses, sit down. I want them bound with their hands behind their backs," Captain Burroughs instructed the armed guards.

"Now I will ask the questions. Moe, tell us what happened."

"Those two came sneaking out of the woods. I told them to get the hell out of here, that I didn't want them around. They wanted something to eat. I told them they could starve for all I cared. I told them to make tracks, and I reached for my musket, but they got the drop on me. They were going to make me load my canoe with my own furs, but I kicked the canoe out into the river and it floated away. Then I made a break for the woods. They shot me in the back and smacked me in the head with a musket butt. I don't remember anything else until I came to in Bucky's cabin with one hell of a headache."

Turning to the jury, Captain Burroughs said, "I think we have heard enough. Are you ready to give a verdict? Do you want to talk it over?"

"No, Captain, we are ready. We find the Morses guilty," said a juror, who took it upon himself to act as spokesman for the rest of the jury.

"Ike and Jim Morse, you have been found guilty of the murder of the Smiths, and attempted murder and robbery of Moe Hood. I sentence you to be hung by the neck until you are dead. Sentence to be carried out at six o'clock tomorrow morning. This trial is over. Take them back to the fort," Captain Burroughs ordered the armed guard.

Clem, Johnny and Bucky stood beside the wheelbarrow that held Old Moe, and watched Jim and Ike walk out of the courtroom with Captain Burroughs close behind.

"Bucky, will you wheel me back to your cabin? I am real tired, and I would like to lay down for a spell," Moe asked.

Walking over to the group, Doctor Hastings said, "I'll take him back, Bucky. I would like to check him over."

"Fine, I will be there later."

"Don't hurry, Bucky, I will be all right," Moe said.

Bucky walked outside and looked around at the crowd. It had started to take on a carnival atmosphere. Some of the women were spreading blankets on the ground and putting homemade items out for sale, while the men were standing around in small groups, passing jugs of hard cider and rum back and forth. In a few hours most of the men would be roaring drunk. Some would be docile as little kittens, while some would be walking around looking for a fight. Many of the women would be going home tomorrow carrying the makings of babies in their bodies. Bucky could see Mary's red hair bobbing along, stopping every now and then to talk to the ladies and look over the items they had for sale. The thoughts that Bucky had of Mary he knew he shouldn't be having, for she was married and nothing could ever come of them. She made strange feelings go through his body; feelings he had never felt before; feelings that were not entirely of a sexual nature. Bucky had taken plenty of girls, mostly Indian girls, and might even have an Indian papoose or two running around somewhere, but no one made him feel like a lovesick moose like Mary did. As Mary walked toward Bucky in her homemade dress, he wondered what she would look like in a store-bought blue or green dress with a hat with a pretty feather sitting on top of her head, like he had seen the ladies wear in Boston and Montreal.

"Hi, Bucky, you look deep in thought. What are you thinking about?" Mary asked.

"You," Bucky replied.

Mary looked at Bucky and didn't know what to say; her cheeks turned as red as her hair. Turning away, she asked, "Have you seen Ben?"

"I haven't really been looking for him," Bucky replied with a grin.

"Hi, Mary, are you looking for Ben?"

"Yes, Johnny, have you seen him?"

"He is over there. They are getting ready to have a knife throwing contest," Johnny said, pointing to a crowd of men and women standing by the stockade wall of the fort.

"Come on, Bucky, let's show them our stuff."

Bucky, Mary and Johnny walked over to the crowd. Someone had drawn a picture of a man on a large board and wrote "Frenchie" above the heart they drew on its chest. The crowd roared with laughter when they hung it on the stockade fence. They drew a line in the dirt about twenty-five feet from the target. The frontier farmers and trappers took turns throwing knifes at the "Frenchie" target, some missing, some hitting it with the back of the knife handle, which drew some good-natured laughter from the crowd. Ben hitched up his britches and stepped up to the line and threw his knife. It flew through the air and landed an inch to the right of the heart. He turned and looked with a look on his face that looked almost like a smile to Bucky. Bucky stepped up to the line and drew his knife from its case and threw it all in one motion. It arched through the air and landed in the right-hand side of the heart. Johnny stepped to the line and drew his knife from its case and threw it just like Bucky. It turned once in mid-flight and struck square in the center of the heart. Walking over to retrieve their knives, Johnny said, "You let me win."

"No, I didn't, Johnny. We both threw well. We learned from the same man. You threw well, Ben."

Ben just grunted and walked away. They heard him say to Mary, "Just a couple of lucky throws."

"God, Bucky, what a poor loser. How could Mary have married him?"

"I don't know. I have been asking myself that for quite a while."

Bucky and Johnny entered many contests and games, winning some and losing others. Johnny won the ax throwing contest, Bucky came in dead last. Bucky won the tomahawk throwing and musket shooting. The big contest of the day was the canoe paddling contest on the Connecticut River. Twenty two-man teams paddled a mile up the river, where the finish line was the boat landing by the fort. The canoes lined up across the river. When it looked like they were all lined up, Captain Burroughs, who was standing in the fort tower, raised his pistol and fired a shot into the air. The race was on. Bucky and Johnny dug in their paddles and shot ahead with the others close behind. The lead changed back and forth many times the first half-mile, and then the others started to fall farther and farther behind. Buck and Johnny took the lead. Bucky could see out of the corner of his eyes that the prow of a canoe was slowly gaining on them. He didn't dare to chance a look to see who it was. He could hear the crowd yelling encouragement from the riverbank. Bucky could sense more than see the finish line, when the other canoe suddenly shot ahead and beat them by a foot. The crowd grew silent. Bucky turned around to see who had beat them. He rocked the canoe, and over he and Johnny went into the Connecticut River. The crowd on the river bank hooted and hollered and thought that a good end to the race. The winning canoe turned around and helped Bucky and Johnny and their canoe get back to the boat landing. It was then that Bucky learned the team that beat them was made up of two Indians who stayed around the fort all year long. Reaching shore, Bucky tipped the Indian's canoe over, dumping the Indians into the water. Putting his arms around their shoulders, all four of them walked ashore, soaking wet.

Chapter Seven

"Bucky, you're wet."

"Yup, I took a bath in the Connecticut River."

"I have been meaning to tell you that you could use one. Must be all of those years you spent with the Indians. Their ways are beginning to rub off on you," Clem said, and gave Sue a slap on the bottom as she walked by.

"Don't pay any attention to him, Bucky," Sue said as she rubbed her backside.

"I don't, Sue. Believe me, I don't," Bucky replied with a grin.

Leaning against the trading post's open doorway and watching the frontier farmers and their families walk by, Bucky could hear the sounds of sawing and hammering being carried by the summer breeze over the stockade wall from inside Fort Number Four.

"They building the hanging tree?" he asked.

"Yup, while you have been playing, some of us have been working. It's too bad we have to hang them, but I guess they deserve it. Such a waste. They aren't worth the price of the lumber to build the hanging tree."

"I guess it is the times. Clem, I am tired of all of this killing. God knows I have done my share and probably will do more before it is all over. We have been fighting for as long as I can remember. The French and English go to war, then they sign a treaty. One of them breaks it and they start fighting again. This is the fourth time, and I hope it is the last. I know good French people, and I know good Indians, and they would like to see this end too. Most of the tribes are friendly. They like the French better than they do us. The French are not after their land. They trap the beaver and other fur-bearing animals. They live with the Indians, marry the Indian girls, have children, and some stay until they die. They leave the land the way they found it.

"Now the English move in and push them off of their land and build cities and towns all over the place. Just like here at Number Four. They cut down the forest, build homes, till the land, plant crops and stay. When the Indians complain, the English make war on them. Men, women and children, those that survive, are forced to give up the land that has been theirs for centuries. I don't know when it will all end, but one thing I do know is that the Indians will fight to the last man. Those snooty English bastards don't think any more of us than they do the Indians. They think of us as ignorant piles of shit. I think we should grab them by their royal asses and throw them into the ocean and go our own way."

"Jesus Christ, Bucky, don't say that out loud. If someone should hear you they would arrest you for treason and hang you alongside the Morses."

"Clem, if they hang everyone who is thinking and saying what I just said, they wouldn't have anyone around here to kiss their asses. Mark my word, Clem, someday it will happen."

Clem didn't say a word. He leaned on the counter and nodded his head in agreement.

Bucky watched a farmer he had seen a few times around the fort take a fiddle out of its case and start to tune it up. A young man walked over to him with a fiddle under his arm. They talked a few minutes, then started to play a few practice tunes. Bucky listened to the sweet sounds coming from the fiddles floating on the late afternoon air. Men, women and children started to gather around the two men and asked them to play their favorite tunes. An old man from the crowd joined the two fiddle players and started beating time with two metal spoons. A man tapping a harmonica in the palm of his hand walked up and joined the group, and a frontier dance band was born. The crowd was in a happy mood, singing, dancing and clapping their hands in time to the music. By looking at the crowd of smiling faces you would have thought you were at a wedding instead of a hanging, where two men would die in the morning. On the frontier you took your good times when and where you could find them, for you never knew when your hair would be on its way to Canada on some buck's belt. Bucky's eyes wandered over the crowd until he saw Mary standing by the band, swaying back and forth to the music.

"Clem, why don't you stop being such a cheapskate and close this place down. I'll bet Sue would like to have some fun."

"That is a good idea, Bucky. I will do it," Clem said as Bucky stepped outside.

Walking over and standing next to Mary, Bucky asked, "Would you like to dance, Mary?"

Mary looked all around for Ben, but since she couldn't see him, she said, "Oh, I guess it will be all right."

Bucky and Mary joined the square dance group as they were circling to the left. They hopped, skipped and twirled to the music and the caller's directions. Bucky had never seen the sparkle of blue like the color in Mary's eyes. Her happy laugh whenever they made a mistake was contagious, and everyone seemed to be having a better time with Bucky and Mary in the group. If Bucky thought of Mary in only a sexual way before, it suddenly dawned on him as he looked at Mary that he was head over heels in love with her. She made his blood flow through his veins like the Connecticut River during the spring floods. Every time they tried to leave the so-called dance floor, someone would grab them and bring them back. They danced a good many fast and lively dances. Bucky was glad when they kept dragging them back again and again, because he didn't want to let Mary go. He knew he could never have Mary. On the frontier you never stole another man's wife unless you wanted to be hunted down for the rest of your life. The band started to play a slow waltz. Bucky held Mary in his arms and guided her into the circle of dancers. To Bucky, with his hand on Mary's small waist, she guided like a canoe on the waters of a calm mountain lake. Neither Bucky or Mary noticed Ben as he walked up and stood by the edge of the crowd. They didn't notice Clem and Sue as they walked up and stood beside Ben.

Neither of them heard Clem say to Ben, "Look at Bucky and Mary. Don't you think they look nice together?"

Ben's head snapped around to look at Clem. He gave him an icy stare.

With a grin, Clem took Sue's hand and guided her into the circle of dancers.

"Clem, you shouldn't have said that. You will only make it hard for Mary."

"Oh, I don't think so. I think Mary's making it hard for Bucky."

"Stop talking like that. Mary's a nice girl," Sue said, giving Clem a good-natured slap on the shoulder.

Bucky was snapped from his time in heaven by someone pulling Mary from his arms.

"Come on, we are going home," Ben said.

"Oh, Ben, I am having such a good time. Can't we stay a little longer?"

"I said we are going home," Ben said, giving Mary a shove and almost knocking her down.

"Ben, take it easy," Bucky said as he put his hand on Ben's arm.

"Mind your own damn business. She's my wife, not yours."

Bucky stood and watched them walk away. He felt a tug on his hand. Looking down, he looked into the shining eyes of a little girl.

"I will dance with you, Bucky."

The people standing nearby smiled as Bucky swept her up in his arms, put her on his shoulders and danced away.

Chapter Eight

Bucky was on his back, listening to Old Moe snore, as he watched the sky lightening up in the east, bringing on the dawn of a new day. He was not looking forward to the hanging, but it was something that had to be done. Bucky was interrupted from his thoughts by a knock on the door and someone whispering his name. Bucky swung his feet to the floor, put on his pants and opened the door to see Ensign Sartwell facing him.

Startled, Bucky asked, "What's wrong? Is there something happening at the fort?" Although he knew as soon as he got the words out of his mouth that if there was the bell would be ringing, calling everyone to the fort.

"No, everything is fine. Captain wants to know if you will help with the hanging, just in case the Morses should put up a fight when it comes time to put their necks in the noose."

"Sure. Tell Burroughs that I will be there if he needs me. Come on in and kick up the fire and make yourself a cup of tea and anything else you can find."

"Thanks, Bucky, but I have already had breakfast. I will tell the captain that you are coming."

Bucky stepped outside and stripped his pants off and took a

sponge bath with the cold water from the barrel by the side of the cabin. Drying himself off, he went back into the cabin and gently shook Johnny by the shoulder.

"I'm awake, Bucky, I heard. I will get Moe there if he wants to go."

"You're damn right I want to go," Moe said from the bed in the corner of the room.

The two large double doors to the fort stood wide open. Bucky, with his musket cradled in his arms, walked into the fort and stood at the end of the parade ground. He surveyed the people inside the fort. The first thing to catch his eye was the hanging tree sitting ominously in the center of the parade ground. Those who had slept the night away inside the fort were starting to stir. Bucky watched as they stood up, coughed, spit and farted. It was repeated over and over again around the parade ground. The women grabbed their young daughters by the hand and hurried to Clem's store, where Clem had put up a makeshift outhouse in back of the store for them to use, for a small fee, of course. The men and small boys headed for the woods. Bucky started to walk slowly across the parade ground toward the storeroom where the Morses were being held. He stopped and watched a young man light a small cooking fire using gunpowder spread on dry tinder, and using the flint and the pan on his musket to set the gunpowder on fire. The boy then blew gently on the sparks it created until the dry sticks burst into flames. A smile spread across Bucky's face as he thought back to a time in the past when he, Charlie, the Morses and the Frenchies where trapping up in the Thunder Bay area. One morning, Ike Morse was starting a fire using gunpowder and his musket. He forgot the musket was loaded with powder and ball shot. When he pulled the trigger the musket discharged. Charlie, who was sitting a few feet away, had just stoked up his corn cob pipe and, putting his hands behind his head, took a big pull on the pipe. He was slowly blowing the smoke out of the corner of his mouth when the musket went off and blew the pipe out of his mouth. Charlie didn't say a word. He slowly got up and walked over to Ike, pulling him to his feet, hitting him with everything he had right on the jaw. Ike didn't come to for fifteen minutes. He ate nothing but watered down soup for six weeks. The way things turned out, it might have been better if Charlie had killed him. Bucky walked up to the small group of men standing in front of the storeroom door and joined in the small talk about the weather, crops, news of the war, anything to keep their minds off the unpleasant task they were going to perform. They watched in silence as Clem's horse and wagon came through the gate and parked beside the hanging tree.

Captain Burroughs walked up and, looking the small group over, took a deep breath and said, "OK, boys, we can't put it off any longer. Lets get it over with."

The hanging party consisted of six people. They were Captain Burroughs, Lieutenant Parker, Captain Spaffard, Ensign Sartwell, Doctor Hastings and Bucky. Captain Burroughs unlocked the storeroom door and stepped inside, followed by the rest of the hanging party.

"Jim and Ike, it's time. Would you like to spend five minutes with a preacher?" Captain Burroughs asked.

"Fuck the preacher. We don't need him," Jim replied with a nervous laugh.

Ike's eyes opened wide. He dropped to his knees on the floor and grabbed Captain Burroughs by the legs.

"Captain, don't! Please don't hang me. I don't want to die. I won't do it again. I didn't do it this time, Jim did it," Ike cried, shaking and sobbing like a baby.

Jim stepped forward and kicked Ike in the ribs. Ike let out a yelp that reminded Bucky of the camp dogs in an Indian village when the Indians kicked them out of the way.

"Shut up! Shut your fucking mouth, you yellow bastard! Act like a man. They are going to hang us and that is it," Jim yelled, as Captain Spaffard and Ensign Sartwell pulled him away from Ike.

"Pull him away from me, Bucky. Get him the hell away from my feet," Captain Burroughs ordered as he tried to move his feet from the grasp of Ike's death grip.

Bucky reached down and pulled Ike away from Captain Burroughs' feet and stood him up. Ike was so scared he could not stand up on his two feet. He fell to the floor at Bucky's feet and curled up into a ball.

"Jesus Christ, I have had enough of this. Pick him up, Bucky. If we have to, we will carry him to the gallows."

"Like hell, Captain. He has shit and pissed in his pants. Can't you smell him? I'm not going to put him on my shoulders."

"Jesus, Sartwell, you take one side, and Bucky, you take the other and drag him out," Burroughs ordered.

As they stepped out of the storeroom, the sun was just starting to rise out of the east. It looked like the promise of a good day for everyone but Ike and Jim. The crowd got so quiet you could have heard a fart from the far end of the fort. Captain Burroughs led the way, followed by Sartwell and Bucky dragging Ike, who was as limp as a rag doll. Then came Jim with Parker and Spaffard on each side of him. Doctor Hastings followed close behind.

"Make way, make way. Give us room to get through," Burroughs ordered.

The crowd moved back, making an aisle from the storeroom to the gallows. Captain Burroughs tried to block out the wailing of Ike from his mind.

Ike was crying, "I don't want to die!" over and over again, and Burroughs had already made up his mind that Ike was going to be first. Bucky noticed Moe sitting in the wheelbarrow with Johnny standing beside him as they passed.

Moe clapped his hands and laughed. "Hey, Jim and Ike, you are headed straight to hell, and you are going to get a ride to your graves in Clem's shit wagon. What could be more fitting for a couple of pieces of shit like you two?" Moe shouted.

"Shut up, you old son of a bitch. I should have smashed your head to mush when I had the chance," Jim shout back.

"You bastards tried, and now you are going to pay for it," Moe replied.

When they reached the bottom of the steps, Doctor Hastings went and stood to the side of the wagon. Sartwell and Bucky dragged the sobbing Ike up the stairs and held him on the trapdoor. Captain Burroughs walked over and put the noose around Ike's neck.

"Ike, is there anything you would like to say?" Burroughs asked.

The wet spot on Ike's pants got bigger. All he could say was, "I don't want to die. I don't want to die." Captain Burroughs walked over to the trapdoor lever. The last thing Ike said was, "I don't want—" as he slid out of Sartwell and Bucky's hands.

The rope squeaked as it stretched. It bounced a couple of times, then there was nothing but silence throughout the fort until Doctor Hastings said, through the open door, "He's gone, Captain."

There was an uneasy stirring throughout the crowd. Even Moe was lost for words. Captain Burroughs cut the rope, and Bucky heard a thud as Ike's body hit the ground. The trapdoor was shut. A new rope was thrown over the stanchion and tied to the railing near the lever that opened the trapdoor.

Jim was brought forward and placed in the center of the trapdoor. Captain Burroughs placed the noose around his neck and asked, "Jim, do you have any last words to say?"

"Only that I will see you all in hell." Out of the corner of his eyes, Jim saw Burroughs reach for the lever and give it a yank. Quick as a cat, he jumped backward and stood about a foot from the opening, staring wide-eyed at the ground. Burroughs reached up, grabbed the rope, and pulled with all his strength. Jim's neck stretched. His eyes bulged out, and his feet lifted a few feet off of the floor. He slowly swung out over the open trapdoor. Captain Burroughs let go of the rope. Jim shot out of sight, followed by a snap that could be heard throughout the fort.

A few minutes later Doctor Hastings called up, "It's all over, Captain."

"Take them down by the river and bury them. They are not fit to be buried with decent folks," Captain Burroughs instructed the burying detail.

Bucky stood on the gallows platform and watched the wagon carrying Jim and Ike's bodies move slowly through the crowd. As it went by, the people in the crowd stretched their necks to look in the back of the wagon. He looked out over the crowd hoping to spot a patch of flaming red hair in the sea of black and blond heads bobbing toward the fort's main gate.

"What's wrong with Johnny?" Captain Burroughs asked.

Looking in the direction that Captain Burroughs was pointing, he saw Johnny gagging and throwing up.

"He is a good boy, and you can count on him when you need him, but killing makes him sick when it's over," Bucky replied with a grin.

"Hey, Burroughs, you did a good job. If you and Bucky want to come over to Clem's, we will split a bottle of rum," Moe offered.

"Too early for me. Some other time, maybe," Burroughs said, and walked toward his quarters. He didn't want anyone to know, but he wasn't feeling too good in his stomach either.

Bucky sat in Sue's dining room, nursing a drink from Moe's bottle of rum and watching the men coming and going, listening to the talk about the hanging and how the war was going. It seemed to be going in England's favor when they took Fort Ticonderoga. They now controlled Lake George and the lower part of Lake Champlain. If rumors were true, there was a big battle looming for the city of Quebec. Maybe the war wouldn't last much longer. Bucky looked at Johnny. He was sound asleep, with his head on the table, snoring loud enough to wake the dead. His belly was full of hot rum toddies that Moe had been buying him. He knew Johnny would be sick again, but this time he would have a headache to go with it. Bucky glanced at Moe sitting across from him with a silly grin on his face. He knew that before the day was over he would be bringing them both to the cabin in the wheelbarrow.

Moe interrupted Bucky's thoughts when he asked, "Bucky, will you do me a favor?"

"Sure, what is it?"

"Would you ask Clem if he could pay me for my furs? I am a little low on cash."

Bucky nodded his head. Getting up from the table, he walked from the dining room and through the large double doors leading into Clem's store. His heart skipped a beat when he saw Mary standing by the counter, watching Clem count the eggs in her basket she had brought to Clem to sell in his store. Walking over to the counter, Bucky tapped Mary on the shoulder and said, "Good morning, Mary."

Keeping her head down, Mary replied so softly that Bucky could hardly hear her. With a puzzled look, Bucky looked at Clem.

Without stopping to count the eggs, Clem glanced up at Bucky and tapped the side of his face with his finger. Bucky looked closely at the side of Mary's face and saw a mark just below her eye. Taking his finger, he moved the hair from Mary's face and saw a large bruise on the side of Mary's face.

"How did this happen, Mary?" Bucky knew even before he asked.

Mary raised her head and looked at Bucky with tears in her eyes. "I was splitting wood and got hit in the face."

Feeling anger welling up inside him, Bucky said through clinched teeth, "The son of a bitch hit you, didn't he?"

Without waiting for Mary to answer, Bucky spun around and headed for the door leading to the outside of the trading post. It was at that time Ben had the misfortune of walking into the trading post. Bucky met him by the door, and without saying a word he swung and hit Ben on the side of the face, knocking him to the floor.

Blinking and rubbing the haze from his eyes, Ben looked up at Bucky and asked, "What did you do that for?"

"You bastard. You hit Mary, didn't you?" Bucky asked, fire in his eyes.

"That is none of your business. She is my wife, not yours. I can do anything I want to her. Keep your Goddamn nose out of my business."

Ben was not a small man, but Bucky, with all the pent-up anger inside him, reached down and grabbed Ben by the front of his shirt, grabbing hair and all, and pulled him from the floor. With his other hand he grabbed the front of Ben's britches, held him up in the air and hung him by the rope he was using as a belt to a wooden peg that was sticking out of the wall.

With Ben hanging there, eyes as big as cannon balls, Bucky said through clenched teeth, "If you ever hit Mary again I will kill you." Turning away, Bucky stomped through the door.

Ben started yelling, with his arms moving in all directions. He looked like one of those dolls the kids played with on a string.

"Get me down!" He yelled so loud that everyone in the dining room ran into the store to see what was going on.

Laughing, Clem walked over and cut the rope holding Ben up. Ben dropped to the floor with a thud. When he jumped up, his britches dropped to his ankles. Clem pointed with the point of his knife, saying loud enough so that everyone in the room could hear, "Kind of small, isn't it, Ben?"

The crowd roared with laughter.

"It isn't funny," Ben replied. He reached down and pulled up his britches before he ran from the store.

"Now I know why you don't have any kids, Mary," Clem said with a laugh.

"Oh, leave Mary alone," Sue said, giving Clem a stern look.

Mary reached up and took the rope from the peg, turned and gave Clem a big smile, then walked from the store with a bounce in her steps.

Bucky left the trading post, looking neither to the left or right. He pushed the canoe out into the Connecticut River. Letting his anger flow from his body through the canoe paddles, the canoe shot swiftly up the river. Completely exhausted, Bucky steered the canoe toward a small island in the middle of the river. Pulling the canoe ashore, Bucky made a quick search of the island to make sure he was alone. He sat on a small log by the river and let his mind wander. *What a fool I am*, he thought to himself. *Mary's married, and I can never have her. Today I made a big fool of myself. I have made it worse for Mary. People are going to talk. They are going to say that we have been meeting in the brush and fussing around. They will make her out a bad woman, and it just isn't so. Oh, what a mess I have made of things.* Bucky cut a small branch from a tree, tied a string on the end, put on a hook and found some fish worms. When he was feeling low, fishing always made him feel better. He tossed the baited hook out into the river, and in a few minutes he pulled in a nice bass. Bucky fished most of the day, catching fish and letting them go. It was late in the afternoon when he kept the last two fish for supper, rolled up his line and hook, then started back down the river.

Chapter Nine

Bucky wasn't in any hurry to get back to the fort, so he just let the canoe drift with the current. He watched a deer come down to the river's edge to get a drink. Lifting his head, he watched Bucky and the canoe drift closer and closer, his ears and tail twitching. Bucky raised his arms up in the air. The deer spun around, and with one leap was out of sight in the forest. He glided close to a beaver, who slapped his tail and dove under water. He saw muskrats, mink and birds of all kinds. Bucky rested the paddle across his knees and thought to himself what a beautiful country he lived in. He thought it was like heaven, if only the war would end. What more could anyone want?

As he neared the fort, his thoughts changed to his present dilemma. *I have got to get away. I guess I will take Johnny and head up the river and check out Old Moe's cabin to make sure nobody has moved in. Then I'll head up the Wells River and over to my old Indian buddy. If I bring along a couple of jugs of good rum he will be glad to see us.* Bucky was jolted from his thoughts. Looking down the river, he saw someone standing waist deep in the water, waving his arms and shouting. A few good strokes with the paddle brought Bucky close enough to see that it was a young boy. The young boy climbed into the canoe, almost tipping it over.

He cried, "Indians! Indians! Bring me to the fort."

Bucky looked but couldn't see anything. The young boy kept screaming, "Indians!" over and over again. Bucky dug the paddle in and pushed the canoe toward the fort.

"What in hell is this all about, Bucky?"

"I don't know, Captain. I picked him out of the river across from the fort. He was yelling, 'Indians!' He told me to take him to the fort. Even before we got to shore he was out of the canoe and running. I caught up to him just as he was pulling on the rope to the bell."

"Christ, we will have everybody here within earshot in fifteen minutes. He's just a kid. How old do you say he is?"

"I would say about nine, maybe ten years old," Bucky replied. Folding his arms across his chest, he continued, "I would say he is from the Grants. There is a small settlement about five or six miles from here with about five families living there, spread over a couple of miles. There is a family named Scott that seems to be the center of everything. They built a house of field stone. It seems to me that the people thought of the place as a meeting house and church. The house is strong enough to hold off a hundred Indians. Scotty, that is what everyone calls him, brags that no Indian will ever get his scalp. Your wife seems to have the kid calmed down a little."

Captain Burroughs went over and sat down on the bench beside the young boy. He was shaking so bad that Burroughs could feel the bench shake. He put his arm around the boy's shoulder.

"Don't be afraid. You are safe here, son. What is your name?" Burroughs asked gently.

"Thomas Brown," the boy replied.

"I bet they call you Tom."

The boy nodded his head in agreement.

"Where do you live, Tom?"

"Over in the Grants," the boy said, pointing toward the Grants with his finger.

"Do you live in that small settlement where Scotty lives?" Burroughs asked.

For the first time since they laid eyes on the young boy, he had a smile on his face.

"Do you know Scotty?" Tom asked.

"No, but Bucky does."

"I have seen you at Scotty's," Tom said, noticing Bucky for the first time.

"If you have any sisters you've probably seen a lot of him," Clem said with a laugh.

For the first time Bucky looked up and noticed the fort filling up with people. Everyone was asking each other what was going on.

"What is going on, Captain?" Clem asked.

"Shut up, Clem, we are trying to find out. Can you tell us what happened, Tom?"

Tom's eyes got as big as saucers as he exclaimed, "Indians!"

Captain Burroughs couldn't help but laugh.

"I gathered that, Tom. Why don't you start from the beginning and tell us everything. Do you think you could do that, Tom?"

"Yes, sir, Mr. Captain."

Alice Burroughs sat down beside Tom and handed him a large molasses cookie, then put her arm around his shoulders and held him as only a mother can. Tom took a bite of the cookie and moved closer to Alice.

"Pa heard about the hanging and wanted to go to it. I wished I had stayed home, because I didn't like it, but Pa wanted to go. We got up early in the morning, did our chores, milked our cow and put her out to pasture. After the hanging we came back home. We got back about noon. I remember because the sun was right overhead. Pa was the first to notice that the cow was missing. Pa and I found where she had broken through the fence. He told me to hunt her down and bring her home. I followed her trail through the woods over to Seth Noyes' homestead. I was just going to step out from behind some bushes into their field when I saw about ten or twelve Indians run out into the hayfield from the other side, yelling and war whooping. Mr. Noyes was piling hay with his two little girls. They were two and three years old. He grabbed them and stuck them under a pile of hay. He grabbed his musket and shot one of the Indians. He was reloading when a big Indian came from the side and shot Mr. Noyes. Mr. Noyes started to crawl toward his cabin. This big Indian walked slowly over to Mr. Noyes and turned him over, then stuck a big knife into his belly. Mr. Noyes screamed. I could see him twisting the knife, making Mr. Noyes scream louder. Then he put his foot on his face and scalped him. I could hear a ripping and sucking sound when he pulled his hair off. Then he walked over to the pile of hay where the two girls were hiding and set it on fire. When the little girls crawled out, he threw them back in, over and over again until they didn't crawl out anymore. Then he held up the bloody scalp, gave a war hoop, and they all rushed toward the cabin where Mrs. Noyes was loading and shooting, but not hitting anyone. She ran into the cabin and shut the door. They broke the door down. That is when I crept back into the woods and started running for home. I could hear Mrs. Noyes screaming. That made me run faster. Pa sounded the alarm and told me to run to the fort and get help. He said to tell you they would be at Scotty's house. You will send help, won't you, Mr. Captain?"

"Yes, we will send help, Tom."

"I will never forget that Indian. He was big, like him," Tom said, pointing at Bucky. He had a big black feather sticking out of his hair," Tom added.

"Black Hawk!" Bucky exclaimed.

"Do you know him?" Burroughs asked.

"Yes, I know him. He is the most vicious Indian you could ever come up against. He enjoys killing."

"Do you think he is part of a larger group?"

"I don't know, Captain, he has traveled both ways. His own people don't like him around. He is like a mad dog. He will turn on anyone, and he likes to be in charge. So I think it might be a small raiding party made up of his own hand-picked killers."

Captain Burroughs stood up and looked at the crowd. They were all bunched together. The women were holding tightly to their husbands' arms, and some were brushing tears from their eyes.

Captain Burroughs took a deep breath and said, "You heard I need volunteers. Who will volunteer to go help our friends in the Grants?"

"I will go," Bucky volunteered.

"Me too," Johnny said, stepping forward and standing next to Bucky.

"Count me in," Clem said, stepping forward.

"How about you, Ben?" Captain Burroughs asked.

"Oh, ah, I can't. I have got things to look after here."

Someone in the crowd started to cluck like a chicken. Ben's face got red, and he walked away from the crowd. A young man stepped forward and joined the small group.

"I am going," Tom said.

"No, I don't think so. I think you better stay here with me," Captain Burroughs said, putting his hand on Tom's shoulder.

"No, I'm going. I know a shortcut. I can get us there quicker."

"We'll take him, Captain."

"I will send Ensign Sartwell with you, but I can't spare anyone else. I don't know what we have coming at us. I can't leave the fort undermanned."

Turning to the small group, Bucky said, "Meet me in fifteen minutes down by the river with two muskets, plenty of ball and powder, a hatchet and a knife." Turning to Sue, he asked, "Will you take care of Moe until I get back?"

"Yes, Bucky, I will watch the old goat for you. If he gives me a hard time I will dump him out of the wheelbarrow."

Turning to Clem, Sue gave him a kiss on the cheek and said, "Be careful."

"Don't worry, Sue, I didn't run a trading post *all* my life."

Chapter Ten

Bucky and his small group huddled together in the bottom of a small gully, listening to the war whoops from the Indians and an occasional shot being fired. The smell of smoke was strong in the air. Bucky knew that burning and killing was Black Hawk's favorite pastime.

"Tom, as I remember, Scotty's house is here with a large field in front and a small clearing on both sides and in back," Bucky said as he drew a diagram in the dirt.

"That is right, and there is a small barn right here beside the house," Tom said as he drew a small square in Bucky's diagram

"Where are we now?"

"We are opposite his front yard."

"Everyone stay here. I am going up and take a look."

Bucky crawled up the small hill on his hands and knees. When he reached the top, Bucky fell to his stomach and crawled to the edge of the woods and looked out into the clearing. To his left was the house. Beside the house was a pile of smoldering hay and timbers, which Tom said was the barn. There was an ox and two cows laying out in the front yard with arrows sticking out of them like needles in a pin cushion. To his right, at about half the length of the field, stood ten or twelve Indians milling around, jumping up and down, waving their arms and yelling and laughing. Behind them near the back of the clearing stood Black Hawk and two other Indians having a powwow. Bucky backed away from the clearing and crawled back down the hill and joined the others. Nobody said a word; they all looked at Bucky, waiting for him to speak.

"Here is what is happening up there. They don't suspect any help for Scotty and his people. They are standing right here," Bucky said, drawing a line in his diagram. "I counted ten of them, and up here near the back of the clearing is Black Hawk and two more. Now here is what we are going to do. They are just out of range of Scotty's guns and jumping around like a bunch of kids. So we are going up this gully until we are opposite the first group. We will get into position, and when I give the order we will fire on the first group. Then, with your other musket, we will all swing to the right and take out Black Hawk and the other two."

The small party of men and one small boy crawled up near the edge of the clearing and poked their muskets through the berry bushes. This was better than Bucky had hoped for.

They were slightly behind the first group of Indians. Bucky looked down the line and could see that they were all waiting for his order to fire. Bucky took aim at the back of a short, husky Indian, yelled fire and squeezed the trigger. He saw Indians dropping, but didn't stop to count. He grabbed his other musket and started to turn toward Black Hawk, when he saw Clem jump up with a yell and run out into the clearing toward the other Indians that were still standing.

Bucky yelled, "Clem, don't!" But it was too late. He saw an arrow sailing through the air toward Clem. He staggered and fell to the ground. Bucky saw the Indian reach for another arrow, but he put a ball into the Indian's chest. The rest took their cue from Clem and finished off the first group of Indians. Bucky ran to Clem, picked up his musket and turned toward Black Hawk.

"Bucky, so we meet again. Someday your hair will hang from my lodge pole," Black Hawk said, shaking the bloody scalp at Bucky.

"You son of a bitch," Bucky shouted, as he snapped off a shot at

Black Hawk. The Indian jumped behind a large pine tree and disappeared into the forest.

"Damn!" Bucky exclaimed, throwing the musket to the ground. "What in hell did you do that for, Clem? If you had held your ground we could have got them all, including that Goddamn savage, Black Hawk. We could have ended his murdering days once and for all."

"I'm sorry, Bucky. I just got excited. Jesus, it hurts. Pull the damn thing out, it's killing me," Clem cried, holding onto his leg and rocking back and forth.

"My God, you're actually hit!" Bucky exclaimed, noticing for the first time the arrow sticking out of Clem's thigh.

"Oh, I am going to die. I am going to die! Someone pull that Goddamn thing out of me," Clem cried.

Bucky took his knife and slit Clem's britches up the front and back.

"Damn, Bucky, those are new britches."

"Stop your crying. Sue will sew them back up so that they will look just like new."

He looked at Clem's leg and didn't like the looks of it. If the arrow had gone all the way through they could cut the point off and pull the shaft through. Bucky guess that this one was about halfway into Clem's leg. He had seen wounds like this turn bad. If he pushed the arrow through, he could cut an artery and Clem could bleed to death or get infection without proper care and be dead in a week.

"No, Clem, we are not going to take it out. We will get you back to the fort and let Doctor Hastings take care of it."

"All right, but lets get with it. It hurts like hell."

Scotty and his band of settlers came running up and started to talk all at once.

"Hi, Bucky, we didn't expect anyone until tomorrow at the earliest," Scotty said, offering Bucky his hand.

Taking Scotty's hand, Bucky said, "You can thank that boy over there. You can be proud of that one." Taking Scotty aside, Bucky asked, "Can you help us out? We have one wounded, and I would like to get him back to the fort as soon as possible."

Just then, one of the Indians sat up and started to mumble something. One of the settlers' wives walked over to him and put the barrel of her musket against his forehead, pulled the trigger and blew the back of his head off. Johnny started to gag and throw up.

"What is wrong with him?" Scotty asked.

"Nothing, killing makes him sick."

"Don't you think he is living in the wrong place?"

"No, Scotty, he is tough as nails in every place but his stomach."

"Follow me. I will fix you up with a stretcher."

Johnny followed behind them, gagging and throwing up all the way to Scotty's house.

The stretcher was a blanket tied between two poles. Bucky laid the stretcher down beside Clem. They picked him up and laid him on the blanket. Clem let out a yowl that sounded like a mountain lion in heat.

"Need any help with them?" Bucky asked, nodding his head toward the dead Indians.

"No, we will take care of them," Scotty replied.

Bucky knew how. They would drag them out into the woods and bury them in a shallow grave, and before the night was over the animals would dig them up and have a feast.

Scotty bent down and handed Clem a gallon of hard cider.

"Here, this is to help ease the pain." Clem pulled the cork out and took two big swallows from the jug, put the cork back in and laid the jug beside him. Clem's friends from the fort picked up the stretcher and started at a fast pace toward the fort. It was getting dark, and they could see lightning flashes off in the distance. About two hours down the trail, the rain caught up to them. In a few minutes they were soaking wet. The rain ran in their eyes and down necks. They were cold, and with Clem yelling and swearing at them every time they slipped on the muddy and slippery forest floor, nobody was in a very happy mood. Bucky noticed that during the last hour Clem was getting more talkative. When they came to a large tree with branches that gave some protection from the steady downpour, Bucky suggested that they stop to rest and take a couple of swallows of hard cider to warm up. Johnny reached over and picked up the jug and shook it.

"It's empty!" Johnny exclaimed with a surprised look on his face.

"Goddamn it, Clem, you drank it all?"

"There you go, mad at me again, aren't you, Bucky? Well, I know what is wrong with you. You are all flustered because you want some of that red-haired pussy at the fort. You can't have any, and it is making you ugly."

"Clem, shut your mouth or I will leave you right here and let the wild animals feast on you."

Clem let loose with a hardy laugh, belched and started to sing every song he knew in a voice loud enough to wake the dead. After suffering through Clem's singing for about an hour, Sartwell asked, "Bucky, is it too late to bring him back and bury him with those redskins?"

"Yes, I'm afraid it is. I can see the river just ahead."

Chapter Eleven

"Oh Clem, does it hurt much?" Sue asked, rubbing Clem's head. Bending down, she kissed him on the forehead.

Clem, laying on Doctor Hasting's kitchen table, was enjoying the attention and playing it to the hilt.

"God, Sue, it hurts awful," Clem said, holding Sue's hand and squeezing it tight.

Turning to Captain Burroughs, Bucky said with a laugh, "He is so full of hard cider he won't feel anything until tomorrow morning."

"Doctor, is he going to be all right?"

Putting his arm around Sue's shoulder, Doctor Hastings replied., "He is going to be just fine. I am going to cut the arrow shaft below the feathers and push it out the other side. I will bandage him up, and he should be just fine in a couple of weeks."

"I want that arrow, Hastings."

"Don't worry, Clem, you can have it. I don't want it."

"Jesus, Bucky, you know what he is going to do? He is going to hang that arrow on the trading post wall and bore the hell out of everyone who comes into the place about his exploits as a great Indian fighter, until the day he dies."

Bucky laughed at Burroughs' remark while watching Doctor

Hastings cut the arrow shaft with a tool that looked like a pair of pliers. He poured alcohol from a bottle of good corn whiskey over the arrow shaft and Clem's leg. He then put the palm of his hand on top of the arrow shaft and pushed the arrow point through the other side of Clem's leg. With his other hand, he pulled the arrow shaft through the leg. Clem raised his head. His eyes got as big as pumpkins, and he fainted dead away. Johnny saw the blood spurt out and drop to the floor. The sight of the blood on the floor made Johnny gag.

Doctor Hastings turned and looked at him. "What's wrong with him?" he asked.

"The sight of blood makes him sick," Bucky said with a little grin.

"Get him the hell out of here. I don't want puke all over my floor."

Bucky took Johnny outside. While Johnny went away to be sick in private, Bucky stood and breathed deep of the rain-cleansed air. He stood and thought how good Mother Earth smelled after the rain washed her face.

Sue walked out of Doctor Hastings' quarters and over to Bucky. She put her hand on Bucky's arm and asked, "Will you carry Clem over to the trading post?"

Yes, I will. Sue, I hate to ask, but could you look after Moe for me for a couple of weeks? I have just got to get away for a while."

Sue knew why Bucky had to get away, and her heart just ached for him.

"Oh, that's no trouble, Bucky. We have another cot in the store. He will be good company for Clem until he gets back on his feet."

"You are going away? We will miss you," said a voice behind Bucky.

Bucky turned around and looked straight into Mary's blue eyes.

"You will?" he asked, surprised at what he was hearing.

Mary just stood and looked at Bucky. She thought to herself, *If only I could tell you how much.* Her whole body ached. She wanted so much to reach out and pull him toward her and press her body close to his. He was always on her mind, even when she was having sex with Ben, which wasn't very often anymore. She fantasized that it was Bucky. Just thinking about it now made her blush and feel ashamed. He was always in her dreams. Mary would wake up feeling hot and excited, get up and go outside and cry softly to herself, sometimes staying outside all night long. It was better than laying beside Ben and listening to him snore and fart the night away. She didn't love Ben, and never had. It was a marriage arranged by her father. He had too many mouths too feed, and it was his way of getting rid of one. If only she could talk to someone, tell somebody how she felt. Maybe Sue. Yes, she could trust her. *God, if he would ask me, I would run away with him tonight.*

Bucky looked deep into Mary's eyes. If he didn't have his musket cradled in his arms, he would have reached out and pulled Mary into his arms. If only he could tell her how he felt, but she would probably laugh at him. She had never made any advances toward him or given him any reason to think that she wasn't happily married, except for the glances she gave him whenever he was around, and the times he had caught her looking at him. She would smile and get red in the face. Sometimes the little remarks that Sue and Clem said made him think that she might want more than friendship. *God*, Bucky thought, *I would like to take her and run far away.* Bucky knew she was too much of a lady to do that. Maybe he should talk to Sue. No, Bucky knew what she would say Mary was married and to leave her alone.

Standing there looking at Mary, Bucky knew now more than ever that he would have to leave in the morning.

"Come on, Mary, it's safe to go home," Ben called from a safe distance away.

Mary reached up and put her hand on Bucky's face and said, "Thanks to you, Bucky."

Bucky watched Mary walk away into the darkness.

Sue came over and put her arm around Bucky's waist.

"God, Sue, I love her," he said.

"I know, Bucky, I know," Sue replied in a motherly fashion.

Mary got up early the next morning, before Ben woke up. She had made up her mind; she was going to talk to Bucky and tell him how she felt. When she got to Bucky's cabin, there was no one there. Bucky and Johnny were already miles up the river.

Chapter Twelve

Johnny noticed a change in Bucky. He had not said a word all morning long. That was unusual for Bucky. He was a ways a happy-go-lucky type of a person. Johnny noticed the change began the day he hung Ben on the peg in Clem's store. He guess it had something to do with Mary. If that is what they called love, he guessed he didn't want any of it.

Bucky was the first to break the silence.

"See those crows flying around over there?" Bucky asked, pointing toward the Grants side of the river.

"That is one way to tell that you are not alone in the wilderness. It could be man or beast, one Indian or a hundred, a mountain lion or a fox."

They sat in the middle of the Connecticut River and watched the crows circle closer and closer. Suddenly the bushes along the river bank parted, and a small bear walking on all fours walked to the riverbank and started to drink. Catching their scent on the gentle breeze, he stood up on his hind legs and stared at Bucky and Johnny, made a *woof* sound and walked back into the forest. For the rest of the day Bucky taught Johnny how to survive in the wilderness. It made Bucky feel good to be able to teach Johnny all of the tricks to survive in the wilderness that Charlie had taught him.

Bucky and Johnny stood on the riverbank and looked up toward Moe's cabin.

"It looks all right to me, Bucky. The only footprints are yours, mine and Jim and Ike's," Johnny said, pointing to the prints in the sand.

"I think you are right, Johnny, but keep your eyes open and be ready for anything."

They walked toward the cabin with their muskets swinging back and forth in front of them. When they reached the cabin door, Bucky gently pushed it open with the barrel of his musket. Johnny jumped when a little chipmunk ran from the cabin and stood in the clearing, chattering at them.

"That is another way you can tell if someone else is around," Bucky said, laughing at the startled look on Johnny's face.

Bucky and Johnny stood inside Moe's cabin, looking at the mess Ike and Jim had made of Moe's meager belongings. They had strewn everything around in their attempt to steal any money Moe might have hidden.

"At least they didn't get this," Bucky said as he walked over to the fireplace, removed a stone and pulled out a small bag full of coins.

"Is that his bank? They must have been stupid not to check there. Everyone hides things behind the stones in their fireplace."

"That's a yes to both of your questions," Bucky replied. Then he added, "You get a fire started and I will go down to the river and get a couple of fish for supper."

When Bucky returned with four nice rainbow trout all gutted and cleaned, Johnny had the cabin all cleaned and also a fire going in the fireplace with a big pot of tea brewing. After eating their fish with a nice mug of strong tea. They sat by the fire, sipping on a second mug, deep within their own thoughts. Bucky thought of Mary, while Johnny was thinking, *Boy, this sure has got shoveling horse shit in Boston beat.*

Bucky and Johnny stayed at Moe's cabin for a week. They cut him a supply of wood for winter heat. They put a flat rock over the chimney to keep the animals and snow out. They left the cabin in fine shape to stand the harsh Northern Grants winter. "I guess that will take care of Moe if he decides to come back this winter."

Do you think he will?" Johnny asked.

"I don't know; he isn't one to hang around large crowds of people very long. Says he likes to breathe fresh air every day."

Johnny turned and took one last look at Moe's cabin as they floated back down the White River. He didn't ask Bucky where they were going. He figured he would tell him when he was ready. They spent all that day paddling up the Connecticut River, joking and splashing each other with their paddles. They stopped here and there to fish. They had enough for supper when Bucky headed the canoe toward the Grants side of the river. Pulling the canoe ashore and hiding it in the bushes, Bucky and Johnny climbed a small ridge to an opening that to Johnny looked like it had been used as a camp before.

"Your pa and I used to stop here on our way to Canada," Bucky said, answering Johnny's question before he asked it.

"Come here, take a look at this."

Johnny walked over and looked down on the Connecticut River winding back and forth like a snake, sometimes not more than a hundred feet apart, as it wound its way down the Connecticut River Valley.

"My God! Bucky, we aren't going to paddle up that, are we?'

"No, we will keep to the high ground and walk until we come to where the Wells River runs into the Connecticut. Then we will head west into the Grants. There is some territory I would like to check out to see if would pay us to trap this year."

The next day found Bucky and Johnny deep in the forest of the Northern Grants. It was late afternoon when they came to a small cleaning in the forest.

"Let's stop here for a few minutes to rest and get our bearings," Bucky suggested.

Johnny sat on a log and looking around, sniffing at the air. "My God, Bucky, what in hell is that?

With a grin on his face, Bucky said, "Stay here and I'll go check it out."

Johnny watched Bucky step back into the forest and fade from sight as if he had never been there. Johnny sat on the log, still sniffing the air. He could not figure out where the smell was coming from. It seemed to be moving around. He got up from the log and started to walk toward the edge of the clearing, where the smell seemed to be the strongest. Bucky suddenly popped into view with his musket pointed at the ground.

"Get up, you stinking redskin. Thought you could sneak up on us? I should put a ball into your stinking hide and leave you for the dogs."

A short, stocky, dark-haired Indian dressed in buckskins stood up.

"You are not so smart. Look behind you," the Indian said with a grin.

Bucky turned and saw a young Indian brave standing behind him with a bow in his hand and a quiver of arrows strapped to his back. He heard the sound of a musket hammer being pulled back.

Bucky spun around and shouted at Johnny, "Don't shoot, they are friends!"

Bucky and the older Indian embraced each other, laughing and pounding each other on the back. The young Indian was about Johnny's age and size, and he resembled the older Indian. His straight black hair was braided in the back, and a fox tail was tied to the braid. They stood and looked each other up and down like two roosters before a fight.

"Come here, Johnny, they won't bite you," Bucky said.

Johnny wished Bucky hadn't said that. He wasn't afraid. It made him feel embarrassed in front of the young Indian.

"Johnny, this is Cross Toes and his son, Fox. Johnny is Charlie's son."

"Ah, Charlie. How is the old son of a gun?" Cross Toes asked.

"He died last fall," Johnny replied.

"Too bad. He was a good man," Cross Toes said, patting Johnny on the shoulder. Then turned to Bucky and asked, "You bring whiskey?"

"Sure did," Bucky answered.

"Good, then I guess I will let you spend some time at my place."

"I don't know that I want to. When was the last time you washed? We could smell you a mile away."

"Let me see, I did fall in the lake the first part of the summer. I don't like water. It makes me all wrinkled," Toes said with a sly grin.

Cross Toes, Bucky, Johnny and Fox walked for about a mile down a narrow path through the forest, until they stepped out of the forest into the sunlight and stood looking at a small lake with a log cabin and a wigwam made from poles and tree bark sitting near the edge of the lake.

"How did you ever find this place, Toes?" Bucky asked.

"When we lived in St. Francis, my woman and I used to come down this way to spend the summer along the river you call the Connecticut to fish for salmon. Fawn liked this place so much that every year we would spend a few weeks. This is where we made Fox. When Black Hawk and his band of killers forced us to leave the St. Francis village in the middle of the winter, Fawn wanted to come here. It was the only place where she was truly happy. The trip was too much for her in the middle of the winter. She took sick and died. I buried her over there," Cross Toes said, pointing to a small mound of rocks on top of a little hill that presented a view of the whole lake.

"Why did they make you leave the village?" Johnny asked.

"Because whenever he came back from a raiding party, all his scalps were small and had holes in them," Bucky said with a laugh and slapped Cross Toes on the back.

"I never killed a white man or took a scalp, but there is always a first time," Cross Toes said, glancing over at Bucky.

Cross Toes served up a fine supper of fresh fish, a tasty rabbit stew and corn bread. After eating their fill, Bucky went to his backpack and took out two gallon jugs of hard cider. Handing one to Cross Toes, they sat down by the fire for some serious drinking.

"Mighty nice cider, Bucky," Cross Toes said. Smacking his lips, he took another swallow from the jug. They sat back and, with grins on their faces, watched the two young boys spar with each other. Johnny looked around, faced a small tree, drew his knife from its sheath and threw it at the tree, hitting it dead center. He took a couple of steps to retrieve his knife, when a knife flashed by and stuck into the tree beside his knife. Fox walked to the tree and pulled out the two knives, handing Johnny his with a smirk on his face.

Johnny said to himself, *I'll show the son of a bitch.* He pulled his tomahawk from his belt and threw it at a small log on the ground, hitting it in the center. Johnny swaggered over to the log and yanked his tomahawk from it. He gave the log a kick, sending it rolling through the grass. It made two complete turns, then stopped with Fox's tomahawk in its center. The two boys stood staring at each other. Fox turned away, took an arrow from his quiver, fit it to his bow, and shot at a spot on the cabin wall. The arrow went through the air like a bird in flight and hit the spot in the center. Johnny raised his musket, took aim and split the arrow in half. Fox looked at the arrow, then looked at Johnny, rubbed his chin, turned and walked down to the lake and stood beside the shore. Johnny walked down to the lake and stood beside Fox.

Looking out over the water, Fox asked, "Do I smell?"

"What?" Johnny asked, surprised.

"Do I stink?"

"Well, yes, you do, but not as bad as your pa."

"You could smell us this afternoon?"

"Yes, but I didn't know it was you. Bucky did, but I didn't. Bucky said that is how you can tell if Indians are around. He says that Indians eat with their fingers and wipe their hands on their clothes. The fat turns rancid and you can smell them a mile off."

Fox laid his bow and quiver of arrows on the grass and dove into the lake. Johnny watched as Fox took off his clothes and pushed them up and down in the water. Johnny laid his musket, pouch of lead balls and powder horn on the ground. He ran to the lake and dove into the water, coming up beside Fox, and splashed him in the face with water. Fox dove under and grabbed Johnny by the legs and pulled him under the water. They both popped to the surface, laughing. They swam around awhile, then went up to the fire to dry off. They stood and listened as Bucky and Cross Toes talked about old times they shared at St. Francis.

"I saw our old friend Black Hawk," Bucky said and spit in the fire.

"When? Where?" Cross Toes asked.

"Down south, near Number Four. He was burning and killing as usual. We chased them away. He was the only one that got away."

"The spirits of past warriors are riding on his shoulders right now. When they find out what kind of warrior he is and how he is bringing dishonor to his tribe, they will abandon him. Then he will be vulnerable. The end of a piece of shit."

"You don't like him?" Bucky asked with a laugh.

"You know damn well I don't. He doesn't like me because I wouldn't go on any of his raids on the English settlers, but that is another story. He hates you for making him look bad in front of the whole village. You took every young maiden in St. Francis into the bushes. My God, Bucky! Did you have to take White Dove?"

"I swear to you, Toes, I never touched her. She followed me into the woods one day and told me that her father had given her to Black Hawk for his wife. When she started to cry, I put my arms around her. That is when Black Hawk came on the scene. He pulled her away and said, 'Mine, not yours.'

"He started stealing from our traps and snapping them shut. When we didn't leave, he and his band of cutthroats started to shoot at us. When I called him a thief in front of the village council, he drew his knife on me. I beat the hell out of him and threw his knife into the St. Francis River."

"You made him lose face. He swore that someday your scalp would hang from his ridgepole."

"He will have to get it first." Bucky tipped the jug to his lips. He found it empty and threw it to one side. He got to his feet, swayed back and forth and almost fell down, catching himself. He staggered over to his backpack and came back with two more jugs of hard cider.

Cross Toes threw his empty jug aside and took the full jug that Bucky offered him. "Good cider," Cross Toes said. He took a couple of big swallows, then handed the jug to Fox.

"The best Clem has. He adds a little rum to it, says it gives it a better kick," Bucky replied.

76

Bucky, Cross Toes, Johnny and Fox sat around the fire, talking and passing the jug of cider back and forth. Fox and Johnny sat with silly grins on their faces as Cross Toes and Bucky continued to relate their experiences while at the St. Francis village.

"It is a good thing for you that they didn't find out that you and Charlie were not French until after you left, or there would not have been enough of you two to feed the dogs. That made Black Hawk a big man in the village after that."

"How did they find out?" Bucky asked.

"Black Hawk was part of a small scouting party scouting around Fort Number Four. He saw you and Charlie there. They jumped a wood cutting detail. I guess they didn't have too much trouble making them talk."

The conversation between Bucky and Cross Toes was getting farther and farther apart, with both of them rocking back and forth, staring into the fire.

"How did your pa get the name Cross Toes?' Johnny asked Fox.

"His little toe crosses over on top of his next toe, so they called him Cross Toes."

"Take your moccasin off, Cross Toes, and show him. Hold on to your nose, Johnny," Bucky said as he slapped his thigh and laughed.

Glancing over at Bucky, Cross Toes took off his moccasin and held his foot up fo Johnny to look at. Cross Toes put his foot across his other leg and started to rub his toe.

"What is the matter, Cross Toes, that toe giving you any trouble? Hell, we can fix that," Bucky said. He reached over and grabbed Cross Toes by his little toe. Reaching to his side, Bucky drew his knife. With a swing of the blade, he cut Cross Toes' little toe off and threw it into the fire. He took the knife blade and stuck it into the red-hot coals. Cross Toes was too surprised and drunk to react for a few moments. Then he let out a yell and grabbed his foot as the blood squirted out. Pulling the knife from the hot coals, Bucky grabbed Cross Toes' foot and stuck the red-hot blade onto the spot where Cross Toes' severed toe used to be. He let out a scream and fainted dead away.

Johnny and Fox jumped up and stared at Cross Toes' foot. Johnny started to gag and throw up. Fox looked at Johnny, then at Cross Toes and Bucky.

"Johnny sick on cider?" he asked.

"No, he is all right. Blood makes him sick."

"He must be sick most of the time."

"Yeah, most of the time," Bucky said with a grin. "Take your shirt off, Fox, and give it to me."

Fox took his shirt off and handed it to Bucky with a puzzled look on his face. Bucky cut a sleeve off and threw the shirt back to Fox. Taking Cross Toes' foot, he wrapped the sleeve around his foot and tied it with a piece of rawhide from Cross Toes' moccasin. Coming to, Cross Toes sat up and grabbed his foot.

"Jesus Christ, that hurts. What did you do that for, Bucky?" Bucky didn't answer. He wondered himself why he did it.

"Here, drink this. It is the best painkiller in the world," Bucky said, handing Cross Toes his jug of cider.

Bucky woke up with a start. He was dreaming that Ben was beating him on the head with a club while Mary was trying to grab Ben's arm. He sat up and looked around the campsite.

Cross Toes was laying on his back, snoring, with his bandaged foot propped up on a piece of firewood. He was holding a cider jug in the crook of his arm. Bucky suspected it was empty. Johnny and Fox were curled up like two balls on the ground. Bucky was cold and had a headache that throbbed every time his heart beat. Also, his mouth tasted, as Charlie used to say, "Like someone had shit in it." The fire was almost out. There was just a few hot coals left. He put a few handfuls of dried grass on top of the coals and blew gently on them until the grass caught on fire. He piled some small firewood on top of the burning grass and hot coals, followed by four or five pieces of large chunks of wood, then took a bucket and headed toward the lake. Bucky dove into the lake. The cold water made his aching head feel better. He swished the water around and around in his mouth and brushed his teeth with his finger. Bucky filled the bucket with water and returned to the campfire when he saw Cross Toes limping around, trying to walk on the heel of his bandaged foot.

"Damn it, Cross Toes, I am sorry."

"Ha! Someday maybe I can return the favor."

"Does it hurt?"

"Of course it hurts, you Goddamn fool. It hurts like hell."

"Sit down and let me look at it." Bucky unwrapped the cloth from Cross Toes' foot.

"Hey! That looks good. Doctor Hastings couldn't do any better." Reaching over, Bucky picked up his jug of cider that had only a couple tablespoons of cider in it and poured the cider onto Cross Toes' foot.

"Jesus Christ, Bucky! What in hell are you trying to do, kill me? I thought we were friends," Cross Toes cried, holding his foot up and trying to blow on it.

"We are, but we have got to kill all those little buggers that cause infection."

All the commotion that Bucky and Cross Toes were making woke Johnny and Fox. They came over and looked at Cross Toes, who was fanning his foot with a piece of flat wood.

"I guess you will have to change your name to just plain Toes now," Johnny said with a smile.

"That is not funny," Cross Toes said, then had to laugh himself and agree. "How am I going to get my winter wood and winter provisions in before snow comes?" Toes asked with a straight face.

The old bastard is trying to get us to do all his work for him, Bucky thought to himself, trying hard not to laugh.

"Don't worry, we will get you all squared away before Johnny and I leave."

The old fox. They should have named him Fox instead of Cross Toes, Bucky thought to himself as he pawed through his backpack and came up with a bottle of brandy.

"I have been saving this for a special occasion, but if your toe starts to hurt too much, take a couple of swallows of this. It should help relieve the pain," Bucky said, handing Toes the bottle of brandy.

Bucky, Johnny and Fox worked all morning and part of the afternoon cutting firewood, only stopping because their bellies were growling and they felt the need for food and drink. As they walked into camp, they stopped and looked down at Toes, who was sitting down on the ground with his back against the cabin wall, snoring, with his chin on his chest and the empty brandy bottle on the ground.

"I guess he must have had a lot of pain," Fox said with a straight face.

Bucky spent three weeks getting Toes and Fox squared away for the winter. He had planned on spending a couple of days with Cross Toes and Fox, but under the circumstances he guess he owed it to them. They had plenty of wood and dried moose meat, salted fish, venison and bear meat. Anything else they needed they could shoot in season, like geese and ducks. They had watched Toes fake them out for a week, walking around the campsite like a young colt until he saw them coming, then he would limp all over the place.

Bucky knew they could leave, but was taken by surprise that night when Toes said, "Bucky, I am going to Montreal to get some powder and ball and a supply of good whiskey. That stuff you had ate a hole right through my stomach."

"Can Johnny come with us?" Fox asked Bucky.

"He is his own man. He can go if he wants to," Bucky replied.

Chapter Thirteen

It took two days of steady walking for Bucky to get to the area that he and Charlie had talked about a few years before. Bucky spent five more days checking the area out. It looked real good; the best he had seen in the Grants in a long time. The place was loaded with beaver ponds. He saw where the beaver were working the poplar trees, and the few beaver he did see were very large. There were a few small lakes, and the place was loaded with muskrats almost as big as the beaver. Bucky was very excited about the prospects for a good trapping season. He could hardly wait to get back to tell Johnny. He missed him. The last few years, since Charlie gave up trapping, he had trapped alone. The winters were long and lonely. He had gotten used to having Johnny around. For the last week, being alone, Mary had been on his mind every day. *God*, Bucky thought, *I should get her off my mind. Nothing can ever come of it unless Ben should die, and he is as healthy as a horse. I should get me a place like Toes, where I could fish, hunt and do some trapping. Maybe get me a nice Indian girl. They are strong and don't mind a few hardships. We could raise some chickens, a milk cow and a whole mess of kids, especially kids.* The thought made Bucky smile as he stood on the mountain ridge and looked down on the area he was planning to trap.

Bucky looked off to the west to another mountain ridge about a day's walking distance away. He remembered that Cross Toes had told him to be careful, that there had been, as Toes had said it, "Bad-ass Indians in the area for the last month," including Black Hawk, who threatened Toes and Fox when they wouldn't give them any whiskey. Fox and Toes sent him packing with the threat of blowing their heads off if they didn't leave. Black Hawk swore he would be back and get even. Bucky was not worried; he had kept his eyes open and had not seen one Indian sign since leaving Toe's camp. Bucky stood and looked off toward the distant mountain ridge. The temptation was just too much for Bucky to ignore. He just had to see what was on the other side of that mountain ridge. He reasoned it would take a day over, he could take a quick look around, then a day back, then back to Toes to pick up Johnny. Then they could head down the river to the fort, pick up supplies and traps, and head back up the river to their trapping area. Sounded just right to Bucky as he started toward the distant hills.

Bucky had been walking toward the distant mountain for most of the day. He thought to himself, *This is just like the rest of the Grants. You walk up one hill and down another. You do a lot of walking, but at the end of the day you are not any closer to your destination than when you started.* Bucky walked across a small clearing and stood on the bank of a small stream. The stream was about twenty feet wide and three or four feet deep. He looked up at the sun and estimated the time to be about four o'clock. Looking down at the stream, it was the first time that Bucky noticed the fresh moccasin prints in the sand by the stream. He eased himself backward from the riverbank and stayed flat on his stomach in the bushes that lined the stream's bank. He peered through the bushes with all of his senses to danger on full alert. Bucky's eyes followed the moccasin prints where they went into the water and came out on the other side of the stream. On the other side was a swamp that Bucky estimated to be about three hundred yards wide, then a small row of trees. He could see smoke from a campfire, and movement that he guessed had to be Indians. Bucky knew Indians had to be very near, for the smell of rancid fat and unwashed bodies was very heavy in the air. He thought, *I have got to get out of here without being seen, and soon*. His thoughts were broken into when someone directly above him said, "Bucky!"

Bucky recognized the voice immediately. He looked over his shoulder and started to get up. Black Hawk raised his musket and drove the butt with all of his strength between Bucky's shoulders, driving him back onto the ground. The pain was so severe that the wind was knocked out of Bucky, and he lapsed into unconsciousness for a few seconds. He could hear yelling, water splashing and Black Hawk giving orders. He was grabbed by both wrists and pulled into the stream. Bucky tried to raise his head to breathe, but only sucked in mouthfuls of water. He thought, *God, they are going to drown me*, as he slipped in and out of consciousness. He could hear more yelling as he was dragged across the ground, the bushes digging into his face. The two Indians dragging Bucky, with Black Hawk running behind them, were war whooping and raising Bucky's musket above his head. They dragged him into the center of the Indian campsite. Bucky laid there, spitting up water and trying to catch his breath. The twenty Indian braves at the campsite stood around Bucky, laughing as they kicked him and poked his body with sticks. He heard Black Hawk say something that he couldn't understand. Suddenly it was silent. He felt a sharp kick to his side. With his foot, Black Hawk rolled Bucky onto his back. He looked up through blurry eyes and saw Black Hawk looking down at him. He would never see hate like that on anybody's face again.

Black Hawk knelt down on one knee beside Bucky and pulled Bucky's knife from it's sheath. Holding it up to Bucky's face, he said, "You son of a bitch, I am not going to throw your knife into the river." Grabbing Bucky by the hair, he continued, "I am going to scalp you with your own knife while you are still alive so you will hear and feel it when it rips off, and you will know that it will hang on my lodge pole at St. Francis. I will be an honored brave, and when the old ones die they will make me chief. I will skin you alive, and you will scream and beg me to kill you."

"Kill him! Kill him now! Do it, Black Hawk," the braves yelled and surged forward. Black Hawk held up his hand.

"No, we will wait until Captain Bennett gets here with the rest of the war party. I want him to see how a real warrior skins a rat. I have waited a long time for this. It is Bucky's turn to wait and think about what he has coming."

As Bucky gained control of his senses, he could see that Black Hawk was in complete command of this war party. He watched Black Hawk strut around with his chest sticking out like a rooster in a chicken coop. The braves were in awe of Black Hawk. Bucky doubted that with everything he had heard about Captain Bennett, he didn't command the respect that Black Hawk did, and with one little snap of his fingers he could have Bennett killed. Black Hawk stood over Bucky, and with a few words and a wave of his hands, two braves jumped forward, grabbed Bucky and dragged him over to a pine tree. They picked him up and slammed his back into the tree. They pulled his arms behind the tree and tied them together. Bucky remembered a trick Charlie had taught him years before. You clenched your fist as tight as you can. That makes the muscles in your wrist swell. Then, when anyone gets done tying you, you relax your muscles. The ropes become loose, and the chances of getting away becomes better. The two braves also tied Bucky's feet to the tree. They stepped back as Black Hawk came over and checked the ropes and shook his head in approval.

He stood in front of Bucky with a big grin on his face and said, "Hey, Bucky! How come you don't say anything? You better pray to your god like the black robes do, because you are going to see him pretty soon."

The braves all laughed and stepped closer, which was what Bucky wanted them to do. He wanted them to hear what he had to say.

"Untie me, Black Hawk, and we will fight, just you and I. Are you afraid? Afraid that I will take your knife away from you and throw it in the river like I did at St. Francis?" Bucky looked at the braves standing behind Black Hawk. He knew that most of them had been at St. Francis when he made a fool of Black Hawk, and the ones who were not there had heard about it. He had dishonored Black Hawk.

He was hoping that Black Hawk would want to regain his honor in front of his braves, for honor meant more than life itself to an Indian. He knew he was getting to some of them when he saw them glance at each other.

A few shouted, "Fight him, Black Hawk! Fight him!"

Bucky knew the one thing Black Hawk was not, and that was a fool.

"Shut up, or I will cut your tongue out," Black Hawk said through clinched teeth.

"No, you won't. You want to go back to St Francis and tell around the campfires how you made Bucky scream and beg for mercy, but that will never happen. I will bite my tongue off first. Then these real braves will go back to St. Francis and tell how you could not make Bucky scream in pain and would not fight him to the death. They will tell them how brave I was and what a coward you are. The brave Indians of St. Francis will laugh at you forever."

Bucky was walking a fine line, and he knew it when he looked at Black Hawk's face. His eyes were little slits in his face. He was biting his lips so hard that there was blood mixed in with the spittle running out of his mouth. Black Hawk wanted to kill Bucky so bad that his whole body hurt. Never in all his life did he want to kill someone so bad. He wanted to plunge his knife into Bucky's belly, cut him open and let his guts fall onto the ground. He held himself in check. He knew that if he killed Bucky now, his braves would say that he was afraid to fight Bucky, or that he couldn't make him scream for mercy. They would laugh at him behind his back and never follow him into battle again. They would call him a squaw man. Black Hawk pulled his knife and, holding it in his hand, looked deep into Bucky's eyes.

Bucky's heart skipped a beat. *God, he is going to cut me loose. I will have a chance, a slim one, but at least I will die fighting.* Black Hawk was not going to let him beat him again. His mind was working overtime. He had to get his braves thinking about Bucky and not him. Reaching out, he grabbed Bucky by his buckskins and started to cut them from his body. Black Hawk was not careful; he cut Bucky here and there as he sliced the buckskins from his body. With blood running down Bucky's naked body, Black Hawk, with a smile on his face, picked up Bucky's penis on the flat side of his knife blade and said, to the Indian braves, "Look here, this is the brave Bucky. Does he look brave to you now? This is what he used to make whores of your wives and sisters when he took them into the bushes."

Flipping the knife into the air, Black Hawk grabbed the blade and drove the handle up and into Bucky's testicles. Seeing Bucky recoil in pain, the braves let out a yell and started to dance around. Black Hawk, once again in command, gave the order for the braves to build a large fire in front of Bucky. The heat from the fire was turning Bucky's skin red. Whenever a breeze blew, the flames would lick at his body. He could smell his hair burning. It also made him cough and his eyes run. Black Hawk came over and stood by Bucky.

"Look!" he shouted to the Indian braves.

"The great white warrior is crying. Don't cry, Bucky. Soon it will be all over. I just got word that Bennett will be hear shortly, after first light tomorrow morning." A young brave jumped forward and pulled a stick from the fire. He stuck it into Bucky's hair, but Black Hawk slapped the stick away.

"No! His hair is mine. I want it whole when I rip it off tomorrow."

The young brave tried to push the red-hot tip into Bucky's eye. He pushed his face away, and the stick burned a round spot on the skin below his eye. The band of Indians watching the young brave went into a frenzy. They started dancing and running around Bucky, grabbing burning sticks and sticking them on his body. After the first hour there was hardly a spot on Bucky's body that was not covered with blisters and burn marks. Suddenly bottles of rum started to show up, and as they drank, the Indians got wilder. They danced, yelled, screamed and fought among themselves, and when they needed someone to vent their rage on, they ran over to Bucky and poked him with burning sticks. Bucky watched as a brave walked over to Black Hawk and spoke to him. They both walked over to Bucky.

Pointing down at Bucky's crotch, Black Hawk said, "Tomorrow I am going to cut those off and bring them back to St. Francis to hang on a pole in the center of the village for everyone to see."

"There will not be any hair on them, Black Hawk," the other Indian said. Picking up a flaming stick from the fire, he singed all of the hair from Bucky's genitals. The pain was almost more than he could stand. He had heard people going crazy from pain, and now he could believe it. To keep his mind off the pain, Bucky tried to think of happier times in his life. Charlie always said that women would be the death of him, and he guessed Charlie was right. If he hadn't been thinking about Mary all morning long, he would have had a clear mind and would have noticed the Indian signs before he stepped into the middle of them. It was a mistake that had cost more than one trapper's life. Bucky watched as one by one the Indians passed out from too much rum, snoring and farting. He started working on the ropes that bound his hands. He was glad that it was rope, not rawhide, even though it meant that some settler was probably dead, because rope would stretch. Bucky pulled and stretched the rope with all his strength until he got a strand of rope from his wrist. It wasn't long before the rope fell to the ground behind him. He looked all around. His heart started to beat faster. It beat so hard in his chest that he hoped they couldn't hear it. Bucky bent forward, all the time keeping his eyes on the sleeping Indians. He reached for a stick with red hot coals on its end and pushed the hot tip into the rope holding his feet together. The hot tip burned into his foot as well as the rope. Bucky grit his teeth in pain for the short time it took for the rope to burn through. Moving very slowly, he stepped away from the tree. His legs were numb from being tied to the tree for so long that Bucky stumbled. A drunken Indian lifted up his head, and through blurry eyes grabbed Bucky by the ankle. Bucky reached down and grabbed a rock to hit him in the head. He was at the row of trees bordering the swamp before he heard any yelling from the Indian camp. He didn't stop to turn and look, but kept on running straight into the swamp. Bucky knew that he couldn't outrun them in the condition he was in. He had to find a place to hide and wait them out. He tripped and fell by an old log. Flat on his stomach, he could see that the log was half submerged in the swamp water and was hollow. Without giving it another thought, he crawled into the log. Bucky crawled as far into the log as he could. He just hoped there was not a skunk living there. He could hear feet running through the swamp and talking in loud voices all around him. Above it all he could hear Black Hawk giving orders. Bucky's heart was beating so hard that would feel his heart pounding. He took a deep breath and tried to relax so that he could hear what was going on.

Black Hawk stood near Bucky's log, holding a firebrand in his hand that was casting a small light. He looked around the swamp with a disgusted look on his face as he watched his drunken warriors staggering, tripping and dropping their firebrands into the swamp water, laughing and shouting at each other.

"Look at the fools," Black Hawk said to the few half-sober Indians who had gathered around him.

"They are going to wipe out all the signs he may have left. You two look upstream. The rest of us will look downstream. If you find anything, give a yell and keep a sharp eye out. He is more Indian than white man." With a wave of his hand to send them on their way, Black Hawk raised his firebrand above his head, stepped over the log and started searching for Bucky.

Bucky lay inside the log, the wood inside poking into his cold and aching body. He tried not to shiver as he listened to the night sounds outside his log. He listened to bird calls that he knew were not birds. With a mental picture of the area in his mind, and listening to the fake bird calls drifting back to him on the night air, he knew where Black Hawk and his friends were looking for him. Some of his fears left him as he listened to the bird calls get farther and farther away. After waiting for what seemed like hours to Bucky, crammed inside the log, his ears tuned to a fearful pitch, picked up the sound of feet splashing through the swamp toward his log. They stopped by the log, and someone put their foot on the log. Bucky felt the log move as the extra weight pushed it down into the mucky water.

Black Hawk and his band of warriors stood around the log. Black Hawk surveyed the area as the dawn started to break.

"Damn! We had him, and we let him get away. I will never find him now. It is starting to rain, and it will wipe out any signs that you drunken fools didn't wipe out. I know where he is heading. is making a beeline to Cross Toes."

"Let's go get him. He can't travel fast in his condition," a brave spoke up.

"No, I will get him and that traitor Cross Toes before the summer is over. We cannot go running off. We have to be here when Bennett gets here. We will have to kill him someday too; all white men should die." Black Hawk squeezed the tomahawk handle and, biting his lips, screwed his face into a mask of hate. "Damn!" he said, and drove the tomahawk into the log.

Bucky felt a sharp pain in his head and lost conscience.

Black Hawk stood in the center of the campsite, his eyes darting around. The sky opened up, and the rain came down in a torrent, running down Black Hawk's greasy hair. With his piercing eyes and long nose, he looked like the bird that he got his name from. He surveyed his braves, huddled under the trees to keep dry. Hearing voices, Black Hawk turned and watched as Captain Bennett and a band of over one hundred and fifty French and Indian soldiers stepped into the clearing. Black Hawk looked at Bennett, with a large hat and a cape wrapped around himself, and thought, *Look at the son of a bitch. Wants to be an Indian, but he will always be a white man. Someday I will kill him. If he opens his mouth, I will kill him now.*

Captain Bennett looked around as he walked over to Black Hawk. He knew that something was not right. He looked Black Hawk straight in the eyes and knew that this was not the time to be asking questions. Bennett was not afraid of Black Hawk. He knew that someday he and Black Hawk would tangle, but this was not the time. Black Hawk was just what he needed for the job ahead.

Keeping his eyes fixed on Black Hawk, Bennett said, "I have orders for us to travel down through the Grants without being seen until we get to Deerfield in Massachusetts. Kill and burn everything. Then move back into the Grants and hightail it back to Montreal. There should be lots of scalps. Are you ready?"

Without answering, Black Hawk raised his arm and, with a sweeping motion, started to lead the way down the Grants.

Bucky slowly regained his senses. It was like coming out of a black hole. The pain was so great that he had to fight to keep from passing out. His head and shoulders were all wet from something sticky that tasted salty like blood, and he never had a headache like this before Every time he moved he wanted to scream, the pain was so bad. Bucky knew it had been raining, because he had heard Black Hawk say so.

He knew it wasn't raining now, because he could not hear it beating on his log. He had no idea of the time or how long he had been unconscious. Bucky laid on the log and listened. He couldn't hear anything but birds singing and his heart beating. Gritting his teeth against the pain, Bucky dug a small hole into the side of the rotten old log with his finger. Looking through the hole in the log, he could see that the sun was shining and that it was sometime late in the afternoon. He looked over toward the Indian campsite. He watched for a long time. He could see no movement. With great pain, Bucky dug a small hole in the other side of the log and peered out at the stream and small clearing he had crossed the day before. Bucky laid in the log, trying to muster up enough courage to leave the security of the log. Clamping his teeth together, Bucky started to ease himself from the log. The pain of the burn blisters breaking and being scraped from his body made him want to scream. With tears running down his face, Bucky grabbed a piece of rotten wood from the log and, clamping his teeth tightly around it, eased himself from the log into the sunlight. With tears running down his face, Bucky lay in the mud and fought the dizziness that was trying to send him into unconsciousness. Taking a deep breath, Bucky raised his head and looked all around. His heart skipped a beat. He was all alone. Bucky thought to himself, *I can't stay here any longer. I need help. I have got to get to Toes.* Mustering up all of his strength and blocking the pain from his mind, Bucky struggled to his feet. Walking bent over with his feet spread apart like a duck, he staggered over to the stream and walked into the water up to his neck. After the smarting stopped, the cool water felt so good that Bucky stayed in the water for a long time, letting the burned skin soften until he could almost stand up straight without too much pain. He washed the congealed blood from his wound in his head, making it bleed profusely again. Bucky walked over to the stream's bank and picked some large leaves from a plant that was growing along the bank. Piling a handful over the open wound, he tied them down with a piece of vine wound around his head and tied under his chin. After a couple of tries, Bucky climbed out of the stream and started the journey back to Toes. The wound in his head was making him dizzy and blurry-eyed, causing him to lose consciousness. As Bucky staggered toward safety, he looked more animal than human, with flies starting to swarm around his head and body. He was in too much pain to notice the flies feasting on the open sores.

Chapter Fourteen

Johnny and Fox were sitting on the ground with their backs against the cabin wall, taking in the early morning sun and talking about their trip to Montreal. Toes walked by only God knows how many times. Toes walked up the little hill where his wife was buried. He stood and looked out across the lake.

"What is wrong with the chief? He is wondering around like a cat looking for a place to shit."

"He is worried," Fox replied.

"Worried? About what?" Johnny asked, surprised.

"Bucky, he should have been back by now."

Johnny and Fox watched as Toes walked back toward them. Instead of walking by, he stopped in front of them. Looking down at them, he ordered, "Pack a bedroll and enough jerky to last three or four days. We are going to look for Bucky. I told him not to go near the Winooski River. That is where the bad-ass Indians hang out, but knowing Bucky, he would want to see for himself."

"It has been almost two weeks since Bucky's been gone. We will never be able to track him now," Johnny said to Fox.

"Yes, we will. You have heard stories of how good your father was at tracking? Toes taught him almost everything he knew," Fox said with pride.

Toes had no trouble picking up Bucky's trail. He pushed Johnny and Fox hard, and on the evening of the second day they spent the night in the area that Bucky planned to trap. The next morning they got up before the sun and followed Bucky's trail all over the area until the afternoon. While Johnny and Fox sat on a log, chewing on venison jerky, Toes made a wide circle around the campsite. Toes stopped and looked toward the ridge.

"Damn!" he exclaimed. His worst fears were realized. "Come!" he shouted to Johnny and Fox. He climbed the ride at a very fast pace, leaving Johnny and Fox far behind. He was standing at the top of the ridge, looking out over the valley and the distant mountains that Bucky had looked at a few day before. Johnny and Fox, huffing and puffing, came up and stood beside Toes.

"I guess I better not bring you two to Montreal again if the girls are going to sap all the strength out of you," Toes said with a grin.

Ignoring Toes' remark, Johnny asked, "What is over there?"

"That is where I think Bucky went. The other side of that distant ridge is the Winooski River Valley. It is one of the main Indian trails from Canada, but with the English sending out more and more patrols from Crown Point, they may have changed their routes to this side of the mountain."

They stood looking out over the valley, each with his own fears for Bucky's safety. They watched a flock of crows flying around in a circle about a mile to their left and slightly downhill from where they were standing.

"Must be a bear," Johnny remarked, thinking of the bear he had seen on his way up the Connecticut River.

"Could be an owl. Crows hate owls," Fox said.

Toes, Johnny and Fox started down the ridge. They had walked about half a mile when Toes suddenly stopped dead in his tracks.

"Go back!" he ordered.

They climbed back up the ridge until they could see the crows flying around. Toes had learned to trust his senses. They had saved his life before. He hoped he was right this time.

Chapter Fifteen

Bucky woke with a start. He was freezing cold. Grabbing hold of a small tree, he pulled himself painfully erect from the damp ground, where he had fallen and passed out the night before. His head was pounding so hard that it was making him sick to his stomach. He was so thirsty that his mouth was dry and his lips were all cracked. Bucky stood there until the dizziness went away and his vison cleared. He painfully moved through the forest, lapping the dew from the leaves of the low-hanging branches. He took his bearings from the early morning sun, walking, sometimes crawling, and always staggering toward the east, with the flies and mosquitoes swarming around him. Day two was more of the same. By day three, Bucky was starting to worry. He was experiencing long periods when he didn't know who or where he was or what had happened to him. On the fourth day he lost it all. The lack of food, water and a raging fever had taken its toll on Bucky. It had left him a blubbering hulk. He didn't even have enough strength left to wave the flies away that were buzzing all around his naked body. There were so many that he looked more like a black man than white. From sheer courage and determination, Bucky had wandered into a raspberry patch and started to hallucinate. Bucky opened his eyes and saw Charlie standing in front of him.

"Charlie! Charlie, help me!" Bucky pleaded.

"How could you be so stupid? Don't you remember anything I taught you? And fooling around with a married woman. What have you gone, crazy?"

"I didn't touch her. I didn't touch Marie, I swear," Bucky babbled.

"I don't mean Marie, I mean her," Charlie said, pointing with his finger.

Bucky looked where Charlie was pointing and saw Mary standing in the sunlight. The wind was blowing her shining red hair. "Mary!" Bucky cried.

The vision of Mary smiled and motioned with her hand for Bucky to come to her. Bucky stood up and shouted, "I'm coming! I'm coming, Mary! I love you. Wait for me." He staggered forward a few steps with open arms, when Ben suddenly appeared beside Mary. With a laugh, Ben pulled her away. "No! No!" Bucky cried.

Suddenly the face of Black Hawk was right in front of him. With a scream, Bucky shouted, "You Goddamn redskin. I am going to kill you!" lunging forward, he landed into the arms of Toes.

Toes picked Bucky up and put him over his shoulders and carried him out of the berry patch and placed him on the ground. Johnny took one look at Bucky and started to gag and throw up. Getting control of himself, Johnny knelt down beside Bucky and put his hand on his forehead.

"My God, Toes! He is burning up with fever. Who could have done this to him?"

"I don't know who, but I am ashamed to say it was one of my people."

Toes cut a strip from one of the blankets and made a bandage for Bucky's head. Picking his head up, Toes poured a few drops of water on his lips. Bucky opened his mouth, and Toes poured a little more into his open mouth. With a wet rag, Johnny wiped Bucky's forehead and face.

"Is he going to be all right?" he asked.

"I don't know. He is in pretty bad shape. We can't do anything for him here. We have got to get him back to the cabin," Toes replied.

"Put him on my shoulders," Johnny ordered Toes and Fox. They picked up Bucky and placed him across Johnny's shoulder. Holding his arms tightly around Bucky's legs, Johnny started to walk at a fast pace toward Toe's cabin.

The sun had gone down hours before, and it was starting to get dark in the forest. Stepping up beside Johnny, Toes said, "Stop, Johnny, we have got to rest."

"No, I am going to get him back to your place tonight."

Putting his hand on Johnny's shoulder, Toes said, "Put him down, Johnny. We have got to get some water and food in him and ourselves, or we won't have strength enough to get him there. Besides, we can't go walking around in the forest in the dark. We have got to take time to make us some torches. "

Toes sent Fox and Johnny to get wood and start a small fire, just to get Johnny out of the way while he examined Bucky. Toes didn't like what he saw. Bucky was burning up with fever, and the sores on his body looked like they were starting to get infected. He had not gained consciousness since they found him, and was moaning from time to time. If he came down with pneumonia, there would be nothing they could do. Toes had to agree with Johnny. They had to get him to the cabin even if they had to travel all night. Fox and Johnny got a small fire going. Toes filled a tin cup with water and crumbled a piece of venison jerky into it. Johnny reached into his pocket and took out a small packet.

Handing it to Toes, he asked, "Here, this is sugar. Will it help?"

Toes didn't know if it would help or not, but he poured it in the cup just the same. He held the cup over the fire and stirred the water, sugar and venison jerky with his finger until it was lukewarm. Toes dipped his finger into the sweetened broth and put his finger into Bucky's mouth. As worried as they were for Bucky, they had to laugh as Bucky sucked on Toes' finger like a baby suckling on its mother. They fed Bucky one quarter of the broth, then shared the rest. They made torches out of pine pitch, and with Toes leading the way and Fox carrying Bucky, with Johnny walking behind, the strange procession once again started walking through the forest. Only the forest animals noticed their passing. They came to Toe's lake early in the morning, just as the eastern sky was starting to lighten up. They looked across the lake with the early morning fog starting to rise like fine lace over the water.

"Johnny, go ahead of us and start a fire in he cabin. Make it a big one, and heat up a lot of water."

Johnny handed Toes his musket, ball and powder, then dove into the lake and swam across to the cabin. He got a roaring fire going with a steaming pail of water hanging in the fireplace.

Toes and Fox, even though they had learned a lot of the white man's ways from the black robes, still lived like Indians. The cabin floor was dirt. They didn't sleep in a bed, but on the floor on a bundle of hay with a bearskin over it. In the winter they used homemade blankets stuffed with goose down. Toes and Fox did not eat at a table, but cross-legged in front of a fire, with their fingers as utensils. Johnny thought, *Someday I will have to teach Fox how to eat with a spoon like civilized people do.* They did have a table that they used to pile everything of value on. Johnny took his hand and wiped everything onto the floor, then dragged the table over to the fireplace. Fox walked into the cabin followed by Toes. Fox laid Bucky on the table. Toes reached over and took the blanket from around Bucky. Johnny looked at Bucky and started to gag. Toes looked at Johnny, shaking his head.

"Go outside and get some air," Toes told Johnny. He went outside, then came right back in.

Toes removed he bandage from Bucky's head, and the wound started to bleed. He glanced at Johnny and noticed his Adam's apple going up and down.

"Except for the black flies around the edges, the cut looks nice and clean. Must be from all the bleeding. Looks like he got hit in the head with a tomahawk." Dipping a rag into the hot water, Toes cleaned the wound. Taking his knife, he shaved all the hair around the cut. Taking one of the bottles of whiskey that he had brought back from Montreal, he poured some on Bucky's head. Bucky moved his head to one side.

"Well, I guess he has some feeling," Toes said as he threaded a needle with some fishing line. Dropping the needle into a metal cup,

Toes poured some whiskey into the cup. He then tipped the bottle up and took a couple of big swallows. Taking Bucky's head in his hands, Toes turned his head to the side.

"Come here, Johnny, and hold his head. Don't let him move."

"Toes, do you know how to do this?"

Holding the needle toward Johnny, he asked, "Do you want to do it?"

"Oh! No, no, I know you are going to do just fine," Johnny said. He held tightly to Bucky's head. Every time he heard the needle pop through the skin, his stomach would rise up in his throat, and Johnny would swallow it back down.

Toes patted Johnny on the head.

"You can let go, Johnny, we are all done."

Johnny glanced at Bucky's head and was surprised. There was no blood. Toes had done a good job; it looked just like the job his mother would do on a rip in his shirt.

Toes took another swallow from the bottle and looked down on Bucky's naked body. The fuzz from the blanket had stuck to the sores on his body. Through whiskey-blurred eyes, Toes thought that Bucky looked like a baby duck.

"Johnny, go get something tree branches about the length of your musket," Toes said, taking another swallow from the bottle.

Johnny was glad to get away for a few minutes. When he came back with the branches, Toes had Bucky all cleaned up. To Johnny he looked much better. He helped Toes make a hoop around Bucky with the branches by bending them over Bucky and tying them together under the table. They gently laid the blanket over the hoops, making sure it didn't touch any part of Bucky's body. Toes tipped the bottle up and drained it in one gulp. Tossing the bottle into a corner, Toes wove over to the fireplace, laid down, and in two minutes was snoring loudly. Johnny walked from the cabin. It smelled like the inside of a whiskey factory from all the whiskey Toes had dumped on Bucky, and Toes' unwashed body sitting in front of the roaring fire was more than Johnny could stand. Fox was laying in the grass sound asleep. He had carried Bucky through the forest most of the night, and he was exhausted. Johnny sat down with his back against the cabin wall. He was so bone weary that his body felt numb. It was early morning when Johnny fell asleep. When he slowly awoke, it was late afternoon. Fox was still asleep in the grass. Johnny could hear movement inside the cabin. Stepping inside, he saw Toes spooning some foul-smelling concoction into Bucky's mouth.

"What in hell is that?" Johnny asked.

"It is willow bark boiled in water. It is good for pain and fever."

"Is he any better?"

"No, Johnny, he isn't."

"Is there anything else we can do?"

"No, we have done all we can. All we can do now is hope for the best and keep giving him this willow juice every hour or so."

"Can't you build a fire and dance around it, shaking rattles and signing?"

"Johnny, I would if I thought it would help," Toes replied with a laugh.

Cross Toes volunteered to stay the night with Bucky while Johnny and Fox stayed in the wigwam. Johnny woke up early in the morning to the sound of splashing in the lake. He pulled the flap aside and looked outside.

"Oh my God!" he exclaimed. "Fox, wake up, you have got to see this."

Fox crawled over to the opening in the wigwam and rubbed the sleep from his eyes. Standing up, he walked outside and stood with his mouth open, a look of astonishment on his face. Johnny and Fox watched as Toes washed his body and clothes. With big grins on their faces, they laughed as Toes walked by naked, wringing the water from his clothes.

"Couldn't stand your own smell?" Johnny asked.

Toes gave them a dirty look. He liked the boys picking on him, especially when they called him "Doctor Toes." He liked that; it was better than Cross Toes had been.

The days were going by slowly for Johnny, Fox and Toes as they sat around repairing Fox's and Toes' traps, getting them ready for the fall trapping season. Fox and Toes ran a small trap line, trapping fox, beaver, muskrats or anything that wondered into their traps. A couple of times they would travel to Montreal and trade their furs for supplies. Their wants were very small, just ball and powder, whiskey for Toes, and white sugar and fish line for Fox. Maple sugar and syrup they made themselves. They also bought flour and cornmeal. All Indians led a leisurely life fishing, hunting and laying around all day. It was a way of life that future generations would only dream about. Toes threw the last of the traps into the pile, got up and walked away.

"There he goes, wandering away again."

"Like a cat looking for a place to shit," Fox replied.

"Fox, you are beginning to sound like a white man every day."

"I guess I will go hunting and try to get some fresh meat for us to eat. Want to come?" Fox asked.

"No, I think I will stay around here, maybe go fishing later. Johnny watched as fox, with bow in hand, disappeared into the forest. He was fascinated by the accuracy Fox had with a bow and arrow. Johnny walked to the lake, pushed the canoe out into the lake and paddled out to the center of the lake. He threw in his line, and within a half-hour had three nice bass. Johnny sat in the canoe and tried not to think of Bucky as he watched the clouds drift by. He knew that summer was fast drawing to a close, and soon the trees would start changing color. The English called it "Indian summer." That was when the Indians raided the settlements, which was not a happy thought for the settlers in the Grants, New Hampshire, New York and Massachusetts. The rocking of the canoe put Johnny to sleep just like his mother used to do when she rocked his cradle back at Fort Number Four. Johnny woke with a start when cold water hit him in the face. He looked into the smiling face of Fox. The canoe had drifted over to the opposite shore. Fox climbed into the canoe and held up a rabbit.

"Nice fat one, Fox." Johnny then held up his fish.

"Nice fat ones, Johnny."

They cleaned their catches and threw the guts into the woods for the animals to eat, then paddled back across the lake. Like most friends, they seemed to be able to read each other's mind. Johnny walked toward the cabin as Fox walked toward the wigwam where Toes was sitting beside a small cookfire.

Stepping inside the cabin, Johnny took a piece of cloth and dipped it into a pail of cool water before placing the cool cloth on Bucky's forehead.

"Hi, Johnny, where the hell am I?"

Startled, Johnny jumped and looked straight into Bucky's eyes. "My God, you are alive!"

"I hope so. Why am I tied? Cut me loose, and what in hell is this thing around me?"

Cutting Bucky's wrists loose, Johnny said over his shoulder as he ran to the door, "You are at Toe's cabin."

Toes and Fox ran to the cabin when they heard Johnny shout at them. Big smiles spread across their faces when they saw Bucky squeezing water from the rag into his mouth and saying, "Boy, that tastes good."

Fox dipped a cup into the water and handed it to Bucky. He gulped the water down and handed the cup to Fox and said, "Give me another."

Toes took the cup and said, "No, too much will make you sick."

"God, this place smells. It smells just like Clem's store did when he broke a keg of whiskey."

Toes got a bottle of whiskey, took a swallow, then poured some up and down Bucky's body.

"You Goddamn fucking savage! You are just like Black Hawk. You like to see someone in pain!" Bucky shouted.

"You hurt my feelings. You called me a savage. I am Doctor Toes, and I make you better. I am going to run that fort doctor out of business," he said with a grin from ear to ear. Tipping the whiskey bottle, he emptied the rest of the bottle on Bucky's body, saying, "Remember? You said we had to kill all those little buggers so they won't cause infection?"

Bucky shouted and swore at Toes until the smarting went away.

Chapter Sixteen

Black Hawk had a bad feeling about this raiding party. He was jumpy and irritable ever since he lost Bucky. He and Bennett had nearly came to blows a couple of times. Black Hawk had a feeling that they were being watched. He knew that each side had spies that traveled back and forth, carrying information, and that someone could have heard of their raid into Massachusetts. Black Hawk told Bennett of his fears and sent out scouting parties. When they would return with nothing to confirm his suspicions, Bennett would laugh at him and say, "Black Hawk, you are losing your nerve." Black Hawk hated Bennett, and his remarks were like pouring whiskey on a fire. He hated Bucky because he was white, but he respected him. He was a warrior, and in a lot of ways they were alike. However, Bennett was nothing but pond scum to Black Hawk.

Bennett would live to curse the day he didn't listen to Black Hawk. Their plans had been reported to General Amherst at Ticonderoga. Their progress down through the Grants had been monitored for days, and a large force of English soldiers and militia had set up an ambush for them that they were about to walk right into.

A flash of light caught Black Hawk's eye in the forest near the head of the column. It looked like a piece of metal catching the rays of the sun. Black Hawk stepped to the side of the trail and motioned to four of his most trusted warriors to join him.

"Saw a flash of light in the woods to our left that we better check out. I hope it is just my imagination again."

They walked into the woods about twenty feet, when suddenly a flash of light, a roar of gun fire and black powder smoke filled the air. For a few seconds all was quiet, then the screams of the wounded filled the air. Black Hawk watched in horror as the English soldiers with bayonets flashing descended down upon the helpless Indians. Bending down on one knee, Black Hawk and his small group watched as a large group of Indians ran back up the trail with the English close behind. Black Hawk ran deeper into the forest and didn't stop until they could not hear anymore musket fire.

While Black Hawk was running, Bennett was being marched over to a group of English officers by an English soldier on the point of his bayonet.

"Captain, here is an Indian who says he is a French Officer," the soldier shouted.

"I demand to see your commanding officer. I am Captain Bennett of the French Army. I demand to be treated with the respect and courtesy my rank demands."

"My God! It is Bennett. You will get no respect from me, you murdering bastard. I don't think you will get any from Amherst," the English captain said with disgust. Turning to the captain of the militia, he asked, "Can you take care of the unpleasant business here? I want to get Bennett to Amherst, post haste."

"We will handle it. I will hang around long enough to see if we can round up some more, then we will hang them all and be on our way," he replied with a toss of his head toward the small group of Indians sitting on the ground.

Captain Bennett was relieved when he saw Fort Ticonderoga sitting high above Lake Champlain. They had force-marched him all the way, and when he complained, they gagged him. He would surely let Amherst know of his shabby treatment. Bennett knew that he would be confined to the fort, but he could stand that until he could be exchanged for an English officer of equal or higher rank. His capture had preceded his arrival to the fort. General Amherst was in front of the large open doors leading into the fort. Bennett, with a pleasant smile on his face, walked up to Amherst and bowed.

Amherst looked Bennett straight in the eyes and said, "You French bastard, you will never enter my fort."

Bennett stepped back with a look of utter surprise on his face.

"Sir, I demand the courtesy and treatment of a French officer while under your confinement as a prisoner of war."

"Demand and be Goddamned. I am going to hang you, you murdering bastard."

"General Amherst, my superiors will hear of this outrage."

"I hope so, then they will not be in a hurry to send another of you French bastards in Indian clothes to murder good English settlers."

"I resent the names you are calling me. As a French officer I demand a trial to answer these charges."

"Here I am. God. I say who lives and who dies. Hang him," Amherst ordered.

A detail of soldiers stepped forward and dragged Bennett over to a tree. Bennett screamed obscenities at Amherst as the soldiers tied his hands behind his back and looped a rope around his neck. Throwing the rope over a branch on the tree, they turned and looked at Amherst. General Amherst raised his hand and let it drop to his side. Taking a good grip on the rope, three of the soldiers pulled until Bennett's feet cleared the ground and kept his kicking feet off the ground until he slowly strangled to death.

The fort's doctor turned and shouted to Amherst, "He is on his way to hell, General!"

"Good. Bury the son of a bitch in the barnyard with the rest of the shit."

Chapter Seventeen

The moment Amherst hung Bennett, Black Hawk was over on the other side of the Grants by the falls on the Connecticut River, ten miles below Fort Number Four. He felt a chill go down his back. Black Hawk was superstitious, but he didn't give it a second thought as he looked down at the falls. His mind went back to the last time he had seen the falls. He was a little boy of nine summers. Black Hawk's mother and father had taught him not to fear the white man, to treat them with kindness and they would return the kindness. For Black Hawk, that all changed a long time ago, when huddled behind these same rocks he now stood beside, he watched two white men kill his father and brother, and rape and kill his mother. Then they threw their bodies into the raging river. He watched as they climbed out of the falls, laughing, and disappeared upriver. Black Hawk and his family came to the falls to fish and look at the carvings left by the ancient ones. It was that day that Black Hawk was turned into a killing machine. He swore that someday he would kill all white men. Some friendly Indians found him huddled behind the rocks, too afraid to move. They took him to St. Francis to live with his uncle. Black Hawk killed his first white man when he was twelve. It was a French trapper who was getting a drink of water from a small stream.

Black Hawk shot an arrow into his back and, sitting beside him, watched him die. That was the beginning. Since then there had been more, more than Black Hawk could remember. Now as Black Hawk stood looking down into the falls, he knew that he would not be able to kill all of the white men. When you killed one, two more took his place. There was only one more white man Black Hawk wanted to kill, and that was Bucky. Black Hawk wanted Bucky's scalp hanging from his lodge pole, where he could look at it for the rest of his life. Black Hawk's thinking turned to the present. He turned and started to walk up stream toward Fort Number Four. The four warriors followed close behind. After saving them from being massacred by the English and militia, they would have followed Black Hawk through hell. Black Hawk knew that they were disappointed. They had bypassed a few isolated cabins where they could have taken scalps, but Black Hawk didn't want to alert the settlers and militia that they were in the area. Now they were here, the place where he had heard Bucky lived, the place the English called Fort Number Four.

He would turn his warriors loose on the next settler's cabin they came to. Black Hawk and his small group crossed the Connecticut River up above the falls. They followed the river upstream until they came to a narrow path leading from the river into the forest. Black Hawk and his four Indian warriors followed the path in single file a short distance, until they came to a small clearing with a small cabin in the middle. They stood in the shadows and surveyed the area. Black Hawk turned to the four Indians and said, "Indians have dogs to sound an alarm. This white man is stupid; he has none."

The four, with smiles, shook their head in agreement. Black Hawk, with the four warriors close behind, silently and swiftly walked across the clearing to the cabin's closed door. Black Hawk pushed the door open and stepped inside. A man, a woman and three children sat at a table eating. The man got up from the table and walked over to Black Hawk.

"Come in, brother, and share our meager meal," he said, pointing toward the table.

Black Hawk slid his tomahawk from his belt and split the man's head wide open. The other Indians ran past Black Hawk and pounced on the woman and children. After the screams died down, all was silent, except for the sucking sounds of scalps being pulled from the white settlers' heads.

Black Hawk liked the feeling he got whenever he killed a white man, or an Indian for that matter, but especially a white man. He knew of some people that got sick or fainted at the sight of blood. To Black Hawk it gave him feelings of ecstasy. He loved to go into battle, hear the screams of the dying, smell the black gunpowder, and the killing, especially the killing. Black Hawk liked close combat. He liked looking into a white man's eyes when he drove his knife into his belly. Black Hawk had an appetite for killing that would never be satisfied, but he wanted only one man's scalp. He was obsessed with killing and scalping Bucky and bringing his scalp back to St. Francis. Maybe today he would get lucky. A brave picked up a flaming stick from the fireplace.

"No! We are to near the fort. We don't want them to know we are here!" Black Hawk shouted.

After the braves ransacked the cabin of food and valuables, Black Hawk led them into the forest. They walked slowly and cautiously for about an hour, always in the direction of the fort. Coming to another small clearing, they looked out across the clearing at a small cabin with its door and windows wide open. They stood by the edge of the forest for a long time, looking the area over inch by inch. Black Hawk thought to himself, *Are these English crazy? Don't they know there is a war going on? Two places with nobody on guard. This is too good to be true.* Black Hawk and his warriors walked cautiously out into the clearing. When they were about halfway to the cabin, one of the braves stopped and said, "Black Hawk, look."

Black Hawk looked in the direction he was pointing. He saw a white man standing at the far end of the clearing. He must have been in the tall grass sleeping, for they never saw him. He stood and looked at them for a few seconds, then turned and disappeared like a ghost into the forest, without firing a shot or shouting a warning to anyone in the cabin.

Black Hawk walked to the open door of the cabin and looked inside. He saw a tall woman stirring something in a large pot hanging in the fireplace. When the light from the opened door changed, Mary looked up, expecting to see Ben. Black Hawk, his eyes accustomed to the dark in the cabin, stepped through the doorway and stood inside the cabin, staring at Mary. Never in all his life had he seen a more beautiful woman. He stood and looked at Mary in awe. He was fascinated by her tall, slim body, her blue eyes and long, flaming red hair.

Mary's eyes flashed back and forth from Black Hawk to the other Indians looking through the open window.

"What do you want? Get out of here," Mary said, shaking the spoon at Black Hawk.

Black Hawk looked at Mary with a smile spread across his face. He had faced men with guns, knifes and arrows who had tried to kill him, now here was this white woman with fire in her eyes, threatening with a wooden spoon.

"You better leave. My husband will be here soon."

Black Hawk let out a loud, scornful laugh. "You mean that scared rabbit that ran and left you here alone for us to do with as we please?"

Mary's heart skipped two beats. It skipped once when she heard that Ben had run away and left her at the mercy of these Indians; it skipped again when the other Indians came into the cabin and called the Indian facing her Black Hawk. *My God! This has got to be Black Hawk, that vicious Indian Bucky told us about!*

One of the Indians reached his hand out to touch Mary's hair. Mary whacked his hand with the spoon. He let out a cry, leaped back and reached for his knife.

"Hold!" Black Hawk shouted. Stepping up to Mary, he yanked the spoon from her hand, then slapped her on the head, knocking her to the floor. Mary jumped up with fire in her eyes. Black Hawk grabbed her by the hair and looked in her eyes. He liked the fire in her eyes. She would bring good money in Montreal. Maybe he should keep her. Yes, he would keep her for his second wife. He would bring her to St. Francis to live with White Dove. He would tame her, and she would give him many half-breeds.

"Come, we must go," Black Hawk said, pushing Mary through the open doorway. As they walked toward the Connecticut River, Mary noticed Black Hawk looking at her. She had seen Bucky looking at her the same way when he didn't think she was looking. It made her heart beat fast and her body tingle all over when Bucky did it, but with Black Hawk it left a big lump in her stomach.

Black Hawk was puzzled. He could hear the bell ringing at the fort. If this woman's husband had run to the fort, and Black Hawk believed he did, then the militia and settlers should be hot on their tails. Instead, they were ringing the bell. To English settlers, that meant an attack was coming and to get to the fort, where they would hole up like foxes in a den. When Black Hawk and his party came to the Connecticut, they found that an Indian family had set up camp by the side of the river. Black Hawk hated these Indians, for they embraced the English instead of fighting them. Black Hawk walked up to them and killed the man and woman with his tomahawk, picked the baby up from the woman's back and threw it into the river. A young boy screamed and ran downstream. Black Hawk threw his tomahawk, which sank deep into the boy's back. Black Hawk reached down and pulled the tomahawk from the dead boy's back and put it in his belt. Picking up Mary, who was staring wide-eyed at what had just happened, he sat her in the center of one of the canoes. Black Hawk got in behind her, and another Indian got in front. The other Indians got into the remaining canoe with the stolen goods from Mary's and the other settlers' cabins. Then, keeping to the Grants side of the river, they paddled upstream.

Chapter Eighteen

Ben ran toward the fort faster than a sinner with the devil behind him with his pitchfork. Ben began yelling at everyone he met, "Indians! Get to the fort."

He ran into the fort's parade ground, yelling, "Indians! Indians! Close the gate and sound the alarm."

Captain Burroughs, hearing the commotion, stepped outside.

"What's the matter, Ben?" he asked.

"Indians, Burroughs, lots of them."

"How many, and where?"

"Down at my cabin. I saw twenty-five or thirty in my clearing, and I could see more in the woods behind them."

"OK, Sartwell, sound the alarm," Burroughs ordered.

"Where is Mary?" Clem asked Ben.

"She isn't here?" Ben asked, looking around, trying to look surprised. "I yelled to her and fired off a shot. I think I hit one of them. She was right behind me as we started for the fort."

"She wasn't with you when you ran past me," a man said as he rubbed his chin whiskers and glanced at the man beside him.

"You don't think I would leave her, do you?"

"Yes, Ben, I think you would," Clem replied.

"OK, OK, enough of that. Maybe she is hiding someplace. I pray that she is," Burroughs said, then started to give orders for defending the fort.

They took all of the powder and shot from Clem's store and stored it in the fort's storeroom. The women filled every pail they could find with water. Some of the men went up into the tower, while the rest of the men and women got ladders and stood on the roof of the buildings that made up the fort.

Sue, who was standing on the roof of one of the buildings facing the Connecticut River, shouted, "Clem, look toward the river."

Nobody said a word. They all saw Mary wave to them as the Indians paddled the canoes up the river and out of sight.

"Captain, isn't there something we can do?" Sue asked, tears running down her face.

"I am sorry, Sue, I can't spare anyone. I may need every man and woman here before this day is over."

Everyone in the tower gave Ben dirty looks and moved away from him. They all knew that it was an unwritten law on the frontier that you saved the last shot for your wife if there was no way out. They all knew of the horrors a white woman went through at the hands of the Indians. Ben walked away from the men in the tower and sat down in a corner by himself. Clem walked over to Ben and spat on him, then walked back to the others.

The cooped-up settlers stood and looked for over two hours for any signs of movement in the surrounding forest. They had not seen a thing.

"Captain, something is not right. Do you see any smoke? Have you ever known of a war party that did not burn everything in sight?" Clem asked.

"No, and I have been standing here thinking the same thing. Sartwell, take a couple of men and go do some scouting. Don't go any farther than Ben Stern's place," Burroughs ordered.

They watched as Sartwell and two settlers who had volunteered to go with him moved swiftly into the forest. Captain Burroughs and Clem stood alone in the fort's tower. The rest of the men and women were in the parade ground, eating. Burroughs and Clem could hear voices off in the distance, then talking and laughter came a little closer. Sartwell and the other two men walked out of the forest as if they were taking an afternoon stroll. Burroughs and Clem went down into the parade ground and waited for Sartwell.

Sartwell walked up to Burroughs and the settlers. Someone handed Sartwell a piece of bread and a cup of tea. He took a bite of the bread.

"Well, what did you find?" Burroughs asked.

Sartwell took a sip of tea to wash the bread down, then answered, "Nothing, Captain. There are no Indians. That twenty-five or thirty Indians Ben saw turned out to be only five."

"The same five that we saw going up the river with Mary?" Clem asked.

Everyone turned and looked at Ben.

"We didn't find any signs of Indians until we got to Ben's place. Then only the footprints of five. We backtracked until we got to the Rock family's place. We found them all dead. We gave them a decent burial."

A murmur ran through the crowd. You could hear over and over again, "Oh my God! Emily and George and the kids are all dead. They were such nice people."

Sartwell took a sip of tea and continued. "We saw where they came up from the river. The Rocks were the first ones they hit. We went back to Ben's place and followed their tracks to the river. We found three dead Indians there. We buried them also. That is all I have to report, Captain."

"You bastard! Why didn't you tell us the truth? We could have saved Mary!" Clem shouted, glaring at Ben.

"I tell you there was more than five. They must have gone off in another direction," Ben lied.

The crowd was in an ugly mood. They hurled insults at Ben, threw hot tea in his face, and those who were near him hit him with their fists. Captain Burroughs grabbed Ben and pushed him into his quarters, then dispersed the crowd. The settlers left the fort. A few went home, but most of them went over to Clem's store to drink and talk about the day's events. The women gathered into small groups to speculate about Mary's fate at the hands of the Indians.

After the settlers left, Burroughs let Ben go. He stood in the parade ground and looked all around, then ran from the fort like a whipped dog.

Chapter Nineteen

The early morning sun shining on his face woke Bucky from a sound sleep. He went outside and stretched in the warm sunshine. Johnny and Fox were already up and taking an early morning dip in the lake. Bucky walked down to the lake, thinking to himself, *I feel good. I am just about all healed, thanks to Toes. I have regained all my strength, and I think it is time Johnny and I headed back to the fort.* Bucky dove into the lake, clothes and all. Taking large mouthfuls of water, he rinsed the morning breath from his mouth. Toes came down to the lake.

"Too much water makes you sick," he said.

"You old fake. You have been washing lately. I can tell by the smell and by the number of dead fish floating on top of the water. Toes, I will never be able to thank you enough for what you did for me. I wouldn't be here if it wasn't for you., Bucky said, stepping out of the water and standing beside Toes.

"That is what friends are for, Bucky. I know you would do the same for me."

"Well, I don't know if I would have dumped all of my whiskey on you."

"I didn't dump it all on you; I did manage to get a couple of swallows."

"Toes, I have used up enough of your hospitality. Johnny and I are going to pack up and head back to the fort today."

"Will you be back?"

"In about a month, month and a half," Bucky answered.

"Toes, can Fox come with us?" Johnny asked.

"Fox is a man now; he can do as he pleases."

Johnny had his musket, tomahawk and knife. Fox had his tomahawk, knife and bow with a quiver of arrows. Black Hawk had Bucky's musket, knife and tomahawk, but Toes had lent Bucky a knife and tomahawk. In the hands of Bucky they were dangerous weapons, so Toes was not worried.

Fox had never been this far south before. He was full of questions, especially why the Connecticut River wound back and forth like a snake. Bucky let Johnny answer all of Fox's questions. His ears and eyes were working overtime. He had vowed that he would never be caught off-guard again. They were in sight of where he and Johnny had spent their second night, when Bucky picked up the sound of faint voices. Bucky motioned for Johnny and Fox to be quiet. They crawled behind some thick bushes and peeked out at the camping area. They got on their stomachs as the voices got louder. Suddenly, Black Hawk stepped into the clearing. Bucky could feel every muscle in his body tighten. If he had had a musket he would have killed Black Hawk right there on the spot. He was so busy watching Black Hawk that he didn't notice Mary step into the clearing until Johnny said, "My God, Bucky! There's Mary!"

Bucky was in shock for a few seconds. Mary? How could they have captured her? Did they surrender the fort? As Bucky watched Mary and Black Hawk, four more braves walked into the clearing. Black Hawk said something to the four braves that Bucky could not hear. The four braves laughed as Black Hawk walked out into the forest. Two of the braves walked over to Mary and pointed down at her crotch. One of the braves reached down and started to pull up Mary's dress. Mary hit him and pushed him away. The other braves, with big grins on their faces, laughed until tears started to run down their faces as the brave tried again and again to pull up Mary's dress.

Bucky knew what they were thinking. If it was red on top, was it red below? Bucky had heard the men at the fort wondering to. They would say, "If the chimney's red, what must the fireplace be?" Bucky had to admit he had wondered a few times himself.

It was not a game to the Indian anymore; he was getting mad. He said something to the other Indian. The second Indian grabbed Mary by the waist and threw her flat on her back on the ground and held Mary down while the other Indian got between her legs and started to pull her dress up. Bucky knew they were going to rape Mary. The hair stood up straight on the back of his neck. Bucky jumped up and ran toward Mary. When he was twenty feet from her he threw his tomahawk. It sailed through the air and struck the Indian who was holding Mary's arms down in the middle of his forehead. He released Mary's arms and fell over backward. With his knife, Bucky slit the other Indian's throat from ear to ear with such force that he almost cut his head off. Throwing him backward, Bucky turned to face the other Indians just in time to see one of them raise his musket. Bucky heard something whiz past his head and saw an arrow sticking in the Indian's chest. The Indian's legs got all rubbery, he fell to his knees, then fell over onto his chest, pushing the arrow out through his back. Bucky heard a musket fire and saw the last Indian fall over backward. He bent over to pick up Mary, who was screaming her head off. She reached up and grabbed Bucky by the neck. Bucky looked up and saw Black Hawk pointing his own musket at him, and he was looking straight down the barrel.

Bucky shouted, "Let me go, Mary! For God's sake, Mary, let go of me!"

Bucky saw an arrow flash by and strike the musket barrel just as Black Hawk fired. He heard the ball as it went by his ear. Pulling away from Mary, he ran toward Black Hawk, but he had melted into the forest. Bucky knew better than to follow him. He could pick them off one at a time. Bucky helped Mary to her feet; she was shaking like a leaf. Mary wrapped her arms around Bucky and started to cry. He would have liked to hold her forever, but he knew they had to leave, and soon. They stripped the dead Indians of anything of value. Bucky picked up a musket, powder horn and a bag of shot and handed them to Fox.

"Here, Fox, this is yours." Fox's face lit up like a full moon.

They walked down to the river. Bucky picked out a musket, powder and shot for himself and threw the rest into the river. Mary walked out into the river and tried to wash the blood from her dress, face and hands. When Mary got out of the water her dress clung to her body. Bucky took one look, then took a deep breath and slowly blew it out through his lips. He thought to himself, *It is a good thing the boys are here or I would build Ben a family right here on the riverbank.* He noticed that Fox was fascinated by Mary's red hair. He just kept looking at it. Bucky helped Mary into the canoe.

Fox put his hand on Bucky's arm and asked, "Bucky, she got red hair all over?"

"I don't know, what do you think?"

"I think maybe yes."

Mary, sitting in the canoe, looked back and forth from Bucky to Fox, her face getting redder and redder. Johnny got in the front of the canoe, Fox behind him, and Bucky behind Mary. The four of them started down the river. Bucky couldn't help but smile as every once in a while Fox would glance over his shoulder at Mary's hair.

They decided that they would not stop overnight but would head straight to the fort, even if it took all night. The trip down the river was peaceful. You would never know by looking at the beautiful mountains in the Grants that beyond them, men were killing men just so one king or another could say, "This land is mine."

"Bucky, you lived with the Indians?" Mary asked.

"Yes, I did," Bucky replied.

"Did you know that the Indians believe that dreams fall from the sky and that bad dreams fall from the sky and are caught in a spider web while the good dreams fall through to the dreamer?"

"Yes, I have heard that."

"It is true," Fox said, turning and sneaking a peek at Mary's hair.

"With a smile on Mary's face, she asked Bucky, "Do you know a lot of Indian girls?"

"A few."

"Are they pretty, or are they big and fat like the ones around the fort?"

"Some are fat and some aren't. I know one who is very pretty. Her name is White Dove."

"I know White Dove. She is very pretty, but not as pretty as you," Fox said, turning and smiling at Mary.

Laughing, Mary said, "Fox, I think you and I are going to be very good friends." After a slight pause she asked, "Do you like her, Bucky?"

"Yes, like a sister."

"Oh, where is she?"

"She lives at St. Francis. She is married to Black Hawk."

"He is not nice to White Dove. He beats her," Fox said sadly.

"Do you have a girlfriend?"

"No," Bucky replied.

"There is nobody that you like?"

"Yes, there is someone I like very much."

"Is she pretty?"

"Yes, very pretty."

"Is she tall like me?" Mary asked with a little smile on her lips.

"Just like you," Bucky replied.

"What color is her hair?"

"Red, just like yours."

"Does she know that you love her? Why don't you tell her?"

"Because she is married."

"Oh, just like me."

"Yes, just like you."

"Maybe you don't have to tell her; maybe she knows."

"I hope so." Then the conversation ended.

After walking around what Bucky said was the last of the falls, Mary sat in the canoe and looked at the starry sky and thought to herself, *God, don't let this night end. Let us go past the fort, down the river to New York. There are a lot of people there; they would never find us.*

Mary asked God to forgive her for her thoughts. She was married, and what she was asking for was a sin, and God would never grant her her wish. Mary had thought that Bucky had eyes for her. Now she knew, even if he would not come right out and say so. She didn't love Ben, and the thought of going back to Ben made her sick to her stomach. He was dirty, lazy and selfish. Nobody liked him, so they didn't have any friends, and he was a coward. He left her for the Indians. The thought made Mary shiver. Mary had heard that in the big cities there was a thing called a divorce, where you could leave your husband if you didn't love him anymore. It cost money, and only the rich could afford to do it. On the frontier you were married for life; the only way you left your husband was when you died. She had heard that a long time ago a girl left her husband and ran away with another man. They hunted them down and hung them both. Listening to the paddles dipping into the water and the gentle rocking of the canoe made Mary sleepy, and she dozed off.

Mary awoke with a start when she heard Johnny say, "There is the fort."

The light from the moon cast an eerie glow around the fort. To Mary it looked like a prison instead of a safe haven. When the canoe reached shore, Bucky stepped out and picked Mary up. He held her tightly in his arms. Mary buried her face into Bucky's neck and gave him what most people would call a little peck. It sent the blood rushing through his veins. He didn't want to, but he gently let Mary slip through his arms onto the ground.

"Bucky, I am afraid," Mary said, holding tightly onto Bucky's arm.

"Why, Mary? You are safe now."

"I know, but I am still afraid. The Indians had me for a whole day. What will people say?"

"Maybe a lot of things, Mary, but not in front of me."

"That goes for me too, Mary," Johnny said. A few seconds later it was followed by, "Me too," from Fox.

Mary laughed, but she would not have if she had known that Fox would have protected her honor with his life if called on to do so.

"Johnny, would you run ahead and get Sue and Clem? Tell them to meet us at the fort."

"Sure. What about Ben?"

"To hell with him," Bucky replied as they headed toward the fort.

Bucky banged on the large closed fort doors with the butt of his musket. After a few minutes someone asked, "Who is it, and what do you want?"

"It is Bucky, and I have Mary with me."

Bucky heard the message being relayed.

"Captain, he says it's Bucky and he has Mary with him."

They all heard when Captain Burroughs shouted, "Then for God's sake, let them in!"

They could hear the wooden bars being removed from the large doors. The doors swung open. Bucky, Mary and Fox stepped into the fort's parade ground and faced Captain Burroughs and a small group of settlers who were spending the night in the fort. Burroughs held a lantern above his head. It cast a circle of light around Bucky, Mary and Fox.

"Oh my God! It is you, Mary!" he exclaimed.

Bucky heard Clem shout, "Don't close that door!"

Clem, Sue and Johnny ran into the parade ground. Sue ran straight to Mary. Putting her arms around Mary, she asked, with tears in her eyes, "Are you all right? I didn't think I would ever see you again."

"I am fine, Sue, thanks to Bucky, Johnny and Fox," Mary replied.

"Sartwell, take two men and go get Ben. If you accidentally shoot him on the way back I will make you a lieutenant."

"First or second?" Sartwell asked with a grin.

"Go on, get the hell out of here."

"How long are you going to run Sartwell ragged, Captain?" Bucky asked as he watched Sartwell hurry from the fort.

"Bucky, Sartwell is a gopher. You know, Sartwell, go for this and Sartwell, go for that," Clem said with a laugh.

"It is all part of his training. Someday he will command large groups of men. You have to be able to take orders before you can give them," explained Burroughs.

While waiting for Ben, everyone stood in silence as Mary told of her capture by Black Hawk, her trip up the Connecticut River and her rescue by Bucky, Johnny and Fox.

"What's with the Indian?' Clem asked Bucky as he watched Fox follow Mary around like a little puppy.

"Oh, he's in love with Mary's hair," Bucky replied with a laugh.

Questions where flying right and left at Mary, especially from the woman. All conversation stopped as Ben walked into the fort and up to Mary. Looking her up and down, he said, "You don't look the worse for the wear. Come on, I am losing my sleep."

Mary stood with her hands on her hips and glared at Ben.

"Come on, woman, I said let's go."

Mary took a couple of steps toward Ben, then stopped and turned around. Pulling six long hairs from her head, she handed them to Fox. A big smile spread across Fox's face. Mary bent down and whispered something into Fox's ear, and his smile got even bigger.

"What in hell did you do that for? He is just a stinking Indian," Ben asked with a sneer on his face, looking for support from the crowd.

"A stinking Indian? This Indian helped rescue me and save me from being raped by Black Hawk and his killers. What did you do? You ran and left me to face Black Hawk and his braves alone. This young Indian is more of a man than you will ever be. You are nothing but a coward!" Mary shouted at Ben, then pushed him aside and walked out of the fort.

Chapter Twenty

Bucky was sitting in front of a makeshift table made of two sawhorses and some boards stretching across them. The table was piled high with traps. He was sorting the traps, putting the good ones on the ground to his left. The ones that needed repairing were to his right. He had been back three weeks and everything was peaceful. Old Moe was coming along just fine. He was spending most of his days over at the store with Clem and Sue. Johnny had taught Fox how to shoot his musket; he was a fast learner. He was almost as good as Johnny. They picked on Fox, trying to get him to tell them what Mary said to him the night she gave him the strands of her hair. He wouldn't even tell Johnny, who he loved like a brother.

Johnny tried to coax it out of Fox by saying, "You can tell me! I won't tell anyone."

"Can't, Johnny. Mary said it was our secret. Not to tell anyone."

Fox braided Mary's hair into a fine piece of rope and wore it around his wrist until the day he died.

Bucky had an idea what Mary said to Fox, and he hoped that someday he could find out for himself. He looked up and saw Sartwell walking toward him. *Oh shit, what in hell does Burroughs want now?* he thought to himself.

"Hi, Bucky."

"Hi, Sartwell, sit down and have a drink."

"I can't, Bucky, I am in kind of a hurry."

"Bullshit! I don't even want to hear what Burroughs wants. You come here and deliver Burroughs' messages, then you are gone like a fart in a strong wind. Sit down and have a drink, and fuck Burroughs." Sartwell took a couple of swallows from the jug.

"How's the wife?" Bucky asked.

"Fine," Sartwell answered and took another drink from the jug.

"You don't have her knocked up yet?"

"No, not yet, but I keep trying. You know, Bucky, you are quite the conversational piece to her and the rest of the ladies around here."

"Really, why is that?"

"They are wondering what your balls look like without any hair on them."

"That bastard Clem! He has been shooting his mouth off again. Sartwell, you go back and tell those ladies that tomorrow at one I am going to have a showing. Your wife can be first in line."

"No charge?"

"No charge, for free."

"That is a good deal. I will tell them," Sartwell said with a laugh. He took another sip from the jug, them wiped his lips with the back of his hand.

"Bucky, I am not here for Burroughs. Actually, I am here to ask a favor for myself. General Amherst sent a message to Burroughs with orders to form a party of not less than thirty men and be ready to leave tomorrow morning. Amherst got word from Canada that the French were coming down with a force of six hundred French and Indians. Word from Amherst's top spy is that they are going to split their force three ways once they reach Champlain. Two hundred Indians with a few French officers are going to raise hell with the settlers around the lakes region area of New York. Another two hundred are coming down the Grants to attack here and Fort Drummer. The other two hundred or more are going to attack the fort at Crown Point, then lay siege to Ticonderoga. The French think we will pull ships and troops away from Quebec and release the strangle hold we have on them there. Amherst is sending a hundred Indians and English regulars. Some settlers from Massachusetts are joining the party. We should have a force equal to theirs. Burroughs put me in charge. It is my first command. I need people I can trust. I want to come back alive."

"Sartwell, you make it kind of hard to say no."

"Is that a yes?"

"Yes, I will go with you."

"We will go too," came a voice from behind them.

"I don't think you should go, Fox. You may have friends there."

"I don't have Indian friends anymore. You and Johnny are my friends. They make my father leave their village in the winter, and my mother died. They come to our cabin and call us traitors and threaten to kill us. No, I will go with you and fight to keep Mary safe."

"I can't argue with that, Fox, but you can't go dressed like that. You would be a target for both sides."

"Bucky, I saw a green shirt in Clem's store. Fox, you would look like that ranger we saw this morning."

"I have heard of those rangers. They are brave warriors. I will be a ranger."

Bucky couldn't sleep; he tossed and turned for hours. He wasn't worried about the upcoming battle, but he was getting tired of all the killing. He got up and went outside and stood looking up at the sky. He let his mind wander over the things that were most on his mind. If God can make the stars, why can't He stop the killing? Maybe there isn't a God. If there was a God, would he let it go on forever and ever? He didn't have an answer for that. He had seen Mary only twice since they got back. She didn't act the same; she acted sad and didn't smile. It seemed to Bucky that all the fire had gone out of her. He had a feeling that she was avoiding him.

He asked Sue about it, and all she said was, "You don't understand, Bucky. She is doing what she thinks is best for the both of you."

Bucky was sure that Sue knew more than what she was telling

him. Maybe it was Ben. Clem told him that Ben was there drinking every night. Clem had told him that he had cut off all of his credit, but he thought he was drinking up Mary's egg money. He had also heard that Ben was selling some of their furniture and tools. He said that there were a couple of rowdies who hung around and told Ben how smart he was and agreed with everything he said as long as he bought the drinks. Ben also told everyone who would listen that he had not touched Mary since she came back. That he was not going to take seconds after any Goddamn Indian, or Bucky either. Bucky thought of going to Clem's store and facing Ben. He knew that if he did he would kill him. Looking up at the sky from the hard table, he finally fell asleep. When he woke up, dawn was just breaking. He gathered up his things and walked to the fort. Bucky stood outside and greeted the other volunteers as they arrived. Bucky saw Mary walking toward Clem's store and walked over to her.

"Hello, Mary, I am off to play with some more Indians again," he said, trying to appear happier than he was feeling.

"I heard," she replied.

For a minute they stood and looked into each others eyes.

"I love you, Mary," Bucky whispered.

With tears welling up in her eyes, Mary replied, "I know, Bucky, I know. I will pray for your safe return.

Sartwell's merry men, what Burroughs called them, left the fort at sunrise. For two hours they sat beside an old Indian trail, waiting for the men from Massachusetts. Armies had been hurrying up and waiting for centuries. The men from Massachusetts arrived, and the men from New Hampshire poked some good-natured fun at them, such as, "What's the matter, did you get lost?"

Sartwell and Sergeant Rose of the Massachusetts militia sent out scouts, and the combined groups started up the trail. They were not the type of men you would expect to see on a parade ground. They were a group of armed roughnecks, but they were born for the type of fighting they were going into. After walking up the trail for more than half a day, a scout came running down the trail.

"Redcoats up ahead," he reported to Sartwell and Rose. They

rounded a corner in the trail and saw one hundred Indians and English soldiers looking at them. Sergeant Rose looked at the English soldiers.

"Jesus, they look just like a bunch of sore pricks."

Sartwell and Rose walked up to a small group of English officers.

"I am Captain Perry. You are Ensign Sartwell?"

"I am, sir."

"Do you understand that you are to be under my command?"

"Yes, sir, I was told."

"Are you familiar with this area?" Captain Perry asked.

"No, but I have someone with me who is," Sartwell replied, calling Bucky over.

"I understand that you are familiar with this area?" the Captain asked Bucky.

"I am, Captain. You want a good place to set up an ambush?"

"Yes," Perry replied.

"Then follow me. It is about an hour's walk up the trail. Captain, keep those drums quiet. This forest has big ears."

Bucky, Sartwell, Captain Perry and his officers walked up the trail at a fast pace.

"I don't think the French would have heard our drums," Captain Perry said, looking at Bucky.

"At the last report, where were they?" Bucky asked.

"The report I got this morning from one of my scouts was that they were about fifty miles up the trail."

"Are they Indian scouts, sir?" Sartwell asked.

Bucky thought to himself, *I know what Sartwell is thinking. You can't trust all Indians. If you are going to have someone out there to be your eyes and ears, you damn well better know who they are, because like white men, some are lazy and couldn't find their way out of their wigwam.*

"You been here long, Captain?" Bucky asked.

"About three months."

"You sound like you are not happy to be here."

"I am not! I have friends in high places that are working to have me sent back to England."

"Captain, if you stay here long enough you will get to love this place. It is beautiful, even with all of its dangers."

"Bucky, I have looked, and I see no beauty around here."

Bucky liked this Captain Perry. He did not look down his nose at you. He hoped he lived to get back to England. Bucky raised his hand and stopped.

"Captain, this is it. Look over the lay of the land. I think you will agree that it is a good place to kill French and Indians."

Taking Sartwell aside, Bucky said, "Sartwell, I don't trust his scouts. With your permission, I will take Johnny and Fox and do some scouting of my own."

"I would feel a lot better if you did," Sartwell agreed.

When Bucky returned late in the afternoon, he walked up to Sartwell, who was pacing back and forth.

"Sartwell, what is the matter?"

"Take a look Bucky! That Goddamn Perry's going to get us all killed!" he exclaimed, pointing to a line of red in the forest. "A blind Indian could spot them a mile away."

"Have you talked to Perry?"

"I tried to talk to his officers. They said he knows what he is doing. The arrogant bastards won't let me get near him."

Bucky spun around and walked over to where Captain Perry was standing, surrounded by his officers. Stepping up to Perry, Bucky asked, "Captain, will you take a little walk up the trail with me, alone? I have something I would like to show you."

As Bucky and Captain Perry walked slowly up the trail, he opened the conversation by telling Captain Perry about Indians.

"Captain, there is very little that I do not know about Indians. I have fought for and against them. For the last ten years I have spent as much time with them as I have with white people. I know them very, very well. The Indians coming down this trail are the best you will ever meet. If they spot you first you are dead. Captain, I want to give you some advice. Do not ever trust anyone else's scouts. Cultivate your own people you can trust. Your scout lied to you. I just got back from scouting. There is a large force of French and Indians, as large as ours, maybe even larger, camped just five miles up the trail. They will be here early tomorrow morning. Now turn around and tell me what you see."

Captain Perry turned and looked down the trail.

"I see the trail, trees, and I see red English uniforms."

"What you see is dead English soldiers if you don't do something about it."

"What should I do?"

"First move everyone back into the woods, about seven or eight hundred yards. A large force like this will send out scouts about a mile in front of them. There will be about fifteen or twenty of them. A few of them will walk down the trail. The rest of them will be spread out on both sides of the trail about two or three hundred yards wide. You will have a party of your Indians set up a trap for them down the trail, and Captain, make damn sure they understand they are not to attack until they hear our shots. We want them all in our trap before we spring it. After their scouts pass through, we bring our men up fast and quietly to their positions. You take your redcoats and hide behind that rise over there. When you hear the first shots being fired, you come a charging. When they see those redcoats charging at them with bayonets shining, those French and Indians will shit their pants. Tell your men not to worry, there will be more than enough Indians to go around."

"If this works, Bucky, you know that I will get all of the credit."

"Captain, after this is over, Amherst will think that you are the best Indian fighter in the colonies, and he will never let you go back to England," Bucky said with a laugh.

Captain Perry had Bucky and Sartwell pick out people they could trust to scout the French and Indian camp and let them know when they started to move down the trail. He also gave the order that no one was to fire until Sartwell gave the order to fire.

Everyone was settling in for a long night. They had all sharpened their knives and tomahawks and cleaned their muskets, then did it all over again. The men told jokes and bragged to keep their courage up, but everyone had butterflies in their stomach. Bucky noticed that they all had put their powder horns inside their shirts to keep their powder from getting damp from the night air. The men were laying around, deep within their thoughts. Bucky looked around and wondered how many would be alive after tomorrow. They sky was getting light in the east when the scouts returned and reported to Captain Perry that their enemies were on the move.

The word spread like wildfire up and down the line. Nobody had to tell anybody to be quiet. Bucky had Captain Perry take his hat and had him wrap up in Johnny's blanket to hide his red uniform. Bucky led him up toward the trail and under a low bush.

Bucky said, "Keep your eyes on that small clearing up ahead."

He stared at the clearing for what seemed to him a very long time. The sky was getting light and starting to penetrate down into the forest. Captain Perry sucked in his breath. He though he saw something in the clearing, but when he blinked his eyes it was gone. He caught a movement out of the corner of his eye, but when he looked it was gone also. He thought, I *guess I need some sleep, my eyes are playing tricks on me.* As he stared at the opening, he saw a figure appear and disappear before his eyes. After the Indians passed through, Sartwell and Rose brought their men forward to their passions to wait, with taunt nerves, to spring the trap.

"Good luck, Bucky," Captain Perry said as he headed back to his men behind the knoll.

Bucky, Johnny and Fox were in the center of the line with Ensign Sartwell. They were on their stomachs behind an old log about one hundred feet from the trail.

"Steady, boys, here they come. Hold your fire, let them come into our trap. I want them all," Sartwell said in a whisper.

Bucky could see them coming down the trail. Two single file columns side by side.

"Steady, boys, steady. They are halfway in," Sartwell whispered through clenched teeth.

Everyone held their breath. By looking at them you would have thought they had forgotten how to breathe. The French and Indians were three quarters into the trap when suddenly gunfire could be heard way down the trail. A thought flashed through Bucky's head. *Damn, Perry's scouts have jumped the gun.*

Sartwell jumped up and shouted, "Fire! Fire! Kill them all! Kill all those French and Indian bastards!"

A deafening roar rang out from the forest, and the smell of black powder filled the air. It was so quiet for a few seconds that the silence hurt your ears. The silence was broken by Sartwell screaming, "Charge, boys! Charge! Don't let any of them get away!"

They all jumped up, and the line surged toward the trail. The yelling of the attacking men and the screams of the wounded and dying French and Indians mingled together into one loud, ear-piecing sound. The French and Indians who had survived the first volley regrouped to face the charge. When they saw the redcoats charging toward them with their gleaming bayonets flashing in the early morning sun, in their haste to get away they tripped and fell over their dead and wounded comrades, their feet slipping in the blood-soaked earth of the trail. Bumping and pushing each other out of the way, they tried to run back up the trail. Some took off and tried to run through the open woods on the other side of the trail. The redcoats had a field day picking them off like rabbits. The redcoats were professional soldiers; they could shoot and load three shots a minute. It was a lucky Indian that survived by going that route.

Bucky ran out onto the trail; he wasn't aware of any sounds. He had his musket by the barrel and was using it as a club on the disorganized Indians. He could see bodied falling in front of him, and he liked it. That day all Indians were Black Hawk. He swung his musket and hit an Indian in the face. The wooden stock broke, so he threw it aside and grabbed his knife in one hand and his tomahawk in the other just as a short, stocky Indian came at him with a knife in his upraised hand. Bucky stepped to the side and hit him in the head with his tomahawk and split his head open like a pumpkin. Suddenly, it was over. Bucky was coved with blood. He didn't know how much of it was his. He was tired and breathing hard; killing was hard work. He stood there catching his breath and listening to the moaning and screams of the wounded. He recognized another sound; it was

Johnny, gagging and coughing. He looked over and saw Fox standing beside him. They seemed in good shape. Bucky watched as the Indians went about their grisly task of taking scalps. They started right after the first shots were fired. They were not going to fight as long as there were scalps for the taking. They didn't care if they were friend or foe, living or dead. Bucky watched as a young French officer sat on the ground, trying to hold his guts into his stomach with his hands. A brave walked over to him and looked at him with a smile, ran his knife around his head and scalped him. The French officer let out a scream. The Indian hit him in the head with his tomahawk, and he fell over backward. Maybe the Indian did him a favor; he would have died anyway.

"Come on, boys, let's get them all or chase them back to Canada!" Sartwell shouted.

He tried to get the Indians to join the chase. All they did was laugh at him. One of the Indians walked up to Sartwell and, shaking his bloody knife in his face, said, "You go chase them."

Sartwell pushed the Indian, knocking him down, then turned and shook his head in disgust before walking away. The Indian jumped to his feet and ran toward Sartwell's back with his knife in his upraised hand. Suddenly he stopped, dropping his knife. He fell to the ground with an arrow in his chest. A brave walked over and looked at Sartwell, then down at the dead Indian. Bending down, he took hid knife from his belt, scalped the Indian and went on his way, looking for more. Nodding his head in thanks to Fox, Sartwell gathered his forces and headed toward the shots he could hear farther down the trail. When they got there, they found that Captain Perry had a small group of Indians trapped and was picking them off one by one. A big Indian climbed onto a large boulder and was trying to rally his braves. A shot rang out. A black hole appeared in the center of his forehead, and he toppled off the boulder. With their leader dead, the Indians threw down their weapons and surrendered.

Everyone felt good. The battle was over and their losses were light. Sartwell lost one from his group. Rose lost one of his Massachusetts boys. Everyone had cuts and bruises. There were ten wounded in very bad shape. Bucky was sure that some would die on the way back home. Bucky saw five redcoats laying on the ground; he hoped there wasn't more. The French and Indian losses were great. One hundred and sixty dead, four French officers captured, and twenty Indians. Captain Perry figured about thirty or forty escaped.

Black hawk was with some of the French officers at the rear of the column when the attack started. They were standing around waiting for a report on what was happening, when they were surprised by a large force of militia. The French ran up the trail. Black Hawk ran into the forest with five of the militia close behind him. A shot rang out, and Black Hawk felt a slight tug from his hair. He ran faster. He could hear them yelling behind him. Black Hawk came to a clearing in the forest overgrown with Juniper bushes. He knew that if he tried to run across the clearing they would shoot him down like a rabid dog. Without giving it another thought, Black Hawk dove under a large Juniper bush with branches growing near the ground.

"Where is he? He has got to be here somewhere. I saw him when he ran out into the clearing," Sergeant Rose shouted.

Black Hawk could see their feet. They were so close he could have reached out and touched them. Black Hawk heard a shot, and one of the men shouted, "I've been hit!"

"Where?" Rose asked.

"Jesus, Rose, he shot me in the ass."

"Let me see. Hell, Andy, he just grazed you. It will be a little sore for you to sit down for a few days, but you are all right. Did anyone see where it came from?"

"Yes, I see him. See him? He is over there by that tree, reloading."

Black Hawk counted five shots being fired. He heard someone shout, "We got him! We got him!" He saw their feet running away. Black Hawk stayed under the bush all day and late into the night. Crawling out from under the bush, he set a course for Montreal, Canada.

Chapter Twenty-one

Bucky, Sartwell, Johnny and Fox stood behind Captain Perry and watched as the four French officers bowed and smiled. They did everything but kiss Captain Perry's ass. Captain Perry was very courteous as he accepted their swords in surrender. He told them, as prisoners of war, they would be treated with respect and honor. To himself he thought, *You two-faced French bastards, I hope when we get back to the fort Amherst hangs you like he did your Captain Bennett.*

Sergeant Rose and four of his men walked out of the forest. Rose and three of his men were laughing. The other one was holding his pants away from his left buttock.

"I don't think it is funny," he said.

"What is the matter, Rose, did he shit his pants?" Sartwell asked.

"No, he got shot in the ass by an Indian. We were chasing an Indian through the woods when we came to a clearing. I don't know how he did it, but he disappeared like a ghost. He must be a ghost, because he got to the left of us by the edge of the woods, and when we were looking around trying to spot him, he shot Andy in the ass. We got him. He won't be killing settlers anymore."

"Rose, I don't think that was the same Indian. The one we shot was short and stocky. The one we were chasing was about the size of Bucky and had a black feather sticking out of his hair. The one we shot didn't have a feather."

"How do you know it was a black feather?" Bucky asked.

"Because I shot at him and hit his feather. Cut it right in half," Andy replied, showing Bucky the top half of Black Hawk's feather.

"Come on, Andy, let's take care of your wound. We have got to get him back to Massachusetts so his wife can kiss his boo-boo and make him all better," Rose said with a laugh.

"He got away again?"

"Looks that way, Fox," Bucky replied.

A small group of Indian prisoners, with their hands tied behind their backs, were being herded down the trail by some of Perry's Indians.

Hearing someone call out, "Bucky! Bucky, help me!" Bucky looked up, a look of surprise spread across his face.

"Crow! What in hell are you doing here?" He stepped forward and pulled Crow from the line and cut the rope binding his wrist.

An Indian stepped forward and pushed Crow back into the line, saying, "Mine. He comes with me."

Bucky took his knife and put the point against the Indian's stomach. "No, he stays with me," Bucky said.

The Indian backed away and looked at Captain Perry. Bucky glancing over his shoulder said, "Captain, I will be responsible for him."

Perry shook his head and motioned the Indian away. The Indian, glaring at Bucky over his shoulder, walked away.

"Crow, what in hell are you doing here?"

"I didn't have a choice, Bucky. Black Hawk and some of his followers came to St. Francis and said he wanted warriors for a big raid. We had heard that there was going to be a big battle around Quebec, and we thought that was what he wanted us for, but Black Hawk said we were going to raid the settlements in the Grants and Massachusetts. Most of us didn't want to go. We do not believe in killing women and children. Bright Feather, you remember Bright

Feather? He stepped forward and said he would not go. Black Hawk shot him right in front of all of us. Nobody said no after that."

"Crow, I will take you as my prisoner. I will take you to Fort Number Four. I want your word that you will stay there until the war is over."

"Bucky, you have my word."

"Captain, I have spent many months around his campfire. We have hunted and fished together. His word is good."

"If you say so, Bucky, that is good enough for me."

Captain Perry, Bucky, Sartwell, Johnny, Fox and Crow stood around in a tight little circle. They stopped talking and watched three men in green uniforms walk up the trail toward them. They stopped in front of Captain Perry and gave him a sloppy salute.

The one who seemed in charge said,

"Captain, do you have anyone here called Bucky?

"I am Bucky. What do you want?" Bucky asked.

"We were sent by Major Rogers to bring you to Crown Point."

"Why? It doesn't matter. I am not going."

"Major Rogers doesn't take no for an answer. He told us not to come back without you."

"I don't care what Rogers wants. I am not going."

The man who was doing all of the talking stuck out his chest and folded his arms on his chest. With smug look on his face, he said, "Look, mister, Rogers wants to see you, and we are going to take you to Crown Point even if we have to hogtie you and carry you there."

Quick as a flash, Bucky stepped forward and grabbed the man by the testicles and squeezed. The Ranger sucked in his breath, opened his eyes wide and stood on the tips of his toes. "You are going to take me where?" Bucky asked as he squeezed harder. The other two Rangers didn't make a move to help their comrade, for Johnny and Fox had their muskets jabbed into their ribs.

Captain Perry put his hand on Bucky's shoulder and said, "Bucky, let go of him."

Bucky let go of the Ranger. The Ranger bent over in pain, breathing hard and rubbing his testicles very gently.

135

Perry put his arm around Bucky's shoulder and said, "Bucky, yesterday you gave me some good advice, and I took it. Now let me give you some. I don't know what is going on, but General Amherst has been madder that a hornet for over a week. I have a feeling that Rogers wanting to see you may have something to do with it. I think you should go and talk to him."

Turning to the Ranger, Captain Perry asked, "Do you know why Rogers wants to see him?"

"No, sir, all I know is that when he gave us our orders he said not to come back without him. He said he heard that Bucky knows the area like the back of his hand."

"Bucky, I will send the Indian prisoners back to Ticonderoga with my scouts with orders to send boats for me and my men to Crown Point. I will take the French prisoners and escort you to Crown Point."

"All right, Captain, I will go." Turning to Sartwell, Bucky asked, "Will you tell Burroughs about Crow?"

"Do you want Fox and I to go with you?" Johnny asked.

"No, I will be back shortly," Bucky replied.

He watched as the Indian prisoners and Perry's Indian scouts disappeared into the forest. Bucky knew that he was looking at dead men, for as soon as they were out of sight, Perry's scouts would kill them and take their scalps. News of the battle had preceded the men from Fort Number Four. Their friends, wives and children were lined up outside the fort, waiting for them. Sartwell had the men line up, and they marched up to the fort. They were greeted with shouts and applause. The children ran out and hugged and kissed their fathers while the women waited patiently for their turn. They were proud of their fighting men and had planned a big celebration. Clem had donated a barrel of good hard cider. The women had made kettles of bean hole baked beans, corn bread and bacon and fried salt pork. Some had made butter and cheese, while others brought fresh milk thick with cream on top. The men ate their fill and thanked Clem for the cider. Someone started to play a fiddle, and the men, women and children started to dance.

Johnny, Fox and Crow walked over to Clem and Sue as soon as Sartwell dismissed them.

"Johnny, where is Bucky? Is he all right?" Clem asked.

"No need to worry, Clem, he is all right. He has gone to Crown Point. That Ranger, Major Rogers, wants to talk to him. He will be home soon." Johnny noticed a relieved look come over Mary's face, as she was standing close by, listening.

"Who is he?" Clem asked, pointing at Crow.

"This is Crow, a friend of Bucky's from St. Francis that we took as a prisoner. He is to stay at Bucky's place until the war is over."

"What in hell is he doing, starting an orphan house for Indians?" Ben asked with a thick tongue from drinking too much of Clem's cider. Ben's drinking buddies roared with laughter and pounded Ben on the back. Mary gave Ben a disgusted look and left for home.

The party lasted all day. It broke up just as darkness was setting in. The men left with their wives holding onto their arms, the children walking close behind. You could bet that a lot of children would be born the following spring.

Clem didn't expect much business at the store and Sue's dining room, not with all the free food and drink at the fort. After it got dark a few people wandered in, mostly to talk and sip a few drinks. Ben hung around outside in the shadows, waiting for them to leave. He didn't dare to go in. He knew that they would call him names for abandoning Mary to the Indians and not joining the men for the raid. After the last couple left, Ben rounded up his cronies and walked into the dining room and up to the bar. He ordered drinks for everyone. Clem waited until Ben paid before he poured the drinks. The men were loud and vulgar. They stood around the bar, farting and laughing about it.

Sue said, "Clem, why don't you throw them out?"

Clem hated to as long as they were spending money. He watched as a stranger walked into the room and leaned his musket against the wall, removed his backpack and sat down with his back to the wall. His eyes darted around the room and rested on the men at the bar. Clem gave him the once-over as he walked over to his table. He wasn't a big man, about five feet seven inches, maybe one hundred and fifty pounds. He looked to be in his late twenties and had spent most of his life outdoors and was able to take care of himself if he had to.

Walking up to the table, Clem asked, "What can I do for you, stranger?"

"I know it is late, but do you have anything hot I could put into this empty belly of mine?" he asked.

"We sure do. How does chicken and dumplings, fresh bread and butter with a slab of cheese and a mug of hot cider with a stick of cinnamon sound to you?"

"Boy, that sounds good," the stranger replied.

"I don't believe that I have seen you around here before." It was Clem's nosy nature to pry for information.

The stranger said with a little smile, "I have been through here a few times. Never stayed long. Just long enough to say hello to a few friends. My name is Joe Becker. I just came back from spending a year with the Plains Indians. I thought it was about time I came back and spent some time with my woman."

"Where is home?" Clem asked.

"North," Joe replied but didn't offer any more information.

Clem knew that he was not going to get anymore information from him, so he left to prepare his meal. After setting the food in front of Joe, Clem returned to the bar. He glanced at Joe from time to time and noticed that he was relishing his meal. Joe would look up and stare at the men at the bar, shake his head, then go back to eating.

"Ben, are you keeping that redhead happy?" one of his drinking buddies asked.

"Goddamn it, I told you before. How many times have I got to tell you? I won't have anything to do with her. I will not take seconds after any Goddamn Indian, or Bucky either. It is one thing for an Indian to take your wife, but to have your neighbor rescue your wife from the Indians, then keep her out in the woods and use her like a whore is more than a man can take. When he had his fill he brought her back and handed her back to me and expected me to say thank you! Well, I will not take seconds from Bucky or any other man."

"That is not true," Joe said from the back of the room. Everyone turned around and, for the first time, noticed Joe sitting behind them.

"What did you say?" Ben asked.

"I said that is not true. I know Bucky. He wouldn't do that to anyone who was a friend and neighbor. He is one good fellow."

"I say he did that to my wife."

"And I say you are lying," Joe shot back.

"You talk funny. Are you French?" Ben asked.

"Yes," Joe replied.

"I think you are a Goddamn French spy!" Ben shouted.

"I am no French spy," Joe said, glaring at Ben.

"I think you are a Goddamn French spy, and I am going to bring you over to Burroughs at the fort!" Ben shouted, suddenly finding his courage.

"You are not taking me anywhere, you are drunk." Joe stood up and slapped some money on the table and turned to get his musket and backpack.

"You son of a bitch! You're a Goddamn French spy, and I am going to kill you," Ben shouted. Ben was a good shot and could have shot Joe in the back easily, but he was drunk and wove back and forth. The shot went wide and smacked into the wall beside Joe's shoulder.

Clem had never seen anybody move so fast before. Joe spun around and reached behind his head. Clem never saw the knife flying through the air. It was only after Clem heard a funny noise that he looked at Ben and saw a knife had been driven into his neck, clear up to the handle, with the point sticking out of the back of his neck. Ben's eyes opened wide and his arms fell to his sides. He started to slide down, but the knife point caught on the edge of the bar and held him up. He hung there with blood gushing out all over his chest. Clem looked toward Joe, but he had already run out through the door.

It took Ben's drinking buddies a few seconds to realize what had happened. Then with a shout of, "Lets get that murdering French bastard!" they staggered toward the door. An old Indian, who every day sat outside, begging for money or anything else anyone would give him, said to the men as they ran out the door, "Him go that way." He pointed in the opposite direction that Joe went. The old Indian sat back down with a grin on his face as he listened to them shouting to each other and running in the wrong direction. The old Indian didn't like them. They would spit in his hand when he held it out. The stranger had given him money and called him chief.

Joe had been to Bucky's cabin before, so he made a bee line for it, running as fast as he could. He banged on the door. When the door opened part way, he slid inside and slammed the door shut. Breathing hard, trying to catch his breath, he stood facing Johnny.

"Bucky, where is Bucky?" he asked.

"Bucky isn't here. He's at Crown Point," Johnny replied.

"Joe! For Christ's sake, is that you!" Moe exclaimed.

Looking past Johnny, Joe's eyes opened wide in surprise.

"Moe, what are you doing here?"

"I asked you first," Moe said with a laugh.

"Christ, Moe, I just killed a loudmouth over at the trading post. I need your help, I have got to get away from here."

"Take it easy. You are safe here. That kid in front of you is Charlie's boy. That Indian is Cross Toe's kid. The other Indian is just a tagalong. Johnny, run over to Clem's place and see what is happening."

Johnny saw a few people walking in and out of the dining room. He stepped through the opened door. Captain Burroughs and Clem were sitting at a table. He walked over and sat down with them. Looking over, he saw Ben hanging from the bar with a knife in his throat. He gagged a few times and swiftly turned his back to Ben.

"What happened?" Johnny asked.

"Someone just did us a big favor," Clem replied. "I saw it all, Captain. It was self-defense. Ben was drunk and took a shot at the stranger and missed. You will find the ball over there in the wall. The stranger, who called himself Joe Becker, threw his knife. As you can see, he didn't miss."

"Well, I am not going to get up a search party and go looking for him tonight. I will do a little looking for him tomorrow, but I expect he will be long gone by tomorrow. Will you take care of Ben?"

"Yes I will put him out back for tonight and bury him in the morning. Look at the mess the son of a bitch did to my floor!" Clem exclaimed.

"Put some sawdust on it. It will soak up most of the blood. Will you tell Mary?"

"I will, Captain." After Burroughs left he said to Johnny, "Take Sue to Mary's cabin and bring them both back here. Then tomorrow morning, bright and early, go to Crown Point as fast as you can and get Bucky."

Clem, bitching to himself, wrapped Ben up in an old blanket and dragged him out behind the trading post. After Clem left, the old Indian sneaked behind the trading post and unwrapped Ben's body. He took his knife and scalped him. The old Indian then wrapped Ben's body back up in the blanket. He was buried the next morning without his hair, and nobody ever knew.

Late that night, Johnny and Fox guided Joe to the river and gave him one of their canoes and bid him a safe trip.

Joe paddled up the Connecticut River, and in a few days he was safe back in Canada. After seeing Joe safely on his way, Johnny and Fox headed toward Crown Point.

Chapter Twenty-two

Captain Perry went with Bucky and introduced him to Major Rogers. Major Rogers got three glasses and a bottle of good whiskey. The three of them sat around and sipped the whiskey. Rogers told them that after their victory over the French and Indians, the French abandoned the raid on Crown Point and returned to Canada. Captain Perry finished his drink, shook hands with everyone, thanked Bucky for his help and wished him luck, then left for Ticonderoga.

Bucky liked Major Rogers. He had a good handshake, and he looked you in the eyes when he talked to you.

"You sent for me, Major? What do you have on your mind?"

Major Rogers said, "Follow me." They walked to the center of the large parade ground. Rogers looked all around. They were all alone.

"Only two people know what I am going to tell you, General Amherst and myself. The first week in August, Amherst sent two of his officers under a flag of truce northward down the St. Lawrence to Quebec. As a pretext, they were caring a peace offering to the Indian settlements along the way. They were nothing but damn spies. What Amherst really wanted was to know how Wolfe was doing with his assault on Quebec. About a month later he got a letter from General Montcalm, telling him that a band of St. Francis Indians captured his men and that he was holding them as prisoners. Well, sir, Amherst flew into a rage and threw the men that brought the letter under a flag of truce into the dungeon. He is madder than hell because Montcalm got the best of him. Now he wants to take his revenge out on the St. Francis Indians. Amherst has ordered me to take two hundred and twenty Rangers and proceed to Missiquoi Bay at the end of Lake Champlain and attack the Indian settlements along the south side of the St. Lawrence River. Then he wants me to march to the Indian village of St. France and burn it to the ground, but not to hurt or kill any women or children. Bucky, here is my problem. The French control all of Lake Champlain. If they catch us in our whale boats out on the water, they will blow us all to hell. We will also have to dodge their scouting parties on shore, but I think I can get us to Missiquoi Bay without being detected. We know nothing about the territory above Lake Champlain. The whole area is blank on English maps. I have no idea where St. Francis is, or the course to take. I have only heard that it is above Montreal. That is why I sent for you. I heard that you know the area like the back of your hand. I need you. Will you guide us to St. France?"

"You are right, I know that country very well. It is very wild country and very swampy ground. There is dry ground, but if it has been raining, that will be swampy too. You will never reach St. Francis."

"Why?" Rogers asked.

"Because if you attack any of the villages along the St. Lawrence River, the news will spread like a fire in a strong wind, and before you travel five miles the French and Indians from St. Francis and Montreal and the small forts along the way will descend on you like a swarm of yellow jackets."

"To hell with Amherst. We will bypass the villages and make a beeline for St. Francis. How long will it take us to get there?"

"Getting there and back will take about two or three weeks, if everything goes well," Bucky replied.

"I will issue rations for a month," Rogers said, more to himself than to Bucky.

"They should have a couple of warehouses full of corn at this time of the year. Your men can fill their haversacks with corn. It will keep their bellies full until they get back to Crown Point."

"Will you show us the way?" Major Rogers asked.

"Yes, you get us to Missiquoi Bay and I will get us to St. Francis."

On the morning of the thirteenth, Bucky watched all morning long as heavy whale boats came up the lake from Ticonderoga and were beached on the sandy shore below Fort Crown Point. He stood looking across the lake at the New Hampshire Grants hills and noticed that they were starting to change color. Hearing someone call his name, Bucky looked over his shoulder and saw Johnny and Fox walking toward him.

"What are you doing here?" Bucky asked, surprised at seeing them at Crown Point.

"Clem sent us. Ben is dead. Joe Becker killed him in a fair fight in Clem's dining room. He said that you would want to get back as soon as you could."

Bucky said, "I sure as hell do," and ran to the fort with Johnny and Fox close behind.

"Major, I have got to go to Fort Number Four."

"Bucky, I can't let you go, we are leaving tonight."

"I don't know where you are going, but if Bucky is going, Fox and I are going too," Johnny said, leaning on his musket and looking Major Rogers straight in the eyes.

Major Rogers stared at Johnny for a full minute. He liked what he saw. Finally, he spoke.

"We are going to attack the St. Francis Indian village. I expect you to hold up your end, and Bucky, it you want to write a letter I will have it sent by special courier to Fort Number Four."

Johnny said, "Major, Fox is a St. Francis Indian."

Bucky sat down and started to write his letter while Rogers pumped Fox for information about the St. Francis village.

> *Dear Clem and Sue,*
> *I can't get back to Fort Number Four at this time. I am*

*about to leave on a raid with Rogers and his Rangers.
Johnny and Fox are with me. I can't tell you where we are
going, but I am sure you will hear in about three weeks.
Pray for us; we will need them. Sue, will you speak to Mary
for me? I know that she will have all kinds of offers. Please
tell her to wait for me to get back. I hope it will be within
a month. I don't want Mary to stay in her cabin alone. I
want her to stay in my cabin and take care of Moe. Crow
will protect and help her. Ask her to wait for me until
spring. If I do not return to Fort Number Four by spring it
will be because I am dead. Then everything I own is hers.
There is money in Portland; she will find papers in the
cabin, and Marie will be sending money that is owed me. I
do not want her to go without food or clothing. Give her
unlimited credit and take it out of the money you are
holding for me.*

    Your friend,
    Bucky

On the night of September thirteenth, Major Rogers and his whale
boats shoved off from shore with the others close behind. Rogers put
Bucky in the last boat with orders that if anything went wrong he was
to go back to Crown Point as fast as he could, because he was the only
one who knew the way to St. Francis. They could not afford to lose
him. The Rangers packed the oarlocks with grease and wrapped them
in cloth so they would not make any noise when they rowed. They
would row then glide, listening for any sounds of the French navy.
They last report Rogers got was that they were about fifteen miles
from Crown Point. That report was weeks old; they could be
anywhere by now. They could be five miles or, in this darkness, two
hundred feet. When dawn started to break, Major Rogers guided his
Rangers to the shore of Button Bay and had the Rangers hide the
boats deep in the forest. The men ate a breakfast of cold rations.
Rogers told them to get used to it, because that was all they would
have until they got back. Rogers sent out scouts northward to see if
they could find the French navy.

Bucky settled down on the pine needles and quickly fell asleep. He awoke several hours later with the feeling that someone was standing over him. He slowly opened his eyes and saw the Indian that he took Crow from looking down at him. The Indian slid his knife from his belt and said, "You pricked my belly, now I am going to cut yours."

Bucky smashed his right foot into the Indian's testicles. His mouth shot open and his eyes got as big as saucers. Bucky's left foot shot out and smashed into his stomach, sending the Indian backward, smashing into a tree, where he slid down into a sitting position, out cold. A group of Indians jumped to their feet. Johnny and Fox levered their muskets at them and they backed away. That was the beginning of Major Rogers' problems. Rogers' scouts found the French navy sailing back and forth off the mouth of the Otter River. Rogers knew they could knot sneak past the French ships as long as they were sailing that close to shore. He would have to sit and wait for the weather to change, or for them to sail back to the northern end of the lake. Rogers' luck didn't change for the better as the day wore on. He sent the Indian that Bucky laid low back to Crown Point. He could hardly walk. That afternoon fifteen Indians came down sick, and Rogers sent them back to Crown Point. The night stayed clear, and the French still sailed back and forth. The next day Rogers paced back and forth, watching his Rangers sitting around and nibbling at their rations all day long.

Rogers said to Bucky, "If we don't move pretty soon we won't have enough rations left to get us to St. Francis."

On the third day, another group of Indians and Rangers became sick, and Rogers had to send them back to Crown Point. On the morning of the sixth day, Rogers had to send another group of sick Indians and Rangers back to Crown Point, and the French navy still sailed back and forth, making no move to leave. Rogers got his officers and Bucky together.

"Boys, we are between a rock and a hard place. If we stay here much longer, a French and Indian scouting party will find us. We can't sneak by the French ships until we get a cloudy night. We are down to one hundred and fifty men. If we lose more I will have to call it off and return to Crown Point."

Nobody wanted to turn back. They talked Rogers into giving it two more days. Late that afternoon a cool breeze blew across the lake and rustled the leaves above their heads. As the day wore on, clouds moved in and a cool misty rain started to fall. At nightfall, Major Rogers gave the order to put the boats in the water. The Rangers piled in and started to row toward the French ships. All of a sudden the heavens opened up and the rain poured down so hard that Bucky could hardly see the boat ahead of them. The French ships were laying at anchor, riding out the storm. Bucky could just make out the outline of a ship as they glided by. Dawn found them way up the lake from the French ships. Major Rogers wanted to make up some of the time they had lost, so he took a chance and put scouts ashore and had them scout ahead by land. Daylight found them passing through the narrow body of water between the east shore and Grand Isle, ending up in Missiquoi Bay at the northern end of the lake. Rogers led them to shore. They pulled the boats from the water and hid the boats and supplies in the underbrush. The men were bone tired. Rogers decided they would spend the night at Missoquoi Bay and get an early start in the morning

"I got us this far, Bucky, the rest is up to you," Rogers said.

By the dawn's early light of September twenty-third, the Rangers, with Bucky and Major Rogers in the lead, started their trek to St. Francis. Before they left, Rogers had two Indians stay behind to watch the boats and supplies with orders to stay there until they got back. If the boats were found they were to make a beeline back to them. Late in the afternoon of the twenty-fifth, the two Indians Rogers left behind caught up to them. A large party of French and Indians had found the boats and had burned them. About two hundred French and Indians were hot on their trail about a day's march away.

Major Rogers called a council of war with his officers and Bucky. "OK, Bucky, you know the area. What do we do?"

"Major, we cannot go back, and we cannot go around the swamp looking for dry land to walk on or they will be right on our backs. We have to cut straight through the swamp. It will be hard going, but it will be just as hard on them if that makes you feel any better. After we attack the village we better move out fast, following the St. Francis River's southerly branch to lake Memphremagag, working our way south until we pick up the Passumpsic River and follow it until it empties into the Connecticut up above the Wells River. It will be a fight all the way, but it is the only chance we have."

"I will send a small party back to Amherst, requesting that he send supplies up the Connecticut to the Wells River, for that is the way we will be trying to get back."

Major Rogers and his Rangers, with Bucky leading the way, plunged into the swamp at a fast pace. After a couple of hours the pace slowed down as the mud sucked at their feet and held them in its grasp like glue, sapping their strength. They fell over logs and into sink holes up to their waist. After the first day, all the days were the same. They were forever tired, cold and wet. There was no dry land to lay down on, so at night they tied themselves to trees and caught what sleep they could and started all over again the next morning. The Rangers bitched and complained constantly among themselves, saying that it was a mistake to let Bucky guide them, that he didn't know where he was going and that they were going to die in the Goddamn swamp, but nobody made a move to go back, for they knew it was sure death back there. Nobody knew what day it was since they all seemed to run together. Slowly they walked out of the swamp and stood on dry ground. After a short walk they stood on the bank of the St. Francis River. Bucky looked around.

"Major, we are on the wrong side of the river. We have got to cross and get on the other side. The village is about ten miles below us." Fox shook his head in agreement.

They crossed without losing a man and, for once, the Rangers didn't complain about being wet and cold, for they would soon be sleeping on dry ground. Bucky led them downstream to within two miles of the village. Major Rogers made sure that his men were well hidden before he, Bucky and some of his officers left to scout the village. Bucky led them to the edge of the village, where they peered out through thick bushes at the Indian village. The Indians were having some kind of a celebration. Most of them were drunk and dancing around a large fire in the center of the village, to the beat of drums. Bucky pointed out the important features of the village to Major Rogers.

"The large building is the chapel. Father Roubaud is the priest; he has a room in the back. He is a good man. I don't want anything to happen to him, Major," Bucky said, with a tone of warning in his voice. After a slight pause, he continued, "Those two larger huts beside the church are the warehouses. They will be full of corn."

"I hope so. We are almost out of rations," Rogers whispered.

"At the end of the village near the river is where they keep their canoes."

"I expected the village to be bigger," Rogers said.

"There is another small village downstream on a small island, but this is the main village. I noticed something that does not seem right. Do you notice something missing in this village, Major?"

"No, I don't, what is it?"

"There are only a few young braves. There are mostly old men, women and children here."

"Maybe the young bucks are the ones behind us," Rogers replied.

They stayed late into the night and watched the party slowly wind down. The Indians left by ones and twos back to their wigwams. Everything looked good; the village did not expect an attack. It would be a complete surprise, but Bucky still had a bad feeling he could not get rid of.

A few hours before dawn, Major Rogers brought his Rangers up close to the village. They stacked their bedrolls and backpacks, loaded their muskets and slid on their bayonets. They patted their knives and tomahawks to make sure they were on their belts. Then they quietly crept to the edge of the clearing surrounding the village, waiting for Major Rogers to order the attack. Dawn was breaking when Rogers gave the order to attack. The Rangers rose up from their hiding places and slowly advanced toward the wigwams. The

Rangers saw scalps hanging from lodge poles beside the wigwams, making their blood run cold. They all had friends and family that had suffered from Indian raids on frontier New England villagers. Maybe some of the scalps were from their loved ones. Today they would have their revenge. A dog started to bark. An old Indian come to the door of the wigwam with a stick in his hand to throw at the dog and looked straight into the eyes of a Ranger. The Ranger drove the bayonet into his belly and pushed the Indian off with his foot, sending him backward into the wigwam. Bucky heard a shot being fired from the wigwam, followed by screams. The Ranger ran from the wigwam and into the next one. The scene was repeated over and over again throughout the village. The young braves taken by surprise and realizing that they were no match for the Rangers, ran to their canoes by the river, hoping to escape downstream. Major Rogers had made plans to stop any escape that way, and had a large group of Rangers waiting. In the early morning darkness they had crept over to the canoes and cut the bottoms out of them. When the Indians jumped into the canoes their feet went through the bottom and got tangled up in the wooden ribs. The Rangers shot them like fish in a barrel. Some dove into the St. Francis River and tried to swim to the other shore. They made easy targets for the Rangers. A few survived by playing dead and floating down the river. After the first shots, Bucky stood near the church and stared in disbelief. Rogers had lost control of his men. They had gone crazy with lust and were killing every man, woman and child they could find. It was a scene straight from hell. The Rangers were setting the wigwams on fire and killing the Indian men, women and children as they ran out. Bucky looked toward the church when he heard shouting coming from it

"You French bastard! You are no better than the Indians."

Bucky saw two Rangers push Father Roubaud out of the church. Farther Roubaud tripped and fell to the ground. The Rangers leveled their muskets at him. Bucky jumped in front of Father Roubaud and held up his hands.

"Don't shoot, he is a priest!" The Rangers turned and walked back into the church and ransacked it, looking for valuables.

"Bucky, Fox! How could you be part of this?" Father Roubard asked, surprised at seeing them there.

"It was not supposed to be like this, Father," Bucky replied. He stood looking out over the burning village, hoping White Dove had survived the attack. A young Indian girl about eight or nine years old ran screaming towards them, with a Ranger swinging a tomahawk close behind. The little girl ran to Father Roubard, wrapping her arms around his waist. She buried her face into his stomach.

Bucky grabbed the upraised arm of the Ranger and looked into his glazed eyes and said, "It's all over, Ranger. It's all over."

The young Ranger suddenly stopped struggling and looked around the village at the bodies of the women and children."

:Oh my God! What have we done?" He started to tremble, sat down on the ground and started to sob. The smell of death was everywhere. The smell of blood and burning flesh mingled with the gunpowder and wood smoke. Johnny had been gagging and throwing up since the beginning of the attack. Fox and Bucky walked around the burning village, looking for White Dove.

Fox said sadly, "This is White Dove's wigwam."

Bucky shook his head in agreement. He was sick in his heart. He could see bodies under the flaming coals.

Major Rogers had finely stopped the killing. It had taken about an hour to wipe out everyone in the village, except twenty-five or thirty women and children who were huddled around Father Roubard. Bucky, Fox and Major Rogers walked back to Father Roubard.

"Father, I am going to let you, the women and children leave whenever you want to."

"Are you going to burn down my church?"

"Yes, I'm afraid I have to," Rogers replied.

Bucky let his eyes wander over the Indian captives. Something registered in his brain, and his eyes shot back to a woman standing slightly behind Father, looking down at the ground almost hidden from his view.

Bucky shouted, "White Dove!"

White Dove looked up, a look of surprise across her face. She ran to Bucky and threw her arms around him and started to cry.

"It's all right, White Dove. You are safe now. I am going to take you back with me to Fort Number Four. Black Hawk is an animal; he will never beat you again," Bucky said as he gently brushed his fingers across an old bruise on White Dove's face.

"Pray for us, Father, for a safe return."

"No, Major, not after what you did here today. I will pray that God will forgive you and take your souls into heaven."

Major Rogers gathered his Rangers around the huts that held the corn.

"Men, it is going to be a long walk back to Wells River. Throw most of the booty away and make room for corn. Fill your pockets and everything else with corn. You will need it," Major Rogers ordered.

Most of the Rangers were loaded down with stolen Indian goods they wouldn't throw away, and took only a small supply of corn. Bucky, Johnny and Fox loaded themselves down with corn. Bucky knew the load would get light very fast. Bucky filled White Dove's small pockets with corn. Looking around, he found a small cloth bag and filled it with about five pounds of corn. Handing it to White Dove, he walked over to Father Roubard to say goodbye. As he stood talking to Father, two Rangers walked out of the church. One was holding a small wooden cross in his hand. The other held a silver statue of the Virgin Mary.

"Oh no!" Father exclaimed, and took a step toward the Ranger.

"No, Father, he will kill you," Bucky said, putting his hand out and holding him back.

"Oh God, Bucky! Dear God! Not the Virgin!" Father Roubard cried.

The Ranger looked at the priest with a grin, put the statue inside his shirt and tightened the belt holding up his pants.

"I promise, Father. I promise I will try to get it back for you," Bucky said.

Bucky looked across the St. Francis River from the opposite

shore. The early morning sun was just beginning to shine into the clearing that was once the village of St. Francis. He watched as Father Roubard led the Indian women and children down the trail. Bucky saw the golden kernels of corn strewn all over the ground. The wigwams were burning, and the flames were licking up through the roof of the church. Major Rogers estimated the Indian dead at two or three hundred. He guessed that Rogers was probably right. He looked at all the bodies and the large pile of hot coals in the clearing and thought back to the happy days he and Charlie had spent there. Bucky thought to himself, *I can't think of the past. It happened, and I was a part of it. Now I have got to think of the future. It is up to me to get Rogers and his Rangers to the Wells River, then down to Fort Number Four and Mary.* For the last two weeks, Bucky didn't have much time to think of Mary. He was kept busy just trying to stay alive.

Bucky sat with his back against a tree, watching dusk turn to darkness. White Dove was on the ground beside him, his blanket over her and around his legs. Every once in a while she would twitch and let out a little cry. Bucky knew that she was having bad dreams. He reached down and gently stroked her head. White Dove reached up and took Bucky's hand into hers and held it close to the side of her face. Bucky loved White Dove, but not like Mary. He loved her like he loved his sister when he was little. He loved Mary, but she had him confused. At first he thought of her like the other men at the fort.

"Boy, I bet she would be a good lay," they would say. Then without him knowing it, she crept into his heart. He wanted her for his own, to be able to sit with her in front of a fireplace, sipping tea, talking and holding hands. He did not know if Mary loved him or not.

When he told her, "I love you, Mary," all she said was, "I know." Why didn't she say she loved him too? Well, if their luck held out he would soon know.

Bucky led the Rangers in a southeasterly direction. There were times when Bucky didn't know where they were, but he wasn't lost. They were traveling through wilderness country he had not seen before. He knew that as long as they traveled southeast they would find Lake Memphremagag. They traveled through the thick wilderness for over a week; most of the time it rained. The cold rain drove the wetness through their clothes and chilled them to the bone. To make matters worse, some of the Rangers ran out of food and had not eaten in two or three days, except bark, moss and the leather from their equipment and clothes. There was constant fighting between the haves and the have nots. The French and Indians had no trouble following their trail. As the men got weaker from hunger, they started to lighten their loads by throwing the stolen goods to the side of the trail. The French and Indians dogged the Rangers, picking off the stragglers. On the morning of the eighth day, Bucky was helping White Dove pound a handful of corn kernels into powder. White Dove mixed the powder with water and made an uncooked corn cake. It was better than breaking a tooth trying to chew on a hard kernel of corn. During the night the wind changed direction. White Dove wrinkled up her nose and sniffed the air.

"Bucky, a lot of water close by."

"You are right, White Dove. I can smell it too. It must be Memphremagag."

Early in the afternoon, the raiding party stepped out of the forest and onto the shore of Memphremagag. The Rangers ran to the water, turning over rocks and devouring the fish worms and grubs they found. One ranger found a dead fish and ripped it apart with his teeth, growling like a dog at anyone who came near. Three Rangers found a small turtle, cracked it open with a tomahawk and pulled the flesh out with their hands, eating it raw, the blood running down their chins. A small group of Rangers came over and started to fight over the scraps. Major Rogers and Bucky stood watching.

"I have got to do something. They are starving to death," Rogers said. He called all his officers and men together for a council of war.

"Boys, Bucky says in our condition it will be about six or seven days' walk from here to the Wells River. Now you know as well as I do that we have men who are starving to death. I would like every man here to turn in his rations. Every day I will hand out a small ration to each man, enough to get us all to our supplies at the Wells River."

"No, Major, I will not give up my rations. They had the same chance that we did."

"They choose trinkets over food! Let the bastards starve," were a few of the thing shouted at Rogers, holding up his hands for quiet.

"What else can we do?" Rogers asked.

A Ranger stepped forward. "Major, I think we should break up into smaller groups. That way we could find game." Bucky and Rogers did not like the plan.

Rogers said, "There is safety in numbers."

After a short discussion, Bucky and Rogers lost out. It was decided that in the morning, those who wanted to could break up into smaller groups and go their separate ways. Some wanted to head toward Crown Point, and weeks later some would filter in more dead than alive. Some small groups were never seen again. Some wandered onto Rogers' trail and followed it to the Wells River.

Major Rogers approached Bucky. "Bucky, I need a favor."

"Just name it, " Bucky replied.

"Ensign Parker and that group want to go toward New Hampshire and pick up the Connecticut River, build rafts and float down to the Wells River. I know it is a brainless idea, but will you guide them?"

Bucky looked over at the group and saw the Ranger with Father Roubard's Virgin statue in the group. He had been keeping his eye on him since leaving St. Francis. He was not going to lose him now.

"Yes, I will go with them if you will take White Dove with you, protect her and turn her over to Clem at the trading post at the fort."

Bucky estimated the march to the Connecticut River would take about four or five days. He felt sorry for the Rangers that had not had a decent meal in weeks. They didn't fill out their clothes; they looked like scarecrows. Every day the distance got shorter; today they had traveled only five miles. It was their eighth day of stumbling through the forest. Bucky knew that it was only a two or three hours' march to the river. They still had a few hours of daylight left, but he knew that in the condition the Rangers were in they could not make it before dark. Bucky gathered the Rangers around him.

"We are going to spend the night here. We will reach the river tomorrow morning. I will send Johnny and Fox ahead tomorrow morning to cut logs for rafts."

The men were so exhausted from lack of food that they just stared at Bucky with blank eyes and dropped to the ground. Ensign Parker sat down and leaned his back against a tree. Bucky looked around and leaned against his musket. "Parker, Don't you think you should put out some sentries?"

"I will, Bucky, just let me rest a few minutes."

"I am going to take Johnny and Fox to see if I can find something for us to eat."

Parker just shook his head and said, "OK." Before Bucky had walked ten feet, Parker's chin dropped to his chest, and he was sound asleep.

Unbeknown to Bucky and the Rangers, Black Hawk and twenty of his braves had found their trail that morning and had followed it. When he saw Bucky and Fox with another young man who he didn't know guiding the Rangers, Black Hawk pulled his braves back. They had all lost loved ones at St. Francis. He didn't want hate to take over reason and tip the Rangers off that they were following them. They would wait until tonight when they were all asleep, then kill them all.

Black Hawk sat by himself, alone with his thoughts. He could not understand how Fox could turn against his own. He would pay, and pay dearly. Bucky had taken his wife, but White Dove was not here with him. Black Hawk said to himself, *I don't care, when I find her I will kill her*. He gave orders that Bucky and Fox were to be taken alive; they were his, he would have his revenge. The Indians that were scouting the Rangers came running up to Black Hawk.

"Black Hawk! They have stopped for the day. They are on the ground, asleep, with no sentries."

Black Hawk jumped up. This was too good to be true; he would have to see this himself.

A young Ranger woke up and walked into the woods to relieve himself. He stepped behind a bush and, taking his pants down, sat on a log with his ass hanging in the breeze. The young Ranger sitting on the log was almost too tired to shit. He didn't know it, but he had a ringside seat to the massacre.

Bucky, Johnny and Fox were feeling very happy as they walked back toward the Rangers. They had found a hedgehog and killed it with a rap on the nose. They skinned it and cut the meat from the bones, then cut the meat into strips and put it into their haversacks. Bucky, Johnny and Fox were in sight of the Rangers. They could see them on the ground. Bucky had just sucked in his breath to shout the good news to the Rangers when the woods behind the Rangers erupted with yelling, screaming Indians. Ensign Parker died in his sleep with a tomahawk in his head. The Ranger with Father Roubard's Virgin statue jumped to his feet. Black Hawk shot him at almost point-blank range. The Ranger fell over backward, then jumped back up. Black Hawk looked at him in surprise. He could see the black hole in the Ranger's shirt. The Ranger turned and started to run. Black Hawk threw his tomahawk and buried it deep into the Ranger's back. The Ranger fell forward onto his face. Black Hawk went over and yanked the tomahawk from the Ranger's back. When he straightened up he was looking straight at Bucky. He raised his musket, then realized it was empty. By then Bucky was gone.

The young Ranger relieving himself in the woods fell over backward and crawled to the end of the log. He stayed there, scared to death, and peeked around the log. He watched as the Indians hacked his friends' bodies to pieces. Finally, they expended their energies and started to pick up the dead Rangers' muskets, knives and haversacks. The young Ranger watched as an Indian with a black feather in his hair ran from Indian to Indian, shouting and pointing into the forest. Most of them shook their head, rubbed their bellies and pointed back toward the way they had come. In ones and twos they walked away. Six stayed with the one with the black feather. He talked to them for a few minutes. Then they all ran away into the forest. The Ranger stayed behind the log for hours, too scared to move. Finally, he crawled away, then got to his feet and ran by the light of the moon, until he was out of breath. A few days later he came across Major Rogers' trail and followed it to the Wells River.

Bucky took one look and knew all was lost. He saw Black Hawk level his musket at him. He shouted to Johnny and Fox, "Run!" They ran for an hour until they came to the Connecticut River. They jumped into the icy cold water and crossed into New Hampshire. From a hill a half-mile away, the three watched as Black Hawk and his braves came to the river. Pointing to the river, they started to wade across.

Night fall hid the bodies of the Rangers, but not from the animals. The smell of blood brought many to the area. They fought over the bodies, ripping them apart and carrying the pieces away, leaving the Virgin statue untouched on the ground. Through the years, leaves, pine needles and tree branches covered her. Slowly, through the years they turned into dirt, and Mother Earth held the Virgin tightly to her bosom. Someday, just maybe, someday she will give up her treasure.

When darkness fell, Bucky didn't stop. He knew that Black Hawk would push through the night, finding every rock they turned over, every blade of grass and twig they stepped on. They had traveled three days and nights without rest, and Black Hawk still followed about a half-mile behind them. Bucky tried every trick he knew, but Black Hawk stuck to them like glue. Bucky kept moving toward the White Mountains. He knew it was their only chance. The White Mountains were bad medicine to the Indians. It was the place where evil spirits lived. Only the bravest of warriors ever ventured into the area. Fox guessed where they were going, and he was afraid.

"Bucky, that is an evil place. Evil spirits talk to you."

"No, Fox, that is not true. It is only the wind blowing through the trees and rocks."

"Toes says there is an old evil Indian that looks down on everyone who enters his land."

"That is only a big rock that looks like an Indian. I will protect you from all evil spirits. Trust me, Fox."

The next afternoon found them in the foothills of the White Mountains. Bucky stopped by a large boulder to rest. Fox and Johnny were sitting behind the boulder, Fox shaking like a leaf. Bucky looked down from one of the many hills on their way to the large mountain and saw Black Hawk and his six braves walk into a small clearing. The six braves stayed by the edge of the clearing. Black Hawk walked to the other side, then turned and walked back. He stood talking to them for a few minutes, then turned and started to walk back across the clearing again. The six braves didn't move. Hawk walked back to the braves. There was a lot of arm waving and pointing toward the mountain going on. Black Hawk tried pushing the braves forward, and they pushed him back. Finally, they started to walk away. Black Hawk turned and shook his fist at the mountain, then walked behind them in the direction that Bucky knew would lead them to Montreal.

Bucky, Johnny and Fox stayed on the hill where they could keep an eye out for anything that moved below them. Bucky stood guard that night while Johnny and Fox slept. They stayed one more day and night where they were hiding, watching to see if Black Hawk would try to circle back and surprise them. Three days later they were standing on the bank of the Connecticut River, looking across at the Wells River. There were signs all over the place of a large group of men passing through. They stayed that day and night, waiting to see if any other stragglers like themselves might wander in. What they didn't know was that there would not be any stragglers.

Major Rogers flew into a rage when they got to the Wells River and found no supplies waiting for them. The party with the supplies had waited a long time, and when Rogers and his Rangers did not show up, they thought that they were coming down by a different route and had gone back down the river to Fort Number Four. Major Rogers, two other Rangers and White Dove built a raft and floated down the river to Fort Number Four. Within the hour after Rogers reached Fort Number Four he had men and supplies paddling back up the Connecticut to the Rangers waiting at the Wells River. He was now waiting at the fort, hoping that more of his Rangers would filter in.

Chapter Twenty-three

The next morning Bucky, Johnny and Fox crossed the Connecticut and started to walk toward Toes' cabin. Johnny and Fox joked and fooled around. They were happy to be on familiar ground. As they neared Toes' cabin, Fox stopped and said, "Bucky, you hear that?"

"Yes," Bucky replied. He didn't like it. It sounded like the time Black Hawk had him tied to the tree and the braves were dancing around him. They crept up to the clearing and peered at a sight that made Bucky's heart beat fast.

"That looks like Black Hawk's braves," Fox remarked.

"Where is Black Hawk?" Johnny asked.

"I don't know, but he has got to be around here somewhere. Keep your eyes open," Bucky whispered. He knew what Black Hawk and his braves were up to. He had seen it before. They had Toes staked to the ground on his back. They had bent down a small tree and tied the tip of the tree to a stake between Toes' legs. They had another rope tied around the top of the tree and around Toes' testicles and penis, so that when they cut the rope holding the tree down it would snap up and tear everything away. Bucky knew they had to act now if Toes was to have a chance. Bucky, Johnny and Fox took aim, and when Bucky said fire, they squeezed their triggers and three Indians fell to the ground. They quickly reloaded and fired again. Two more Indians fell to the ground. The Indian that was left turned and ran to the safety of the forest.

Black Hawk, hearing the shots being fired, ran from the cabin. He saw Bucky, Johnny and Fox step into the clearing. Black Hawk knew their muskets were empty and ran over to Toes and, holding up his knife for them to see, shouted, "This is for you, Fox."

He cut the rope holding the tree down.

Bucky saw Toes' body jerk upward and stood looking at Toes' body parts dangling from the top of the tree. Black Hawk ran laughing into the forest.

Fox let out a scream and ran to his father. He held Toes' head in his lap as his father's blood drained from his body. Fox jumped up and started toward the forest where Black Hawk had disappeared. Bucky grabbed him and held him tight.

"No, Fox, not now. We will get him, I promise. When we do he will be all yours."

Fox fell to the ground and cried. They buried Toes beside his wife. Bucky and Johnny left Fox alone by the grave, alone with his grief. They stayed the night alone in the cabin. Johnny's heart was breaking for his friend. He thought, as he lay in the darkened cabin, *Whoever said Indians do not cry didn't know Indians very well.* Johnny knew the pain Fox was going through, and he wished he could share some of the pain. Fox could not share his sorrow; he had to grieve alone. Like Johnny, the pain would go away and the good memories would last forever. Johnny was surprised that he didn't get sick.

He thought back to a few short months ago, which now seemed like a lifetime, when Bucky first told him, "Johnny, someday your stomach will get hardened to it, but if you are human, you never will."

The morning sun was just peeking over the eastern horizon when they left for Montreal.

Chapter Twenty-four

Bucky, Johnny and Fox walked toward an old shack about three miles from the city of Montreal. The shack belonged to Joe Becker. Joe didn't like living near people. He used to tell Bucky and Charlie that he liked to take a piss in front of his shack without everyone watching him. When he wasn't trapping he lived with Rose, a big, fat, full-blooded Indian. She really was a rose. She was as beautiful inside as she was outside. Rose was standing outside the shack, holding an armful of wood, watching them approach. When Bucky was about fifty feet away from Rose, she dropped the wood, threw up her hands and ran into the shack. A few seconds later Joe stepped out of the shack and stared in their direction.

"My God!" he exclaimed, "It is you, Bucky. I thought you were dead."

"Well, I'm not. Do you want to touch me?"

Laughing and pounding them on the back, Joe herded them into the shack. Rose was standing way back in a corner.

Bucky walked over to her and said, "Rose, I'm no ghost," and gave her a big hug and a kiss.

"I'm glad, Bucky, I am glad," Rose said with a big smile.

They sat around the fireplace, sipping a couple of brandies, while

Rose prepared a meal for them. They ate corn bread, thick pieces of fried bacon and potatoes fried in bacon fat. It was the best meal they had had in weeks.

"My God, Bucky, when I saw Black Hawk with your musket, I said to myself, Bucky must be dead, nobody would ever take it from him as long as he was alive," Joe said between mouthfuls of food.

Bucky told Joe of the events of the last couple of months, ending with the death of Toes. Joe was sad to hear of the death of Toes.

"I spent overnight with old Toes after I left Number Four," Joe said sadly.

"Have you seen Black Hawk lately?" Bucky asked.

"Yes, at the Indian camp just outside of town. I was over there trading with them this morning. He was there bragging and drinking."

"I promised Fox I would get him."

"I will help you."

"When?" Fox asked.

"Tonight, when it gets dark," Joe replied.

The fall of darkness found them hiding in the bushes by the side of the Indian encampment.

Joe said, "You three stay here. There are quite a few St Francis Indians here. They won't think anything about me wandering around." A half-hour later Joe came back.

"Follow me, I found him." They skirted around the outside of the encampment. They looked out from their concealment in the bushes at Black Hawk and two other braves sitting around a campfire, drinking whiskey. They passed the bottle around until it was empty, then threw the bottle into the fire. One Indian got up and staggered away. A few minutes later the other Indian got up and followed him. Black Hawk sat alone, rocking back and forth, mumbling to himself.

"I hope the son of a bitch doesn't fall asleep," Bucky whispered to Joe.

Before Joe could answer, Black Hawk got to his feet and staggered toward them. He staggered into the bushes so close to Bucky that if he wasn't so drunk he would have seen him. Black

Hawk stood there, weaving back and forth, and started to urinate. Bucky stood up and hit him in the head with the butt of his musket. Black Hawk fell to the ground, out cold.

They tied his hands and feet, and Bucky handed his musket to Joe, saying, "If he comes to hit him again."

Bucky carried Black Hawk on his shoulders for about two miles into the forest.

"What do you say, Fox, I am not going to carry him all the way back to the Grants."

They were standing in the center of a small clearing. The moon was shining brightly on the clearing.

Fox looked around. "Right here," he said.

Bucky dropped Black Hawk to the ground like a sack of corn. Johnny and Fox climbed to the top of a small tree and hung on until the top reached the ground. Fox drove a stake into the ground and tied a rope to the tip of the tree and stake.

Bucky and Joe sat with their backs to a large tree and built a fire between them. It was the first of November, and the weather was starting to turn cold, with a hint of snow in the air. Major Rogers had returned to Crown Point, knowing that no more Rangers would be returning. If Bucky had known that the word of his and Johnny's demise at the hands of the Indians was spreading all around theFort Number Four area and that Mary and White Dove had shed enough tears over them to cause the Connecticut to overflow its banks, he would have run all of the way back to the fort.

When they left Joe's shack, Joe said, "This will probably be a long night."

He handed Bucky an earthenwear jug of brandy and took one for himself.

Joe and Bucky made themselves comfortable and waited for the show to start.

Johnny helped Fox drag Black Hawk over to the bent tree. Fox stripped Black Hawk of all his clothes and staked him down on the ground, flat on his back. He tied a rope around Black Hawk's testicles and penis and to the tree, just like Black Hawk did to his father. Fox built a fire beside Black Hawk. Johnny walked over to Bucky and took a drink from the jug and watched Fox as he kicked Black Hawk in the side, trying to bring him to.

"I think when he comes to he is going to have one big headache," Joe remarked.

"I believe that you might be right," Bucky said, and took another swallow from the jug.

Fox found water and came back with his haversack dripping. He emptied the cold water onto Black Hawk's face. Black Hawk came to with a start and looked into the hate-filled eyes of Fox. He raised his head and looked down between his legs.

"I am going to make you scream," Fox said, and gave Black Hawk a kick.

"Try your best," Black Hawk said with a sneer.

"I will make you scream and beg for mercy, and then I will feed you to the dogs."

"Go to hell. I will not scream and beg for mercy from you or anyone else, you traitor bastard. May the ghost of the childen and women of St. Francis follow you for the rest of your life," Black Hawk shouted at Fox. He knew he was going to die. He would die with honor.

"He is not going to die easy, Bucky," Joe said, taking another swallow from the jug.

"No, he won't," Bucky agreed as he rubbed his face. He was starting to feel the effect of the liquor.

Fox took a flaming stick from the fire and pressed it against Black Hawk's body over and over again. Black Hawk squirmed but didn't cry out.

"Beg for mercy and I will kill you quickly."

Black Hawk just laughed at Fox.

"He is one tough son of a bitch," Joe remarked.

"He sure is," Bucky answered and took another drink.

Fox took his knife and started to peel the skin from Black Hawk's body. Johnny took a drink from the jug, then walked over to see what Fox was doing. Johnny took one look, turned away and threw up, gagging and coughing.

"That is an awful waste of good whiskey," Joe remarked.

"Blood makes his stomach upset, but he is getting over it a little. He is a good boy. He will stand beside you through thick and thin. Both of them will," Bucky said, sticking up for Johnny.

"No offense, Bucky."

"None taken." They tapped their jugs together and took a couple of swallows.

Fox took his tomahawk and chopped off Black Hawk's fingers, saying, "Now you will wander through the afterlife with no way to protect yourself. You will die over and over again."

The pain was so great that Black Hawk could hardly stand it. He bit his lips so hard that blood ran down his chin. He closed his eyes and drove the pain from his mind.

"Do you wonder where they ever learn this?" Joe asked.

"Well, I have thought about it, and I think they are born into it," Bucky said, so drunk he could hardly see.

Fox jumped up, running his knife ran Black Hawk's head. Putting his foot on Black Hawk's face, he ripped his hair from his head. Bucky heard a sucking sound as Black Hawk's scalp ripped from his head, followed by a high-pitched scream. Fox threw the scalp into the fire, then cut the rope holding the tree. It sprung back up to the sky.

"My God, Bucky! I have never seen flying balls before!" Joe exclaimed, truly amazed.

"Oh, I have seen that before," Bucky said as it was something he saw every day.

Fox came over to the campfire and took the jug from Bucky and started to drink. Bucky was so drunk that everything looked fuzzy to him. He had not been that drunk in years. He grabbed his blanket, pulled it around his shoulders and passed out. He woke up early in the morning with the blanket over his head. He could hear voices. Bucky threw the blanket aside and got a face full of snow. It had snowed about six inches during the night and was still coming down hard. Johnny, Joe and Fox were sitting around the fire. Bucky looked over toward Black Hawk; he couldn't help but feel a little sad. The bravest Indian he had ever known was now nothing but a pile in the snow.

Bucky thought in some ways they were a lot alike. *In another time and place, I think we could have been good friends.*

Noticing that Bucky was awake, Johnny said, "Bucky, Joe has offered to finance us and take Fox and I out to see the Plains Indians. He says the grass grows shoulder high, the beaver are twice as big as ours, and there are buffalo as far as the eye can see. You're coming with us, aren't you, Bucky?"

Bucky couldn't help but laugh at the excitement in Johnny's voice and the sparkle in his eyes.

"No, I have business at Fort Number Four," he replied.

Johnny and Fox looked at each other with big grins on their faces.

Chapter Twenty-five

Bucky spent a week at Joe's cabin, resting and getting supplied for the trip back down to Fort Number Four. It was now close to the first of December. The cold and snow was starting to settle in for the winter. They were all standing outside Joe's cabin to see Bucky off.

"If you are not good to Mary, Fox and I will come back and hang you on a hook," Johnny said with a laugh.

"We won't be leaving before spring thaw if you should change your mind," Joe said, shaking Bucky's hand.

"Thanks, Joe, you never know." Turning to the boys, Bucky said, "You couldn't be going with a better man. Listen to him and keep your powder dry."

Rose handed Bucky a pair of snowshoes she had made for him, then said, "When Joe gone, you come back. I treat you good."

They all had a good laugh. Bucky put the snowshoes on and wrapped a bear skin around himself. It was heavy but would keep him warm. He said his goodbyes and started the long walk back to Fort Number Four. He spent one night at Toes' cabin and another at Moe's to get warm and have a good night's sleep out of the snow. The Connecticut River was starting to freeze. In some places Bucky had to carry the canoe around frozen spots. It was early in the afternoon when he saw the outline of the fort. After spending over a week traveling on snowshoes through the frozen wilderness of Canada and the Grants, it never looked so good to him in all his life.

Bucky saw Mary's flaming red hair outlined against the white snow. It looked like a warm fire; it sure made him feel warm. She had her back to him and was splitting wood. He could see the ax go up in the air and come back down with a thud.

Bucky quietly walked up behind her and said, "Would you like me to that for you?"

Mary spun around with the ax raised in front of her. Her mouth dropped open and her eyes got as big as saucers.

She dropped the ax and screamed, "Bucky, you are alive!" She threw her arms around him, realizing what she was doing. Mary stepped back, her face getting as red as her hair.

"Come in, you must be cold and hungry," she said through the tears of happiness in her eyes.

Bucky walked into the cabin. He had never seen it so neat and clean.

"I am not hungry, Mary, but I would like a nice cup of tea." They sat side by side, sipping their tea in front of the fireplace.

"White Dove and Crow have gone to live with Moe. They didn't think you would ever return. That old man loves them. White Dove used to comb his hair and fuss over him all day. She told him that if she ever had a papoose she was going to name it Moe. I heard him tell Crow to get busy," Mary said with a laugh, getting red in the face.

"I know, I spent a night at Moe's on the way down. White Dove's belly is starting to rise. I have never seen three people so happy. Did you know that Clem and Sue want to sell the store?" Bucky asked.

"No!" Mary answered, surprised.

"Yup, says he and Sue would like to move to Concord, Massachusetts. Clem said it is a nice, quiet town and that nothing ever happens there. It is close to Boston."

"I will miss them."

"Me too. You know, Mary, I have been thinking, it is time I settled down. I don't want to wait until I get like Charlie got, all crippled up from sleeping on the cold, damp ground. Since I took that tomahawk to the head, my eyes are not as good as they used to be. I suppose I could buy the trading post, but I would need help. If I had the trading post I would tear it down and build a new one. When this war is over, people will start flooding into the Grants, and they will come right through here. They will want a nice place to sleep. I would build a nice dining room, a larger store and four or five rooms upstairs to rent, but I couldn't do it alone, so I better forget that." Bucky was just picking on Mary, for he had already talked to Clem and Sue and knew that Mary had never lost hope that he was alive and would return to Fort Number Four to take her for his wife. He handed Mary three packages.

"I bought you something for taking care of Moe. Go try it on." Bucky could hear some oohs and ahs as she opened the box.

"How did you know my size?" Mary asked.

"I should know, I have been watching you long enough."

"You can turn around," Mary said.

Bucky stared at Mary standing in the flicking candle light, dressed in a long green velvet dress. She also had a green box hat with a feather sticking out of it sitting on top of her long red hair. Small green pointed shoes completed the outfit.

Finally, Bucky said, "Mary, you are beautiful. Captain Burroughs is waiting at the trade post. I told him I was going to ask a certain redhead to be my wife, and if she said yes I asked him if he would marry us today. Mary, will you be my wife?"

"Oh, yes! Yes, Bucky!" Mary cried and ran to Bucky.

Bucky picked her up and walked out of the cabin.

The End

WITHDRAWN

Printed in the United States
50139LVS00002B/403-432

9 781413 794649